A SUMMERSTOKE AFFAIR

A tale of passion, power and dirty parsnips...

In the village of Summerstoke it's not only the autumn fireworks that go with a bang. Juliet Peters, soap star and compulsive flirt, and Isabelle Garnett, ex-artist, neglected housewife and mother of two, have nothing in common but are both trying to build a new life in the country. Their husbands seem to be on a collision course too – one, a newly elected MP returning to his family roots; the other a local newspaper editor desperate for a story. Add a wild child teenager, a reformed casanova, and four eccentric ladies at the manor and you've got a recipe for trouble!

A SUMMERSTOKE AFFAIR

A Summerstoke Affair

by

Caroline Kington

Magna Large Print Books
Long Preston, North Yorkshire,
BD23 4ND, England.

British Library Cataloguing in Publication Data.

Kington, Caroline
    A Summerstoke affair.

    A catalogue record of this book is
    available from the British Library

    ISBN   978-0-7505-2857-3

First published in Great Britain 2007 by Orion,
an imprint of Orion Publishing Group Ltd.

Published in Large Print 2008 by arrangement with
Orion Publishing Group

Magna Large Print is an imprint of Library Magna Books Ltd.

Printed and bound in Great Britain by
T.J. (International) Ltd., Cornwall, PL28 8RW

All the characters in this book are fictitious, and any resemblance to actual persons living or dead is purely coincidental.

For Isabel and Adam

Acknowledgements

Particular thanks are due to Dr Andrew Murrison MP for allowing me to trail round with him and bombard him with questions, to his secretary Jackie Packer, and to Robert Pettigrew for explaining backstage at Westminster; to Sam Holliday, editor of the *Bath Chronicle* for giving me an insight into the workings of a daily local paper; to my friend, artist Wendy Hoile, for teaching me about paint; to Adam, my son, for scrutinising the dialogue of Jamie and his friends and generally giving me huge support in the writing of this book; to Isabel, my actress daughter, for generously sharing her experiences with me; to my sister, Belinda, for steadfastly reading everything I sent her; to my agent, Broo Doherty, for her wonderful support; to Kate Mills and Genevieve Pegg for their invaluable input and encouragement; and most particularly to my husband, Miles, whose support services are second to none.

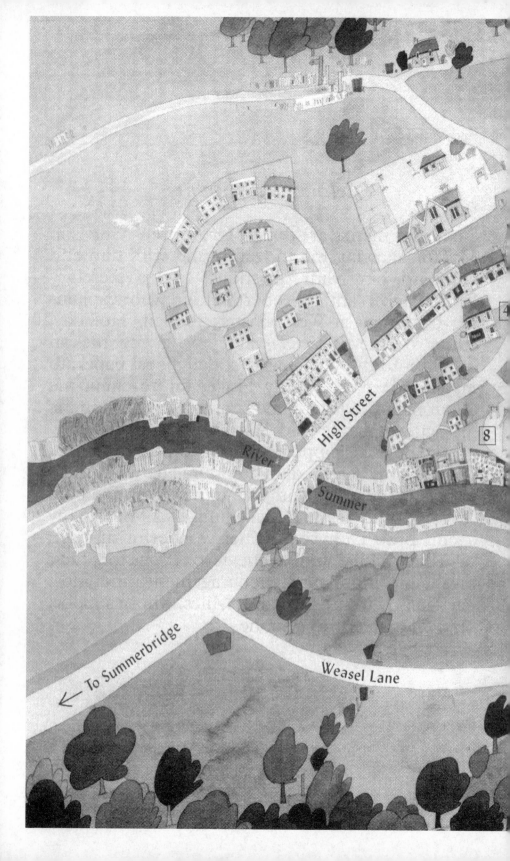

Summerwoods

To Bath

1. Marsh Farm
2. The Manor House
3. Summerstoke House
4. Shop and Post Office
5. Foresters Arms
6. The Old Vicarage
7. The Doctor's House
8. The Village Hall

Summerstoke Ridge

JUNE

1

'Whoa, Sultan, whoa! Steady boy, steady.' The rider astride the tall black stallion brought his nervous mount to a standstill as a car swept past them without slowing down on the country road that led out of the village of Summerstoke.

'Ignorant bastard!' Hugh Lester glared with disdainful superiority after the offending vehicle before urging his horse forward towards the bridge spanning the river.

It was a beautiful Sunday morning and Hugh, as was his wont, had been roaming the country-side around the village for a couple of hours. He was in high good humour. Not only was he happiest – if a man like Hugh could ever be described as happy – when he was mounted on his horse or his wife, but he had seen enough of the shabby condition of the farm, in the middle of the Summerstoke valley, to convince him that it wouldn't be long before its owners succumbed to pressure and accepted his offer.

Hugh owned the other farm in the village, Summerstoke Farm, and he was rich and successful. From the very beginning he'd learned to play the subsidy game and ruthlessly milk his land for all it was worth. His first love was horses and he and his wife Veronica had added to their wealth and prestige by running a livery stables. But, ever restless, he wanted to expand and more than anything else he wanted to open a stud. Studs attracted money and class and Hugh and Veronica were attracted to money and class, and the power that went with that combination.

However there was a slight snag to Hugh's ambition: they needed more land, and land, available land, was in short supply.

The village of Summerstoke sat on the side of a hill leading down to the River Summer. Hugh's land was on the village side, the Tucker family of Marsh Farm owned the pastures on the other side, and the only other landowners of note were the Merfield sisters of Summerstoke Manor – a trio of elderly freaks, in Hugh's opinion. Too old to farm themselves, they leased their juicy pastures to the Tuckers.

After his ride that morning, the way forward became clear to Hugh: if he could persuade the Merfields to sell their land, Marsh Farm would cease to be viable as a dairy farm and then, he was sure, he'd be able to get it for a song.

The church bells started to ring out as Sultan started up the High Street and Hugh, sitting high above the rest of the world, felt very good indeed.

The odd passers-by, walking back from the village shop with Sunday newspapers tucked under their arms and swinging pints of milk, cast admiring glances in his direction. Hugh preened himself. He looked good and he knew it. On horseback the disadvantage of being only five foot six was hidden, and although he was nearly fifty he had a good figure, a full head of wavy black hair, strong features and piercing blue eyes.

When he had reached the age of eighteen and

18

realised he would not grow any taller, he'd nearly despaired. But then he discovered that on horseback he could look down on the rest of the world, and when he'd made a sufficient packet of money the world did not look down on him.

Nearing the lych-gate of St Stephen's, his spirits lifted still further. It couldn't be better. The small congregation was leaving the church and walking down the path, he could see the Merfield crones accompanied by a much younger man and by the tall, lugubrious figure of the vicar.

The ladies, all around eighty, were as tall as the vicar, elegant and thin. On the rare occasions he'd been in their company, he'd felt like a stunted dwarf who'd crawled out of a fairy tale. He knew he'd feel the same way if he went to call on them with his proposal. They'd never seen him on horseback. On Sultan, he was a force to be reckoned with – they'd take notice, of that he was supremely confident.

The group had just reached an old Daimler parked alongside the lych-gate, another elderly lady at the wheel, when Hugh reined in Sultan. At the sound of the horse they were sufficiently distracted from their conversation with the vicar to look up.

'Good morning, ladies,' Hugh attempted a light, jocular note. 'And what a beautiful morning it is.'

The three elderly ladies regarded him silently.

'Ah, yes,' the Vicar hastily filled the void, 'isn't it, Mr Lester. God's in his heaven and all's right with the world, eh? Fine animal you've got there.'

Hugh ignored him and addressed the eldest of the three, whose arm rested lightly on the young

19

man's by her side. She was a formidable old lady, dressed from top to toe in black lace, with a cadaverous face and sunken dark eyes.

'This is a fortuitous encounter, Mrs Merfield.' He smiled – an uncommon experience – till he thought his face would crack.

She did not respond with any warmth. 'Is it?'

'Yes,' he ploughed on. 'I was planning to call round to see you.'

'What on earth for?' enquired one of the other sisters, dressed, Hugh observed with distaste, as if she was half her age, in some light drifty material.

He fought off a scowl. 'I've got a proposition to put to you.'

'A proposition. Whatever next?' drawled the third sister. 'I can't imagine what that could be, can you, Elizabeth? Perhaps he wants to buy the manor. Shall we sell?'

Hugh's attempt at a smile was replaced by a flush. Handsome as his own place, Summerstoke House, was, it was not in the same class as Summerstoke Manor, which he dreamed of owning.

He forced a laugh. 'No, of course not. But I wanted to discuss your pasture land with you.'

'Our pastures?'

'Yes,' Hugh blundered on, refusing to be fazed by her discouraging demeanour. 'This is probably not the time or place to discuss it, but I thought, seeing you here, I would put the idea to you. I need more fields for our horses, and your pastures this side of the river, so close to Summerstoke Farm, would be ideal. I know you lease them to the Tuckers, but I could offer you more, substantially more, and would be more than happy to pay a good price if you were to think of selling…'

His voice trailed away and, feeling hot and desperately uncomfortable, he tried another smile, looking for some sign of encouragement in at least one of the faces staring up at him.

There was none.

Mrs Merfield's voice was icy. 'You're right, Mr Lester. This is neither the time nor the place. Today is Sunday, a day of rest according to the teachings of the Bible, and we have just come from church. If you wish to discuss business with us, I suggest you make an appointment in the usual way. Good day.'

He was dismissed.

The old lady was helped into the car by the young man, and all Hugh could do was control his increasingly restless horse and try to think of a good exit line. One of the other ladies glanced up at him just before she, too, took her place in the car.

'I think you're wasting your time, Mr Lester. It's highly unlikely we'd take those fields away from the Tuckers. There are more important things in life than money, you know.'

The car pulled away; the young man, who had remained behind, shook hands with the vicar, nodded at Hugh, then strolled up the road in the direction of the Manor.

The vicar, looking more uncomfortable than ever and poising for flight, glanced nervously in Hugh's direction. 'Well, er, good day to you, Mr Lester.'

'Who's that?' Hugh stared after the man.

'That? Oh, he's Mrs Merfield's grandson.

21

Oliver Merfield, um … a nice boy, very nice. He and his sister used to stay in the village during the school holidays. Their father is Sir Nicholas Merfield, you know, a diplomat.'

Hugh snorted contemptuously. 'Well, he didn't learn anything about the art of diplomacy from his mother, did he?'

This criticism of his patroness was clearly painful to the vicar. 'Er, well, yes … she can be a little abrasive. However, Oliver is quite … quite different, er… Hopefully, we're going to see a whole lot more of him.'

'Why's that?' Hugh turned his cold stare on the vicar.

'Did you not know? He … er … he's been chosen as the Conservative candidate for Mendip … er, in the by-election at the end of June. He … er … may well be our next MP.'

'Another Merfield to deal with – that's all I need!' seethed Hugh, slapping Sultan's rump with his crop and spurring him on, his face black with frustrated temper. He felt he had, quite un-deservedly, lost the first round to the Merfields.

Hugh Lester was a very bad loser.

Inside the Town Hall, the main council chamber had been turned into the election hall. It was a large, self-important room with yellow oak panels on which hung portraits of all the previous mayors of the town, reduced by oils into a dull, pompous assembly in robes and chains, staring out from their frames without interest or a glimmer of humour.

In the centre of the chamber, rows of trestle

22

tables had been erected, now littered with discarded paper cups, half-eaten sandwiches, crisp packets, empty bottles of water, pens and crumpled paper. The air was stuffy and thick with the fetid smell of stale adrenalin and general fatigue, and groups of tellers, party workers and support staff sat around in various states of exhaustion. Their faces were an unhealthy greenish hue – the elegant crystal chandeliers having been abandoned in favour of strip lights, usually only used by the maintenance staff.

The combination of the harsh blue light and the overwhelming yellowness of the room had caused the more discerning of the cameramen to sigh deeply. They sat in a small huddle on one side of the room: a selection of reporters and photographers too bored and tired to exchange more than the odd quip, and all wishing themselves on any assignment but this one. Camera teams from all the major television stations, who probably felt the same way, kept aloof from the grumbling hacks and occupied a balcony at the back, where they yawned and dozed their way through the long night.

Of all the people in the chamber, only the six candidates continued to smile and chat and move with any animation as if, until the result was declared, any sloth on their part would influence the outcome.

Oliver Merfield, Conservative, and much the youngest of the candidates, stopped to talk to a thin, middle-aged lady with large tinted specs and wearing a shiny purple blouse over tight, black, cropped trousers.

'Rita, hello. How are you? I didn't expect to see you here?'

She beamed back, obviously very pleased to be recognised and said, archly, 'I don't know that you should be talking to me, Oliver. I support the opposition.'

He smiled. 'I don't suppose I'll be shot. Which one?'

'Roy Green. He's his own man, and that's what we need out here in the sticks. No offence, Oliver, but he's one of us. I know he hasn't got a chance in hell, but we're sick of being ignored. Those fat cats in London aren't interested in the likes of us.'

'But your shop's doing well enough, isn't it?'

'For the moment, Oliver, for the moment, but it's a foolish virgin who sells her cow when milk is cheap, as they say.'

Oliver blinked. 'Er, yes, I suppose so.'

'And this government, they say one thing and do another. Trouble with them is they're like fish.'

'Oh?' Oliver gave up the struggle.

'Fish always stink from the head down!' Rita gave a loud crack of laughter and dug him in the ribs. 'You might remember that with your own leader.'

Oliver was saved from comment by the arrival at his side of Keith Mann, his agent, who had picked up signals that a decision had been reached.

On the stage, a weary technician had started fiddling with the microphone. Gathering round him were various officials bursting with self-importance – for a brief moment they, alone, knew the result.

'Looks like we have a decision, Oliver,' muttered Keith, an election veteran. 'Where's Juliet?'

Acknowledging his agent's presence, Oliver smiled at Rita, who had sold him sweets when he was a schoolboy. 'I've got to go now, but I'll come and have a chat when all this is over.'

He turned to Keith, his face composed. 'Right, I'm ready. Let's go and face the music.'

If he was nervous, it didn't show, Keith thought, and not for the first time did he mentally applaud the selection board for choosing such an engaging and likeable candidate.

Oliver Merfield was a gift for any political agent. He was in his mid-thirties, tall, lean and strong, with an open, warm face and engaging grin. Not handsome, but with interesting features, clear grey eyes, a strong chin and a Roman nose, even white teeth, and thick hair, the colour of dark honey, very straight and floppy.

Women flocked to him – the older ones wanted to mother him and the younger ones wanted to bed him. Oliver, Keith was sure, didn't notice, and treated everyone, men and women, old and young, as if he was sincerely interested in their well-being and respected their opinions, however much they diverged from his own.

He was such a refreshing change from the die-hard Tory candidates Keith Mann had worked for in the past, and Keith, now nearing fifty and having grown tired and cynical in the job, could swear he had almost enjoyed this by-election – almost.

The vote was by no means in the bag. Out canvassing, it had been clear the electorate were tired of the present government and were poised to vote tactically, which meant that the Liberal candidate was presenting a real challenge, for the first time ever, in this part of the country.

The knight who had represented the constituency for the last thirty years, and whose death had caused this by-election, had been an old-fashioned Conservative and deeply loved by his constituents, although the records showed he had only spoken in parliament twice in his whole career, once in favour of fox-hunting, and once in favour of bringing back the death penalty.

Oliver, unlike the knight, had never lived in the country and Keith knew that this, together with his youthfulness, weighed against him. They had played the family-connections card for all it was worth – Oliver's family originated from a village in the constituency. Oliver, with his wife and son, was planning to live in the area, so much had been made of him returning to his roots.

'Rather him than me,' thought Keith, who couldn't bear either the country or country people and was desperate to return to London. 'And I can't imagine Juliet being that keen to bury herself down here.'

'Juliet, where's Juliet?' he repeated with increased urgency as more people appeared on the stage and the sound engineer fussed with the positioning of the microphones stand.

Oliver looked around the hall for his wife. 'She said she was going to do an interview for local TV. But that was ages ago, I'm surprised she's not back–'

Keith interrupted, put out. 'Interview? What interview? Why wasn't I told? I should be there.

Juliet on her own is a loose cannon.'

Oliver laughed and put his arm around his agent's pudgy shoulders. 'Don't worry, she's playing the role of the perfect wife tonight. She'll give them twenty seconds of tasty soundbites on how important it is for me to be elected; her life as an MP's wife; and how much she's looking forward to living in the country. Then, politics forgotten, she'll go on for twenty minutes about how she left *Hunter's Way* because she felt she was being typecast; about the roles she's been offered and turned down; and about her planned debut in Hollywood.'

Keith pouted. 'Nevertheless, I should have been told.'

Oliver shrugged, suddenly looking weary. 'You know Juliet, Keith. We can count ourselves lucky she's played ball so far. Shall I go and fetch her? I think they went outside.'

'No, no. I think you're going to be called to the stage any minute. I'll go.'

For a moment, Oliver looked nervous and much younger than his thirty-five years. 'How do I look? Will I do?'

Keith looked him over, critically. Very sensibly, given the claustrophobic heat, he had eschewed the ubiquitous suit and tie and wore a loose white linen shirt sporting a blue rosette, and a pair of dark-blue linen trousers. He looked cool and elegant, and for a moment Keith Mann felt short, fat and greasy, middle-aged and envious. His young charge had a future he once had aspired to but for which he was not, he'd been forced to accept, the right material.

27

He patted Oliver on the arm. 'You look fine. Good luck, Oliver. I'll get Juliet to join you, pronto.'

He hurried to the entrance, mentally cursing himself for having taken his eye off the ball as far as Juliet was concerned. He knew he was the subject of considerable envy for the time he was spending in her company, but he was not one of her fans and even went so far as to describe her, privately, as 'a pain in the bloody backside'.

As Oliver had predicted, Juliet Merfield – or Juliet Peters, as she was known professionally – star of stage and screen, was twinkling for all she was worth into the lens of a television camera on the steps outside the Town Hall.

'So yes, in answer to your question, I'd love to work in the West Country if the opportunity presented itself. You have two wonderful theatres here. But as I said, I'm auditioning for another television series, and if that happens...' She smiled at her interviewer. 'But I'd rather not say too much about that just yet, obviously.'

'Juliet, there you are!' Keith's voice was irritable. 'You really shouldn't go off and do interviews without checking with me.'

A shadow of annoyance passed over Juliet's countenance and she tilted her chin. 'Since we were talking about me and my career, Keith, I don't really see that it's any business of yours.'

Keith glared at her. 'You're new to this game, Juliet. These guys are professional. One unguarded comment, taken out of context, could do untold damage.'

'You forget *I'm* a professional, too.' She turned

to the reporter and smiled. 'And I'm sure you'll vouch for the fact that I've said nothing that could, in any way, be construed as damaging, have I, David?'

He was putty. 'No, no of course not. It was a great interview.'

Keith cut him off. 'We'll talk about this later. Juliet, you're wanted onstage. I think they're about to announce the results.'

The interviewer snapped into action. 'I must be off. Juliet, it was lovely talking to you. Perhaps we could do something else with you in the near future.'

He sped off, his cameraman struggling after him.

Juliet trailed into the hall in the wake of Keith Mann and mounted the stage to join her husband.

'Your rosette, Juliet. Where's your rosette?' Keith hissed.

She had been issued with an outsize rosette earlier in the day, which she'd managed to lose so he'd already had to find her another one for the platform.

'Silly man,' she thought. 'He shouldn't have wasted his time.' There was no way she was going to be seen by the media wearing such a thing.

She smiled at him sweetly. 'I'm so sorry, Keith, I must have left it in the Ladies. But I am wearing a blue dress. Won't I do as I am, darling?' she appealed to Oliver.

He looked down at her and smiled slightly. She was wearing a simple short, sleeveless silk sheath the colour of forget-me-nots.

'You look lovely.'

She did.

She was petite, with clear, creamy white skin, large bright-blue eyes fringed with dark lashes, and an abundance of long, curly, red-gold hair. Her face was heart-shaped and she had dimples, which had melted his heart the first time he'd seen them, cupid lips, a straight little nose and a small, determined chin.

Oliver glanced at his agent, one eyebrow lifting slightly.

Defeated, muttering under his breath, Keith took his place at the back of the stage. Juliet took Oliver's hand and, for the first time since he had been selected as the Conservative candidate for Mendip, whispered, 'Good luck, darling.'

A hundred miles away, lying on his bed in the dark, his face illuminated by the flickering screen of the television, Jamie Merfield watched Juliet take her place on the platform by his father's side. The camera cut to a close shot of her smiling up at his dad, and Jamie caught his breath, as he always did when he spotted her unexpectedly.

When he was a small boy living with his grandparents, it had felt as if his whole being gasped whenever she appeared. For him, then, she was the most beautiful person in the world and she was his mother. His. For that, he forgave her everything – forgave her the times when she said she was coming but didn't; forgave her when she didn't take him on holiday when she'd promised; even forgave her when she came one evening after he'd fallen asleep and went again before he'd woken. (For weeks after that he'd forced himself to keep awake till after his grandparents had gone to bed and there was no chance of her coming.) She was the centre of his universe and when, one day, when he was about five, she had told him he was going to live with her, he thought he'd die with happiness.

He hadn't seen that much more of her after the move, but the nanny brought in to look after him was much younger and more fun than his gran, and his dad was there, too, so he didn't miss Gran and Grandpa hardly at all.

His dad used to visit him at Gran and Grandpa's much more than his mum, in fact, and Jamie thought he was nice. But as Gran used to say, he wasn't special like she was – no, not like her. And at school Jamie knew she was special because of the way the other kids stared and asked, 'Is that your mum?' and wanted to be friends with him.

Throughout his childhood he'd had imaginary adventures in which, invariably, he rescued her from some terrible disaster and she would fold him in her arms, weeping soft tears, telling him she was so proud of him and she could never love anyone as much as her brave little boy.

Then he had graduated to secondary school and Mum became Juliet.

'We're friends, as well as mother and son, aren't we darling? We've grown up together. You're my best friend. You should call me Juliet. Mum sounds so ... so ordinary.'

Sometimes, particularly over the last nine months since he had turned fifteen and seemed to be struggling with so many different things, he found himself wishing that she was more Mum

31

and less Juliet. But then the treasonous thought would be buried and he'd revel in the fact his friends envied him his relationship with the beautiful and famous Juliet Peters.

He hadn't told anyone at school about his father standing for election. He sort of thought the Head might know because of what he'd said to Jamie that afternoon. Jamie shivered at the memory.

'You know this is an expulsion offence, don't you, Jamie? The rules are quite clear. How's this going to affect your father? Eh? What happens when the press get hold of it?' He shook his head. 'You've put me in an impossible position. You've got your GCSEs starting the day after tomorrow so we shall expect to see you in for those and then you must come in, before the end of term, with your parents, to talk to me about your future here. But I warn you, Jamie, if you're caught on the school premises, either smoking cannabis or with it in your possession, press or no press, I will have to expel you.'

He would've loved a joint now, but the bastard had confiscated his stash and he'd finished his last fag hours ago. He'd promised his mother he wouldn't smoke in his aunt's house, but he reasoned that leaning out of the window and flicking the dog-ends onto the adjacent roof was a reasonable compromise.

While his parents were on the election trail, he'd been sent to stay with Aunt Polly, his father's twin sister, who was unmarried and lived in a Victorian terrace near Shepherd's Bush. He'd stayed with her so often in the past – Juliet's career frequently took her away, as did Dad's, he

32

being an international broker – he had his own room at the top of her house. He liked Aunt Polly, who was elegant and bright, but not in the same league as his mum in the looks department.

She'd commented he looked off-colour when she got back from work but assumed he was suffering from a mixture of exam nerves and election excitement. He didn't disabuse her.

'I've got some friends coming over to watch the election on News 24, Jamie,' she said. 'I know it's school tomorrow, but in the circumstances, they'll be understanding. Are you going to stay up and watch it with us?'

Jamie was torn about his father's new career. He was sufficiently fond of his father to want him to succeed at whatever he chose to do, but the only thing of interest about winning the election, for him, was the kudos it might carry. However, he thought, it was more likely he'd be mocked for being the son of a Conservative MP and, worse, a rural one at that. Mendip – Christ, where the hell was Mendip?

His mother had told him if his dad won, it might mean they'd have to go and live in the country, a fate worse than death as far as she was concerned; and so, as he always followed where she led, he agreed. Now, with the threat of expulsion also hanging over him, he hadn't had the heart for partying.

So Jamie had smiled wanly at his aunt. 'No, thanks. My exams start the day after tomorrow. I think I'll have an early night.' And, excusing himself, he climbed the steep staircase to his attic room.

It was hot and stuffy under the eaves, so he pushed open the window, took off his shirt and shoes and flung his long, pale body on the bed. He lay there, absently twisting his thumb ring and staring up at the ceiling, till the daylight turned to night, a city night of dark navy stained with a gauze of orange, and the sound of the metropolis, drifting in through the dormer window, had dulled to a muted, distant roar.

Around midnight he had roused, put the television on with the sound off, changed out of his jeans, and lain back on the bed, defying the tedium of the television pictures to work on his overactive brain and put him to sleep.

It had nearly worked, when suddenly there she was, his mother, Juliet. He caught his breath.

There was a knock on his door. Jamie jumped and zapped the television off.

'Yes?'

His aunt whispered, 'Sorry to disturb you, darling, but I think you'd kick yourself if you missed this moment. They're about to announce the result. Come and join us downstairs.'

For a moment, Jamie hesitated. Then an unexpected excitement took hold of him, banishing the awful grey lethargy that had held him in its grip for the last twelve hours. 'Right, okay, Aunt Polly. Thanks. I'll just grab a T-shirt.'

Inside the hall Dave, the reporter, had made contact with the broadcast van outside who, in turn, had alerted London. He then turned his attention to the candidates lining up on the stage.

Juliet was standing by Oliver Merfield's side

and one or two cameras had already started flashing in their direction.

'If he gets elected,' Dave muttered to the cameraman at his side, 'I reckon there's going to be some fun and games ahead.'

In the well of the hall, the small army of photographers and journalists had muscled their way forward to form a line in front of everyone else, and on the balcony the three rival camera crews were poised, ready for action.

'No prizes for guessing who'd win the beauty prize,' a voice murmured in the reporter's earpiece. 'You ready with your piece to camera, Dave, as soon as we get the result? London don't want to hang about.'

'No more do I,' Dave muttered back. 'I've got to get this little lot edited for the early-morning news. Ah, we have lift-off.'

A small middle-aged man in a dark-grey suit, whose thinning hair was stretched over his scalp, who wore a chain of office round his neck, and who nervously clutched a piece of paper, came to the microphone and tapped it. He cleared his throat, pulled himself up and, puffing out his chest, proceeded to thank the assembly for their hard work and patience.

Then he drew a deep breath. 'In the parliamentary by-election for Mendip, I, Peter James Spencer, being the returning officer for the constituency above mentioned, hereby give notice that the total number of votes given for each candidate at the election, was as follows: 'Robin Atkins, United Kingdom Independence Party, eight hundred and fifty-seven; Penny

Dunford, Labour, three thousand, two hundred and thirty-nine...'

A ripple went round the room. Labour hadn't expected to do very well here, but this was a vote considerably down on the last election. Oliver swallowed and tried very hard to look impassive, but he felt for Juliet's hand.

'...Elliot Flowers, Liberal Democrat, twenty thousand, nine hundred and ninety-two...'

There was an audible gasp, one or two cheers from the floor and some applause. Oliver felt weak. It depended on the turnout, but the size of that vote was going to be very hard to beat. Had he failed to hold Mendip for the Conservatives? Would they find him another seat if he lost them one of the safest in this part of the country?

'Roy Green, Independent, eight hundred and fifty-seven...'

The farmer's supporters cheered and he grinned and waved back, cheerful in defeat.

'Oliver Merfield, Conservative...'

Oliver froze. He had been working for this election for months, had thought of little else, had pinned so much on it, and now that it was upon him, the stress of the moment engulfed him; his ears and eyes played tricks and he couldn't hear, couldn't see. But everyone else could.

'Twenty-one thousand, seven hundred and seventy-one–' His supporters went wild, cheering, shouting and stamping. Oliver stared at them, his heart thumping. Had he done it? Had he really done it? By his side he heard Juliet shriek with excitement, something she rarely did.

The returning officer held up his hand for

silence, his job not quite completed. 'Camilla Upton-Scudamore, the Green Party, two thousand, eight hundred and thirty-seven. I declare that the under-mentioned person has been duly elected to serve as member for the said constituency: Oliver Merfield–'

His declaration about the number of spoilt papers was drowned by shouts and cheers from all round the council chamber.

On the balcony, the reporter was already on camera '...so there you have it. Oliver Merfield has been elected, with the Conservative majority slashed dramatically by the Lib Dems; Labour just held onto their deposit and UKIP lost theirs. The electorate are sending the main parties a message and Oliver Merfield is going to have to listen to them very carefully if he's to keep his seat in the general election next year. But he's definitely going to be a politician to watch: he's now the youngest Conservative MP in the House, and for you TV soap fans, he's married to the actress Juliet Peters, who recently left the cast of *Hunter's Way*...'

Juliet stood at Oliver's side, graciously smiling and shaking hands with her husband's supporters and well-wishers. Her thoughts, however, were not so gracious. She was pleased for Oliver – he was her husband and his success reflected on her – but she was used to being the centre of attention and, although she acknowledged that Oliver had earned that right this evening, she was starting to feel disgruntled and could hardly bring herself to be civil when, for the hundredth time, someone pressed her hand and said, 'You must be so thrilled.'

For Juliet was not thrilled.

Most of her life Juliet had been single-minded in the pursuit of her ambition: to become a star, a real star, of stage and screen. Nothing was going to stop her. Her determination and dimples meant she had been luckier than most other aspiring actors, eventually landing a regular part in a TV soap, *Hunter's Way*. Not quite the level of stardom she wanted but a good step in that direction, so she was devastated when, less than a year ago, they told her audience ratings were dropping so they planned the dramatic demise of a much-loved character – and she was to be the sacrificial lamb. Apart from a number of interviews with Hollywood casting agents, there had been no work since.

In the circumstances the last thing Juliet wanted was to be buried in the country.

She wanted Oliver to succeed, she really did – it was just that she didn't want to have to put herself out in any way. Preoccupied with her own life, she'd been content for him to dabble in politics if it kept him happy. When he told her he'd been selected as a candidate in a rural by-election, she was horrified and threw up all sorts of objections, but Oliver was firm.

On the campaign trail she hadn't let him down, playing the candidate's wife to perfection, triumphantly recording the number of times she was recognised as Juliet Peters and not just as Oliver Merfield's wife.

But Oliver was under no illusions about Juliet. He appreciated how much her presence had helped him to victory but was well aware, standing on the stage receiving the congratulations of the other candidates, that there were going to be some sticky times ahead and the role of MP's wife was not one on Juliet's agenda.

'Oliver.' It was Rita. 'I just wanted to say that if Roy wasn't to win, I'm really glad it was you.' She shook him vigorously by the hand, setting her dangly, brightly coloured earrings dancing. 'There's no loss without gain, as they say. Who'd have thought it? Young Oliver Merfield, our MP... Well, well! We'll look forward to seeing you back in the village, you and Juliet. She must be over the moon!'

Oliver laughed at Rita's excitement. He glanced across at Juliet. She was smiling serenely at a noisy cluster gathered around her. From the enchanting girl he had met when she was sixteen, she had grown into a very lovely woman, but he could tell, from the little tuck in the corner of that lovely woman's mouth, she was building up a storm.

Detaching himself from Rita and the group surging around him, he beckoned to Keith.

'Any chance of us getting out of here, pretty soon?' he whispered. 'I think Juliet's had enough of the Town Hall.'

'I'll get the car round.' Keith needed no prompting. He knew that a discontented Juliet could be dangerous and, although the election was in their pocket, the last thing his party would thank him for would be unwelcome publicity at the moment of triumph. 'Don't forget, though, Oliver, you're expected back at party headquarters. The night's not over yet.'

Oliver manoeuvred his way to Juliet's side and said in an undertone, 'The car's outside when you're ready to go, darling.'

She flashed him a look. 'Need you ask?' she hissed. 'I was ready half an hour ago!'

Making their apologies to the mass of people who still pushed to press flesh, he steered her through the hall and out onto the steps, accompanied by the jubilant cheers of seemingly indefatigable party workers. The cameras flashed, and Juliet smiled and waved as enchantingly as anyone could have wished.

'We must phone Jamie,' Oliver murmured as they made their way to the car.

'Not now, for goodness' sake.' Juliet snapped. 'It's nearly three in the morning. He'll be fast asleep. I'll call him before he goes off to school.'

'I'd quite like to tell him myself.' Oliver replied mildly, as they climbed into the car, still smiling for the few remaining photographers.

'Suit yourself. Are we going back to the hotel now? I'm absolutely exhausted.'

'If you want me to drop you off, I will, but we did promise we'd go and have a glass of champagne at the Conservative Club, and I can't let them down.'

The outside broadcast vans had already packed up and gone but Juliet caught sight of the TV reporter hurrying down the steps. She wound her window down as he drew alongside the car.

'Juliet, I'm so glad I caught you. I wanted to congratulate you. I thought you'd be staying around for a drink.'

'We're going on to the Conservative Club; why

40

don't you join us there?'

'I'd love to, but I'm not a paid-up member.'

Juliet laughed engagingly. 'I'm sure, as my guest, you'd be most welcome. I'll leave your name on the door. That would be all right, wouldn't it, darling?' She turned to Oliver, but he was talking on his mobile and giving his full attention to the call.

'Jamie, hi... How did you... Oh, of course, Aunt Polly would... Thanks very much... Yes, I am excited. It was close. Did you watch all of it? Oh, I see, Pol woke you... How do *you* feel? No, I'm back home tomorrow... Yes, we'll talk, then.'

Having finished the conversation with his son, Oliver spoke to Polly, causing Juliet to sink back into her seat, sighing with exasperation.

'And how's Juliet taking it?' his sister asked.

Oliver glanced at his wife, sunk in the shadows, staring out of the car window.

'Oh,' he said lightly, 'like me, really, Pol, a bit overwhelmed with it all. We've got a lot to discuss. Anyway, thanks for being so supportive. I'll give you a ring when we're on our way back to London.'

The car drew up outside the Conservative Club as he finished speaking. The door was opened for them and they were ushered into the building by a small, cheering crowd.

In spite of herself Juliet brightened when, after having a glass of champagne pressed into her hand, someone asked for her autograph, and then another person wanted one, and then another. She found the reporter at her elbow, glass in one hand, bottle of champagne in the other.

'Looks like you've got quite a fan club, here,' he grinned. 'May I top you up?'

Oliver, glancing across at Juliet, smiled to himself. The centre of attraction, she was sparkling and wouldn't demand to be extricated before he was ready to leave. He himself was being slowly processed around the room by the branch chairman, a rotund gentleman in his early sixties, with a red, round, beaming face that belied a pair of shrewd blue eyes.

He was introduced to so many people and shook so many hands that his head began to spin and his facial muscles hurt.

'Now,' said the chairman in an undertone, 'I want you to meet a chap by the name of Hugh Lester. He's not a member, but he's indicated that he's interested in making us a handsome donation. I don't have to tell you, Oliver, that after this election our coffers are somewhat empty, so I invited him along tonight as my guest. Hugh...' He advanced on two men, standing slightly apart, deep in conversation.

Without horse and riding hat, Oliver recognised the name rather than the man. Hugh Lester was immaculately dressed, with crisp black curly hair, clear brown skin, high cheekbones, a strong jaw, and the coldest blue eyes Oliver thought he'd ever seen. His companion was a thin, dark-haired man in his mid-twenties, who looked vaguely familiar. As the chairman converged on them, the latter stepped away with a self-deprecating smile.

'Hugh, old chap, I'd like to introduce our new member for Mendip. Oliver Merfield, Hugh Lester.'

Hugh Lester's handshake was hard and dry, as was his small talk.

'Congratulations. We met briefly once before. You're related to the Merfields of Summerstoke, aren't you?'

'Yes, my grandmother and my two aunts. You know them, of course?'

'As neighbours. They have some land I want to buy. I haven't given up.'

He didn't look like the sort of person who gave up on anything easily, Oliver reflected. But that, of course, would make his grandmother dig her heels in all the more. He smiled and made some polite reply.

Hugh Lester nodded at him and turned to the chairman. 'I'm going to have to shoot off in a minute, Andrew. Mind if I have a quiet word with you first?'

'Not at all,' replied the chairman smoothly. 'Would you excuse me, for a moment, Oliver? I'll be right back.'

As soon as the two men moved off, Oliver found his hand being pumped by the young man, who was hovering nearby.

'Congratulations, Oliver. Wonderful news.' In spite of the heat in the room, the man was wearing a jacket and tie. Dark patches had appeared under his armpits and body odour mingled with a liberal application of aftershave. His face was bony, pale and sweaty, and his dark hair was short and spiked with gel.

'Thanks. Er ... I'm sorry, I've met so many people over this campaign, I can't remember...'

'Mark. Mark Smith. I work for Alberry Harris,

43

the estate agents. You called us a few weeks back.'

'Oh, yes.' Oliver smiled. 'Well, the need to find somewhere has become all the more urgent.'

'It certainly has, Oliver. And I think we've got just the property for you. The owner came into our office only this morning. Very nice it is, too. Could be right up your street. It was a vicarage, so it's nice and spacious, lots of character and in a village just inside your constituency. Couldn't be better.'

'I'll call tomorrow for the details. Sounds very promising. Thank you, Mark. What's the name of the village?'

'Summerstoke.'

'I am not,' said Juliet, stepping out of her blue silk dress, which had slipped unheeded to the floor, and unhitching her bra, 'going to live in sodding Summerstoke. Not in a million years. Next to those witches! You can't make me, Oliver – I won't!'

She removed the last of her underwear and, tossing her copper-gold curls over her naked shoulders, she pushed past Oliver, and went into the shower.

So beautiful, so desirable – and such a brat! thought Oliver, not for the first time, as he towelled himself dry. He felt exhausted. It had been a tactical error on his part, he realised that, saying anything about the house to Juliet before they were back in London. Particularly mentioning Summerstoke. He hadn't been thinking straight. It was going to be hard enough to persuade her to sell their London home and move to the West Country, but they'd discussed it when he was selected and he knew she realised, when he won, the move was inevitable.

He had fond memories of childhood holidays in Summerstoke. His grandmother and aunts still occupied the house that had been in his family for over two hundred years. It felt the most natural move in the world for him to settle in the village, but he had no intention of doing so.

Juliet did not view his family with any warmth. In awe of both his parents, she disliked Polly, his twin, and positively loathed the old ladies who inhabited Summerstoke Manor.

He was dozing when Juliet climbed into the bed beside him. He reached out to her, running his hand gently down the curvature of her body. She responded, turning to him and returning his kisses, moved her fingers gently down his chest to his groin.

He shivered.

She gave a little giggle. 'I've never made love to an MP before. I wonder if it will be any different?'

'The MP and the actress – shall we find out?' he whispered, kissing first one small plump breast and then the other.

He thought she was fast asleep, her head nestling on his shoulder, when he reached out to turn off the light.

'Oliver.'

He turned to find a pair of brilliant blue eyes fixed on him.

'Promise me we'll not move anywhere within

45

spitting distance of the old harpies.'

He groaned. 'Juliet...'

That was it.

'Goodnight, Oliver,' she said coldly, and turning her back on him she rolled over to the far side of the bed.

AUGUST

2

Thwaack!

At an indecent speed the ball whizzed across the court, barely skimming the net and landing just inside the line, with a slight puff of red dust, bounced away into the back of the court.

'Forty-thirty. Match point.'

Richard Garnett wiped the perspiration out of his eyes, smeared the palms of his hands on his crisp white shorts, gripped his racquet, and, with his knees slightly bent, danced on the balls of his feet, watching his opponent.

In spite of the fact that he was overheated and so whacked he didn't think he could run another length of the court, he felt an inner glow of satisfaction. He might be unfit but he'd played a good game, and in front of a pleasing number of onlookers who always collected around Number One court when the club's top seeds were playing.

He cut a dashing figure and he knew it. He might be forty-nine – how would he cope with admitting fifty? – but he was tall, well-built, had a pleasing tan that came quite naturally with the summer; thick hair, strong features without being fleshy, all his own teeth – although they were a bit too yellow for perfection – and dark, mocking eyes. Both men and women admired him, and his easygoing manner and fund of good stories meant that he was a welcome guest at many tables, quite apart from the fact that being the editor of the only local daily newspaper in the region gave him a kudos he relished.

Thwaack!

The ball hurtled over the net with such speed it was barely visible. He just got there – thwaack.

Thwaack.

Feeling every sinew in his body stretch to breaking point, he got there again: thwaack.

Thwaack.

The ball shot past him far to his left, and he turned just in time to see the tiny telltale dust cloud.

'Game, set and match, I think,' shouted his opponent triumphantly and ran towards the net to shake his hand.

He grinned at her. 'Well done, Vee. You're some player.'

It was unfortunate she managed to look so smug, he reflected, as they left the court to a smattering of applause.

He'd known Veronica Lester and her husband, Hugh, ever since he'd moved to Bath after the collapse of his first marriage, ten years ago. Richard had been introduced to Hugh as 'someone it would be useful to get on your side, old chap.' His adviser had been right. Hugh Lester knew everyone who was anyone and could open doors normally closed to members of Richard's profession.

Richard had cultivated the friendship and it gave him a valuable finger on the pulse of the region. If, on occasion, he buried a story that might have made headlines, he was more than compensated for the favour by inside information he could use.

Richard was well aware that Hugh Lester was formidable in his ruthlessness, certainly not the sort of person to cross, and he was equally aware that, while he might flirt with Veronica (which she encouraged), anything more would be fatal.

Not that he was tempted. Veronica was younger than him by a few years, and though she was tall and slim, her hair thick and blonde, and there was a latent sensuality about her, she wasn't at all pretty – he found her nose rather long, her teeth slightly prominent and her chin a bit too underhung. Also, he noticed as he walked off the court with her, her skin was starting to look a bit lined and weathered, probably as a consequence of the time she spent with her horses.

But he liked her. She was as strong and as ruthless as her husband, but unlike Hugh she had a sense of fun and their friendship had flourished. All in all, he was glad he didn't find Veronica more attractive (although, of course, he gave her no inkling of that) because it meant that their relationship remained on a refreshingly platonic level – something quite rare for Richard.

Showered and changed, they met for the obligatory G and T in the club bar.

'God, I'm unfit!' Richard groaned, stretching out his long limbs.

'Well, thank goodness you are, darling. I might not have beaten you otherwise. So far,' she said, preening, 'I've had a good summer. I've not lost a singles yet.'

'You put me to shame. I need to get up here more.' He took a long, appreciative sip of gin. 'It's such a pity Isabelle's no interest in tennis.'

Veronica eyed him curiously. 'Do you know, Richard, in the ten years I've known you, eight of which you've been married to Issy, I've never been able to work out what drives you as far as women are concerned. I mean, I'm sorry if I'm speaking out of turn, but I like to think we're the best of friends...'

'I like to think so, too.'

'Well, then, darling, you'll forgive me if I say I just don't understand why you married her.' She shrugged. 'I know I've said this before, countless times. You're an attractive man; you came down here footloose and fancy-free, the sort of man who'd never be short of a girlfriend, or a mistress if you prefer, then out of the blue, you marry a girl eighteen years your junior.'

'Seventeen.'

'Who's pretty and arty, I grant you that, but hardly says a word, looks out at the world with those huge eyes of hers as if she's going to burst into tears any minute, and in whose company, quite frankly, I die of boredom after five minutes. And you can't deny you're bored, too, Richard. I'm not blind.'

'Oh?' Richard lifted his eyebrows, a slight smile playing over his lips.

'I know you've had affairs.' Veronica paused and studied the slice of lemon stuck on the ice at the bottom of her glass. 'Rosalind Harris, for example.'

Richard looked surprised. 'That was four or five years ago.'

'But it wasn't the first, was it, and I don't suppose it'll be the last.'

52

'No,' he said candidly, 'I don't suppose it will. What's this, Vee, an expression of outrage at my immoral behaviour? I wouldn't have expected this from you.'

'No, of course it's not,' she replied, testily. 'Far from it. Having saddled yourself with Issy, I'm not at all surprised. But why did you do it in the first place? You've never given me a satisfactory explanation and I think you owe me one.'

'Why's that?'

'Because,' Veronica breathed in deeply, 'whenever I have a dinner party, like the one next Saturday, small, select and important, I choose my guests carefully. You'd always be one of the first to be invited...'

'Why, thank you.'

'Except that then we're stuck with Issy.'

There was a moment's silence.

Richard got to his feet and held out his hand.

For a moment Veronica thought maybe she had gone too far, but before she had time to apologise, or tick him off for taking offence, he smiled. 'Another gin, Vee?'

She watched him walk across to the bar, greeting other members with an easy bonhomie as he went. She meant what she had said. He really was an attractive man, both physically and temperamentally. If it wasn't for Issy... They couldn't even go out in a foursome any more because Hugh would be stuck with her, and after the last occasion he had refused, point blank, to do it again. Now, if she even suggested including them on her guest list, he pulled a face or made a fuss.

Richard was thoughtful as he made his way to

the bar. He was well aware his marriage to Isabelle puzzled his friends.

She had been such an independent spirit when they first met. There was something wild and elusive about her and she had a fragility that he found utterly enchanting. Richard had never wanted anyone so much, and pulled out all the stops to make it happen. An inexperienced twenty-two-year-old, she hadn't been able to resist him, but with marriage and babies she'd become a pale shadow of herself, lost those qualities he'd found so alluring, and yes, Vee was right, become a bit of a liability.

When he returned with the drinks, he smiled his most rueful smile and leaned towards Vee, confidingly. 'I'm sorry, Vee. Issy's never at her best in company, and since the girls were born she's become even more introverted. Truth to tell, the girl I met is chalk and cheese with the one I'm married to now. Believe me, she really was something – and so different from Clare, my first wife, who was an organisational freak.' He sipped his gin, reflecting. 'I met her in an art gallery, in the company of some tiresome gay friend, as I recall. It was her first exhibition. She was wearing this fiery red dress and looked wild and, well, bloody sexy. I found her paintings remarkably odd. Great splashes of colour – a load of bollocks, I thought, but everyone was raving about them, said she had great talent.' He shrugged and continued, dryly, 'I was lonely after Clare booted me out; I suppose I was vulnerable; I fell head over heels.'

'But why did you marry her. Why couldn't you have done what any sensible person would've done and had an affair till passion had run its course?'

Richard grimaced. 'You're right. But I did marry her, and I've two lovely little girls–'

'And a washed-up artist for a wife. Does she do any painting now?'

'Nothing since Becky was born. Six years it's been. But I've not given up. And I reckon once she starts painting again, she'll regain her old fire.'

'And in the meantime you, we, have to put up with a limp rag.'

'That's the way it is, Vee.' He smiled at her, twinkling. 'But she's not that bad. There are ... compensations.'

A twinge of jealousy caught Veronica unawares and, swallowing too large a mouthful of gin, she choked. When she had caught her breath, she said acerbically, 'Well, I'm glad there are compensations for you, Richard, I really am. What a pity we don't get to share them.'

Richard gave her a wicked look. 'What? Are you suggesting four in a bed, Vee?'

'Oh, shut up, you horrible man,' Vee laughed, her good mood restored. 'I certainly am not. There are limits to friendship.'

'So what are we to do? Are you uninviting us to your dinner party next weekend?'

'No, of course not, don't be silly. I need you. I've finally managed to get *Country Houses and Gardens* interested in our plans for Summerstoke House stud. That sort of publicity's priceless. Their chief feature writer, Harriet Flood, is coming to check us out. Une dame un peu formidable, I'm told and I know I can rely on you to

55

charm the spots off her.'

'Who else is coming?'

'A rather delicious young man I played tennis with last week, by the name of Simon Weatherby – he's only just joined the club so I don't suppose you'd have met him – and Marion and Gavin Croucher. I know Gavin will wield that old-school charm, but he really only has one line of conversation.'

'Horses.' Richard laughed.

'Exactly.'

'Then, my dearest Vee' – Richard lifted her hand and kissed it – 'I am yours to command. And as for my poor little Isabelle...' He shook his head. 'She doesn't always have to accompany me, you know. I suspect she'd much rather stay at home with the children. Actually, Vee.' Suddenly he looked serious. His voice deepened and, not for the first time, Veronica Lester entertained thoughts of infidelity. 'I was going to consult you. I'm thinking of moving her and the children out of Bath altogether. She doesn't like living there, I know. It's too ... too precious for her. I think she'd be far happier in a village environment. What do you think?'

As Hugh Lester entered the hall of Summerstoke House, he could hear his wife's voice floating from the kitchen. Hanging up his crop, he sat on a large oak settle to remove his riding boots, half listening to his wife's conversation through the open door.

'Yes, I'm sure. Absolutely... I'll check with Hugh, but I can't imagine he'll put up any opposition.

Fine … see you both this evening... Oh, the usual, seven thirty for eight. See you then. Bye.'

His second boot came off with a clatter on the highly polished tiled floor and Veronica Lester appeared at the kitchen door. 'Hello, darling. I was thinking of making some iced coffee. D'ye want some? It's too hot for anything else.'

'Thanks.'

He padded across the floor, his sweaty feet leaving damp prints in his wake, and followed her into the light, airy kitchen in which all the surfaces gleamed and all the pots and pans knew their place. Hugh never came in here during the week, when their daily was in residence, but it was the weekend and so he slumped down at the long oak table.

'I've never known August so hot,' he said. 'The ground's like concrete. The horses are miserable.'

She placed a tall glass of black coffee and cracked ice in front of him. 'You should try taking Sultan out just before dawn. I had a great ride this morning.'

He looked up at her. Tall, shapely, not a hair out of place, immaculately turned out even though she was in the middle of cooking for a dinner party, she defied her forty-odd years. He raised his brows. 'Your stamina's an example to us all. Either of our useless offspring up?'

Veronica brought her coffee over to the table. 'Not yet. Anthony didn't get back till really late last night – I heard his bike in the yard sometime after one o'clock – and you really don't expect Cordelia to be up before midday, do you? She's a teenager!'

57

Hugh snorted and sipped his coffee. 'Who were you talking to on the phone just now?'

'Marion, Marion Croucher.'

'What did she want?'

'We were discussing a business proposition.'

Marion, an interior designer, was the wife of a crony of Hugh's, and Veronica's closest friend. Hugh had the highest opinion of his wife's business acumen, but this morning he was too hot, he hadn't much enjoyed his ride, and he was not looking forward to having to entertain Harriet Flood, due to arrive later that afternoon, so he snapped, rather aggressively, 'What sort of business proposition?'

Veronica raised her eyebrows and surveyed her husband coolly. 'She wants to open a shop.'

'Bloody hell! What sort of shop?'

'Interior design, of course: that's her business. She says there's so much more she could do if she didn't operate from home, and I see her point. The logical place to open a shop would be Bath, but premises there are expensive and it would be a long haul in every day, so she's looking round the villages.'

'And?'

'And what, darling? You sound so cross.' She got up, went to the fridge and got out a pitcher of black coffee.

'I heard you say something about checking with me, that's what.'

She topped up his glass and trailed her fingers through his mane of black hair, which even though he was nearly fifty barely showed any sign of silver. Hugh was secretly very proud of his

58

thick mop, seeing it as a statement of his virility.

'You're going to have to get your hair cut soon, my sweet. It's amazing how quickly it grows.' Veronica's tone was light and teasing, and she dropped a kiss on the top of his head before continuing with her tale. 'So I suggested she had a look at the village shop, here in Summerstoke.'

'It's not for sale, is it?' Hugh ran his fingers through his hair, his irritability fading.

'No. But you know that dreadful Godwin woman's always complaining we don't use it enough – as if we'd want to buy the things she stocks. I think the business is teetering, so I suggested Marion made a pre-emptive strike – you know, go in there, say she'd be interested in buying if the woman was interested in selling; hint she'd give her a good price, but say she's in no hurry for a decision.'

'But Marion hasn't the kind of money to buy a place in Summerstoke. I know you say her business is doing well, but from what Gavin says, not so well that they can afford to fork out the sort of money the Godwins would ask for. The Godwins aren't stupid. They'd have the place properly valued.'

Veronica leaned forward in her chair, her long nose twitching slightly with excitement. 'That's where we come in, Hugh. We'd put up the capital to buy the building.'

'What!' Hugh almost exploded with disbelief. 'Vee, are you mad? What on earth would we want with a fucking shop?'

Veronica smiled. 'Listen, dearest, we can't lose. As I see it, the scenario goes like this. We put up

59

the money, Marion buys and she does all the alterations, etc – that's her part of the deal. I tell you, darling, I'd give her no more than a year – that's generous – before she folds. The building is then ours.'

'But what would we want–'

Veronica held up her hand to silence him. 'We buy the building as a shop; now, as you know, retail premises are considerably cheaper than residential to buy; so the shop doesn't work – it closes – we apply for planning permission for change of use – granted. Happens all the time, and we've acquired a valuable property in Summerstoke that, with a minimum of effort, we sell on as a residential property in what is a very desirable part of the country.'

Hugh was impressed, in spite of himself. 'Does Marion know the whole of it?'

Veronica gave a dismissive little laugh. 'No, of course not. And don't you say anything to Gavin. For this to work to our advantage, we must be the only signatories on the property.'

'I thought she was your best friend?'

Veronica shrugged. 'She is. And I'm helping her get what she wants, aren't I? I'm just using a little speculative sense.'

'So you are. You're a clever thing, aren't you?' Hugh looked at his wife with admiration. 'Supposing the Godwin woman won't sell?'

Veronica gave a short laugh. 'Then we lose nothing. But she will. That shop's on its last legs and if people are encouraged not to shop there... We could start a little rumour about Health and Safety. You know what this village is like – a tiny

60

pebble tossed into a pond becomes a tidal wave.'

'My God, Vee.' Hugh gave a short, harsh laugh. 'You'd outclass Machiavelli with your machinations.' He ran an immaculately manicured finger down his wife's bare arm. 'I'm going to take a shower. Fancy scrubbing the parts I can't reach?'

Veronica recognised the invitation for what it was and shook her head, smiling at him. 'I don't think I could risk it, Hugh. We might disturb the children.'

'For Chrissake, Vee, Anthony's nineteen and if Cordelia's not asleep, she'll be plugged into her iPod. Don't you want to?'

'Of course I do, darling.' Her lips brushed his hair and she slipped her hand inside his shirt. His chest hairs were slimy with perspiration. She gave a nipple a playful tweak and withdrew her hand as tactfully as she could. 'But later. Go and have a shower now and we'll have a rendezvous with a bottle of bubbly this afternoon, before our guests arrive.'

'What time's this Harriet woman getting here?' He drained his coffee and got up.

'We arranged about six, so I can show her around. She wasn't specific, so she'll get a taxi from the station. The others are coming at seven thirty.'

'Who are the others? I know the Crouchers are coming, but who else?'

'That guy I met at the country club, Simon Weatherby. He's interesting – works as a business trouble-shooter. Very high-powered.'

'Good. Perhaps he can help us do some shooting of our own.'

61

'And the Garnetts. Richard will charm the socks off Harriet; he's worth his weight in gold.'

Hugh groaned. 'Pity you can't say the same about his wife. Just don't sit her anywhere near me.'

Veronica smiled at him. 'I won't. But I'm relying on you to work your own personal magic on Harriet Flood, darling, so don't end up talking horses with Gavin Croucher all evening.'

Isabelle Garnett stared at herself critically in the mirror. God, she looked washed-out.

'Thirty-two and already over the hill,' she muttered, picking up a make-up palette. Selecting a silvery grey, she smeared the lids of her huge blue eyes, blackened her fair eyelashes with mascara, patted her cheeks with some rouge powder and sat back to look at the result.

A waiflike creature stared back. The make-up sat like a layer of paint, emphasising the fine lines and the shadows of fatigue, rather than concealing them, and with her cropped blonde hair, she looked, she thought, like a tragic clown.

'Oh, sod it.'

She rifled amongst the clutter on her dressing table, the surface of which was a chaotic jumble of make-up, ribbons, little porcelain dishes overflowing with pins, earrings, slides, brooches and buttons, and found a crimson lipstick, which she creamed over her lips. She loved the colour and it matched her dress: layers of light drifting chiffon, a whirl of orange and red.

Having sprayed herself cautiously with Jo Malone, a present from her husband but a bit fierce for her, she thought, she adorned her bare arms with brightly coloured bangles and selected a pair of long red coral and silver earrings that dangled from the thin metal arms of a miniature clothes dummy balanced on a box, a present from her eldest daughter. It immediately toppled over, dislodging a curled photograph from a small gilt letter rack stuffed with dusty cards and fading snapshots she'd not looked at for ages.

She glanced at her watch. Nearly seven. Richard was cutting it fine, even by his standards.

She stood up from her dressing table and, picking up the photograph from the floor, crossed the bedroom to the long glass that Richard had salvaged in the division of spoils when his first marriage collapsed.

Critically she examined herself. Yes, the espadrilles worked and she liked the fact they added a couple of inches to her five foot five inches. Richard was over six foot and she hated having to crane her neck to talk to him. Not only that, but Hugh Lester, their host that evening, hated being the shortest person in the room. She disliked him enough to enjoy the prospect of looking down at him. Her outfit was faintly bohemian but, she reflected, that was what people expected of her, even though she hadn't produced a painting for years.

She glanced at the photograph in her hand, intending to stuff it back in the rack, but the picture caught her attention.

'Joe,' she said softly, and smiled.

It was a snapshot, taken eleven years ago, of her and Joe, her best mate at art school, at their final exhibition. She was holding aloft the Steel Cup, awarded to the most promising graduate of the year, and Joe, with a mop of ginger hair and a straggly beard, was pulling an appalling face, pretending to stab her in the back.

She sat on the edge of the bed, gazing at the picture.

She'd met Joe shortly after she joined the school and he'd told her on their first encounter that he was going to become the most important sculptor of the century.

Life as an impoverished art student had been difficult, particularly as her parents were un-comprehending and unsympathetic. For three years, she and Joe had supported each other through the knocks and the low points of student life, and together they had celebrated the highs.

He had been there when she first met Richard.

It was in a small but prestigious gallery off London Bridge where her work was being shown alongside a well-known painter's, and the gallery was packed. Joe had come along to lend moral support.

They were standing together, clutching their wine glasses, watching the crowd and straining to catch comments on Isabelle's paintings when Joe nudged her elbow. 'Who's that guy over there, Isabelle? The tall one, dark, wavy hair. Do you know him?'

The man he pointed out was a good bit older than her, but looked, she thought, very romantic. He was lean and tanned, with dark, intense eyes, wearing a loose linen open-necked white shirt. And he was staring across the room at her. She caught his eye and blushed.

'No,' she said and turned to Joe, 'I don't know him. I wonder why he's staring at me? He's a bit of all right, isn't he?'

Joe looked across at Richard. 'He's too old for you,' he said, 'and he looks as if he's used to getting what he wants. He'll eat you alive. I wouldn't go near him, if I were you.'

Joe had been right. Richard *was* used to getting what he wanted.

She stroked the photograph. She'd insisted on Joe coming to the registry office as her witness, even though she knew he was unhappy about it.

When she left London to move into Richard's house in Bath, she and Joe kept in touch, and shortly after the birth of Clemmie, her second daughter, he phoned to say he was coming to see her.

She'd been full of mixed feelings about his visit. She so wanted to see him again, but she was afraid he would shake his head at the way her life had worked out – a mother, a housewife, but no painting, nothing, her talent wasted.

She'd shown him round the house, they played with the children, and over lunch sat and chatted about past times and old friends.

Then he took her hand and gave her a searching look, 'Do you belong here, Isabelle?'

She made some prevaricating reply, but he was right. Even now, after eight years of it being her home, she still felt as if the house, a tall, four-storeyed Georgian terraced house, had not fully accepted her right to be there.

She looked up from the photograph and gazed

about her.

Their bedroom, in particular, reflected that feeling. A large, airy room, with the evening sun pouring through long sash windows, picking up the dust on the cluttered dressing table. That was indubitably her, but the rest of the room, with its polished oak floor, large deep-pile rugs, elegant iron bed and white furnishings, the white walls and white-painted shutters at the windows, the much-coveted original Lowry on the wall, the fitted wardrobes with polished brass handles – all that was Richard.

Richard was Georgian, neat, orderly, everything at right angles, everything in its place; whereas she was Victorian, spiral staircases, turrets and dark, spidery corners.

'What do you mean?' she had said to Joe, not wanting to meet, head on, the implication of his questioning. 'What do you mean? I've a lovely house, two beautiful daughters and my husband loves me–'

'Does he? Or are you one of his possessions? Aren't you completely subsumed by him? Where are *you* in all of this?'

'Joe was right,' she mused, as she gathered her discarded clothing off the floor with one hand, holding the photograph in the other. 'He could see what I wouldn't.'

Even the friends they had – no, she corrected herself, especially the friends – were Richard's. Following his lead, they insisted on calling her Issy. 'That's not my name. My name is Isabelle. I hate being called Issy; my friends call me

66

Isabelle.' But it didn't matter how hard she tried to make herself heard, they called her Issy, infantilising her.

Defensive, she had grown angry with Joe. 'You don't know what you're talking about. Richard loves me for what I am, and I'm more than just my painting. I've two children, Joe. You may consider it a cliché, but they're part of me – don't you see *that* as an achievement? If I do nothing else with my life, at least I've produced them, and that's something you'll never do.'

He'd looked sad and said he had to go and that he'd come to say goodbye as he had been offered an artist's residency in Australia. At that she'd burst into tears and the two had hugged each other, made promises about writing and to see each other again, one day... Then the taxi came to take him to the station.

She looked closely at herself in the photo. She was wearing a short red dress and black net tights, her hair was streaming wild over her shoulders, her head was thrown back, her face full of laughter and–

She started, hearing the hall door slam, stuffed the photo back into the rack, and bundled the clothes she had recently discarded into the bottom of her half of the wardrobe. She'd just managed to squeeze it shut when the bedroom door opened and Richard entered.

One quick glance told her he was in a filthy mood, a frown marring his features. She went to give him a kiss, but he brushed her away with a perfunctory 'Not now, Issy, I'm late and I'm not in the mood. Start the shower for me, would you?'

He started to remove his clothing. 'Where's the shirt I asked you to iron?'

'It's hanging up in the bathroom.'

In fact, Isabelle had only remembered about his shirt at the last minute, after the babysitter had arrived, and it was the babysitter who had pressed it for her, making a far better job of it than Isabelle, who hated ironing.

'What kept you?' she asked tentatively. 'You know the Lesters are expecting us at seven thirty?'

'Sodding meeting overran and then the bloody traffic had come to a standstill at Cleveland Bridge. On a Saturday evening – I ask you! Some fucking lorry had broken down. Go get the car out. I'll phone ahead when we're on the road. If Vee's making one of her fucking culinary master-pieces, she'll need to know we're late.'

Isabelle followed him into the bathroom, a frisson of apprehension making her stumble over her words slightly.

'I'm afraid we'll have to go in your car tonight, Richard. Mine's not back from its MOT. The garage phoned to say collect it on Monday.'

In fact, she'd only taken the car in late that morning, knowing full well the chances of them being able to complete the MOT before lunch-time, when they knocked off for the weekend, were remote.

'What?' he shouted. 'You've got to be joking! What a fucking useless bunch they are. I've had a fucking day and now I won't be able to have a fucking drink!' Richard's car was a sleek, silver, classic Jaguar and he didn't allow anyone else to drive it.

She left him to work out his fury under the shower and went downstairs, into the playroom. It was a small room at the back of the house. Isabelle had decorated it herself and the walls were a cheerful deep yellow. On one she'd painted a mural of a fairy castle, unicorns, a dragon and other fantastical creatures. On the others she'd pinned family photos, prints of favourite cartoon characters and all the drawings her daughters had produced.

The floor was covered with an assortment of brightly coloured, plastic toys (Clemmie's); a large dolls' house (Rebecca's) stood in one corner, the front open to reveal every room neatly arranged and a family of miniature dolls sitting round a miniature dining table.

Her two little daughters, washed and ready for bed, were sat on the sofa cuddled up to Angela, the babysitter, watching a cartoon.

Rebecca looked at her anxiously. 'Is Daddy cross with you, Mummy? We heard him shouting.'

'He swore. We heard Daddy swear,' chimed Clemmie, with a certain satisfaction.

'He's had a bad day so he's a bit cross. Don't worry, Becky, it's nothing to do with me. Now, be good children for Angela, won't you, and go to bed when she tells you to.'

She collected the obligatory offering of a bottle of wine and a box of expensive-looking truffles they'd recently been given. (Isabelle sometimes fantasised about how many times a box of chocolates would be passed from dinner party to dinner party before someone actually took the

69

plunge and opened them.) As a precaution, she checked the sell-by date. Still okay, just.

'Come on, Isabelle. What the hell are you doing? I thought you were ready?'

She trailed out into the hall and arrived at the front door just in time to hear Richard explode with fury.

'They've done it again – the bastards have done it again! I'll kill 'em! Just wait till I get my hands on them.'

He was standing by his car, looking at his right hand, the fingers spread out, smeared, golden brown, sticky and dripping.

Isabelle sighed deeply.

Periodically, Richard insisted that his newspaper conduct 'name and shame' campaigns against things as diverse as drinking on the streets, traffic flow, litter-louts, pigeon nuisance, Asbo terrors, *leylandii* hedges, homelessness, and drink-drivers. Someone had taken offence at being pilloried, blamed Richard and a number of times, Richard, who liked to drive his very distinctive car around town, had found honey liberally smeared all over his door handle.

With an oath, he pushed past her and headed for the downstairs cloakroom.

She wanted to laugh, but knew that would be a huge mistake.

'Shall I call the police?' She couldn't think what else to say.

'What fucking for? We'd waste a whole evening waiting for them to arrive just to hear them say they wouldn't be able to do anything unless I caught the bastards red-handed, and then they'd probably let them go because it would only be my word against theirs. Fucking useless. Go and wipe the rest of that shit off would you, and then we'll get going. My God, I am sick and tired of this fucking city.'

This was a cry she was hearing on a regular basis these days, she reflected as she went and collected rubber gloves, hot soapy water, and a wet cloth.

When Richard started a mantra like that, it usually meant that he was building up to doing something. She wouldn't be directly included in the decision-making process but would be presented with the results as if she had been.

He'd bought the family car on that basis, swapping her neat and dearly beloved elderly Morris Traveller for a second-hand Discovery; the old Aga had been ripped out and replaced by a huge gleaming gas range; a conservatory had been built in place of the terrace at the back of the house. (The terrace had been a suntrap and a wonderful place to sit in the evening; the conservatory was too hot for comfort.)

Even her short hair was the result of a decision by Richard. After Clemmie was born, she had been tired and depressed, and her long fair hair had gone thin and lank. After making a number of comments about how she might look better if she had it cut, he'd made her an appointment with his hairdresser without telling her, and delivered her up to the scissors.

And now this.

She didn't want to move out of the city. She wouldn't mind moving house, preferably to the southern side, where the architecture was more diverse and the countryside more accessible. But move out of the city altogether? The thought was appalling.

3

Richard and Isabelle were half an hour late when Richard drove the Jaguar through a pair of high wrought-iron gates into the courtyard of Summerstoke House and parked it next to an ornamental fountain.

Summerstoke House, a self-important residence that had belonged to the Lester family since Hugh was six, was on the outskirts of Summerstoke at the end of the High Street.

The village had grown up on the steeper side of a river valley, which, in times gone by, had flooded badly in the winter and become a breeding ground for mosquitoes in the summer. Inevitably the homes of the wealthier villagers were built on the higher ground and, needless to say, Summerstoke House was the highest of them all, looking down over village, river and water meadows.

Veronica, elegant in an expensive black silk shift, met them as they entered the hall. 'Richard, at last! No, no excuses. You can tell me later – I'm in the middle of a culinary crisis. Issy, darling, you look lovely, so bohemian! Go and find Hugh in the drawing room. Everyone else is here.' So saying, she disappeared back into the kitchen.

'This is the sort of house that Richard would like ours to look like,' thought Isabelle, not for the first time. Victorian, it had been built with money and no taste and converted by the Lesters, who had plenty of both, into a stylish, beautiful home.

The drawing room, where the party was under way, had light cream walls adorned with gilt-framed oil paintings of horses. The carpet was the colour of old gold; in the window bays, expensive cream silk and linen drapes hung from ceiling to floor; even the lilies in the fireplace matched the décor of the room and added to the air of discreet elegance and wealth.

The guests had formed into two loose groups. Isabelle recognised Gavin and Marion Croucher, whom she'd met before at similar gatherings. Gavin, tall, thin, slightly stooped, in his early fifties, was an ex-Olympic show jumper. Isabelle thought him an old bore, with no conversation apart from his prowess with horses, how many he owned and how much he sold them for.

His wife, Marion, in her late forties, short and plump, wearing layers of chocolate, tan and cream silk, ran a very select interior-design company. With Isabelle her manner was invariably patronising.

'Darling Issy, how nice to see you,' she murmured. 'What an interesting combination of colour, orange and crimson, very bohemian, but then you do have youth on your side.'

She was talking to an unpleasant-looking woman, with artificially black hair, skin the colour and texture of china clay, and sharp, malicious eyes.

Isabelle was introduced to her, but their introduction was so perfunctory that she forgot her name immediately. The woman, displaying no interest or curiosity in Isabelle, resumed her conversation with Anthony, the Lesters' son, who was nineteen and the only one of the Lester family Isabelle liked.

'Hi, Anthony,' she said, lightly.

He gave her the glimmer of a smile, which faded on the approach of his mother, and the next time Isabelle turned in his direction he'd vanished.

The champagne cocktail Hugh had pressed on her when they arrived, quickly went and was followed by another, so by the time Veronica seated them round the dining table she was starting to feel light-headed.

'So, tell me, what boring old story kept you in the office on a Saturday, and made you so late, Richard?'

Aware Veronica had cast him in the role of chief entertainment officer, Richard rose without hesitation to her challenge and, seeking to draw the attention of the whole table, slightly raised his voice in reply. 'I'll tell you if you want me to, Vee, but I should warn you, it's not a subject for polite dinner parties or for those of a squeamish disposition.'

It worked. Immediately there was a general exhortation to tell them the worst.

Sipping her glass of wine, Isabelle didn't join in; she was starting to feel a bit dizzy.

'A nasty substance smeared on the handle of

74

my car.'

The delicate ambiguity of the words he had chosen, with just the right tone of light good humour, produced a gratifying reaction. Ignoring his wife's gaze, Richard responded to the shrieks and requests for elucidation, turning his sticky encounter into a gripping, but entertaining story of being stalked by someone who he suspected was out for revenge because Richard, as editor of the local paper, felt it was his duty to expose those who'd done wrong.

Social nicety meant that he was never actually asked to describe what the substance was. He left it to the guests' imaginations and was well rewarded by their cries of horror.

The crabmeat ravioli, Vee's triumphant offering as the first course, was replaced by champagne sorbet, and every last drop of the white wine Hugh was willing to part with was drunk before the discussion finally turned to other things.

Veronica excused herself and went to oversee the main course.

At her departure, smaller conversational groups formed. Marion talked to the other female guest about the use of colour in Victorian homes, very much a one-sided conversation as the woman displayed more interest in the contents of her wine glass than in listening to Marion; and Hugh and Gavin became involved in a deep discussion about the merits of Hugh allowing a client, from one of the oil-rich Arab states, to invest in his proposed expansion.

Isabelle, realising that no one would be interested in a more truthful version of Richard's experiences, had remained silent while he held centre-stage, but two glasses of fine chardonnay plus two champagne cocktails made her feel bold enough to sit back in her chair and say, lightly, to no one in particular, 'Well I, personally, think any self-appointed guardian of public morality deserves the shit they get thrown at them.'

She was aware of a startled look from the man on her left – he'd been introduced to her earlier as Simon Weatherby and she had immediately liked him – and Richard, turning to join in the conversation with the two other ladies, looked back sharply.

Unperturbed, she carried on. 'The trouble is that newspapers, or rather their editors, have muddied the waters, don't you think?'

Simon, with a glance at Richard, gave a guarded reply. 'How do you mean?'

'Yes, darling, what on earth do you mean?' There was a warning note in Richard's voice.

'Newspapers should reflect the news – tell it how it is as far as possible, and not indulge in ridiculing or pillorying individuals. That's what I mean. What gives them the right to do that? And what defence do people have against such a powerful and arbitrary exposure? It's hardly surprising, in the end, that the worm turns.'

They were interrupted by the return of Veronica, bearing outsize white plates on each of which was arranged elegantly sliced breast of duck, nestling on a bed of puy lentils, accompanied by little parcels of fine green beans fastened with chives. As the guests were served, and Hugh filled their glasses with a fine Bordeaux, Richard leaned

76

across the table to his wife.

'Your use of the epithet "worms" is very appropriate, darling. That's what the majority of these people are, worms.'

'Some of them may be, but a lot of the time they're just ordinary people who've made a mistake and their lives are made hell by the sort of campaigns you run against them.'

Veronica, about to embark on a flirtatious exchange with Simon, at least ten years her junior, immediately tuned in to the tension growing between husband and wife.

She laughed gaily. 'Come on, you two, you must try this duck. It's the first time I've tried this recipe.'

But her attempt to divert was in vain.

'How do you mean: "ordinary people"?' Richard scoffed. 'We don't target people who've done nothing wrong. You may sneer, sweetheart, but I'm proud of my paper's record.'

'Well, I hope you never get caught doing something wrong. Anyone can make a mistake and I think the sort of naming and shaming campaign run by your newspaper is horrid.'

She drank deeply from her glass, aware that Veronica was looking at her coldly, aware of the quietness of the man on her left, aware that Richard was getting increasingly irritated with her.

He shook his head dismissively. 'Like it or not, we have a lot of support for it. Don't you think people who drink and drive, for instance, ought to be identified, Issy, darling? After all, they could easily kill someone.'

'The fact that they could is taken into account

77

by the punishment they receive from the court.' Isabelle was aware that her voice was getting louder and shriller and that others round the table had stopped talking and were listening to their conversation, but she carried on, past caring. 'Why should you take it upon yourself to punish them further? What you're doing is little better than shoving them in the stocks, and the only reason you're doing it is to sell newspapers.'

'And if we sell newspapers because of our campaign, doesn't that mean we have public support?' Richard's voice was cold.

Isabelle felt a little bubble of anger grow inside her. He was so complacent – they were all so complacent.

'You're playing to the lowest common denom-inator, to the prurient spectator who gloats over the discomfiture of others while probably offend-ing in the same way.' She glared round at the rest of the table, all of whom were now listening. She knew she sounded pompous, but she didn't care. 'I bet there's nobody here who can say, hand on heart, they haven't driven under the influence of alcohol.'

There was an uncomfortable silence.

Veronica was the first to speak. Her guests had been made to feel awkward; Isabelle had trans-gressed an unspoken rule.

'Most of us are a good bit older than you, Isa-belle. In *our* student days, attitudes were different; but I'm sure, now, no one round this table would dream of taking the risk. The ones who appear in court deserve everything they get. In irresponsible hands, the car is a lethal weapon. We magistrates,

78

you know' – Veronica was a justice of the peace and liked being so – 'feel very strongly about it. Richard's naming and shaming campaign has our support, one hundred per cent.'

Richard sat back and sipped his wine as the party, with the exception of the bloke between Isabelle and Vee, and of the Lesters' star guest, Harriet Flood (who, he noticed, leaned across Hugh to help herself to more wine and quaffed it with evident enjoyment), joined in the demolition job on his wife.

Issy must be pretty drunk to speak out like that, he thought. She rarely criticised him openly. Silly bitch. But his annoyance stemmed as much from the fact he'd have to drive them home and Hugh always produced the finest *appellations*. He'd allowed himself two glasses and was about to finish the second. His resentment grew. The wine was bloody wasted on Issy; she might just have well got drunk on cider. He toyed with the idea of leaving the car overnight and getting a taxi back, but then he'd have the drag of having to rescue it the next day.

When Isabelle was humiliated to the company's satisfaction, the conversation shifted and Richard was drawn in to entertain them with stories from his newspaper, which he did with aplomb, provoking much laughter.

He felt better, and, draining the last of his wine, turned to Veronica, 'Would you mind very much, Vee, if I leave the car here tonight? We'll get a cab back, then I can pick it up tomorrow.'

She smiled, 'I should have suggested that

earlier, Richard, of course. Look, Harriet's staying till after lunch. Why don't you join us, then you could give her a lift to Bath station? Oh no, you can't. Your car's a two-seater, isn't it?'

'That's no problem,' he replied smoothly. 'Isabelle couldn't come anyway – she'll have to look after the girls.'

Veronica looked delighted. 'That's great!' Dropping her voice, she confided 'I could do with a bit of help with Harriet – she's not the easiest customer in the world. You can use your charm on her.'

'Nothing would give me greater pleasure,' he grinned, glancing across at the lady in question in time to see her helping herself to another glass from the bottle in the middle of the table. He whispered to Veronica, 'I say, she's knocking it back a bit, isn't she?'

'Yes, and it's starting to get to Hugh. It's a particularly fine red, from a small vineyard in the Bergerac region, and I don't think he has much left. I'd better get you a glass before it all disappears down her gullet.' Raising her voice, she asked Hugh to pass the wine so she could fill Richard's glass.

Isabelle looked up, startled. 'I thought you were going to drive back, Richard?'

'I was,' he replied coldly, still wishing to punish her for her outburst at his expense, 'but it seems daft to ruin the evening, so we're getting a taxi.'

She stared at him then flushed, as, snubbing her, he pointedly turned away to Veronica.

'Whereabouts in Bath do you live?' Simon came to her rescue. 'Is it one of those grand

80

Georgian houses the city's famous for?'

'In a way. It's one of the terraces on the northern side of the city. Very tall, with a long, thin walled garden.' Gratefully, Isabelle turned to talk to him, shutting out the sight of Richard blatantly flirting with their hostess.

Vee looked particularly elegant this evening, Richard thought, in a little black number, backless and very flattering, with her thick blonde hair – a little too blonde for his taste – held back by a black silk band. He suspected that she'd invited this Simon fellow because she fancied an evening's dalliance with him – he certainly was a good-looking bloke. Richard's competitive spirit was roused and, exerting all his charm, he derived a huge amount of amused pleasure from keeping Vee's attention focused on himself.

He glanced across at Hugh. With barely a rudimentary attempt to include the two women either side of him, he was deep in discussion with Gavin about local land prices. As far as Richard could tell, Hugh had only two loves in his life, horses, and Vee. Hugh knew what he wanted and he almost always seemed to get it. Richard admired that. He himself cared too much about what others thought to develop that ruthless streak; he got his way, instead, by exercising an engaging, easy charm.

'So Richard, how's the house-hunting going?' Hugh had broken off his conversation to pour out a dark-red dessert wine to accompany the chocolate maquise with strawberry coulis that was their dessert.

81

Richard ignored the gasp of pained surprise from Isabelle. 'Early days yet, Hugh. I've put a few feelers out, but nothing suitable so far.'

'What sort of place are you looking for?' Marion Croucher gave up trying to impress Harriet Flood and turned to Richard. 'I'd no idea you were thinking of moving. You've got a lovely house in Bath. It's so central, and with a garden. Why are you thinking of selling it?'

It was a good question; as ever with Richard, there was more than one explanation.

He assumed a serious expression. 'Isabelle and I haven't discussed it in depth yet, but we're worried about the girls. This business of the stalking is probably nothing, but it could be the thin end of the wedge. I'd never forgive myself if they became targets.' (Okay, okay, he thought, it was only honey, but it could have easily been something nastier, and someone *is* targeting me.)

He hit the right sombre note and with the exception of Isabelle, who sat mutinous and seething, there were sympathetic murmurs all round.

'Plus,' he improvised, playing the role of caring father in a cruel and wicked world for all that it was worth, 'life in the city is becoming all the more precarious for children, no matter how much we try and protect them.' He allowed his voice a slight wobble. 'There are so many pitfalls – kids from decent homes, decent schools, exposed to drugs, alcohol, whatever.'

A fleeting image of the comprehensive his eldest two had attended, in King's Cross, flitted into his mind: drugs and alcohol weren't the half of it. How much of the deprived inner city had this lot ever experienced?

He continued in a lowered voice, looking solemnly round the table, 'And I don't want that for my little girls.'

'So what are you looking for?' Marion asked.

'Oh, I don't know. Somewhere like Summer-stoke, I suppose. Not too far out of Bath so I can commute – a village with a small school, perhaps.' (And, he thought, one with no fees to find.)

He'd die rather than admit it to this well-heeled lot, but his finances had reached crisis point. His salary was handsome, but Isabelle wasn't earning anything; that little pre-prep school he'd insisted Rebecca went to was bloody expensive and with Clemmie soon to join her there... *And* Clare was permanently on his back to cough up for their two kids. Daniel, thank Christ, was in his last year at Warwick, but Abigail, who had been off back-packing somewhere in Australia, was returning home, expecting to be put through university, and where was he going to find the extra funds for that?

He lived well, he admitted it – he worked damned hard so why shouldn't he enjoy what he earned? But he had to find a way round this shortage of the ready. His house was worth over a million, but he was blowed if he'd move into a cheaper house in Bath. That would hand his enemies a juicy bit of speculative gossip, and anyway he didn't want to live anywhere smaller or with less prestige. Out of the city, houses became cheaper the further away they were. If he could find one at half the price of his own, his problems would be sorted.

But he dithered. He liked living in the city, he liked the buzz, the social life, the immediacy of everything, and he didn't see why he should sacrifice all that. It was the honey that had finally stirred him into action. The first couple of times it happened he'd been annoyed, but got over it. The third time it rattled him; he didn't like the idea of being targeted. Moving out of the city became an appealing imperative.

He glanced at Isabelle; she was pissed off. Maybe he should have mentioned his plans before tonight, but he was seventeen years older than her – it was natural for him to take the lead and make decisions. Sometimes, admittedly, he did things without first consulting her, but that was how their relationship had evolved. When they married she'd made it clear she had little regard for convention. Her life was led in a chaotic way Richard admired but did not understand, as he hadn't understood the great sweeps of abstract colour she used to produce and the critics so admired.

Maybe a move to the country is what she needs, he thought, halfway to convincing himself he was going to put the whole family through this great upheaval for her sake. Maybe she'll become revitalised; lose that wan, washed-out look, start painting again.

'How quickly do you think you can sell?' Hugh asked.

Aware of Isabelle's reproachful stare, Richard replied lightly, 'The estate agent has a buyer lined up as soon as we give the word. Marion's right.

The house, apparently, is considered very desirable, even though the market's damned slow at the moment.'

'Well, if you're really interested in a house in Summerstoke, you should get your skates on.' Hugh poured himself another glass of the dessert wine. 'The Old Vicarage has come up for sale. It's not been advertised because there's a buyer already interested, but if you were to move quickly and gave them something near the asking price, I'm sure they'd consider the offer.'

'Oh, Richard, how brilliant!' Veronica enthused, and turned to Isabelle. 'You'll love Summerstoke, Issy, and the school has a very good reputation.'

'Do you know who's in the running to buy at the moment, Hugh?' Gavin asked, stifling a yawn – it was getting late. 'Anyone we know?'

'Oliver Merfield, our new MP. He's the grandson of the chief witch in the manor. God forbid we should have another Merfield in the village. But he's got a house to sell in London, Richard, so get moving.'

SEPTEMBER

4

Angry and humiliated, Oliver Merfield could not remember a time when he had felt so wretched. He stared bleakly at the man opposite him, who had his back to the window so the September sunshine, streaming in, cast his face and form in shadow and fell. like a spotlight, on Oliver. Oliver could have shifted his chair but he was in a state of shock and incapable of anything so assertive.

For a moment the room was silent. A pendulum clock ticked heavily somewhere behind him; through the open window, he could hear the continuous roar of the traffic on the Westway; in the depths of the building a bell sounded and moments later, Oliver heard the scuffled hurrying of myriad footsteps.

'I'm really sorry, Oliver, Juliet.' The headmaster had said this a number of times and seemed to mean it. He turned to Juliet sitting beside Oliver. 'I've bent over backwards. In June, I told you it was a final warning. If we were a state school, I'd be under an obligation to inform the police. As it is…'

'The police?' Juliet quivered.

Oliver's insides seemed to go very cold. He couldn't bring himself to look at Jamie who was sitting, shoulders slumped, staring intently at the grey-flecked carpet.

Graham Whittaker, the headmaster, was a

pleasant-faced man in his late forties. During the years Jamie had been attending the school, Oliver and Juliet had got to know him quite well. He had taken advantage, many times, of Juliet's star status to fund-raise for the school, and when Oliver became an MP the head had been among the first to congratulate him. Now, although apologetic and rueful, he was distancing himself. No longer to be fêted and fawned over, they were the parents of a problem pupil and as such he addressed them, as he had never done before, from behind the deep expanse of his desk.

He leaned forward, hands clasped together. 'Possession is a criminal offence, Juliet. What makes it worse is that, according to the other two boys involved, Jamie brought the cannabis into school and shared it with them. As the law stands, that makes him a supplier.'

'What?' Oliver was horrified. 'That's dreadful. How can sharing...? That's what boys do, share.'

Juliet moaned softly.

'I know, Oliver. But it's the law, and these lads are old enough to know that. Jamie has fully admitted everything to me, haven't you, Jamie?' The head paused and waited for Jamie to reply.

'Jamie?' Juliet prompted him softly.

'Yeah, yeah. Whatever.' Jamie shrugged and continued to stare at the carpet.

The headmaster sighed. 'It's a very difficult situation. I know what I ought to do...'

'Oh, please, please, don't bring the police into it. I couldn't bear it. He's only sixteen. I'm sure they all do it.' Juliet was close to tears.

'I don't know about that, Juliet. I hope you're

wrong. But we've made it clear to all the boys that expulsion will follow if they're caught with cannabis on the premises. I gave Jamie a second chance and he's let me down. What's worse, he's let you and himself down. I've no choice.'

'Oh no!' Juliet let out a little scream.

The head raised his hand in a placatory gesture. 'Rightly or wrongly, I'm not going to report Jamie to the police. At heart, I believe he's a nice boy. As you say, he's only sixteen – it would be a tragedy to criminalise him at such an age. However, I've no choice but to ask you to remove him from this school. I've a duty of care to my pupils and must do all in my power to protect them; if I allowed Jamie to remain on the school roll, it would be a dereliction of that duty. You do understand, don't you?'

'What I don't understand,' said Oliver bitterly, some time later, 'is why I was never told about the first warning.'

He had followed Juliet up to their bedroom, where she had gone to shower and change as soon as they got home. It was something she always did when particularly upset, as if the force of the water could purge the nasty experience.

She was sitting at her dressing table, surrounded with powders and cosmetics, carefully applying a bold red lipstick to her cupid lips; her golden hair, curly with damp, tumbled down her naked back, smooth and cream-coloured. But Oliver was not in the mood to succumb to his wife's attractions, and asked again, 'Why, Juliet? Why didn't you tell me?'

Juliet, having recovered from the shock and, worse, from the humiliation, was bouncing back. 'Because, Oliver,' she said, still concentrating on her image in the mirror, 'in June, your mind was on other things.'

He stared at her. 'What?'

'Your silly election – playing at politics. You'd time for absolutely nothing else.'

Oliver was used to Juliet's dismissive way of referring to his political aspirations, but this time a firework went off in his brain.

'That's just not true. Something as important as this, involving Jamie and his entire future, for God's sake... You should have told me.'

'And what would you have done? The school had already decided to give him another chance. Why make a fuss?'

'Because it's important that I know what my son's up to. I should've been given the opportunity to intervene. I don't suppose this incident at school is the only time he's smoked dope. He's just lucky he wasn't picked up by the police.'

'Because if he had, it would have been nasty for you, wouldn't it, Mr newly elected MP? That's what you're worried about.' Juliet swung round, her eyes glinting. 'MP's son done for dope – the papers would love that!'

Oliver was the closest he'd ever been to hating his wife. He stood staring down at her. Even at her most bitchy, she looked beautiful, her face flushed, her eyes sparkling. But he was angry and replied frostily. 'Yes, yes, they would. But actually that hadn't occurred to me. I'm just worried about Jamie.'

He sat down on the corner of the four-poster bed, breathed in deeply and moderated his tone, knowing he would get nowhere, otherwise. 'He talks to you. Do you know, is it just marijuana, or is it other things as well? How serious a problem do we have here?'

Juliet shrugged and turned her back on him to brush out her hair. 'I think you're making too much of this. It's a bit of dope, that's all. Most of the kids of his age are using it. He was unlucky to get caught. After all I've done for that stinking school, you'd think Graham Whittaker would have been more sympathetic.'

'It seems to me Jamie pushed the sympathy vote to the limit. Taking it to school – what on earth possessed him?'

Juliet shrugged again, her hair crackling and gleaming under the brush strokes. 'It was probably his turn. Jamie says there's a group of them who get together, in and out of school. If clever Mr Whittaker thinks by expelling Jamie he's expelled the problem, he's very much mistaken.'

Incredulous, Oliver ran his fingers through his hair. 'I can't believe you've let this go on and not done anything about it.'

Juliet got up from her toilette and surveyed him coldly. 'Really, Oliver, I don't know what you expect of me. Jamie confides in me because he knows I won't snitch on him. If I did, that would be it between us. We'd become just another mother and son who never talk, never share things. As it is, we're friends.'

She selected a sage-green linen dress from the fitted white wardrobe dominating one wall of their bedroom, and stepped into it, sliding her arms into the sleeves and hitching it up over her shoulders.

'I respect his confidences, and that way, Oliver, I'm sure, if there was ever anything wrong – I mean really wrong – I would know. At the moment it's a phase he's going through. He's got this group of friends and he's desperate to keep up with them, and if that means smoking a little dope, then that's what he'll do, whatever I say. Would you zip me up, please?'

Oliver did as she requested, then sat in silence, as she pulled out a matching jacket and looked for a pair of shoes. But his anger at being kept in the dark, at being marginalised yet again by Juliet in the upbringing of their son, bubbled up. 'Didn't it occur to you the move to the country would've been a good opportunity to remove Jamie from the influence of this group of friends?'

Juliet made no reply, studying in her long mirror the effect of the shoes she'd put on.

Oliver tried to keep his voice even. 'Juliet, when the Old Vicarage came on the market, you made such a fuss, I delayed doing anything until it was too late.' He paused, knowing it would be counter-productive to get too angry. 'So we decided to take our time finding somewhere, not in Summerstoke, leaving Jamie to do his exams in London. And now, you do realise, don't you, his expulsion has changed all that.'

'Has it? I don't see how. He could go to a local sixth form college. I know his GCSEs weren't brilliant, but they weren't that bad, either.' She glanced at her watch. 'Look, Ollie, can we continue this discussion later. I've got to go.'

'Go? Go where?'

'I've got an interview with a casting agent. Louis says I'm in with a good chance. They're looking for an English actress to front a new detective series set in Louisiana. If it goes well, we'll go on to the Ivy, so I might not be back until quite late.'

Oliver closed his eyes. 'Juliet, we need to talk. This is important.'

'And so is this interview. We can talk later.'

For a long while after the front door had closed behind her, Oliver lay on the bed, staring up with unseeing eyes at the muslin canopy.

From the moment he'd met Juliet, when he was just eighteen, it had always been the same: no matter how wrong she was, she dictated the terms. When she became pregnant he'd wanted to marry her, but she'd refused; she wanted to go to drama school and nothing, absolutely nothing, was going to stop her. Marriage and babies simply weren't on her agenda. He was halfway through university and, although he was passionate about her, she didn't encourage him. She accepted his claims to Jamie, but wouldn't let him do more than visit the baby at her parents' house. Determined to support Jamie as best he could, he'd taken a well-paid path into the City rather than follow his father into the diplomatic service as he'd planned; a decision, he knew, that disappointed his family. When she finally agreed to marry him, Juliet made it quite clear her career was always going to come first, and as far as Jamie went she knew best.

But did she? Did she? Until now he'd been so busy he'd been content to play second-fiddle parent. But Jamie was in trouble and maybe it was his, Oliver's, fault as much as anyone's? Maybe Jamie deserved more than he'd been given?

From across the landing, a low, thudding, electronic bass came from his son's room, an inescapable, insistent soundscape. Getting to his feet, Oliver went and knocked at Jamie's door.

'Jamie? It's Dad. May I come in? There's something I want to discuss with you.'

It was very late when Juliet let herself into their little house in Barnes. Exhausted, but elated, she was looking forward to sharing the triumphs of the evening with Oliver.

The interview had gone well and she knew it.

It had been all too familiar: a hatchet-faced Englishwoman who asked her to read a ridiculously insubstantial piece of text in an unlikely number of different ways, watched by a short, fat man with boiled-egg eyes, who occasionally interjected, in a Californian drawl, to ask highly personal questions. Juliet was skilled at playing both sides simultaneously and within a short time the casting director had visibly thawed, and the producer was talking about the places he would take her to in Hollywood. Louis, her agent, had wangled her the last slot of the afternoon, so when he called to pick her up it had been a relatively easy task to persuade the interview-drunk couple to unwind with them over a meal at the Ivy.

Louis only ever took his clients to the Ivy when he was pleased with them. It was clear he had high hopes of this interview and was going to play his part, if Juliet played hers. At the end of a long, tiring evening in which she sparkled, flirted, and was oh so serious about the quality of the writing she'd been asked to try out earlier, Louis put her into a taxi, kissed her on the cheek and murmured reassuringly, 'If they don't invite you over to La La Land, my sweet, I'm in the wrong business.'

To her chagrin, the house was in darkness – both Oliver and Jamie had gone to bed. On the kitchen table she found a note from Oliver asking her to wake him up as soon as she got in as they 'had important things to discuss, which couldn't wait'.

Juliet didn't want to wake him. She didn't want to run the risk of another scene casting a dampener on the success of her evening. She reasoned that if it was that urgent Oliver would have waited up for her, so she crumpled up the note and raided the case of champagne she and Oliver had bought for special occasions.

Then she sat at the kitchen table, opened the bottle of champagne and toasted her future.

Oliver didn't wake when she tiptoed into the room, so she slid into bed and fell into a deep sleep, only to be woken almost immediately it seemed, by Oliver's alarm.

She felt him get out of bed; sensed him looking down at her; heard him say softly, 'Juliet, are you awake? Juliet?' Feigning sleep, she did not stir. She listened to him moving around in the bathroom and then downstairs. Opening one eye, she registered the time on the clock. It was just after six. Oliver must be mad – there was no way she was going to wake and start talking at this hour.

She had passed the age when she could party half the night and look as fresh as ever the next morning. She needed sleep.

Slipping into a comfortable doze, she thought she heard Jamie's voice and would have roused herself, but hearing Oliver returning to their room, she maintained her deception and resisted all his attempts to wake her. Only when she heard the front door shut, and the sound of the car driving away, did she relax and fall back into a genuinely deep sleep.

In spite of Oliver's determination to make an early start, there was a lot of traffic about and it wasn't until he finally got onto the M3 that he allowed his mind to drift over the events of the last twenty-four hours. Jamie was asleep, but Oliver had every intention of waking him up when they reached the services so that they could have a more purposeful discussion than the one they'd had the day before.

He'd gone to Jamie's bedroom intending to have a sensible talk with his son about drug taking and its consequences and then to discuss, calmly and rationally, what options were open to him concerning his education. But in the event he got absolutely nowhere. Jamie refused to answer any of his questions, shouted at him to leave his room and then climbed, fully clothed, into his bed, turning his back on Oliver and pulling the duvet over his head.

Faced with an obdurate Jamie and an absent Juliet, Oliver could have shrugged his shoulders and gone back to the Commons and the more peaceful cut and thrust of Prime Minister's Questions. But he was not a quitter and, having decided the time had come to cast off the secondary role they'd assigned him, he was determined to do everything he could to prevent Jamie from sliding into a useless, wasted adolescence.

So he'd made a number of calls, and when everything was in place he'd poked his head round Jamie's door and told him to be ready to leave at six thirty the following morning.

To Oliver's amazement, Jamie had got up when requested, swallowed a bowl of cereal and got into the car without any protest or any apparent curiosity as to where his father was taking him.

Oliver glanced at his sleeping son and sighed. The time when *he* could hand over the responsibility for his movements to somebody else, without question, was long gone.

He'd endured a lengthy and sticky conversation with the Whips, trying to extricate himself for the next two days from his obligations in the House and from the various committees to which he'd been detailed. He was a new boy; they owed him no favours and seemed to enjoy making him squirm. They were unimpressed by the argument that he had to sort out his son's schooling. Where was the boy's mother? Wasn't that her role? He'd stuck to his guns and finally, grudgingly, they accepted his absence, but being out of favour with the Whips was not a good idea and could result in his being cast into outer darkness.

That was a chance he was prepared to take. He was ambitious, but not ruthless. Living with Juliet, he'd experienced – time and again – the sacrifices, in pursuit of her goals, she demanded of those who loved her, and he was not prepared to go that far, not with Jamie.

But it seemed, he reflected with a deep sigh, as he turned off the motorway to the service station, that ambition and parenthood were hard to reconcile.

He knew, although they were far too discreet to utter a word of criticism to him, his family thought Juliet completely self-centred, but how was he any different? Juliet had emphasised, often enough, that if she was to succeed she had to be completely single-minded. Now he'd embarked on a career which would be as all-consuming as hers.

He drew up the car and nudged his son's arm. 'Jamie, wake up.'

Jamie stirred and, peering round the hood of his sweatshirt, grunted, 'Where are we?'

'Motorway services. I'm going for a coffee. Is there anything you want?'

'Burger and chips.'

'Jamie,' Oliver groaned. 'It's only eight thirty – you don't want burger and chips!'

'I'm hungry,' Jamie whined, 'and I don't know what we're doing here and why I'm not still in my bed. The least you can do is buy me burger and chips. And a Coke,' he added as Oliver, sighing, climbed out of the car.

'Right,' said Oliver firmly, as they set off again. 'Time to talk, Jamie.'

'What's to say?' replied Jamie, staring out at the woodland bordering the motorway.

'We've got to sort out your future,' replied

Oliver mildly. 'You must feel rock bottom, at the moment.'

'Nope. Why should I?'

'Being expelled is not a pleasant thing, not for anybody.'

Jamie made no comment and Oliver pressed on. 'The thing is, Jamie, we've got to find somewhere else for you to finish your education. I've been thinking things over, and I worry that, with your mother's career and me so busy, it would be all too easy for you to drift, and I don't want that to happen to you. Since I need to spend any time I'm not at Westminster in my constituency, that's where we're going to make our home – you, me and Juliet.'

He could feel a sudden tension in Jamie, but went on, 'I've thought it all through. I can use Aunt Polly's spare room when I have to stay up during the week, or when Mum needs to be in London. We'll put the house on the market and find somewhere in or around Summerbridge. I've spoken to the principal of Summerbridge College. We've got an appointment with him at ten thirty this morning, and someone's going to show us round before that. Assuming we like what we see and your chat with him is okay, he says you can start in the sixth form straight away. It's important, Jamie, you don't lose too much time starting your course.'

He paused and glanced at his son. He was slumped into his seat, looking stunned and almost close to tears.

Oliver softened. 'It's lucky it's the start of the conference season next week. Apart from the conference itself, I'd planned to spend as much time down here as I could, so I'll be around to begin with. I don't suppose we'll find anywhere to buy very quickly, but we'll look for somewhere to rent. In the meantime, we'll stay at Summerstoke.'

At this, Jamie exploded. 'Stay with those old witches? I won't. You can't make me. It's not fair. You can't sell the house – Juliet wouldn't let you; she doesn't want to go to Summerstoke, Summerbridge, or anywhere in the stinkin' country, and nor do I. It's a dump, the dead end of nowhere. It's not fair. You're buryin' me alive just because that's where *you* want to be. You haven't asked me what *I* want, have you? Well, I don't want to leave London, and that's that. You can't do this to me. Juliet won't let you – she can't stand those weird old hags and nor can I. You can't leave me with them, they're mad.'

Oliver didn't attempt to interrupt his outburst, and allowed him to rant on about the unfairness of life in general and how his mother would react when she found out.

When he finally fell silent, Oliver said coldly, 'When we go to Summerstoke, Jamie, I'd be grateful if you keep your opinions about my grandmother and my aunts to yourself. They deserve your respect, if nothing else. As to our plans, your mother agreed it will be in your interests to make the move here.'

He glanced across at Jamie, who was gazing moodily out of the car window, and said more softly, 'I'm not abandoning you, old chum. I shall be staying at Summerstoke with you, and until the house is sold we can go back to Barnes at the weekend – you can meet up with your mates then.'

But Jamie was not mollified. He hated the idea of his home being sold, and of leaving London and his mates and so fought back the only way he knew how: he refused to have any further conversation with his dad, lapsing into a resentful, sulky silence until they reached Summerbridge.

Summerbridge was a busy market town, not large, with a main street that crossed over the river just below the market square and curled up a steep hill to the more residential areas beyond. The buildings were mostly Georgian, built of the local sandstone with plenty of Victorian adornment and enough sixties infill to make the town more utilitarian than charming.

Summerbridge College, which turned out to be a large comprehensive school with a separate sixth form, lay on the outskirts of the town on the edge of a housing estate. Functional in design, the school consisted of a cluster of two-storey buildings set out in grounds of mature shrubs and trees.

A sixth-former had been appointed to show them round, and to Oliver's relief Jamie thawed sufficiently to ask his guide one or two questions and to greet the principal, when the time came for the interview, with a degree of civility.

Jamie was not going to give his dad an inch, so no way was he going to admit he liked the principal of Summerbridge College or that he thought the school seemed cool.

It was co-ed for starters and everything seemed a lot more relaxed than at his old school. No mention was made of his expulsion, and the

103

principal seemed to bend over backwards to give him the courses he wanted, including, which Jamie thought was awesome, the opportunity to do drama and in a fully equipped theatre – that just didn't happen in his previous school.

He'd often been ribbed about 'following in mother's footsteps' and, though he fiercely denied it, he dreamed a dream. The scenario: Juliet would be sitting in a theatre watching a play unaware that he was in it. He'd appear onstage and she would sit up in her seat – there was something familiar about him. 'Who is that young actor?' she would whisper to her companion. 'He's very good.' 'Don't you recognise your own son?' came the shocked reply. 'Jamie!' she'd gasp, staring at him, full of wonder and pride.

Oh yes, one day, one day he'd blow her away.

Yeah, considering his old school had chucked him out, this one was not a bad alternative. But there was no way he would give his dad the satisfaction of knowing that. No way!

His dad, the MP ... it was a new experience for Jamie to see his father treated like a celebrity. His mother, yes: everyone wanted to talk to his mother, bees around the honey pot; even if they'd no idea she was somebody worth knowing, they'd queue up to shake hands with her, get her autograph. But his dad ... even the principal wanted to pump his hand and was all smiles when they left. And then afterwards, going round Summerbridge, so many people approached them and Oliver insisted on giving them all the time of day, whatever they looked like. It was really embarrassing, particularly as some, in Jamie's opinion, had more than one or two screws loose.

After leaving the school, they'd gone into Sum-merbridge to start traipsing around the estate agents. He'd not been involved in anything like this before; he hated it, deeply pissed off by the whole process, so by plugging in his iPod and reducing all conversation to a series of grunts and shrugs, he made it quite clear to his Dad he was well hacked off.

It was not a successful expedition from Oliver's point of view, either, and Jamie could see his father becoming increasingly dispirited.

'Serve him right,' thought Jamie viciously. 'Playing at being someone important. Who does he think he is? It's all his bloody fault.'

They went to an Italian café for lunch. It was full of bustle, chatter and laughter, but Jamie was not going to enjoy anything and sat hunched, enjoying his misery, a black crow of doom over a Coke and sandwich, ignoring all his father's attempts to involve him in sifting through the various house details.

Eventually, to Jamie's relief, Oliver gave up and decided there was nothing with sufficient promise to demand an immediate inspection. It was time to visit the old ladies in Summerstoke.

The afternoon was getting on when they left Summerbridge and Jamie was puzzled. Juliet hadn't called. He'd read the note Oliver had left for her and had recognised it as a red rag. He'd fully expected her to phone, hours ago, to demand their immediate return to London. But she hadn't. By the time they reached Summer-stoke and drove over the river into the village, he was getting quite desperate.

Passing the village shop and church, they turned into a long, narrow, gravel drive, bordered on one side by a vast yew hedge and on the other by a high stone wall. Two great stone gateposts flanked the entrance to a courtyard and there they pulled up in front of the sort of house Jamie had only seen in the movies.

He'd been there before, he knew, but he'd been very young and so caught up with being his mother's son that anything she didn't like he hated, without question, so he'd only the dimmest memory of the house and its occupants.

Oliver smiled encouragingly at him, then crossed to an ancient oak door and pulled at a bell.

Jamie lingered, looking up at the mellow honey-coloured stone manor house, covered with a creeper that was just turning red and yellow. It was only two storeys high, but it stretched out on either side, its façade dotted with millions of mullioned windows all twinkling in the afternoon sun. Clumps of chimneys sprouted from the stone roof, and at regular intervals, poking out of the roof, were a number of small plain sash windows.

'Servants' quarters.' Jamie, impressed in spite of himself, refused to view it in anything but a negative light. 'I bet that's where they'll put me.'

The door opened and Oliver hugged the old lady who appeared. He turned to Jamie, 'Come on, Jamie, come and say hello to Nanny. She's not seen you since you were six or seven.'

With bad grace, Jamie joined his father. Nanny – what a stupid thing to call this old woman. There was no way he was going to hug or kiss her, no way! She was tall and thin, slightly stooped, with short grey hair and nondescript spectacles through which a pair of shrewd hazel eyes looked him over. Her face was round, she had thin lips and a long nose, and her skin was weathered and wrinkled, devoid of make-up.

''Lo,' he grunted.

'Jamie,' she smiled, and even in his sulky state he noticed her smile. It was warm and welcoming, and she didn't look so old. 'I'm afraid, pet, you'll have to put up with us remarking on how much you've changed. Why, you're quite grown up. Come in, come in. Take Jamie into the sitting room, Oliver, and I'll bring in some tea. Or would you rather have squash, Jamie?'

'I don't want anything,' replied Jamie and then, catching his father's creased brow, he added a belated 'Thanks.'

It seemed to Jamie, stepping over the threshold into a huge, square, flagstoned hall, the whole day was an obstacle race. First the drive down at the crack of dawn and long lecture from his father; then the interview with the principal, followed by house-hunting; then Nanny, and now he had to face his great-grandmother and his great-aunts.

Oliver led the way into a long, low-ceilinged room.

The afternoon sun sparkled through the whorls of glass in the windows, teasing the shadows in the darker corners of the room. Everything, to Jamie's eye, seemed to be a silvery grey: the painted wooden panels on the walls, the thick carpet underfoot, a heavily ornamental plastered ceiling, and three huge sofas grouped round a cavernous fireplace in which a small fire burned. A number of ornamental and very uncomfortable-looking chairs were scattered round the room; three tall bookcases stood against the wall facing the windows, their glass fronts reflecting twinkling contortions of light; a gigantic Chinese vase occupied one corner and various incidental tables displayed ornaments, bronzes, vases of flowers, and countless family photographs.

The room teased his memory. He didn't know how old he'd been when he was last there, but he'd come down with Oliver and remembered spending an endless afternoon sitting in one of the window seats, pretending to look at a book and feeling miserably homesick.

Nothing much had changed, Jamie felt, slowly trailing in his father's wake to greet the elderly ladies who were seated round the fire, upright and expectant.

'Grandmère.' Oliver bent and kissed the proffered cheek of the oldest of the three ladies.

Grandmother Merfield, or Grandmère as her grandchildren called her, was thin and elegant, dressed in a high-necked black dress that finished just above a pair of bony ankles to reveal silky black stockings and the highest pair of black stilettos Jamie had ever seen. Her hair was iron grey, long and swept up in a coil at the back of her head; her nose and chin dominated her face, reminding Jamie of Mr Punch, and the white face powder she wore increased the similarity. Any thought of laughing at her, however, was quelled by the look in her eyes, which were large and hooded, their darkness accentuated by the almost black shadows scoring the eye sockets.

Oliver turned to kiss the cheek of the elder of his two aunts. She wasn't as tall and formidable as his great-grandmother, but she looked, Jamie thought, extraordinary for someone who must have one foot in the grave.

Her hair was astonishingly blonde; quite thin but whipped over her head as if she'd been caught in a strong sideways wind. Long silvery earrings, a bit like the sort his last girlfriend used to buy in Accessorize, dripped from her ears to her shoulders; her eyelashes were suspiciously dark and curled upwards to meet thin, arched black eyebrows; her eyes, heavily made-up, were green and mocking, and her mouth was a vivid slash of red. She had a long, thin neck around which she'd wound a number of silk scarves, all different shades of red, and a dress, also red, of a silky material which shifted and shimmered when she so much as twitched. Jamie was fascinated and appalled – she was unreal.

The youngest aunt rose to her feet to hug Oliver – as if she was a serious contender, thought Jamie with disgust, rather than someone who'd been drawing her pension for the last fifty years. She was not much taller than him and had a frailty about her that made Jamie think of butterfly wings. She was as gross in her appearance as her sister, he felt, if not grosser, floating about in a strange pink dress that fluttered just below her knees, drawing attention to a pair of long, thin legs in shiny flesh-coloured tights and sporting a pair of high-heeled sandals the same colour as the vivid pink flash in her cropped silver hair. Like her sister, she was heavily made-up, but her face and features were smaller, her cheekbones more dramatic and unlike the beaky nose of her sister, hers was small and delicately turned up at the tip. Large rings of beaten silver dangled from her ears, whispering to themselves every time she turned her head, and numerous light silvery bracelets ran up and down her wrinkly arms, ensuring that every movement she made was accompanied by a tinkling percussion.

The Black Witch, the Red Witch, and the Pink Witch.

'And this is Jamie.' Oliver drew him into the circle.

Given the warmth of the welcome he'd witnessed being given to his father, Jamie braced himself to fend off hugs and kisses from these extraordinary old women, but none made a move towards him. He had the uncomfortable feeling of being scrutinised, appraised, and found wanting.

'Well, Jamie.' It was his great-grandmother speaking, 'we're glad to see you. It's been so long since you were last here, I don't think I would have recognised you.'

'Oh, you would, Elizabeth,' breathed Pink Witch. 'He's the spitting image of Oliver, at his age.'

'Yes, you're right,' agreed Red Witch, 'which is surprising, considering Juliet's colouring. He's so lucky not to have ended up a carrot top.'

Jamie bridled, but the entrance of Nanny bearing a large tray interrupted them. His father went to meet the old woman, taking the tray off her, and placing it on the low table by his grandmother.

'Thank you, Oliver. Now then, sit down and tell me what you want. Is it something to do with the fact that Jamie is not in school?'

Jamie looked at his father, alarmed, but Oliver appeared unperturbed. 'Got it in one, Grand-mère.' He smiled across at Jamie, who still stood, awkwardly, outside the circle of sofas. 'Jamie, you can either come and join us or go outside and get some fresh air. You haven't been here for years. You might like to go and have a look around.'

Jamie hovered between feeling if there was to be any conversation concerning him he ought to be present to hear it, and the overwhelming need to escape.

Nanny smiled at him. 'You won't miss anything in here, pet. I'm sure your dad will fill you in. I'll show you the way out to the terrace. There's a path that runs alongside the river and if you're lucky you might spot a heron or a kingfisher.'

When Juliet woke again, half the morning had gone. The sun was beating hot against the closed curtains, the bedroom felt stuffy, and her head gently throbbed. The distant sound of children's voices floated across from a school playground, high and twittery, like caged budgerigars; the noise of the traffic in the nearby street had sunk from the rush-hour snarl to a midday drone; and from next door came the strains of a local music station accompanying the scream of an electric saw and the reverberating thumping of a hammer.

Her own house seemed very quiet.

She sat up and called, 'Jamie?'

There was no reply, so she got out of bed, drew

111

back the curtains and stood for a moment, relishing the heat of the sun on her skin, then slipped on a white silk dressing gown and went to Jamie's room.

It was in the usual chaos – duvet thrown back, sheets screwed in a bundle on the floor, the carpet invisible under layers of clothes, shoes, books, comics, magazines, empty beer bottles, crisp packets and half-eaten sandwiches, now dried and curling – but no sign of Jamie.

Juliet was puzzled. If he didn't have to get up to go to school, there was no way he'd be out of bed before noon.

She went to the top of the stairs and called again, but again no response. She padded down the staircase, stopping at the bottom to pick up a pile of letters on the mat.

Sorting through them, she went into the sitting room, a comfortable space with stripped pine floorboards, thick rugs, and two deep cream sofas. The television, which she had half expected Jamie to be watching, sat in the corner, its screen darkly reflecting the emptiness of the room.

The dining room, too, was empty. The contents of Jamie's schoolbag lay on the polished walnut table where Jamie, the previous day, in an expression of anger and frustration, had tipped them before stalking upstairs to his room, refusing to talk further.

In the kitchen, the champagne bottle and her glass had been moved from the table to the sink and the table bore evidence of a hasty breakfast. Jamie's favourite cereal packet stood open beside a bowl containing a pool of chocolaty brown milk and a half-drunk glass of cranberry juice.

Against a mug of black coffee, barely touched, a note had been propped. Juliet threw the letters on the table, put the mug of coffee into the microwave, then read the note.

It was brief:

Dearest Juliet,

I'd hoped to discuss the latest developments with you last night. Tried to wake you this morning before we went. I've taken Jamie down to Summerstoke. He's going to see the head of Summerbridge College this morning. They're optimistic about offering him a place, but he must start ASAP as they've been back over three weeks already. I'll ring when I've any news.

Oliver

'I don't believe it! I simply don't believe it. How dare he!' Juliet exploded.

The microwave pinged and with trembling fingers she withdrew the mug and went to pick up the phone. Oliver never did anything concerning Jamie without consulting her and she was determined that was the way it was going to remain.

The first time she'd discovered Jamie had been caught with marijuana at school was shortly after the election, when Oliver was almost always away, either in his constituency or striving to set up his office in Norman Shaw South, the grim office block assigned for the use of lowly MPs.

She and Jamie had agreed not to tell him, but Juliet privately came to the conclusion Jamie's friends were an unsavoury lot and it might be a good idea, after all, to move into the Old Vicarage.

113

Her dislike of Summerstoke stemmed from the time she'd gone there, as a teenager, with Oliver. An only child of elderly parents, Juliet had been adored all her life. The family at Summerstoke Manor, however, were resistant to her charms; she found them cold, and believed they looked down their long noses at her. She was an outsider; she didn't fit in; she wasn't wanted. They made her feel inferior and she couldn't forgive them.

But she was concerned enough about Jamie to entertain moving to Summerstoke, particularly as the Old Vicarage turned out to be a very handsome late-Georgian house, considerably larger than their semi-detached in Barnes. When the sale fell through, she'd brushed her unease aside and decided to leave Jamie at his school in London for his A-level course. The best solution, she argued, for Jamie was a city kid through and through, and she'd no idea how he'd cope with being in the country, let alone living so close to Ollie's freaky relations. Besides, Jamie in London gave her a cast-iron excuse to remain in the city herself.

The fact that it was Jamie's behaviour that had upset her plans and Oliver had come up with a solution, did not appease Juliet. She should have been consulted. She ignored the fact she'd not allowed Oliver the chance to talk to her. His actions were high-handed and unforgivable and she was going to insist they came back to London immediately.

Before she could dial Oliver's mobile, the phone rang. It was Louis.

'Darling,' he purred, 'I just wanted to tell you how wonderful you were last night.'

Juliet's mood immediately changed. She beamed down the phone. 'Thanks, Louis. And thank you again for the Ivy. I just hope it pays off.'

'Well, that's why I'm phoning you, darling.'

Juliet's cheeks went pink, her legs gave way and she sank into the nearest chair. 'Have you heard something? Surely they won't have made any decisions yet?'

'They don't hang about. Time is money – it's a favourite studio cliché, but it drives everything. I rang Sarah Mackintosh this morning to say she'd left her scarf at the restaurant and she gave the strongest possible hint that you could be winging your way this weekend.'

'Oh, Louis!' Juliet could hardly speak.

'You've no other commitments, have you? Oliver's not going to throw a fit?'

'No, no, of course not. Why should he?'

'Well, initially it could be for a week. There'll be a shortlist of three or four actresses and you'll be expected to meet the writer, the studio bosses, the director, probably the lead male, although they are being very cagey about who he is, but his opinion will count for a lot, as well as the producer's and the designer's. It'll be a busy week, baby, and they'll be watching you all the way.'

'If I get it, how long will I be in Los Angeles?'

'Depends on the success of the pilot, sweetheart. That'll take about six weeks, but of course, the contract they'll ask you to sign will be for six years.'

'Six years?'

'Yep, that's why I asked about Oliver.'

Juliet gulped. Everything she had dreamed of

115

was suddenly possible. She was going to get her chance, nothing could, or would, stop her.

'Don't worry about Oliver; he knows I've always wanted to go to Hollywood. He'll be as excited as I am.'

5

'What about Juliet? Where does she fit into all of this? Or have you two finally separated?'

There was a moment's stunned silence. It was a question they all wanted to ask and would have spent a great deal of time speculating about in private, but, outspoken though the Merfield sisters were amongst themselves, Charlotte's blunt question broke the niceties they observed when dealing with their family.

'Charlotte!' Mrs Merfield's tone was reproving.

Oliver was equally taken aback, but he quickly recovered. The old ladies were a formidable team, but he was at ease with them and, spiky though she was, Aunt Charlotte had always been his particular favourite.

He laughed. 'Don't worry about Juliet. She's fine – we're fine. In the end she was quite keen to buy the Old Vicarage, remember? Now that it's not possible for Jamie to stay on at school in London, she agrees with me a change of scene would be the best thing for him.'

The memory of Juliet pretending to be asleep in bed that morning flitted through his mind.

'She's got an important audition on at the moment, otherwise she'd be here herself. With any luck, we'll find somewhere pretty quickly, even if we just rent to begin with, so I won't need to impose on you for very long.'

'It's no imposition, Oliver,' replied his grandmother with a slight air of reproof. 'We haven't seen enough of Jamie.'

'Though what a teenage boy will make of living with us crones, I can't imagine,' Louisa tittered.

'It'll be nice to have some young blood around. I look forward to getting to know the young man better,' said Nanny warmly, reaching for a plate of shortbread and passing it to Oliver. 'Here, I baked these this morning. You used to love shortbread when you were a boy.'

'And I still do. Thanks, Nanny.' He nibbled the biscuit. 'It certainly beats anything in the shops. You'll have to try it on Jamie. I don't suppose he's ever eaten homemade shortbread.'

'He certainly is rather pale and skinny.' Louisa gave a little laugh. 'And so stern! Does he ever smile, Oliver? I remember the last time he came here with you he scowled the entire time. Quite unnerving.'

'He doesn't smile a lot, but that's not to say he doesn't appreciate things. Teenagers tend not to smile – it's not their way, it's not cool. Underneath all that moodiness he really is quite nice, believe me. He didn't say much, but I could tell he was impressed with the college and starting tomorrow won't allow him too much time to brood.' He pulled a face. 'The most important thing now is to find somewhere to live.

It's a pity the estate agents didn't come up with anything halfway decent.'

'How are you going to find the time for house-hunting? As far as I can work out, you're run ragged as it is – stuck in Westminster all hours of the day and night during the week and at everyone's beck and call when you're down here,' said Charlotte.

'It's a shame you didn't buy the Old Vicarage. You'd have been right next door to us,' commented Louisa. 'That would have been fun.'

'Not for Juliet,' Charlotte observed wryly. 'In spite of what you say, Oliver, I could never see her settling in Summerstoke with any enthusiasm.'

Oliver sighed to himself. Charlotte was right, of course. It was going to be incredibly difficult to find the time to do more. He'd always worked hard, but even the pressure of life in the City hadn't prepared him for the lifestyle of an MP. If it was just him... But it wasn't. He had to settle Jamie, make a proper home for him and one where Juliet would be content to live for at least part of the time; she would never give London up completely, he knew. If he could find somewhere she liked... But there was no way she'd help him find such a place. He thought briefly of the MP who shared his shabby and cramped office in the basement of Norman Shaw South. *His* wife had done the house-hunting and moving single-handed, but then she wasn't a Juliet.

He shrugged. 'The right place will come along, eventually. I'll get Susannah, my constituency secretary, on the case, and in the meantime

118

'perhaps we'll find somewhere to rent.'

'Well now, I've got an idea,' Nanny beamed. 'I didn't realise you were considering renting, Oliver. I've just the place for you, and what is more, it's in the village.'

Jamie couldn't care less about herons or king-fishers – he wasn't sure if he'd ever seen either in his life – but he'd taken Nanny up on her offer and within five minutes of leaving the old crones he was at the water's edge. There, safely out of his father's sight, he lit the first cigarette of the day.

Inhaling deeply, he stared down at the river, the level of which was a good five feet below the edge of the bank, its flow barely perceptible through the clumps of reeds and mats of water-lily leaves decaying on the river's edge. The water seemed almost black, mirroring patches of blue sky and white clouds. A few ducks foraged among the weeds, taking no notice of him. A water bird, with a flashy black-and-white tail and spindly legs, took fright at his arrival and ran across the water's surface to the protection of the opposite bank, screeching alarums as it went, and a large golden dragonfly detached itself from a tall flower hanging over the river and ambled past Jamie, before settling on a browning teasel.

He finished his cigarette and flicked the stub in the direction of the ducks. There was a moment's flurry as the nearest drake thought he was in for a titbit and the others rushed over to grab their share. Disappointed and quacking expressively with much fluttering of feathers, they turned their backs on him and returned to the reeds.

Jamie pulled out his mobile and dialled Juliet. The phone flashed momentarily then went dark. Jamie stared at it in disbelief. No sodding signal. He looked round for higher ground. The lawn rose slightly towards the house, but then the massive bulk of the manor would cut out the signal, so he turned and walked along the river-bank in the direction of the village, which lay beyond a line of willows.

His luck was well and truly out. A high stone wall bordered the edge of the garden and ran right down to the river, disappearing from view under a turbulent mess of ivy, brambles and nettles. There was no way through.

Built into the bank close to the wall, its roof half covered with ivy, was what looked like a summerhouse, but on closer inspection Jamie realised the summerhouse, which had little glass doors opening directly onto a wooden verandah and deck, was part of a boathouse. He could just see the prow of a boat at the waterline, and just visible over the edge of the railing was the top of a ladder.

The planks of the deck were green, slimy and a bit rotten, but Jamie, stepping cautiously, made his way to the ladder and looked down. The rungs were iron rather than wood, and rusty, but other-wise looked intact. The bottom of the ladder rested on a rock just above the water and from there he saw it was possible to reach the boat-house without getting his feet wet. The boathouse entrance faced away from the bank, towards the middle of the river, and Jamie could see the rowing boat was afloat.

For one wild moment he dreamed of escape, of getting into the boat, rowing to the village, and hitching a lift back to London. He'd disappear long enough for his parents to understand they couldn't pack him away; that he would not, absolutely and definitely not, be buried alive in this godforsaken dump.

'Hi, Jamie. I see you've found the boathouse.' His father came up behind him. 'We used to camp out here when we were kids. I loved it, although it could get very cold and spooky at night.'

Jamie said nothing, continuing to stare down at the river. He was not into having any chummy chats with his dad at the moment, and least of all did he want to listen to tales from his dad's childhood.

'This decking doesn't look very safe. I should think it's years since the old dears came down here,' his father continued, trying, Jamie realised, to be friends.

'So?' he turned and, not looking at Oliver, walked past him back onto the grass. 'What have you fixed up? What have you told them? Do they know I'm a drug dealer. Are they preparing my prison cell right this minute?'

'Don't be absurd.' Oliver followed him. 'You're no such thing. I just told them you'd got into a bit of difficulty in London and we thought it best if you went to the local school, particularly as we're going to be living down here. Since it's important you start as soon as possible, you and I are both going to stay here until we find somewhere to live.'

'Juliet will love that!' snorted Jamie.

121

'Mum will stay in London till we've either sold or rented the house and found somewhere here.'

'Great!' Jamie was so miserable that he threw himself on the grass, rolled over and stared, unseeing, up at the scudding clouds.

Oliver sat down next to him.

'It's not that bad, Jamie. They're eccentric and they've very strong views about things; but be straight with them, and polite, and you'll get on very well. It's likely we'll not be here for long. I came to tell you that I'm going to look at a house in the village. It's not for sale, but Nanny tells me that the owner, who's a retired doctor, is going off to live with his daughter in Canada and wants to find a tenant. Let's go and have a look at it together.'

The request was more of a plea but the day, in Jamie's opinion, had been bloody and, above all, he didn't want to stay in Summerstoke. Holding Oliver entirely responsible for the change in his fortune, he turned his head away, saying coldly, 'No, thanks. Leave me out of it.'

Oliver sighed and got to his feet. 'Nanny's preparing your room. She says if you're hungry make your way to the kitchen. In any event, supper's at seven. I'll see you then. I've got a lot of calls to catch up on, so I'm afraid I'm going to be busy most of this evening.'

As he walked away across the grass, Jamie sat up and called after him. 'Have you spoken to Juliet yet? Does she know we're here?'

'I've left a message on her phone. I'll try again when I get back.'

Jamie waited till Oliver had disappeared into the

house, then got to his feet and made his way back to the boathouse. He swung his legs over the verandah, holding on tight to the edge as he tested the rungs of the ladder. The metal bit into the soles of his trainers, but the bars held and he slowly lowered himself down onto the slab of rock at the water's edge. Rubbing his hands on his jeans to get rid of the rust and muck from the ladder, he cautiously edged his way along the platform of stones. Although they were caked with mud and weed, they were quite dry and not at all slippery so he reached the boathouse with ease and stood on a concrete shelf looking down, not at a rowing boat, but at a wide, old-fashioned punt.

'Wicked!' he breathed and looked round for oars or something to steer it with.

At the back of the boathouse, a pile of faded, mouldering cushions was stashed against the wall next to a small staircase that clearly led to the summerhouse above. Apart from that, there was nothing else there. The water slapped against the stones, and the boat bobbed temptingly at the end of its moorings. Jamie climbed the little wooden stairs, which protested loudly under his weight. The door at the top was locked. If the oars or whatever were kept in there, he'd have to go and ask for a key. No way.

Back by the punt, he squatted down and pulled the mooring rope till the boat was alongside the shelf and he was able to scramble in. The punt tilted alarmingly but didn't sink; nor, Jamie noticed to his satisfaction, did it let any water in.

He had no plans; he wasn't really thinking through what he was going to do next. He sat in the gently rocking craft, lit another cigarette and smoked it, feeling considerably more cheerful than he had done all day. He looked around. The boathouse was little more than a shed, open on one side to the river, but it felt like a place apart, a place of secrets, a place unobserved and forgotten. This would be his place – no one would find him here. He'd keep his magazines under those cushions; he could smoke unobserved; he could get hold of some beer and stash it here; and if he was able to get hold of any ganja, he could smoke it here and no one would be the wiser.

He finished his cigarette and peered out. A little way along the bank from the boathouse, on the same side, a line of willow trees had been stripped and a pile of branches had been left stacked on the bank. One or two looked quite long and sturdy – ideal punting poles. He got quite excited. If he worked the punt along the water's edge, holding onto the bank as he did so, he should be able to reach the stack without too much difficulty.

Two ropes held the punt in place. From the tightness of the fastening and the way the knots had grown into themselves, the punt had not been taken out for a very long time. Persevering, he managed to unfasten one, but then the craft swung on the axis of the other, tightening it still further. Nothing Jamie did would release it. Frustrated, he gave a mighty yank on the rope. The ring to which it had been tied came away and Jamie, rope in hand, fell back into the middle of the punt. The violent movement sent it spinning and before he could grab the edge of the concrete sill, it floated out of the boathouse and, still spinning, was borne by the current into the centre of the river.

Jamie regained his balance and viewed his situation with dismay. Fortunately, the river was not flowing very fast, but it was quite wide. A number of trees grew over the water, but unless he stood up, their branches were out of his reach.

He tried standing up, once, but the punt lurched so violently he was convinced he'd end up in the river and sat down immediately.

The water was reedy and he toyed with the idea of trying to grab hold of a clump, but as he leaned over the side the shallow craft started to ship in water, so he was forced to abandon that idea as well.

Up to that point the excitement of the adventure had temporarily banished the various humiliations of the last twenty-four hours, but now, finding himself sitting helplessly in a boat, in the middle of the river, drifting downstream with the craft moving faster and, it seemed to him, increasingly out of control, Jamie's misery welled up and over.

'It's not fair, it's not fair. Why me? What have I done?' he moaned. 'Why doesn't someone help. I'm going to drown and nobody cares.'

His one hope was that he would be spotted from the riverbank. But the bank was high on both sides, and thick clumps of rushes, large, mauve-headed flowers, shrubs, brambles and briars, teasels, and tall plants with heads clouded in seeds, grew in such great profusion along the water's edge that his view of the world beyond was obscured.

'Help!' he shouted, hoping that someone on the bank, out of sight, might hear him. 'Help me. Help!'

The river rounded a bend. The bank on the left was cliff-like, but on the right it was much lower and a small inlet had been beaten down to form a muddy beach. If only he could steer the boat over to that side, maybe he could... But the current took him closer to the cliff and all Jamie could do was to look on helplessly as a black-and-white cow, its legs sinking in the mucky gloop, came down to the water's edge to stare at him as he floated past.

He was coming to another bend and the river's current was taking him over to the other side. It was definitely getting faster.

'Help,' he wailed. 'Help me!'

'What's up? What's wrong with you?'

Never had the sound of human voice been so welcome. In front of him, over on the right-hand bank, there was another muddy indentation. In the middle of this, sitting astride a fat pony, was a girl about the same age as Jamie.

'I've got no oars,' he squeaked. 'I can't steer the boat. Help me.'

She didn't hesitate. 'Throw me your painter,' she shouted back. 'Come on, Bumble,' and she urged the pony into the river.

'My what?' Jamie started to panic. The boat was almost parallel with the girl now and would soon be past her.

'Your painter. The rope attached to the boat, stupid. It must have one.'

Flushing with resentment, Jamie leaned for-

126

ward and, gathering up the rope at the front of the punt, still with the metal ring attached to it, threw it in the girl's direction.

It splashed into the water, well short of the pony.

'Pathetic!' she snorted. 'Try again, quick! Forward, Bumble. On, boy!'

But by the time he had pulled the dripping rope back into the boat, he had floated beyond her and was closer to the opposite bank. It was hopeless.

Jamie let out a whimper. Sodding boat, sodding river, useless girl. He was going to end up in the water, the weeds would pull him under and he would drown. Serve them all right!

'There's a group of alders hanging over the river round the next bend,' the girl shouted. 'The current will take you right under them. Stand up and grab a branch, then hold tight.'

'The boat'll tip over if I stand up,' wailed Jamie.

'Don't be stupid, it's a bloody punt. When you grab the branch, try and steer the prow into the bank. There's a weir round the next bend, that *will* tip you into the water. Look, I'll follow you along the bank, this side.'

She urged her pony out of the river and onto the bank. Ahead of him Jamie saw, as she had predicted, a group of thickly foliaged branches hanging over the water. His punt floated on serenely, straight towards it. The first branch nearly knocked him backwards, but he recovered himself in time and made a wild grab at another. The trees overhung the water sufficiently for him not to have to stand, which was as well, because the sudden braking of his body and the forward motion of the boat resulted in a wild gyration. Jamie held on grimly, and more by luck than design the twisting of his body caused the front of the boat to turn its nose into the bank and wedge itself amongst the tree roots.

'Well done!' shouted the girl. 'But don't let go, whatever you do.'

'What do I do now?' shouted Jamie back, suddenly angry. 'There's no way I can get through these trees onto the bank this side. I'm stuck.'

'Just hold on. I'll be back.' And digging her heels into her pony's sides, she trotted off back along the riverbank.

Time passed.

With leaves in his face, his arms scratched by twigs, his muscles aching from the effort of not letting go, Jamie's mood spiralled still lower. Supposing she didn't come back? He couldn't see what she could do by herself– as far as he'd been able to tell, she looked quite small and thin. Maybe she'd bring someone back with her and Jamie would find himself in trouble with the grown-ups yet again. And anyway how would they rescue him? A motorboat? Jamie strained his ears. There was no sound of a motor but he detected, for the first time, the sound of rushing water. It was ahead of him, out of sight around the bend. The weir. She wasn't kidding.

Tears started in Jamie's eyes, his nose ran. This wasn't funny. He wasn't sure how long he could hang on like this. Where the fuck was she?

Behind him he heard a splashing.

'Sorry I took so long,' the girl called, sounding

indecently cheerful to his jangled spirits. 'It's ages since anyone's used this and I had a real struggle to untie the mooring rope.'

Jamie surreptitiously wiped his nose on his sleeve and looked over his shoulder. She was rowing towards him in the most battered old boat he'd ever seen.

Deftly, she manoeuvred herself upstream of him, closer to the bank, and grabbed hold of the side of his punt. The weight of the rowing boat made the punt's stern swing out towards the centre of the river.

Jamie let out a yelp.

'Listen, it'll be all right,' she said with confidence. 'Don't let go just yet but hold on with one hand and pass me one of the mooring ropes – there's one just behind you.'

Holding on for all he was worth, Jamie leaned backwards and groped for the rope. He felt her take it from him and then felt the punt shifting its position as she fastened it to her own boat.

'There, that should hold. Now all you've got to do is climb across into my boat.'

'What?' Jamie almost shrieked. 'I can't do that.'

'You've got to,' she replied firmly, 'unless you want to stay here, clinging to that tree.'

'Why can't you tow me? I thought that's what you were going to do?'

The girl started to sound exasperated. 'How can I possibly do that? The punt will be heavy enough to pull upstream without a lump like you weighing it down. I need you to help me row. Come on, get moving, time's getting on. And you needn't worry about drowning. The water here's quite shallow.'

The punt rocked wildly as Jamie cautiously rose. Still clinging to his branch, he edged his way along the punt until he was close enough to step across. He hesitated. He didn't see how he could do it without being tipped into the water and he didn't relish the idea of getting wet, even if there was no danger. The sun had dipped below the riverbank and a slight breeze had picked up. The air no longer felt warm and the river looked cold and uninviting.

'Oh, do come on.' The girl was getting cross. 'For Chrissake, there's nothing to be scared of.'

He scowled. 'I'm not scared,' he said resentfully, and for the first time looked at her properly. Her hair, blowing around her face, was long, blonde and quite fine. She had a delicate face, lightly tanned, with a little nose and a small, pointed chin and the most extraordinary green eyes Jamie had ever seen. They were glaring at him, and the corners of her mouth were tucked in with annoyance.

Jamie let go of the branch, made a grab at the side of the rowing boat, simultaneously flinging himself into it. The tub rocked violently, shipping a large quantity of water and the girl shrieked as, nearly unseated, the oars slipped from her grasp.

She grabbed them, shouting, 'What on earth are you doing? You'll capsize us, you great idiot.'

She pulled on the oars, the boat steadied, and Jamie sat at the bottom of the tub in a pool of water, gazing up at his saviour. He was right: she was about the same age as him and really, quite slight. She was rowing hard, but he could see they'd make little progress unless he helped. The trouble was he had the haziest idea of how to row, only ever having done it once before, when he was quite small, in a boating lake.

'When you're quite ready,' she said, with sarcasm, 'you can take over. I'll move up to the prow. Where are we going, by the way?'

'What?'

'This punt – it must have come from some-where. Since you don't have a pole or oars, I guess you must have nicked it. Were you planning to take it back after your little jaunt?'

Jamie flushed. 'I didn't nick it. It belongs to my family. I need to take it back.'

'Your family? Do you live in the village?'

'My great-grandmother does. The boat's hers, I suppose.'

'Your great-grandmother... Is that Mrs Merfield?'

'Yes. How did you guess?'

'We live on the other side of the river; you can see the boathouse from ours. So we've not too far to go, but if you don't take over from me, at this rate we'll not get there before dark. Here, take the oars and I'll move back.'

Before he could say anything, she had thrust the oars into his hands and moved to the front of the boat. Having no alternative, and not wishing to lose any more face in front of her, Jamie levered himself onto the bench, clutching the oars tightly, as the boat rocked violently again.

'For God's sake, whatever you do, don't let go of the oars. You're so bloody clumsy! We've already got half the river in the bottom of the boat.'

'Are you sure it's not leaking?' The water lapped over Jamie's feet. The varnish on the seats was peeling, the wood looked old and grey and cracked.

'It's not,' she snapped. 'Come on, start rowing. We're drifting back downriver.'

So, thinking it couldn't be so hard, and trying to imitate people he'd seen rowing, Jamie had a go. The result was nearly disastrous. One oar skimmed the surface of the water, sending a drenching shower over both him and the girl; the other dug deep, causing the boat to lurch sideways. An oar flew out of his hand as he tried to regain his balance; fortunately for him, it fell in the boat and the girl grabbed it with a shriek.

'What the fuck are you doing? Are you trying to capsize us? Don't you know how to row?'

'No, I bloody well don't,' Jamie replied through gritted teeth, completely humiliated.

'Great! Why didn't you say so? Shit, this is going to take us an age. Look, shift your bum. I'll sit next to you, and we'll take an oar each.'

Patiently, she showed him how to use the oar, and at last they started to make progress. Jamie, aware of her proximity and the feel of her body moving in unison with his, slowly fell under her spell.

As they laboured to tow the punt up the river, he told her of the circumstances that had led to the moment she saw him drifting down the river; proudly he told her about his mother; casually he mentioned his father's new status; and, with great relish, he described the four witches with whom he was doomed to live.

When he finished his tale of woe, she showed scant sympathy but looked at him disdainfully. 'I don't understand what you've got against the old ladies. They may be ancient, but they're pretty sparky. My gran's as old as them and she's brilliant. For Chrissake, will you pull harder? We're gonna hit that branch!'

Jamie pulled at his oar with renewed vigour and managed to avert the disaster.

'So how do you know my family?'

She shrugged. 'The Merfields aren't the only people to have lived in this valley since the dawn of time. We may not be as posh, but we've farmed on the other side of the valley for ever.'

'You haven't told me your name.' Jamie felt very humble. He'd never met anyone quite like her.

'Alison.'

Alison. What a cool name. He sneaked a look at her profile. The exertion of rowing had brought a flush to her cheeks, her eyes glinted, her hair wrapped itself round her face like wet strands of silk. She was the most beautiful creature he'd ever seen.

'Do you ... er... Are you at university?' He felt like a nerdish geek.

'No, not yet,' she replied crisply. 'I'm in my last year at Summerbridge, doing my As.'

By the time they reached the boathouse and she had left him to tie up the punt as best he could, Jamie was completely reconciled to the idea of staying at Summerstoke Manor, of living in the village, and of going to Summerbridge College because, for the first time in his life, he was smitten by someone other than his mother.

In bemusement, Oliver put the phone down and sat on the window seat, staring out at the blackness. Nothing was visible in the dark; it had started to rain, and little silver beads shivered down the thick, mullioned panes. In the quiet of the night he could hear the creaks and moans of the old house, but apart from his own breathing there was no sound of anyone else to disturb the cadence of Juliet's voice in his ear.

When he had finally finished working through his pile of papers, everyone else had long gone to bed and he had tried, once more, to get hold of Juliet on the phone before going to bed himself.

He was puzzled by her elusiveness. He had fully expected her to phone, demanding their immediate return to London, the moment she found his note. Every time his mobile rang he braced himself for the scene that would follow. But she hadn't called, and, what was odder, she hadn't rung Jamie. At least, he'd told Oliver she hadn't and from the hurt note in his voice Oliver had no reason not to believe him.

For a while he'd worried something might have happened to her, but then he dismissed the thought. It was the sort of game Juliet would play if she were displeased – do the unexpected, not get in touch, punish him.

The day, in every other way, had gone so smoothly. True, Jamie was in a terrible sulk, but the principal of the College hadn't raised any difficulties over Jamie's expulsion, and the school seemed a nice enough place, well equipped, and the students friendly. His elderly relatives hadn't

134

let him down and were as welcoming as four such formal old dears could be. He had no qualms about leaving Jamie with them, and although Jamie might put up a fight about being left in Summerstoke, he knew he could trust him to behave circumspectly, at least while he was there. He'd been disappointed, but not surprised, when Jamie refused to go with him to look at the old doctor's house, but that visit, also, had paid off.

It was a nice house and Oliver had liked it and the elderly doctor who showed him around. The house was double-fronted, virtually opposite the church. The room that had once been the surgery would make an ideal study for Oliver, and the waiting room, on the other side of a wide hall, had been converted into a comfortable sitting room. There were four bedrooms, and, if the bathrooms and kitchen were somewhat old-fashioned, the doctor indicated he would be happy to finance any modernisation, within reason.

The house was to be let, unfurnished. The doctor didn't plan to return to England but was reluctant to sell, he told Oliver, in case his move to Canada didn't work out. Oliver was tempted to sign with him immediately, but he knew if he did, Juliet would never be reconciled to the place. He would have to exercise great diplomacy with both her and Jamie. But he was used to doing that and told the doctor that, if Juliet agreed, they'd be ready to move in by the middle of October.

He'd returned to the Manor half an hour before supper to hear nothing had been seen of Jamie since he'd left to view the house. Worried, Oliver had gone to look for his son and met him racing over the lawn towards the house. Since Jamie habitually walked with a discontented shuffle, this was different enough; but Jamie, although his jeans were muddy and wet through, and his trainers squeaked with water, had an animation about him Oliver hadn't seen for years. His normally pallid face was flushed with exertion, and the dull, dead shutters had lifted from his eyes.

'Jamie, there you are. Supper's nearly ready. I was coming to find you.'

'Cool. I'm starving.'

'What have you been doing all this time? You're soaked.'

'Oh, nothing much. Messing about on the river. Hey, Dad, what was the house like?'

The enthusiasm with which he made this enquiry took Oliver by surprise.

'Er, I liked it. It's in the middle of the village. The front door opens onto the pavement, but there's a wild, overgrown garden stretching right up into the hillside at the back, and there are plenty of bedrooms so if you want to have any mates to stay...'

'Nice one, Dad, that's cool. Will you have time to take me round there tomorrow, when I get back from College?'

And he had led a bemused Oliver back into the house where, if not exactly an active participant in the conversation over supper, he ate his food with every show of enthusiasm and replied politely enough whenever a question was directed at him.

Now, to cap it all, there was his conversation with Juliet. His final attempt to get hold of her had been successful and instead of some frightful scene down the phone, she'd apologised for not being available and listened, in comparative silence, when he told her about the College; about staying at Summerstoke Manor until they could find somewhere to buy or to rent; and about the availability of the old doctor's house.

'What's it like?'

'Well, I liked it; but the decision is yours. Until you've seen it, I won't make any moves.' He paused, but as she said nothing he proceeded cautiously, 'I had thought, though, if we rent somewhere, we wouldn't have to sell Barnes. We could let it instead, and use the rent to finance this place. We could bring all our stuff down here, as the doctor wants to let it unfurnished, and then we wouldn't have the worry of a tenant ruining our things. What do you think?'

'I think it's a brilliant idea, Ollie.'

'Pardon?' Oliver was so taken aback, he thought he hadn't heard her properly.

'Darling, it's a perfect solution. During the week, when you're not there, Jamie will be at that college and he can go over to the Manor to eat and sleep. You go back to your constituency on Thursday night so he's got you at the doctor's house until Monday. We can always make other arrangements during the holidays. I'm glad we're not selling our little house – after all you're not going to be the honourable member for Mendip for the rest of your life, are you?'

Oliver struggled for a moment. 'Juliet, where do you figure in this equation? Why should Jamie *need* to stay at the Manor?'

'Ollie' – the excitement emanating from Juliet

137

was so physical, Oliver could feel it pulsating down the line, buzzing in his ears –'this might be it! I could be on my way! I can't believe it. I'm so excited – that's why I've not been able to talk, I've simply been rushed off my feet getting ready.'

'Getting ready for what? Sweetheart, what are you on about?'

'Hollywood, darling. That's what I'm on about. That interview I had yesterday afternoon... Louis says they loved me. It's for a new television drama series – I'm up for the lead: a detective who realises she's psychic.'

Oliver, who had long since learned not to say anything disparaging about the quality of the parts Juliet auditioned for, tried to sound enthusiastic. 'That's really great, but why should it prevent you coming down here?'

'Oliver,' Juliet almost shrieked with excitement, 'Louis says I've got to be prepared to leave for LA this weekend, and if I get the part it could mean staying there for a least six weeks while they shoot the pilot. Then, if it's successful, I'm contracted for the next seven years.'

'What?' It was Oliver's turn to shriek, but with dismay. 'You're kidding? How certain is this?'

'I expect I'll hear tomorrow. These guys don't hang about. Louis says if I get through to LA, I'll be one of two or three they'll be looking at and the whole process of the final selection will take about a week.' Juliet's tone changed, and she continued soberly, 'I'm not going to blow this one, Ollie. It's what I've been waiting for and it's finally happening. Look, we'll talk some more tomorrow. Are you staying down there?'

'Yes. I had to put a whole load of meetings on hold today, to sort out Jamie, so I shall be really tied up for the rest of the week. Can you come down?'

'Darling, be reasonable. If I'm flying out at the weekend, I shall be in a flat spin.'

'Have you spoken to Jamie? Does he know any of this?'

'No, not yet. I'll try and get hold of him tomorrow. Don't say anything to him, will you? I want to tell him, myself. He'll be so thrilled!'

Oliver somehow doubted that. Poor Jamie, in one week he'd lost his old school, his friends, his home, and now his mum.

'What about packing the house up? Will you be able to make a start on that?'

'Don't be silly, Oliver. Get Polly to help you. She's Mistress Efficiency.'

The conversation ended with Juliet still in a buzz and Oliver feeling increasingly dazed.

He sat in the window for a long time, trying to sort his thoughts. On the plus side, Jamie seemed more reconciled to his change of fortunes and they had a house they could move into. But, and it was an overwhelming but, he had not imagined life without Juliet, or at least, without Juliet being substantially present.

The beautiful, winsome person Juliet presented to the world concealed a ruthlessness that brooked no opposition in pursuit of her goals. He had learned that the hard way. He loved her dearly but he accepted, with equanimity, the knowledge that Juliet's love for him, deeper than his family gave her credit for, was not as great as her love for herself. Undoubtedly she loved Jamie, but he knew she wouldn't hesitate to put them both on one side if the stakes were high enough. And Hollywood...

There was no contest. It was a dream powerful enough for her to leave him and Jamie behind, apparently without a qualm.

Maybe, he thought, getting up and stretching, she won't go. Nothing's certain, after all. She's been for auditions before and it may well be she'll not get the part.

Taking comfort from these disloyal thoughts, he made his way through the dark reaches of the house to his bed.

EARLY OCTOBER

6

'So Richard and Issy are moving in next week, are they? How do you feel about them living practically next door?' Marion Croucher, sipping her glass of chilled Chardonnay, eyed her friend with interest.

Veronica shrugged. 'It'll be fun to see more of Richard. He's always so busy it's hard to pin him down. I didn't know they'd moved until yesterday, but since we only got back from the Seychelles the day before, that's hardly surprising.'

'You've obviously had a good holiday, Vee, darling. I'd give my eye teeth for a tan like that.' Marion's admiration was tinged with envy. There was no way that she and Gavin could afford three weeks in the Seychelles at the drop of a hat.

'I needed it. This place is so parochial at times, it drives me mad.' It was a warm evening, early in October, and the two were sitting on a terrace in the garden of Summerstoke House, enjoying the last of the sun.

'The village should get a bit livelier with Richard in residence.' Marion smirked. 'He's an attractive man.'

'Mmm.' Veronica smiled slightly. 'He is, but more importantly he's good fun.'

'Goodness only knows what he sees in Issy.'

Veronica shrugged. 'Hugh and I have never been able to work it out. Actually I once asked

Richard just that—'

'Vee, you didn't! What did he say?'

Veronica's smile was enigmatic. 'Said she was very different now from the girl he'd first met. But he did imply there was some sort of sexual chemistry between them – she is seventeen years younger than him, after all. But whatever it is, I don't think it's strong enough to hold him. I think he sees she's a liability.'

'Do you think he has affairs, Vee?'

'Probably, but he's very discreet.'

Marion darted a curious glance at her friend. 'Would you have an affair with him?'

Veronica was amused. 'I might flirt with him, Marion, darling, but an affair? No, I know on which side my bread's buttered. More wine?'

'Thanks. And where's Hugh this evening? Out riding?'

'No, he's pursuing the latest bee in his bonnet. He's gone to see Andrew Hill.'

'Oh, yes, Gavin mentioned Hugh wanted to become chairman of the Landowners. He thinks he'd be ideal – all that wheeling and dealing, right up Hugh's street. Is he getting Andrew to propose him?'

'I suppose so.' Veronica poured herself another glass of wine. 'Quite frankly, Marion, I'm not terribly interested. Hugh's become obsessed with the idea, though. Gavin's right: he likes being in the control seat, and becoming the county committee chairman would give him so much power and influence. He'd love it.'

'He's going to have to lobby all the other members of the committee, though, isn't he? It's not

144

going to be easy.' Marion drained her glass and looked meaningfully at the bottle besides her hostess.

'He'll get it.'

'Andrew Hill's also chairman of the local Tories, isn't he? Why did Hugh encourage Richard to pip Oliver Merfield over the sale of the vicarage? Surely having Oliver Merfield as a neighbour would be more use to Hugh?' Marion twirled her empty glass then put it down with a sigh.

'An MP more useful than a newspaper editor? That's a debatable point. As it happens, Hugh doesn't like the Merfields; they've never done him any favours. But funnily enough we've got the best of both worlds – that's the other bit of news I picked up when we got back. Oliver Merfield's renting a house in the village. We're throwing a little party on Friday to welcome them to the village. Should be entertaining.'

'Yes, it should,' Marion tried not to show she minded not having been asked. 'Your neighbours have suddenly taken a turn for the more interesting, darling. Perhaps I should drop them my card and remind Issy, as well.'

'She couldn't afford you, Marion. So tell me, how far have you got with our shop plans?'

'I phoned when you were away to tell you I'd called in at the Summerstoke shop.'

'What success?'

'None. The woman was quite rude, actually. Said she'd no intention of selling. I left my card, but I honestly don't hold out much hope. That's what I wanted to talk to you about. Should I start looking elsewhere, do you think?'

145

Veronica sipped her wine, thoughtfully. 'No harm in doing that. In the meantime, I'll put into action a little plan I dreamed up. If the shop's customers start drifting away, she'll have to sell. We'll just have to be patient for a while longer. More wine, darling?'

Isabelle was on her knees in a sea of crumpled paper, unpacking a tea-chest of china, when the doorbell rang, summoning attendance like a little church bell. For a moment she squatted back on her heels, listening with pleasure as the brassy notes echoed around the half-empty house. Getting to her feet, she padded across the broken linoleum of the kitchen floor to the hall, following a shaft of light falling on the bare floorboards from the fanlight over the front door.

Standing in the porch was a tall, thin man in his fifties, with a large head and a shock of grey hair. She thought, as she opened the door, she detected a hint of disappointment in his demeanour – with one foot on the doorstep and one on the drive, he looked as if he'd been about to flee.

'Ah. Good morning,' he said, putting his hand to his head as if he were going to tilt his hat, except he wasn't wearing one, and nervously fiddled with the steel frame of his spectacles instead. 'Mrs ... er...'

'Mrs Garnett,' Isabelle replied cautiously. She took in the shabby tweed jacket, the stained grey garment not quite covering the sloping bulge of his stomach, and his collar, which unequivocally stated his profession.

'Ah, yes. Well, erm ... I'm the vicar of St

146

Stephen's, the parish church of Summerstoke, and, er...' his voice faded away and Isabelle sensed he was waiting for her to make the next move. She'd never had a vicar calling on her before – as far as she was concerned, it was something that happened in old-fashioned books when, she vaguely remembered, they would be invited in for tea, or a glass of sherry.

She viewed him curiously. His head was very big – almost too large for that long, thin body; he had big ears, too, and large nose and chin and mouth. In fact, it was as if his head had been designed to fit a frame of entirely different proportions and his body was finding it a struggle to support such a weight: his shoulders were stooped and the eyes peering at her anxiously from behind his specs were watery and tired.

'Er...' He sighed, deeply, and resumed his speech. 'I've called to welcome you to Summerstoke. Mrs, er...'

'Garnett.'

'Yes ... and to tell you St Stephen's is always open and we, er, very much hope to see you there, you know, as part of the congregation, or at one of our coffee mornings. You'd be very welcome.' Relieved at having completed his mission statement, he allowed himself a weary smile.

To her surprise, Isabelle felt touched.

They had only been in Summerstoke for a week, but already it felt as if she was starting a life sentence in a penal colony. Once the removal vans had gone and the excitement of the move was replaced by the almost Herculean task of making the house their own, all Isabelle's reservations about living in the country came back to taunt her.

She hadn't many good mates in Bath – she'd never been one to make close friends, anyway – but she'd an easy camaraderie with the other mums, both from the birth group and from when Rebecca had started school.

In Summerstoke not only did she not know anybody but in the school playground she had the distinct impression the other mothers were either avoiding her or discussing her unfavourably, and all her attempts to be friends were ignored. Within the space of a few days, collecting the children had become something of an ordeal.

As Richard left earlier for work and returned later, she calculated that on some days she could go twelve hours without speaking to another adult. It was not as if she could take herself out shopping. Summerstoke had only the one shop and the silence that fell the first time she went in was almost as intimidating as the reaction to her in the school playground.

It didn't matter the vicar was only doing his job. He was the first person to welcome her to Summerstoke and that affected her.

She smiled back at him. 'How very nice of you. Thank you. Would you like to come in? I mean, if you have time. I was about to make myself a cup of tea, if you'd like...'

He looked taken aback, then alarmed. 'Er, thank you, that's very kind, but, er ... Mrs ... er...'

'Isabelle. My name is Isabelle.'

'Isobel?' His face suddenly lightened. 'That was my mother's name.'

'Oh.' Isabelle couldn't think what else to say, except 'Easy to remember, then. Easier than Mrs Garnett, anyway.'

'Yes. Well, thank you for the offer, of tea. Another time, perhaps.' His manner became almost brisk. 'I've got a churchwardens' meeting in half an hour and I've got to get my papers together.'

'Thank you for calling.'

'Very nice to have met you, er ... Isobel,' he half laughed, uncomfortable with the intimacy of her name, then plunged on, becoming quite chatty now he'd got an exit strategy established. 'That's my house over there.' He waved at a stone wall that skirted the drive, forming one boundary of the Old Vicarage's front garden. Isabelle could just see the roof of a building beyond.

'It used to be the stable block of this house, you know, in the days when clergymen could afford horses. Then the church sold this lovely house and converted the stable for the likes of me. Very appropriate, you may think.'

Isabelle felt guilty. 'Of course, the Old Vicarage – it never occurred to me. Did you use to live here?'

'Oh no. But my wife was very friendly with the previous owner, Mrs Delaney. She's going to miss her very much. She used to spend quite a bit of time here, particularly in the garden. She loves gardening, you know.'

'Oh.' Again, there seemed little else she could say. She certainly didn't want to say anything that might encourage the vicar's wife to think she still had freedom of the garden, although she suspected that was what was being hinted at.

'But she hasn't got the time any more, even for

our meagre plot. She's working as the receptionist for the doctors. I expect you'll have met her?'

'No, I don't think I have. I haven't signed on yet. We've hardly been here...'

'You'd be well advised to. It's a good practice. We're very fortunate in all we have in this village, what with the surgery, the shop and the school, but, as my wife is the first to say, if we don't use it we'll lose it. Oh, my goodness, I nearly forgot. She asked me to give you this.' He groped in the pockets of his jacket, finally producing a folded piece of paper. 'She thought you might find it useful. It's a list of our local suppliers and, you know, odd-job men, the chimney sweep, that sort of thing. Well, Mrs ... er ... I must be going.'

He thrust the paper in her hands, went to tip his non-existent hat, then, nodding his farewells, turned and shambled down the drive as if he was carrying the woes of the world on his shoulders.

Isabelle stood at the door and watched him leave. I wonder if all vicars are like that, she thought. This must be the first time in my life I've ever had a conversation with one. What a strange man. When he was out of sight, she shut the door. You should have asked his name, she reproached herself. What do you call vicars? What do I call his wife? Mrs Vicar?

She returned to the kitchen, put the kettle on and settled down to finish the task in hand. Eventually the chest was emptied, the floor covered with scrunched-up newspaper, and the kitchen table, which appeared to have shrunk since they moved it from Bath, covered in china. She was pouring boiling water onto a teabag, when the doorbell clamoured for her attention a second time.

'I bet that's the vicar's wife, coming to have a look for herself,' she muttered, going to answer the door.

Nobody could have looked less like a vicar's wife than her new visitor. She was tall and willowy, her height accentuated by a pair of very high heels. She must have been in her mid-twenties, Isabelle guessed, but although her entire appearance was designed to leave nothing to speculation, she looked as if she'd blown in from another era: a Hollywood starlet from the 1960s. She wore her hair, black and brittle with lacquer, in a beehive; her almond-shaped blue eyes were liberally outlined with mascara, and her mouth was painted into a glossy pink cupid's bow. Although it was mid-October, her legs were bare, a denim skirt just covered her bottom and a white frilly blouse revealed her shapely bosom.

Isabelle blinked. 'Er...'

But before she could say anything, the starlet beamed at her. 'Hello. Sorry to bother you, but I'd heard as how you'd just moved in so I thought I'd drop by and see if you can use my services.'

It was the first time Isabelle had properly met the full roundness of the soft West Country accent and she listened, fascinated.

The vision continued, 'I live in the village, down by the river, and I've got my own cleanin' business. I've just finished my mornin' at the manor – Mrs Merfield, she's one of my clients – and seein' as you're so close, I thought I'd leave my card.'

A more unlikely cleaning lady Isabelle couldn't

151

imagine. Weakly she accepted the piece of cardboard extracted, with some difficulty, from the pocket of the girl's skirt, and glanced at it. It advertised the cleaning, ironing and baby-sitting services of Paula Spinks. In case she was in any doubt, the starlet pointed to the card and then at herself.

'Paula Spinks: that's I; and my Lenny said to say if there was any odd jobs goin', he's your man. He's good with his hands, is Lenny.'

Isabelle thought of all the odd jobs that needed doing; of the dust and dirt piling up as she struggled to bring the house into some sort of order; of the heap of ironing that grew in the waiting.

'I was just about to have a cup of tea. Would you like one?'

Unlike the vicar, Paula didn't hesitate. 'I never say no to a cuppa. Thanks very much, Mrs, er...'

'Garnett. But please, my name is Isabelle.'

'Isabelle – that's dead romantic, that really is. Joan Collins played a girl called Isabelle in *Tales that Witness Madness* only they called her Bella. Does you get called Bella?'

Isabelle looked at her sharply, suspecting her of taking the piss, but she clearly wasn't. 'No. I get called Issy, but I prefer to be called Isabelle.'

She led the way to the kitchen, aware Paula was staring around her with open curiosity.

Pulling out a chair at the kitchen table and removing a large oval dinner plate Isabelle had placed there for safety, Paula remarked with a certain sympathy, 'Blimey, you've got a bit of a job on your hands, ain't yer?'

Isabelle gave a wry laugh, 'I suppose I have. Have you been in this house before, Paula?' She poured the water into mugs as she spoke. 'It's only teabags, I'm afraid. I've no idea which packing case the teapot's in. Milk, sugar?'

'Oh, both please, lots. I like my tea sweet and milky. No, I've never been in here before. Mrs Delaney weren't the sort of person to invite the likes of I to tea. It's a fair old size, ain't it?'

'Yes. Do you want to have a look round? It's a tip, at the moment, but...'

'My house is always a tip,' said Paula cheerfully, apparently unaware such a confession was not the best way to advertise her services as a cleaner, but Isabelle warmed to her, and the two women, mugs in hand, set off to inspect the house.

It was a rambling house. Isabelle and the girls had been thrilled with the number of rooms, the outbuildings, and the size of the garden. Richard had shaken his head over its general state, but Isabelle hadn't at all minded the terribly old-fashioned decoration, the archaic plumbing, the kitchen cupboards that had been fitted in the 1950s, and the ancient Aga which belched poisonous, oily fumes when the wind blew in the wrong direction. She loved the fact that there were open fires in all the rooms; that the staircase went up through the centre of the house, and that there was a cellar *and* an attic.

Between them, she and Richard had managed to get the right furniture in the right rooms, but everywhere there were boxes, tea-chests, rolled carpets and stacked pictures. The rooms were generally large, but looked very shabby: the floral

153

wallpaper much favoured by the departed Mrs Delaney was faded and torn, with darker patches where pictures or mirrors had once hung; the uncarpeted floors were grey and dusty, and the curtainless windows, smeared with grime, added to the dilapidated feel of the house.

Paula was impressed by the number of rooms and appalled at the state of them. 'My goodness, Isabelle, have you got to get this little lot sorted all by yourself? Where's your man?'

'Richard? He's at work. Anyway, he's not particularly practical. We're getting the decorators in as soon as possible and once each room is finished we can carpet it and sort out the furniture. Until then, it's going to be a bit like camping.'

She led the way into her daughters' bedroom. 'I've tried to make this a bit cosier, though, for the girls. They were upset at leaving our old house.'

The room glowed with colour. Isabelle had thrown a number of rugs over the floor; soft toys were piled on a long wooden chest; there were bright cotton duvets on the beds and a number of crystals, suspended from the ceiling, caught and refracted the light from the window. She had roughly whitewashed the walls, covering them with posters, and started painting a mural of a fairy castle.

'Wow!' said Paula, admiringly. 'I like that. Who's done that, then?'

'Me. I did one for them in their old playroom. I haven't had time to get very far with it, though.'

'I think it's lovely. You are clever. You should be an artist.'

She followed Isabelle out of the room. 'Is it just

154

the two kiddies you've got?'

'Yes, Becky's six and Clemmie's four.'

'You going to send them to the local school?'

'They're there already.'

'Oh? They must be in the same classes as my eldest two. Ryan, he's six, and Kylie's four – she only started in September, bless her. What did you say their names was?'

'Clemmie, short for Clementine, and Becky, or Rebecca.' She felt a pang.

Clemmie had coped with the change of schools with total equanimity and came back, each day, armed with pictures she'd drawn and models she'd made and with tales of the friends she was making. Becky, on the other hand, heart-broken to leave her old school had made no friends, clung to Isabelle when she tried to leave her in the playground in the morning, and came home tearful in the afternoon.

Isabelle had tried to share this with Richard but, although sympathetic, he believed it was simply a matter of time and Becky would get used to it.

'Is it a good school, do you think?' she asked, as she and Paula returned to the kitchen.

'No idea,' came the cheerful reply. 'Teachers seem nice enough though my Ryan does his best to run them ragged. He's a little rascal, that boy. Takes after his dad.'

Paula put her mug in the sink and patted the pile of ironing balanced on the ironing board. 'Do you want a hand with this little lot? Me mum's looking after the littlies till dinnertime, so I could do this now – if you'd like us to, that is? As a one off – you don't have to say about the cleanin' if you don't want.'

Isabelle didn't hesitate. 'I'd love you to, Paula, if you don't mind; but you haven't told me what your rates are?'

Paula hesitated for a fraction, and then said, with a hint of defiance as if she would be challenged for asking too much, 'Six pound an hour.'

Isabelle's eyes widened. Her cleaner, in Bath, had charged nearly twice that amount. 'Fine,' she said faintly. 'You're on. Another cup of tea?'

'Never say no. Now, where's this iron to? And I'm gonna need some hangers.'

As Paula ironed and Isabelle washed and put away the crockery, they continued to chat. Isabelle learned Paula had been a devoted fan of Joan Collins since she was fourteen; she'd met Lenny, who was a bit older than her, when she was fifteen and still at school, and they'd married when she was seventeen. She was now in her mid-twenties and had four children.

'Four?' said Isabelle faintly. 'How do you cope? I find two bad enough.'

'Oh, we get by. They're a handful, but they mind Lenny – and me mum helps out.'

'How do you manage to do babysitting? I'd have thought you'd have enough with your lot.'

'But I don't get paid for minding 'em, do I? Me mum comes over, or Lenny stays in, or Ali comes over from the farm.'

'The farm?'

'Yeah, Marsh Farm, that's where my Lenny works. Charlie Tucker farms it with his brother, Stephen, and Ali's their little sister. The whole family's really nice. Charlie's Lenny's great mate,

156

he's good fun. A terrible flirt, mind. Lenny says he's had more girlfriends than he's had hot dinners.' Paula chuckled.

Having endured Richard's flirtations, Isabelle disliked the Charlie Tuckers of this world and grimaced.

Paula didn't notice and burbled on. 'Ali, she's seventeen an' studying for her exams, so she's happy to come over when I needs her.'

'Would you be able to babysit for me this evening?'

Paula looked regretful. 'With a bit of notice, I could've got something sorted, but Lenny's out tonight with Charlie, me mum's got bingo, and I know Ali's off to see her boyfriend – he's in hospital.' She brightened. 'But you could bring them over to mine, if you like. I wouldn't charge yer.'

Isabelle smiled at her. 'That's really nice of you, Paula. Another time, perhaps, when the girls are more settled. It's only a cocktail party. I can take them along for a bit. It'll be a good excuse for me to leave early.'

'Why would you want to do that? Don't you like parties?'

Isabelle pulled a face. 'Not much. Lots of boring people I hardly know, talking in very loud voices, never really listening to anything anyone says, chucking as much booze down their throats as they can till they can hardly walk and think everything they say is incredibly funny.'

'I used to love parties,' Paula said wistfully. 'Dancing, that's what I like. We had a big disco in one of Charlie's fields in the summer. Me and Lenny bopped till dawn. It was fab.'

157

'Perhaps we should have a house-warming party when everything's finished,' Isabelle suggested. 'The front sitting room's large enough for dancing. Would you come?' Isabelle could visualise Richard's reaction to Paula. She smiled.

'You serious?' Paula looked a bit startled.

'Yes, I'm serious. You're the nicest person I've met in Summerstoke so far. I'd like you to come. And Lenny.'

Paula looked pleased, but said nothing, concentrating on pushing the nose of the iron round a shirt collar. 'Your husband, he's got a lot of shirts. Does he wear a clean one every day?'

'Sometimes two. Particularly if he's got to go to a function in the evening, which can happen three or four times in a week.'

'You're jokin'! I heard he was a reporter. Is that right?'

'He was once. He's a newspaper editor now. That's why he gets so many invitations.'

'No wonder he's got so many shirts!' Paula's eyes were round. 'He must be really important.'

Isabelle looked askance, but said nothing.

'That's two important people on my client list now. Brilliant!'

'Who's the other one? You mentioned the Manor House?'

'Well I s'pose they're important, too, in their way. D'yer know, Isabelle, your house *seems* big; the Lesters' house *is* big; but the Merfields' house is enormous. They could employ us for the whole week and it would be like painting that bridge, you know, the one in Scotland; as soon as I'd finished it, I'd have to start all over again.'

'So who's your other client?'

'Oliver Merfield – he's our MP and married to Juliet Peters.' The reverential way she pronounced the name Juliet Peters clearly indicated who Paula considered to be the more important member in that household.

Isabelle wrinkled her forehead. 'Juliet Peters? Should I have heard of her?'

Paula was aghast. 'Isabelle, you can't be serious? She's really famous – she was in *Hunter's Way*. She's beautiful.'

Isabelle shook her head. 'I've never watched *Hunter's Way*, I'm afraid. I've seen pictures of Oliver Merfield, though. He's quite young, isn't he? And very good-looking. Pity he's a Conservative.'

'He's very nice and polite. Which is more than can be said for that son of his. How two such lovely people can have such a piece of work...'

'They were going to buy this place originally, but their sale fell through and Richard bought it. I felt quite bad about that.'

'Don't see why. Anyway, they've got a nice house – it's Dr Lessing's old house. He's gone off to Canada, more's the pity. I liked Dr Lessing – he was our doctor for years. But I don't think he's sold it to them, just rentin'. They moved in a week ago and I spent days before that cleanin' it out, good and proper. A right pickle it was, but that's doctors for you.'

Isabelle grinned. 'What's it like, working for a star? Is she very demanding?'

Paula shrugged. 'I ain't met her yet. She's in Hollywood. Oliver's sister helped him set up shop. But Oliver said she could be coming back

159

any day now. I do hope so. I'm dying to meet her.'

She flicked the switch on the iron. 'There, all done.'

Isabelle could have wept with gratitude. All Richard's shirts were on hangers, beautifully pressed, and a pile of the girls' clothes as well as her bits and pieces were neatly folded and placed in the ironing basket. Paula had saved her hours of anguish.

'Oh Paula, that's terrific. Thank you. You will ... you will come again, won't you? I know this house is a mess and we're not beautiful or famous...'

Paula grinned, 'But you're nice and that, as I told Lenny, is important. I made a solemn promise, after I left the Lesters, I'd never work for nobody I didn't like again.'

At the mention of the Lesters, Isabelle felt the grey edge of depression start to creep over her. 'The Lesters? Did you work for the Lesters?'

'Yeah. For years. They was horrible. It was the best day's work I ever did when I walked out.' She caught the set expression on Isabelle's face and said, awkwardly, 'Sorry, 'ave I said something I shouldn't 'ave? Are they friends of yours?'

Isabelle was torn between loyalty to Richard and wanting to tell Paula what she really thought. Richard wouldn't approve of a friendship with the likes of Paula, she had absolutely no doubt about that, and he wouldn't understand her impulse towards such a friendship. She wasn't sure she understood it herself. Paula wasn't bright, and was unlike herself in every way, but the last hour had been refreshing and fun, and the intense loneliness of the last week, which had been

160

growing day by day, had dissipated a little.

She bit her lip. 'Don't apologise. They're old friends of my husband. Actually, Paula, they terrify me, and you're right, they're horrible. We're going there this evening – this cocktail party, I mentioned. They're giving it to welcome Oliver Merfield and his family and us, to the village. Can you imagine? It's going to be awful. The Merfields have every reason not to like us – after all, we've got the house they wanted – but Veronica Lester rides roughshod over all that and insists we're going to be bosom buddies.'

Paula looked sympathetic. 'That's one party I'm glad I'm not going to, not even if Juliet Peters was to turn up. You can tell us all about it next time I'm round. Let's see. It's Friday today. How about Tuesday morning, nine to twelve, or Thursday morning, same time? They're both free.'

'Make it both,' said Isabelle, 'for the moment at least.'

After Paula had gone Isabelle took the pressed clothes up to the children's bedroom and lingered for a moment, looking out of the window.

Their room was at the back of the house, and she could see across the lawn and shrubbery to the river and the valley beyond. To the far left, on the other side of a clump of trees, she could glimpse the river as it curved to meet the end of the ridge, and in the field below the ridge she could make out a cloud of seagulls following the progress of a tractor as it turned the silver-grey ground dark brown.

The valley was dissected by a hedgerow that

ran from the point where the river disappeared under the cliff, right across the valley floor to meet, she guessed, the road to Summerbridge on the other side, although she couldn't see round that far as a bend in the river and the houses of lower Summerstoke obstructed her view.

'I could get some good photographs to send Joe from up here,' she thought, gazing across the valley. Just visible, beyond the river, a farmhouse sat on a slight rise, surrounded by outbuildings and barns. 'I guess that's the farm where Paula's Lenny works,' Isabelle muttered. 'I ought to go and explore. That hedge probably runs along a footpath, or a lane.'

She glanced at her watch. It was a little after twelve. She could do with a break. She opened the window and leaned out. The air felt warm on her skin; the sky was blue, with white, scudding puffs of cotton wool and, as if to tempt her, the sun suddenly threw off the cloud it had been lurking behind for most of the morning and the landscape sizzled with colour.

Charlie Tucker, sitting in his tractor and ploughing a stubble field, sang lustily. The liver and white spaniel lying on the floor of his cab was a recent acquisition but already adored him without qualification. He was thirty-two, tall and lean, his skin weathered but not yet leathery; he had short, nut-brown hair, a pair of merry brown eyes under dark brows, a long, square jaw and a slightly hooked nose. He was restless, full of energy, and found it hard to take anything seriously, whether it was work or women.

He shared the farming with his younger brother, Stephen, and at the moment his mind was preoccupied with a scheme that would relieve him of the more tedious aspects of farm life.

Born into farming, Charlie had a restless nature which did not suit the role of farmer, unlike steady and reliable Stephen, so Charlie had opted to try and develop the farm's potential in other ways. He had already started converting unwanted out-buildings into studios and workshops – one already was as good as let. Their grand plan was to move away from conventional farming, the kiss of death for small enterprises like theirs, and turn Marsh Farm into a rare breeds centre.

'We could set aside a field, have demonstrations of ploughing through the ages, get some antique tractors, and a pair of those whacking great shire horses with an iron plough. Get the punters to pay to turn a furrow. That'd be a laugh, eh, Duchess?'

The dog could not hear Charlie's voice over the roar of the tractor, but she sensed she was being addressed and her tail thumped enthusiastically.

Charlie liked ploughing and he was good at it. He took pride in the straightness of his lines; he loved the way the earth curled, rich, brown and shiny as it was turned; he even liked the flocks of gulls that screamed and swooped in his wake. Most particularly, he liked ploughing at this time of year.

The hedgerows were a profusion of colour, with leaves turning every shade of yellow, orange, red and brown. There were more berries than the birds could eat: impenetrable bushes of green, purple and red blackberries; sprays of orange and scarlet rosehips; vermilion necklaces of bryony which was deadly poisonous and hung like droplets of blood from the twigs and stalks of the hedgerow; great drooping fronds of dark purple elderberries; tight, bright green flowering ivy, the intensely sweet fragrance of which attracted a million bees, setting the entire hedge buzzing; the whole lot topped by the wild candyfloss of old man's beard.

Charlie had nearly completed the field and was thinking about lunch when the weather changed and the light breeze brought with it a series of showers that rapidly settled into a steady downpour. He finished the field and decided to make a start on the next the following day.

Locking the cab of his tractor, he dashed to his battered old van parked in a lay-by on the edge of the field, Duchess running joyfully alongside him. Once in his van, he decided to finish off his flask of tea and the large piece of chocolate cake his mother had included with his elevenses. It didn't look that appetising – cakes weren't his mum's forte – so he decided the birds could have it and tossed it onto the passenger seat. He poured out his tea, smiling at the dog behind him, whose eyes were fixed steadfastly on the cake.

'I know you'd wolf it down in a sec, Duchess, but we've got to watch your figure. Hey, who's that?'

Ahead, sheltering under a copse of trees, was the figure of a girl or a boy – he couldn't make out which through the rain teeming down his windscreen. He shrugged. Probably someone from the village, walking a dog. It was the only reason for anyone to come down Weasel Lane, which only provided access to the fields and petered out before the river. He could just see Stephen, at the far end, about to herd a small group of heifers down it.

Suddenly the figure abandoned the shelter of the trees, darted to the middle of the lane, turning this way and that as if looking for an escape route, and then pelted towards him. He didn't recognise the woman but hardly had he time to register this when she wrenched open the passenger door and threw herself into the van, slamming the door shut.

Deafened by a cacophony of barking, Charlie attempted to calm the dog down before he turned to stare at her. She was in a state of collapse, drenched through, trying to catch her breath, shaking and whimpering with shock.

It was impossible to tell her age. Her hair was very short, and plastered to her head like a cap; she was of medium height, but thin, and her cotton shirt and gipsy skirt, soaked by the rain, clung to her, making her look like a colourful stick insect, an impression accentuated by her face, which was small and delicate, and dominated by a pair of huge, round, soft blue eyes.

Startled and wary, they turned on him when, after what seemed a decent interval, he spoke.

'Er, something wrong, miss?'

'What? Oh, er, I'm sorry.' Colour flooded her face and she struggled to retrieve the situation. 'I'm really sorry. It's just that I was so wet and I ... I was going to walk back when I saw... It's just that I'm not used to ... and you hear such things...

165

There was no way past. I didn't know what else to do. I'm so sorry, I didn't mean to startle you, or your dog.' She had an unexpectedly low voice for one who looked so frail, with a slight twinge of an accent that Charlie was not familiar with.

'What were you running from?' Charlie was puzzled.

She hung her head and blushed even more. 'Those cows. They were coming straight for me. I didn't know where to go, so I ran.'

A great bubble of laughter welled up inside Charlie but some instinct made him hold it in check.

'I've never really seen cows close to before. They're so big. I panicked. I'm sorry, you must think me very stupid.'

He did, but didn't let it show, and said consolingly, 'If you're not used to them, they're pretty big. But those are only heifers – very docile, you know. They'd have looked you over and passed on.'

'Oh, I didn't know.' She looked so wet, so wretched, that Charlie felt an unexpected surge of sympathy.

'If you don't live in the country, no reason why you should. Would you like some of my tea? You look as if you need it.'

'Thank you,' she replied, subdued, and took the proffered mug.

Duchess was still grumbling so he leaned back and ruffled her head. 'That's enough, Duchess. Enough!'

Out of the corner of his eye he could see the woman take a mouthful of tea, then grimace. She attempted a smile as she handed the mug back. 'Sorry, I'm not used to so much sugar. But it was very kind of you.'

'No probs.' He wound down his window and, throwing the residue away, suddenly remembered the chocolate cake. Again the bubble of laughter welled and threatened to burst. He grinned: the damage was done, nothing he could do about it.

'D'ye want a lift back to the village? Or to your car? This rain has set in for the rest of the day.'

She hesitated.

He smiled at her encouragingly. 'My name's Charlie. This is my land. I've been ploughing the field back there. The cows that gave you such a fright are part of our herd. Stephen, my brother, was driving them into a field up the lane.'

At this she frowned slightly, hesitated, then gave a slight smile. 'Thank you, I'd love a lift, if you're sure. And I'm sorry I was so... You're very kind.'

He shrugged and turned on the ignition. 'Where to?'

'Oh, the village, please, if it's not too much trouble.'

'No trouble at all. Save you getting completely drenched.'

'It was so sunny when I set out. I walked further than I intended.'

'Not exactly dressed for walking, are you?' he said, glancing at her. Apart from a small purse slung over her shoulder she was not carrying anything, and her clothes and flimsy sandals didn't seem the right sort of gear for going for a walk in mid-October, however tempting the weather.

'What?' She looked startled. 'No, I suppose

not, but then I didn't expect...' She lifted her chin and replied with something of a spark, 'Is there a regulation uniform for walking in the country?'

He laughed. 'No, no – wear what you like, be my guest. It's just that lanes like these can get pretty muddy, particularly now the weather's changing.'

Charlie's laugh was infectious and she smiled, rather reluctantly, back. 'I must make sure I get out my green wellies next time.' She gazed out of the van at the passing hedgerow. 'This lane's beautiful, isn't it?'

'Is it?' Charlie grinned faintly. The idea of Weasel Lane being beautiful was a new one on him.

'Yes, particularly the hedges. I don't think I ever realised how many different plants make up a hedgerow. It really is old England, isn't it?'

'Old England?' Charlie chuckled. 'I'd never thought of Weasel Lane being *that* before, but I suppose it is pretty ancient. Most of the other hedges have been grubbed up.' He cast her a sidelong glance. She was an attractive woman, not pretty the way Charlie normally liked, but with those huge blue eyes, high cheekbones and long slender neck... 'You're not from these parts, are you?'

'No. I've lived mainly in London or, more recently, Bath.'

'Visiting friends in Summerstoke, then, are you?'

'No.'

They reached the junction with the main road. It was raining so hard that Charlie could hardly see through the windscreen.

168

'So what brought you to the village, then, apart from wanting to go for a walk?'

'We've moved here. Last week, in fact.'

'Oh, I see. Shall I drop you at your house, then?'

'Thank you, that'd be brilliant. It's the Old Vicarage.'

'The Old Vicarage? I heard that our new MP was gonna move in there, but he got gazumped.' He glanced across at her. 'So, you're the new owner, eh?'

She was embarrassed and replied awkwardly, 'Well, yes. He wasn't gazumped exactly. We made an offer and, er, that was the one that was accepted.'

'Well, all's fair in love and house-buying, that's what I say, although the Merfields are a local family and everyone thought the Old Vicarage was as good as theirs.'

She was silent and stared out of the window.

'You, er, gonna live here full time, or is it back to the city during the week?'

She smiled faintly. 'If you mean are we week-enders, no. We, which includes my two little girls, are making a home here full time – unlike Oliver Merfield and his wife, who'll be in London for most of the week.'

'Fair enough. It looks like we'll be seeing you around quite a bit, then. Better get yourself some decent walking boots.' He laughed. 'My name's Charlie Tucker, I live at Marsh Farm, and you are...?'

'My name's Isabelle, Isabelle Garnett, and my husband's called Richard.'

'Pleased to meet you. So why have you decided to come and live here? Absolutely nothing going on for you, I'd have thought. Won't you miss town life?'

She sighed and gazed out of the windows as he drove over the river bridge and into the High Street.

'Probably. But my husband wanted to move and he's got friends here.'

'Oh?'

'You might know them, I suppose. I expect everyone knows everyone else in this village. Their name is Lester, Hugh Lester and his wife, Veronica.'

'That toerag! Bloody hell!' Charlie couldn't help himself. 'Know him? Yes, I know him all right and I wouldn't give him the time of day, him or his wife – they're as bad as each other. Look, I'm sorry, but as far as I'm concerned your friends are bad news.'

An embarrassed silence followed this outburst and it was with relief that Charlie turned the van into a narrow drive and pulled up in front of the Old Vicarage.

A Discovery stood in front of the garage. He glanced at it.

'I see you've got your four-wheel-drive already. Nice and handy for all these country lanes.'

'Yes, it will be, won't it? Lucky we had one already, wasn't it?' she said stiffly. 'Thank you for rescuing me and thank you for the lift.' Opening the door, she climbed out, then looked across at Charlie.

'As it happens, I think your assessment of Hugh

170

and Veronica Lester is spot-on. Aren't you lucky you don't have to have anything to do with them?'

She gave him a bleak smile, slammed the van door shut and ran across to the porch, fiddled with the lock for a moment, let herself in and was gone without a backward glance.

Charlie pulled a face, then his glance fell on the chocolate cake. It was well and truly flattened – God knows what sort of mess it had made of her skirt. But the impulse to laugh had vanished. Something about her had got under his skin: he felt sorry for her, ashamed and irritated at the same time. But since she moved in Lester circles, it was unlikely he'd have much to do with her and so, driving back to Marsh Farm, he put her out of his mind.

7

Oh God! Isabelle groaned inwardly as, holding her little girls by the hand, she walked through into the Lesters' courtyard. Trust Richard to leave us to come on alone. I'm not going to enjoy this, not one little bit. What on earth am I doing here? I don't belong with these fat cats.

As far as Charlie Tucker was concerned, she was one of them and the dismissive way he'd reacted to her, and the hint of contempt she'd detected in his manner, riled her. She'd stormed to the bathroom, stripped off her wet clothes and soaked in a hot bath, simmering with anger. Why should she care?

Hadn't Paula said he'd had more women than hot dinners? The bastard, he probably boasted about it! She despised him and fervently hoped she'd never meet him again. If it was up to her, she wouldn't. But his comments rankled.

Rebecca hung back, dragging on her arm. 'Mummy, do we have to? It's gonna be so boring.'

'It might not be,' Isabelle replied brightly but with no conviction. 'You've been here before. Remember Cordelia? Perhaps she'll show you the horses. They've got lots of horses here, and if you're very good perhaps they'll teach you to ride, now we're neighbours.'

'Oh, goody,' shouted Clementine. 'I'd like that. And will there be ice cream, Mummy? There should be ice cream if it's a party, and pizza...'

Other guests were arriving at the same time, some on foot, most by car, and the courtyard was nearly full. Stepping around a badly parked monster, Isabelle had barely time to register tyres crunching on the gravel behind her, before a hand grabbed her arm and pulled her aside. A gleaming BMW stopped just short of where she and the girls had been and the driver glared at her through his windscreen.

Isabelle turned to her rescuer. He was tall and lean, a little older than her, with dark auburn hair that fell into his eyes, an open, friendly face and warm smile.

'Sorry about that.' His voice was pleasant and definitely a bit posh, she thought. 'I hope I wasn't too rough, but that idiot didn't look as if he was going to stop in time. You all right?'

'I'm fine, thank you and I'm very grateful for

you saving my life, although I'm sure he *would* have stopped before he mowed us down.'

He laughed and Isabelle thought how ... well, how *nice* he looked. He wasn't handsome, but there was something very attractive about him.

She held out her hand. 'I'm sure we'll get introduced again, but I'm Isabelle Garnett and these are my daughters, Rebecca and Clementine.'

His grasp was warm and firm. 'Pleased to meet you, Isabelle. I'm Oliver Merfield, and this–' he half turned and Isabelle saw he was accompanied by a pale, thin youth clad in black, a smattering of adolescent acne somewhat spoiling the cool rebel image he was trying to affect – 'is my son, Jamie.'

'Hi, Jamie.' She smiled at him but his expression didn't lift, he merely nodded. ''Lo.'

Isabelle turned back to Oliver, and said rather self-consciously, 'I'm really sorry about ... about the Old Vicarage. You must have been very annoyed?'

He smiled down at her. 'At the time, yes. But actually, things have turned out very much for the better. I don't think we're really ready to buy somewhere in Summerstoke, particularly as Juliet, my wife, may be away for some time. We're renting a very nice house in the village, which doesn't need so much doing to it and it suits Jamie and me. We'd have rattled around in the Old Vicarage. So please, don't think any more of it.'

'Thank you.' She looked around. They were the only guests left in the courtyard. 'I suppose we ought to go in. Veronica must be wondering why on earth we're lingering out here. Your wife's not in Summerstoke at the moment, then?'

'No. She's in Los Angeles, making a pilot for a television series. Initially it was for six weeks so I'm hoping she'll be home by the end of the month. You must come round and see us when she's back.'

'I'd love to, thank you.'

They joined the queue of guests pushing into the drawing room and as soon as they were spotted Oliver was borne away by Hugh, leaving a sulky Jamie to be chatted up by Cordelia Lester, who, seeing a boy near her own age, had pounced.

For a second or two Isabelle stood by the door with Clemmie and Becky. Most of the faces looked depressingly familiar but they weren't from the village, she was certain. She looked around for the vicar. Surely he'd be here?

'Issy, darling.' It was Veronica. 'For goodness' sake don't linger by the door. You look as if you're about to bolt.'

Spot on, Vee, thought Isabelle, giving her hostess a faint smile.

'You've brought your two little girls – how nice! Where's that dreadful husband of yours? Not late again?'

Why does she always manage to wrong foot me? Isabelle squirmed and said, brightly, 'Yes, I'm sorry. I thought you meant us to bring Becky and Clemmie. Richard phoned. One of his bosses called, from London. He's on his way now.'

'Good. Now I really want you to meet some of our locals. Cordelia?'

Cordelia, in the process of trying to impress Jamie, resented the interruption and turned

174

impatiently. 'Yes, Mother, what is it?'

'Take Issy's two little girls to the playroom, would you? They can watch a video. And find them some squash and biscuits.'

'But I was just about to show Jamie the stables.'

'I'd much rather watch a video,' her victim muttered.

Becky showed every sign of not wanting to leave Isabelle's side, but Isabelle gently urged her after Cordelia, who flounced out with an unabashed Clemmie dancing at her side, demanding to be shown the horses.

Jamie, ignoring Veronica, addressed Isabelle. 'Tell my dad I've gone home, will you? This is just not my sort of scene.'

Veronica watched him cross the hall and turned back to Isabelle. 'Well! How graceless can you get? I hope my children have better manners.'

'I suppose,' said Isabelle, feeling briefly both sympathetic and envious of Jamie, 'it's all a bit strange for him. It's hard, not knowing anyone.'

'Come on, Issy, we've all got to start somewhere. Now, I'm going to introduce you to the Hills. They live near Devizes.'

'That's a good thirty miles away, isn't it? I thought this was going to be a party for local people?'

'It is. But he's the chairman of the local Conservative Party and his wife, Audrey, is a love. A bit eccentric, mind you – she writes the most dreadful poetry, and insists on riding, though she's far too fat for her mount...' And she steered the hapless Isabelle across the room.

To Isabelle's relief and pleasure, they found Oliver in conversation with the maligned Audrey Hill, a pleasant-looking, plump woman, in her late fifties.

Veronica stopped short and turned to Isabelle, looking concerned, 'Oh, Issy, just one thing before I introduce you. I've been meaning to warn you before, but I just haven't seen you. The village shop.'

'Yes?'

'I hope you haven't used it?'

'Well, yes. I was posting a letter to Australia so I bought one or two bits and pieces while I was in there. Why?'

'Because–' Veronica's voice dropped dramatically, – 'I happen to know they have rats in their basement; in the storeroom, to be precise. By rights, they should be closed down but nobody in this village will make the effort. It's so parochial – they like the shop the way it is. But I'd hate to think of you ... especially with your little girls. You can't be too careful.'

Isabelle stared at her, aghast. 'Rats? How do you know that, Veronica?'

'The cleaning lady who used to work for me lives in the village. Utterly useless girl – I had to fire her – but she told me about the rats coming up from the river and nesting in the basement. I've no reason not to believe her.'

'Bloody Vee,' Richard growled; as he slammed the office door behind him and sped across the nearly empty car park. 'Fancy starting a party at six thirty. It's not so easy to get away when you're at other people's beck and call.'

He thought fleetingly of the conversation he'd just had with his boss and felt a twinge of unease. He'd have to look into those figures, but not now. Not now.

The Lesters had invited them for six thirty and Vee had made it clear as the party was in his honour, she expected him to be there on time. Thanks to that call from head office, he was already running late, and Issy had not been pleased, he could tell, but it couldn't be helped.

He'd just turned on the ignition when his mobile rang. 'Oh, for Christ's sake, what now?'

He didn't recognise the number and was curt. 'Yes?'

'Daddy, it's me, Abi. I'm back.'

Richard sighed deeply. This was not going to be a quick call. 'Abi, my darling, how lovely to hear you. How long have you been back? Where are you, at Mum's?'

'Yes. I got home a few days ago. I would have been in touch sooner, but I've had loads to sort out. Hey, what's this I hear about you moving?'

'Yes, we have. It's a lovely ... a small village called Summerstoke.'

'Can't imagine you living in a small village, Dad – not your sort of scene at all. I've heard there's lots of inbreeding in West Country villages. Have you met any halfwits yet?'

'Abi, for goodness' sake.'

'Only teasing. Have you got a space for me?'

An image of uncurtained rooms full of packing cases flashed across Richard's mind.

'Eventually,' he said cautiously. 'Everything's in a real mess at the moment – we've only just moved in.'

'Mum says it's an old vicarage. Sounds cool. Is it okay if I come down tomorrow?'

'Abi!' Richard couldn't disguise the note of protest in his voice.

Abigail's response was inevitable and typical. 'I don't believe it! You haven't seen me for six months and you don't want to now. I'm your daughter, for fuck's sake, in case you've forgotten. Setting up your little love nest with whatsername and your two little chicklets ... you've no time for Danny and me, any more, have you? Have you?'

Fighting an urge to throw his mobile into a nearby holly bush, Richard set about placating his daughter. By the time he succeeded, not only had he agreed that she should come down the next day and be received with open arms, but he'd also promised that in the evening he'd take her to her favourite restaurant in Bath.

'So I can have some time with you, Daddy, just you and me. After all, I haven't seen you for six months. She wouldn't begrudge me an evening of your time, would she?'

Why she insists on casting Issy in the role of wicked stepmother, I do not know, he fumed, finally turning on the ignition. Anyone less like a wicked stepmother... He pictured how Issy would look when he told her about Abigail's imminent arrival and feeling guilty, then resentful. For Chrissake, it's only for a weekend, and she is my daughter. She's entitled...

By the time he turned into the drive of the Old Vicarage, he was nearly an hour late and in a thoroughly bad temper. Stopping only to change

178

his shirt (noting, with a certain surprise, that Issy had ironed a whole pile of them), he walked swiftly up the road to Summerstoke House.

The front door was ajar and Richard, entering the empty hall, stopped for a moment to absorb the restrained elegance of this house and to compare it, discontentedly, with the shabby chaos that awaited him at the Old Vicarage. One day, perhaps... But Issy was no Vee and he doubted her home-making would ever achieve this degree of sophisticated comfort.

The noise of the party poured from the open doorway of the drawing room. He smoothed his hand through his hair, took a deep breath and, with the practice of time, replaced his frown with an engaging half-grin, then went in and stood by the door, looking for his hostess.

'Darling, there you are, at last!' Vee, in a short, close-fitting, strapless dress of velvet the colour of rich cream, showing off her tan to perfection, manoeuvred her way across the crowded room summoning, as she did so, a woman carrying a tray of glasses brimming with a vivid blue liquid.

'You poor old thing. Fancy getting stuck at the office on a Friday night. Issy said you had the head beaver pinning you down. Nothing nasty, I hope. Here, you need one of Hugh's cocktails. He's christened it the Blue Flash, but basically it's champagne cocktail with a splash of blue curaçao instead of brandy. It's lovely.'

He accepted a glass and as he sipped he could feel himself relaxing. Unlike his wife, he loved parties. He got a buzz from meeting lots of different people and engaging effortlessly with any

179

topic of conversation going; he loved the feeling people wanted to meet him, that he was somebody, and that status was what being the editor of a paper gave him – albeit a regional rag with a falling circulation.

'I'm very glad you made it,' said Vee, smiling up at him, 'considering this party was meant to introduce Mr and Mrs Merfield and Mr and Mrs Garnett to Summerstoke's polite society. With a partner missing from both sides, it was starting to look like anything but happy families.'

He grinned and helped himself to another glass. 'Well, come on, Vee, darling, get it over with. Let's take the bull by the horns. Introduce me to whichever Merfield is here.'

'It's Oliver Merfield; his wife's still in Los Angeles.' She gave a light laugh. 'From the look of it, Issy's got him by the horns already.'

Richard followed Vee's gaze.

Isabelle was standing in a window bay on the far side of the room. The silvery curtains were drawn and provided a perfect backdrop for his wife. She was wearing a short, slate-blue dress with long, glistening earrings and a necklace made of layers of little multi-coloured mother-of-pearl buttons. Her blonde hair shone like a halo round her face, which was flushed and animated, and as he looked on, the man, who stood with his back to Richard, said something that made her laugh. Richard hadn't seen her look so good for ages.

She used to look like that at him.

A fierce, unaccustomed stab of jealousy suddenly hit him.

Resisting a primaeval urge to go and punch his

180

rival on the nose, he turned to Veronica with a smile. 'I'll introduce myself later. Issy seems to be doing a good job and I want to catch up with you, Vee, while I've got the chance. I've hardly seen you since your dinner party, in the summer, when Hugh encouraged me to go for the Old Vicarage. How are things?'

'Oh,' Vee said lightly, sipping her blue drink, 'it turned out to be a pig of a summer. You heard about my son nearly killing himself on his motorbike?'

'Yes. You poor thing, it must have been awful for you.'

'It was. So when Cordelia went back to school, Hugh and I took ourselves off for a much-needed break in the Seychelles. Hence my tan.' She preened herself. 'Three weeks in the sun can cure most ills.'

'Did anything come of Harriet Flood's visit? Wasn't she planning to do a feature on your stud idea?'

Veronica's eyes flashed with anger and for a fleeting moment her face turned ugly. 'We couldn't get the land we wanted and then, with Anthony's accident, it was all put on the back burner. Ms Flood' – she sneered the name – 'wasn't interested if we weren't going to develop the stables. Personally, I'm glad she wasn't – the woman was a lush, and one evening in her company was as much as I could take.'

She collected herself, laughed lightly and took him by the arm.

'Now, how about you? Am I going to get an invite to look around your house? Issy was very unforthcoming when I dropped a hint.'

Again the vision of his shabby and unprepossessing house flitted across his mind. 'She's got a lot to do to make it habitable. We need to get the workmen in as soon as poss.'

'Let me help, I'm good at that sort of thing. Or you could think of using Marion. But I can put you onto a good builder, if necessary – not one of the oicks from around here – and an excellent decorating firm from Bath.'

He smiled his thanks. 'That'd be brilliant, Vee. Issy's a bit at sixes and sevens.'

He looked across at his wife, who, catching sight of him, beckoned him over. 'Looks like I've got the royal summons. Anyone else I don't know here, Vee? Most of the faces look familiar and I thought this was a meet-the-neighbours do?'

Vee laughed, 'Richard, darling, the people here are ones you'd like to meet. You wouldn't have thanked me if I'd invited the vicar, the baker, and the candlestick maker, would you? Anyone who's anyone is here. Go and say hello to our MP.'

Richard took a fresh glass and made his way across the room.

Isabelle grabbed his hand. 'Thank goodness you're here. I'd just about given up on you and I want you to meet Oliver.' She smiled, almost shyly, at the man standing by her side.

Richard looked at him appraisingly. Clear grey eyes, steady and confident, looked back at him. His skin was unblemished and unlined, his hair thick and free of silver. He was not as well built as Richard, but he was lean and youthful.

Not that much older than Issy.

182

'Richard, pleased to meet you at long last. My secretary makes sure I have my daily copy of the *Wessex*.' His handshake was dry and strong, and his voice had the accent of the well-educated upper middle class.

Richard snarled inwardly. He'd met this type before. Arrogant twats – they thought they owned the world and behaved like it. He forced a smile. 'Ah, do you read it, though? Pleased to meet you, Oliver. How's things on the Opposition bench?'

'Interesting, frustrating; never enough time. Much the same as any job, I should think.'

Typical politician's reply, thought Richard. Thinks he can smarm his way into people's good books with this fucking false egalitarian modesty. Well, it won't wash with me.

'Surely not,' he replied, lightly. 'A lot of people wouldn't mind swopping their situation for yours.'

'They might get a horrible shock.' Oliver laughed and turned to Isabelle with a smile. 'Talking of shocks, Isabelle was telling me I might've had one if we'd bought the Old Vicarage instead of you. Sounds like an awful lot of work.'

Isabelle, Richard noticed, smiled back. She really was looking incredibly pretty. How dare she make eyes at him? How dare Merfield encourage her?

'It is,' he said, his eyes narrowing, 'but it'll be worth it. And you've bought this old doctor's house?'

'Rented, not bought; it's a good solution.'

'Well, that must make your family happy – you're an old Summerstoke family, aren't you?' (His thoughts rumbled on antagonistically:

privileged, living off the fat of the land, by the sweat of other people's labour.)

'Yes, my grandmother and my aunts still live in the village.'

'In the Manor?'

'Yes. I sort of grew up there.'

'Oh?'

'My father's in the diplomatic service, so we were sent away to school. My grandmother took pity on us in the holidays. Summerstoke is very much part of my childhood.'

(And so, with a deft flick, Richard seethed, he makes a privileged childhood, fucking public school and holidays at the Manor, sound like deprivation. Bloody hell, he's a complete prick!)

'That was nice for you.'

This last comment sounded so belligerent, that Oliver was momentarily shaken. He gave a polite smile. 'Yes, yes, it was. It didn't entirely make up for not seeing our parents, which is why I'm keen our son, Jamie, has more access to both his parents.'

'Where's your wife, then?'

'Away, working.' Oliver laughed uneasily. 'That's the trouble with being married to an actress – their work can take them anywhere. You're lucky.'

(This guy, really takes the biscuit. How dare he patronise me like this) 'Am I? In what way?'

'Well, being an editor, you have an office, set hours, one location, a house in the country, a wife at home. I'd say there were more people who'd rather swap with you than me.'

Richard stared at him and took a sip of his cocktail. (He's talking a load of bollocks, and he knows it. What have I got for working my fingers to the bone. A wife who, on the face of it, is a sandwich short of a picnic, and debts that continue to rise. I bet he wouldn't swap places with me, except to get into Issy's knickers!)

'I don't think so. I've had to work hard for the jam on my bread – council estate, comprehensive, sixties university. I wasn't born with a silver spoon in *my* mouth.'

By the time Richard finished this exchange of pleasantries with Oliver, has voice had lost its neutral, carefully cultivated, slight estuary twang and had thickened with bellicose Nottinghamshire vowels.

It was clear to Isabelle he'd taken a powerful dislike to Oliver Merfield.

'Why?' she asked, as she and Richard walked back to the Old Vicarage. 'Why did you dislike him so much?'

'Quite frankly, Issy, I'm surprised you need to ask.'

'Well, I do need to. I liked him.'

'I could see that!'

'I don't know what that's supposed to mean. I thought he seemed very nice.'

'Nice! He's an oily politician, for Chrissake. Being nice is the one thing they can do – turn on the charm whenever it's needed. The next thing you'll be telling me is you thought he was sincere!'

'Well, he was. We were talking about our new cleaning lady and–'

'What? You were talking to Oliver Merfield, a Conservative MP, about a cleaning lady and he was interested?' He gave a harsh, sarcastic laugh. 'I

185

think that proves my point, don't you? In a million years I cannot think why anyone *but* a politician should pretend to be interested in talking about a cleaning lady. Issy, darling, you need to grow up.'

'You're wrong. I think you're being incredibly aggressive and I want to know why. And why all that guff about council housing? *I* was the one brought up in a council house, not you, and as for that sneering reference to a sixties university, Sussex was one of the most sought-after universities when you went there.'

'He got up my nose, that's why. Typical Tory. He's had everything handed to him on a silver plate and, still wet behind the ears, he thinks he can run the country. His sort don't know the meaning of graft; think they can oil their way in and get anything they ask for. Well, he don't cut the mustard with me.'

'I think you're being incredibly unfair and I don't understand why. You rub shoulders with politicians all the time. Do you always make it so blatantly clear when you don't like them?'

'Don't be absurd.'

Isabelle was stung. 'I'm not being absurd. You were bloody rude. This is our neighbour we're talking about here, Richard. I don't understand why you took against him but you were really embarrassing.'

'I don't think *I* was the embarrassing one, Issy.'

'What's that supposed to mean?'

'You.' Richard's lip curled in disgust. 'The way you threw yourself at him, hanging on his every word.'

This suggestion so angered Isabelle that by the

time they got home the shouting match had been replaced by an icy silence that followed them to bed.

The following day was one of the worst she could remember. The girls were upset by the discord, she and Richard barely spoke, and then Abigail, Richard's older daughter, arrived on the doorstep expecting to be given a good time and Richard made no attempt to apologise to Isabelle for not having told her of Abigail's planned visit.

Abigail resembled her father physically, but she had inherited none of his charm. She'd been eleven when her father married again and had never made any secret of the fact that she resented the existence of her stepmother and the subsequent arrival of her two half-sisters. At her mother's insistence she spent part of her holidays every year with Isabelle and Richard, and, as nothing Isabelle did could ever redeem her in Abigail's eyes, those times had been purgatorial for Isabelle. She was hugely relieved, therefore, when Abigail decided to go back-packing in her gap year, and nurtured the hope that if Abigail survived the experience, and wasn't eaten by an alligator or married to a Maori, she would return a kinder, wiser person.

Sadly, that was not the case. Abigail immediately cottoned on to the tension between her father and stepmother and made hay. She flattered and fawned over her father, paid barely any attention to Rebecca and Clementine, criticised almost everything about the Old Vicarage, complained of boredom but wouldn't go out as it rained all day and finally, when Isabelle had finished peeling the vegetables for the evening meal, announced that Richard was going to take her out to a restaurant in Bath.

Sickened by the smug malice on her stepdaughter's face, Isabelle turned to Richard.

He had the grace to look a little ashamed. 'Sorry, Issy. Perhaps I should have mentioned it before, but you might have known I'd take Abi out tonight.'

'Fine. Suits me.' Stalking past them both, she went to the kitchen door. 'Becky, Clemmie, put your coats on.'

Richard's eyes widened slightly. 'Where are you going?'

Trying to stop her voice wobbling with anger and misery, she replied, as coolly as she could manage, 'The girls have been cooped up all day. They need some fresh air, and so do I.'

Sitting on one of the swings in the playground, feeling utterly miserable, Isabelle watched the two little girls who, disregarding the drizzle, rushed from swings to slide to roundabout in the fading light.

'Isabelle?'

She hadn't noticed him approach and at the sound of his voice she jumped.

'Oliver?'

'Sorry, I didn't mean to startle you. I've just been to have a chat with Mrs Godwin and I saw you sitting here. Not the nicest weather for the playground, is it?'

She looked up at him and read the sympathy in his expression. She tried to smile. 'No, but the girls have been stuck inside all day and I needed some fresh air.' She got up. 'But you're right, it's pretty nasty and it's getting dark; time we went.'

She called the girls. As she turned to go, he said, 'I'm expected for supper at the Manor tonight, so I'll walk along with you, if I may.'

Clemmie came dancing up to him. 'Hello. We saw you at the party, last night, didn't we?'

Oliver smiled at her. 'Yes. I had my son, Jamie, with me. Did you enjoy the party?'

Clemmie thought for a moment. 'Not much. We didn't see no horses an' there was only borin' old squash an' biscuits an' a bossy girl an'–'

'Okay, Clemmie, that's enough,' Isabelle hastily interjected. 'You and Becky run on ahead. It's getting quite wet now, we must hurry home.'

'How did you find the party last night?' Oliver began lightly. 'I suspect we didn't meet too many real locals.'

'No, but then I never thought we would. She's not bothered with ordinary, decent people. That's not Vee's style.'

'You sound bitter.'

'Do I? Sorry.' She bit her lip. 'She's always been very hospitable as far as we're concerned. She and my husband are great friends.'

'And you? Are you great friends with her?'

'I'm one of those ordinary people, and I can't stand her guts. But now we're neighbours all that may change. Listen, it's not fair of me to slag her off. After all, yesterday evening was the first time you met her, and for all I know you got on like a house on fire.'

'Well, she was very amiable, but–' Oliver broke off and grinned. 'I met her husband, Hugh, once

189

before. He's terrifying, isn't he?'

The gateway to the Old Vicarage in sight, Becky and Clemmie ran on ahead and disappeared.

Isabelle gave a short laugh in agreement, then stopped and turned to face her companion. 'Isn't he? But, talking of husbands, Oliver, mine behaved like a pig last night.'

'Did he? I didn't notice–' Oliver began, but Isabelle interrupted him.

'Yes, you did notice. He was horrible. All I can say is I'm really sorry. He's such a charming person normally. He was late and tired, but that was no excuse.'

Oliver gently squeezed her arm, 'Please, Isabelle, you don't have to apologise.'

Coming out of the drive, the headlights of Richard's Jaguar caught them in their beam, but the car hardly paused before sweeping out onto the road and disappearing up the hill.

'You've got to come, Isabelle, next Monday even-ng, in the village hall. We've all got to go. We've got to show our support, Rita says, or we'll lose the shop. It's all right for people to say we can use the supermarket at Summerbridge, but that's miles away, and what happens to people who can't drive?'

Paula dipped a choc chip cookie into her tea and looked earnestly across the kitchen table at Isabelle. 'I've got Lenny, but he can't drop every-thing just to get me a tin of baked beans 'cos I've run short for the kiddies' tea, can he? And what about people like poor old Mrs Long? She needs the shop.'

Isabelle shook her head. 'I'd use it more, Paula, but if it's got rats… I'm surprised they're allowed to continue trading.'

Paula stared at her. 'Rats? What yer talkin' about, Isabelle? What rats?'

It was Isabelle's turn to stare. 'Rats from the river, nesting in Mrs Godwin's storeroom. I understood you knew all about them.'

'Me? I don't know nothin' about no rats.' Paula shuddered. 'Can't abide them, meself. Lenny was all for getting Ryan one for his birthday, but I said, "Over my dead body you will". Give me the shivers, they do, them and mice. Ugh!'

'But I thought *you* said the Godwins were having trouble with rats in their storeroom, in the basement.' Isabelle was puzzled.

'Well, for one, the Godwins ain't got no basement, and for another, they've never said nothin' about rats to me, so it must have been someone else.'

Isabelle frowned. She hadn't dreamed it. At the party, when Veronica warned her off using the shop she'd definitely said it was Paula who'd told her about rats coming up from the river and nesting in the basement storeroom.

Picking the girls up from school, later that afternoon, she called in at the shop to post a letter to Joe. It was like stepping back in time, she thought, as she stepped over a large and rather smelly brown Labrador lying panting across the entrance.

With a cry of delight, Clemmie immediately started patting him. 'Er, I'm not sure you should do that, darling,' Isabelle murmured. 'He might not like it.'

191

'He loves it, dear. Don't worry.' Rita looked up from serving a customer. 'He's an old gent and sweet as honey.'

'What's his name?' asked Becky, timidly joining her sister stroking the dog.

'Chocolate. He's meant to be my guard dog, but he wouldn't say boo to a goose.'

As Isabelle waited her turn, she looked around. It wasn't the sort of enterprise that would have survived in an urban environment.

The shop was long and narrow. The counter, running down one side, displayed items to attract tourists rather than locals: West Country shortbread, jars of local honey, handmade fudge and a basket of knitted hats resembling strawberries.

A securely partitioned section at the far end formed the post office; beyond that was a door to the sorting room and storeroom. Next to the door stood a cabinet containing dairy products and soft drinks, and a freezer carrying a limited selection of ice cream and frozen food.

On both sides of the shop, from ceiling to floor, shelves upon shelves carried a whole variety of products, pushed in together in a seemingly random display. There were bottles of bleach alongside tins of strawberries, boot polish and jars of honey, paper towels next to packets of biscuits, pet food alongside jars of coffee and boxes of tea bags, sweets, bottles of wine, tights and pop socks – anything a household could want, including a display of magazines, newspapers and comics, which spilled over the floor.

Isabelle selected a roll of Sellotape, a can of tomatoes and a bottle of fabric conditioner –

items that could pose no threat if there *were* rats – and wandered down to the back of the shop where a display of paintings struggled for attention above the freezer.

They were the creations of the Summerstoke Art Group, flagged 'SAG's Summer Exhibition'. Isabelle bit back a giggle and inspected the pale watercolours of the village and the countryside around. These timid offerings were dominated by a number of oil paintings of dogs – not whole dogs, just their heads, painted by Rita. A faded notice indicating her willingness, for a reasonable fee, to paint a similar portrait of anybody's pooch.

Isabelle regarded them with awe; she had seldom seen such dreadful pictures.

At the counter Rita was in full flow.

'Of course, I know it's still only a rumour, but there's no smoke without fire, as they say. Neville Jones told me – you know, Mrs Grey, he's one of our regular postmen – he's heard back at the depot they're going to cut all rural sorting offices. Well, that's an important part of my income. If I lose that, I'm not sure I can keep the post office open, and if *that* goes, why then I really will start losing customers hand over fist.'

Mrs Grey made sympathetic noises. 'Well, Rita, now it's on the agenda of the parish council AGM. The word's out and I'm sure you'll get a lot of support.'

'Which is just as it should be. The village shop is vital to the well-being of any village, in all sorts of ways. I mean, Mrs Garnett, would you have moved to this village if there hadn't have been a shop?'

193

Isabelle, who had been appalled at the prospect of moving to a place with just one shop, could only shake her head.

'No, of course not. And I'll tell you, if this shop goes house prices will fall, as sure as eggs is eggs. There won't be such a scramble to buy houses here, and it won't be so easy to sell. People don't think of that when they drive their whopping four-by-fours to fill up at Sainsbury's or Tesco's, do they?'

'No, I suppose not,' replied Isabelle faintly, wondering how on earth she could broach the subject of rats.

'I really must be going,' interjected Mrs Grey. She picked up her bag and turned to Isabelle. 'I've been meaning to call on you, Mrs Garnett, to welcome you to our village. I know my husband's been already, but that's no excuse for my tardiness.' She held out her hand. 'Lavender Grey.'

Isabelle took her hand. A plump middle-aged lady, she had a face like a currant bun. 'Your husband?'

'Yes,' said Lavender Grey briskly. 'The vicar of St Stephen's. You must come round to one of our coffee mornings. You'd be most welcome and I shall look forward to a proper chat. As Mrs Godwin will tell you, this village is divided into doers and non-doers. I do hope you're a doer.'

Giving Isabelle no chance to reply, she walked briskly to the door, patted the children on the head and stepped over the dog, bidding them all, 'Good afternoon.'

'Mrs Grey's a doer,' remarked Rita, turning to Isabelle. 'Give a job to a busy person, as they say

194

– she knows as well as anyone this shop is the heart of our community, more than the church these days. If people want something, need a bit of advice, or a bit of help, they come here first. All the children in the village pass through here. I know them all. I watch them grow up; stop them nicking sweeties when they're younger and buying fags when they're older. You can't put a price on that, can you? And once it's gone, it's gone. Too late to shut the stable door.'

She paused for breath long enough to take the items Isabelle had selected and enter them in the till. 'Is that all, dear?'

'I need to send this to Australia.'

'Righto. Pop it on the scales.'

Isabelle followed Rita to the post office counter, desperately searching for a way into the subject of rats.

Rita took the envelope from her and read the address as she stuck on the postage. 'Melbourne. That's a nice place, I've heard. A relative?'

'No, a good friend. We were at college together. I'm sending him some photographs of Summer-stoke.'

'Old England, eh? Make him homesick.' Rita counted out her change. 'Now, if that's all, perhaps your two little girls would like to choose a lollipop.'

She held out a large jar of brightly coloured, sticky sweets.

Isabelle froze. Oh my God, they're not wrapped. Do rats eat sugar? Her brain raced.

'Er, there was something else, Mrs Godwin,' she blurted. 'Er … do you have any experience of water rats? Only,' she continued in a sudden, creative rush, dropping her voice so the girls, intent on which colour lollipop to have, couldn't hear, 'I'm worried they might come up from the river and nest in our basement.'

Rita shook her head, regretfully. 'Can't help you there, dear. We sell mousetraps, but they wouldn't be any good for rats, would they?'

'You don't have any trouble, yourself, what with all your food and stuff in the basement?'

'We don't have a basement, and our storeroom's completely secure against vermin of any sort. Has to be, otherwise we'd have the environmental health department down on us like a ton of bricks. Hang on, I'll ask Rob what you should do – he's in the storeroom right now.'

Before Isabelle could stop her, she went to the back and yelled for her husband. Isabelle's heart sank. Rita was one thing, but Rob, her husband, was a taciturn man by reputation, who treated all customers as time-wasters.

'What now?' were his first words on appearing. 'I'll never get this stock-taking done if you keep interrupting.'

'Mrs Garnett here is worried about what to do if water rats nest in her basement.'

Rob Godwin looked at her, a faint sneer on his face. 'Well, for one thing, there ain't such things as water rats. They's brown rats and black rats, but not water rats – they's water voles, but they nest in the riverbank, those what have survived the mink, that is. If you've got rats, missus, you need to get hold of the ratcatcher. He'll sort you out. Phone the council, they'll tell you how to get hold of 'im.' And without waiting for her to

196

stammer her thanks, he turned on his heel and disappeared back into the storeroom.

'There,' said Rita, triumphantly. 'Isn't that what I was just sayin'? Where else in the village would you have got that information from, eh?'

8

'Jamie, just cool it, eh?' drawled one of the boys in the theatre studies class. 'We know you don't rate Summerbridge as a source of front-line entertainment, but it's what we're used to and we like it, okay?'

'Yeah, just shut it!' growled another. 'We're sick of your smart-arse comments.'

It was the end of the afternoon at Summerbridge College and in the theatre Jamie and his fellow students were hanging on for the drama teacher to come back with copies of a text he wanted them to prepare for auditions the following week.

A lot had happened to Jamie since he'd fallen for a girl called Alison that day on the river. Bombarded by emotions entirely new to him, he was also overwhelmed by the novelty of almost everything else in his life.

The school was much larger than Jamie was used to and although he was constantly on the look-out for Alison in the sixth-form block, he was disappointed. Occasionally he thought he caught sight of her at a distance, or in a group, or hurrying to class. He asked about her but since he didn't know what her surname was, or what she was studying, he met with unhelpful shrugs.

And so the encounter took on a dream-like quaity. He nurtured every moment he'd spent with her; cherished and revisited every tiny detail; polished his memories of her so that she shone, like starlight, in the daydreams he frequently retreated to as solace for the bumpy ride he was getting both at college and at Summerstoke Manor.

Initially his fellow students had been interested in him, and he'd tried to impress them with descriptions of his life in London and what it had to offer over a hick town like Summerbridge. But they soon made it clear that it wasn't enough that his dad was the local MP and his mother was Juliet Peters, and all too often Jamie found himself on his own.

Waiting for the teacher, the group had been discussing the movie on that week and Jamie, railing against the limitations of a town with only one cinema, discovered just how unwelcome his opinions were.

'If Summerbridge is so fucking awful,' said another, 'why don't you sod off back to the big city? You won't be missed.'

Jamie flushed, but was saved from having to respond by the return of the drama teacher.

'Sorry to keep you, lads and lasses,' he said cheerfully, 'but the key to the book cupboard required some skilful sleuthing on my part. Read the play carefully, decide which parts you want to audition for, be prepared to read anything and we'll discuss the play next week.'

Jamie stuffed a copy in his bag and glanced at his

watch. The school bus left for Summerstoke fifteen minutes after the official end of school. If he missed that, he was scuppered. Public transport was useless – the only other ways of getting back were a town bus, which left mid-evening, or a taxi.

He yelped when he saw the time, shot out of the theatre and ran as fast as he could to the car park. He was just in time to see the tail lights of the Summerstoke bus as it paused before turning onto the main road.

He tore after it, but it was no use. By the time he got to the road, it was out of sight. With a groan he slumped on a bench by the side of the road and put his head in his hands.

'What the fuck do I do now?' he muttered. Bloody, sodding bus – why hadn't it waited for him? Now he was stuck. Shit! His dad had supplied him with an emergency fund to pay for a taxi, but he'd spent that on fags. There was no help for it, he'd have to leg it and try hitching. Shit! Shit! Shit!

'What's up?'

Sunk in gloom, Jamie hadn't registered the sound of the bike and looked up, startled. Sitting astride a battered Vespa was Tish, a girl from his drama group.

She was someone he'd steered clear of, she looked so fierce. She was not very tall, with dark curly hair, intense brown eyes, a pierced nose and a wide mouth. He knew everyone thought she was the best actor in the group, a position he longed to occupy himself.

'Something wrong?' she asked.

'I've missed my bus. I didn't realise Mr Theobald was gonna be so long collecting the scripts.'

'Isn't there another one you can catch?'

'Not for five hours.' He sighed heavily and stood up. 'I'll have to walk.'

'Where do you live?'

'Summerstoke.'

She shook her head. 'That's a bit of a slog. It's about eight miles once you get up to the main road. Hang on a minute.' Turning her bike round, she went back into the college grounds. She rode up to a group of students and minutes later returned with a helmet dangling over her arm.

'Here,' she said, 'put this on. I'll give you a backie up to the main road. I can't take you any further because Adam needs his helmet.'

Stammering his thanks, Jamie climbed on the back of her bike.

She dropped him off at a lay-by. 'Good luck. Oh, one piece of advice: don't hitch with your hood up like that – you'd never get a lift.' Before he could say anything, she'd turned and roared away.

Thumb out, hood down, Jamie started walking. The traffic was fairly heavy as it was the main road to Bath and, cheered by the unexpected help he'd been given, he was hopeful of getting a lift pretty quickly.

His optimism proved ill-founded. Car after car passed him, often pulling wide, making a point: they wouldn't give him a lift, no way.

After a while the grass verge disappeared, the road narrowed and steep banks overhung with trees bordered the road. With every passing car Jamie had to press himself against the bank and for his pains was splattered with mud thrown up from the damp surface. His mood darkened and he started to see all car owners as enemies, cursing each one under his breath as they passed. After nearly an hour of walking, and with the turn-off to Summerstoke still nowhere in sight, he was feeling really sorry for himself.

A car hooted behind him. Jamie turned, intending to make a rude gesture, but he saw that the white, battered van had stopped. Almost hysterical with relief, he ran and opened the door.

The driver gave him a friendly grin. 'I'm turning off to Summerstoke, a bit further along the road, but you can have a lift as far as the turning, if you like.'

Jamie could have kissed him. 'Summerstoke's where I'm heading.'

'Hop in then, mate. It's your lucky day.'

Jamie scrambled in. 'Thanks. I was beginning to think I'd have to walk all the way.'

As the van moved off, the man casually remarked, 'Don't often see hitchhikers these days.'

'I missed the bus.'

'Oh.' The man glanced at him, curiously. 'You new to Summerstoke? I don't think I've seen you around before.'

'Yes,' replied Jamie. 'I've been parked on some elderly relatives while my parents house-hunt.' Although he was relieved to have got this lift, Jamie felt rock-bottom and not in the mood for explanations.

'That's a bit tough. How're you finding Summerstoke?'

'Difficult,' Jamie mumbled.

'How's that, then?'

'It … it's so different. There's nothing to do in Summerstoke. I mean, there are no kids of my age to hang about with – leastways, I haven't met any. And there are no shops, no cinemas…'

'There's one in Summerbridge.'

'Yeah, but the last bus goes before the end of the movie. What's the good in that?'

'I take your point.' The man's sympathy touched a chord and Jamie, bitterly fed up with everything, exploded.

'I can't believe how anyone can live here and like it. I miss London so much. It's bright and noisy and busy, and there's loads to do, and stuff going on all the time, and you can always get a bus or tube somewhere, no worries. Here it seems to rain all the bloody time, it's cold, there's nobody about; and it's so spooky, particularly at night, it's so fuckin' black. I hate it.'

'It's 'cos you're not used to it, that's all. You not got any mates here?'

'No.' Jamie thought bleakly of the general un-friendliness of his classmates and of the friends he'd left behind in London.

'Hmm, that's a shame. I don't know where I'd be without my mates,' the man said cheerfully. 'You ought to get some of your friends down from London. Show them how the other half of the world lives. Have a laugh.'

He pulled the van up short of Summerstoke Bridge. 'This is as far as I go. You shouldn't have too far to walk now.'

'No. Thanks, thanks a lot.'

'And lighten up, mate,' the man smiled. 'You'll get used to Summerstoke by and by. It may seem small and boring, but there are worse places to live. Cheers.'

Jamie watched the van disappear through an open gate and down a rough track. He felt slightly regretful. Although the man was nearly as old as his dad, Jamie liked him and he was the first person he'd really spoken to in Summerstoke, apart from the weird witches, that is, and Alison, of course.

He glanced at his watch. It was nearly six thirty. He was normally home by four thirty. He quickened his pace. Supper was at seven and under no circumstance, it had been made clear to him, was he to be late for that.

When his father wasn't about, mealtimes had become a test of endurance for Jamie. They always followed the same pattern.

'So, Jamie, what did you do at school today?' His great-grandmother would inevitably ask, looking down her hooked nose at him, her dark eyes glittering.

'Double English, double theatre studies, double history, double free,' mumbled Jamie, spooning up the soup, which might be parsnip, or carrot, or cauliflower or some other mucky liquid, which he would swallow with horror while craving a burger, or chips, or pizza, or anything halfway decent.

'Did you finish that history essay you mentioned yesterday?'

'Yes, Grandmère.'

'Has it been marked?'

'Not yet.'

'You must show it to me when you get it back. What homework have you got this evening?'

203

And so it would go on.

Then Aunt Charlotte, the Red Witch, would question him about his reading habits. 'What are you reading at the moment, Jamie?'

'Um, *Jane Eyre.*'

'That's what you're reading for your English studies. What are you reading for pleasure?'

'Er ... you wouldn't have heard of it.'

'Try me.'

'It's called *Amara*. It's by a guy called Richard Laymon.'

'What's it about?'

And reluctantly he would be drawn into describing the latest book he was reading by his favourite gothic horror writer, and endure the shudders of disapproval, which came particularly from Aunt Louisa.

The Pink Witch would then ask him about his friends and tease him about girls. 'I am surprised you haven't got a girlfriend yet, a good-looking boy like you. Haven't you met anyone you especially like, is that it?'

He probably disliked her more than the other two.

Nanny proved an unexpected ally, often intervening in the middle of a bout of relentless cross-questioning with 'Now, now, Miss Louisa, that's enough' or 'I'm sure he's worked harder than we ever were, Mrs Merfield. I think we should let him finish his supper in peace' and the amazing thing was that the three witches always seemed to listen to her, even the Black Witch, his great-grandmother, whom Jamie found terrifying.

That particular evening, following the advice of

204

the man who'd given him the lift, he sent a text message to two friends in London, urging them to pay him a visit.

He heard nothing back.

Then, as September made way for October, life for Jamie started to change.

He was sitting curled up in his armchair in the kitchen, late one afternoon, struggling with the text of Sophocles' *Antigone*, the play he was to audition for, when Nanny had a couple of visitors. There was nothing remarkable in that – quite a few people drifted through the manor kitchen and this pair, although younger than most, were as uninteresting to Jamie as the rest.

'Jamie, this is Stephen Tucker and Angela, his fiancée.'

''Lo,' said Jamie, without enthusiasm.

Stephen Tucker was a well-built man in his late twenties, fresh-faced and ruddy, of cheerful countenance, with twinkling brown eyes and a mop of brown hair. He nodded at Jamie in a friendly fashion.

His fiancée Angela, at his side, seemed tiny and looked, Jamie thought, like a little grey mouse, an impression accentuated by her enormous spectacles.

She smiled. 'Hello, Jamie. I'm pleased to meet you. Nanny has told us you're living here for a while.'

'Oh.'

There was a short silence. Jamie knew he should probably make the effort to say something more, but he couldn't see that this couple were worth bothering with.

205

Nanny sniffed reprovingly. 'Stephen runs the farm on the other side of the river, Jamie, and he leases the fields from us on this side. You may have seen him bringing the cows through the village.'

She turned to Stephen and Angela and beamed. 'Now, then, sit yourselves down. Tea's nearly ready. I want to hear all your news.'

At the mention of the farm, Jamie's ears pricked up and, although he tried to concentrate on his script, he found himself listening to their conversation, waiting for a mention of Alison.

He was disappointed. It was all about weddings, and animals, and someone called Charlie putting in a planning application to develop holiday cottages and workshops. He bided his time and when there was a lull in the conversation he said casually, 'I met someone not long ago, a girl called Alison. D'yer know her?'

'Alison?' Stephen paused in the process of eating a large piece of fruitcake. 'She's my kid sister. She hasn't mentioned meeting you.'

'Oh.' Jamie didn't know whether to be disappointed or relieved – he wasn't too proud of the circumstances surrounding his meeting with Alison. 'Well, um, I thought she seemed very nice.'

Aagh! I sound so lame! he thought savagely.

Angela looked at him sympathetically. 'Yes, she is nice; very busy with her exams, though. You go to Summerbridge College, too, don't you? Did you meet there?'

'Er ... not exactly. I saw her on her pony one day, and we ... er ... talked a bit. She said,' Jamie continued blindly, 'I should call round and see her, but I couldn't remember where she said she lived.'

'Well, that's easy,' said Stephen cheerfully. 'She lives at Marsh Farm and you can call round any time you like. We'd be pleased to see you.'

The following day the auditions were held and, to his great joy, Jamie was given the part of Creon. From the muttering and the black looks cast in his direction, he knew it was not a popular decision, but he didn't care – he'd show them. His impulse was to text his mother, but he held back, thinking of the moment he would surprise her.

Following the auditions, the group were given a rehearsal sheet. Glancing at it, Jamie groaned: many rehearsals were scheduled after school hours and at weekends.

'What's your problem?' sneered the boy sitting next to him. 'If you can't hack the rehearsals, do us all a favour and jack it in now.'

'It's not that, it's transport that's the problem, that's all. The school bus goes at four fifteen and there's not another till nine.'

'What you need,' said Adam, who everyone had thought would be given the part of Creon, 'is wheels. Lots of kids have problems getting about – it's why the car park's full of bikes. Get your daddy to buy you one. He's loaded, isn't he?'

By this time Jamie had been at Summerbridge College for three weeks and that weekend he and his father, with the help of Aunt Polly, were moving into the old doctor's house.

In a break between heaving furniture and boxes, Aunt Polly asked him how he was getting on at Summerbridge College.

'S'all right,' he said, shrugging. Then the

207

bubble of pride he'd been nurturing, ever since he'd been cast, could be contained no longer. 'I've just been given the part of Creon for my theatre studies practical.'

The effect was gratifying. Amid cries of 'Well done, Jamie, that's brilliant!' Aunt Polly hugged him warmly.

His father beamed.

'Only trouble is,' Jamie continued, 'I'll probably have to turn it down, take on something smaller.'

The two adults stared at him, aghast.

'Why, Jamie, why? Don't you think you can do it?' his father enquired anxiously. 'I know it's a big commitment, but if the teacher thinks you've got the ability...'

'It's not that, Dad. It's just most of the rehearsals take place early evening and at weekends. I wouldn't be able to get back to Summerstoke.'

'I could pick you up at weekends,' Oliver ventured.

'Yes, but that's only at the weekends, and supposing you're busy opening something, or visiting somewhere. You often are.'

'What a pity you're not old enough to drive. I can see transport is a real problem, stuck out here,' said Aunt Polly sympathetically.

Jamie seized his opportunity. 'I'm old enough to ride a motorbike, though.'

The expected protest came, but Jamie had done his homework. Not only had his father roared around the countryside on a motorbike when he was young, but, as Jamie pointed out, quite a few of the students at the college, similarly placed, had bikes.

Nanny, carrying a tray of tea and cake, came into the sitting room where they were pushing the big sofas into position and added her penny-worth. 'That's how young Alison Tucker, from Marsh Farm, gets to college. She's got a moped her brother did up for her. It doesn't have to be very powerful, Oliver.'

Jamie could have kissed her.

By the end of the weekend and after a long call to Los Angeles, he had secured the promise of a moped, and with that prospect in his sights Jamie felt his world opening up. That night, alone in his bedroom, he dreamed of visiting Marsh Farm, fantasising about the moment he would roar up the drive, resplendent in leathers, and sweep an admiring Alison off her feet.

The bike made a huge difference to Jamie in many ways. Not having to dash off to catch the bus immediately classes had finished meant he started to spend more time with the other students. Spending time chatting with them, he discovered they weren't so Neanderthal as he'd dubbed them and they, in turn, decided he wasn't such a stand-offish prick. Slowly but surely invitations followed, first to join a group going to a coffee bar, then to a pub, the cinema, bowling, someone's seventeenth birthday.

More significantly, Jamie was admitted to a small coterie of drama students who took their work seriously and were considered to have talent. They had made one of the dressing rooms in the theatre their base and here they gathered between classes and after school, drinking coffee, smoking and talking.

Jamie particularly admired a couple of them: Adam, who was playing Haemon, Creon's son, and Tish, the girl who'd given him a lift on her bike, who was Antigone. Gradually he became included in their regular circle of friends. In a rare moment of self-analysis Jamie admitted to himself he was enjoying himself in a way he'd never done before.

One evening in the middle of October, when he let himself into the Manor after eleven o'clock, he found Nanny waiting for him. 'Sit down, young man,' she said sternly. 'We've got to talk.'

He slumped into a kitchen chair, his face a picture of sullen resentment. 'What about?'

'I think you know, Jamie, I completely approved of your father getting you a bike. I do not approve of the hours you're starting to keep.'

'What's it to you?' he said, more aggressively than he'd intended.

'How very rude he is,' said a voice behind him.

Turning, Jamie saw the Red Witch standing in the doorway to the hall. She looked at him contemptuously and drifted into the room.

'I should have thought it would be obvious, even to someone as apparently ignorant as you, that there are certain rules of courtesy to be observed, whoever you are with, wherever you happen to be.'

She sat down at the table next to Nanny and drawled, 'You are our guest, in our house, and are our responsibility. For some extraordinary reason, Nanny has grown very fond of you and when you don't come home in time for supper and you don't phone to say you are going to be late, the silly darling worries about you, frets about motorbike accidents, that sort of thing. We had one in the village not so long ago, and the boy was lucky to escape with his life. Strange though it may seem, Nanny doesn't want the same thing to happen to you.'

Jamie flushed and glanced across at Nanny who sat looking at him, her face lined and weary. He dropped his gaze feeling ashamed, an unfamiliar emotion.

'I'll away to my bed, now that the prodigal son has returned.' Charlotte rose and stretched elegantly. 'Oh, and Jamie...'

He looked up.

'If you must smoke, please use an ashtray – your cigarette stubs do nothing for the rose bushes. Next time you want a cigarette, come and join me in the smoking room. It'll make a change to have some company. Good night.'

Jamie watched her segue her way out, fascinated and resentful at the same time.

'What does she mean, the smoking room?'

'All the big houses have them. When smoking was confined to the gentlemen of the house, they would change their jackets, put on these funny hats and retire to a smoking room. When the habit became more general and women smoked as well there was little point in having a separate room.'

Jamie turned to her, interested. 'So why do we have one? None of you lot smoke.'

'Oh, once upon a time I think everyone did, even your great-grandmother; but then poor Mr Douglas, your great-grandfather, came back from the war so ill, she gave up and so did everyone else, all except Miss Charlotte, that is.'

'Why didn't she?'

Nanny cast Jamie a look that he found hard to decipher. 'When she came back at the end of the war, she was in a bad way – not ill, exactly, but her nerves were all over the place. She'd spent a lot of time in France, behind the lines, and I think she must have seen some terrible things. She said if she couldn't smoke, she'd probably hit the bottle, so we put aside a room where she could.'

Jamie knew very little about the Second World War, but had gleaned enough from films to be intrigued by Nanny's references. 'Behind the lines? Was she a spy? Did she work with the Resistance?'

But Nanny had said all she was going to on the matter. 'That's her business. If you want to find out more talk to her. Not that she'll tell you, necessarily. She's always been very reluctant to say much about it.' She yawned. 'I'm more than ready for my bed and it's time you were asleep, too. Be a pet and put some milk to warm on the Aga.'

'I don't like warm milk.'

'No, I didn't imagine you would, but *I* do.'

Jamie got to his feet, once more feeling a twinge of shame. Nanny watched him as he got the milk out of the fridge and set some to warm.

'Why do you smoke, pet?'

Jamie shrugged; there was no obvious answer. 'Helps me relax, I s'pose.'

'Do your parents know?'

'Juliet does and says she doesn't mind so long as I don't do it in the house.'

'And your father?'

212

Again Jamie shrugged. 'I dunno, probably, but I don't smoke in front of him. Is this hot enough?' He carried the pan over to her.

'That'll do fine. Now, if you wouldn't mind, in the cupboard next to the fridge you'll find a bottle of whisky. That's it.' She took the bottle from Jamie, poured a good measure into her milk, took a sip and smiled. 'That's better. Now, pet, a few house rules: back by seven for supper, and if you're going to be late, I'd like to know beforehand. In any event, while you're staying here you must be back by ten.'

'Ten!' Jamie was aghast. 'That's really early!'

'Nevertheless, with college the next day, it's plenty late enough. I can't believe your parents would let you stay out all hours, especially when you've school the next day.'

Jamie thought about Juliet. In spite of opposition from his dad, she had set no rules and he had come and gone as he pleased. He sighed. He really missed her. Nice as Nanny was, the difference between life under her regime and life with Juliet was so acute, he felt as if he'd wandered into an unreal world; he was part of a fantasy game and he didn't know the code for getting himself out.

Oh, Mum, oh, Juliet, he sighed to himself, come home, soon, please.

Nanny got up stiffly from the table. 'Well now, Jamie, you look as if you need your bed as much as I do.' She looked at him closely. 'By the way, have you been to see young Alison Tucker yet?'

Jamie found himself blushing under her scrutiny. 'Er, no. What with these rehearsals and stuff, I've been busy.'

He'd thought about her endlessly, though, but his imagination could take him no further than skidding to a halt in the farmyard, sending ducks and hens screeching and flapping across the yard, taking off his helmet to reveal his identity, and then ... and then ... all he could see was the scorn in those green eyes.

'Never mind. She'll be at the bonfire, the weekend after next. You can see her then. It's a big village do: lots of fireworks and a huge bonfire. Everyone will be there.'

Unusually for a meeting of Summerstoke Parish Council, every seat in the village hall was taken. The hall, a simple Victorian building, had originally housed the village school and consisted of one large, high-ceilinged room, with narrow stone-mullioned windows, a small kitchen and storage room at one end, and the entrance hall and lavatories the other. It was just large enough to seat a hundred people, and Isabelle, considerably delayed by Richard's late return home, squashed in at the back, behind a small group forced to stand because of the lack of chairs.

It was a diverse mixture of people, some very elderly, who considered a public meeting an occasion for which they should dress up but couldn't quite disguise their struggle with poverty. A number of younger couples in shell suits or sweatshirts and tracksuit bottoms, chatted loudly, revealing the poverty of their generation in a different way. Various generations of the farming community assembled with nods and muttered exchanges, the older men ruddy-faced in brushed-

214

cotton check shirts and corduroy trousers; their wives in sensible skirts and jumpers, and the younger ones uniformly attired in jeans and shabby waxed jackets. There was also a smattering of middle-aged, middle-class members of the community, hair carefully groomed, neatly pressed denims, cashmere jumpers, lipstick, hairbands, scarves and gleaming Barbours.

Isabelle knew very few of the people, but the group at the back made room for her, nodding in welcome as if they knew who she was and accepted her right to be there.

She craned her neck and could just make out Paula's beehive next to a more diminutive leather-jacketed figure with a blond ponytail.

At the other end of the hall the parish councillors occupied a semi-circle of chairs, self-consciously reading, in turns, sub-committee reports which were listened to with barely concealed impatience by the parishioners.

'Old windbag,' Isabelle heard a young man by her side mutter as, yet again, Major Tenby, the chairman, formally congratulated a sub-committee on their achievements. 'Why doesn't he get on with it?'

'I thought they was giving us a glass of wine and nibbles?' whispered his companion. 'I don't see no sign of it.'

'That's for after. It's a bribe to keep us here to the end.'

'Well, if we have to listen to much more of this, it ain't worth it,' she grumbled.

'So that's our committee reports for the year completed and once again, on behalf of the

215

village, I would like to thank you all for your sterling work. We're very fortunate to have such a conscientious group of councillors on the team. Now, then.' Major Tenby coughed self-consciously. 'We turn to Any Other Business, under which there is just the one item and which is the reason, I suspect, we have such a good attendance from the village tonight. So much so,' he gave an arch smile, 'we might not have enough wine to go round, so we'll have to pop down to Tesco's for a few more bottles, eh? Ha ha.'

But his joke went down badly; his audience were clearly impatient so hastily he handed the floor to Rita Godwin.

Rita sketched out the doom-laden story that everyone in the village was now familiar with, and then the debate began: what, if anything, the village could do to influence the Post Office to change its mind; what the village could do if that proved impossible; and whether or not the village wanted the shop enough to take action to keep it going.

'Because I can tell you, there's people in this village who've never even been in the shop, and there's customers, good customers, who've stopped coming – without as much as a thanks-but-no-thanks. So the first thing I wants to know is, do you want this shop or not? Or should I sell it to the lady what's come in and made me a decent offer 'cos she wants to open an Interior Design Shop. Just what Summerstoke needs, perhaps?'

There was an indignant growl. Something went click in Isabelle's brain, but her attention was drawn back to the meeting.

After a vociferous exchange, in which Major Tenby's attempts to control the discussion became increasingly marginalised, a diminutive elderly lady stood up and addressed the assembly.

'Right, I think we've all had enough talk for one evening, don't you?' Barely waiting for the growls of assent, she carried on, 'I think we need a bit of action here. First things first, though. Do we want to fight for the shop, or don't we? Because if the majority don't – and I've heard some views leaning that way this evening – we might as well bite the bullet and go home now.'

'Not afore our free glass of wine, Elsie,' someone shouted.

The old lady smiled grimly. 'I'm sure the Major won't keep you waiting much longer, Lenny. But in the meantime I think we should test the water, eh? Who wants to keep the shop going? Put your hands up. Rita, Stephen, help us count.'

Some hands shot immediately into the air, others went up more tentatively, joined, after further whispering, by others. It was by no means unanimous. When the young man, who'd been roped into helping, agreed his count with the shopkeeper, the old lady encouraged those who felt closure was inevitable, and not worth the fight, to vote. One or two hands waved bravely and more went up for the 'don't knows'.

A brief animated discussion took place between the old lady, Rita, and Major Tenby.

Isabelle watched the old lady, fascinated. She was very neat, in a high-necked blouse with long sleeves, a padded waistcoat and pleated plaid skirt, a silk scarf loosely knotted round her neck and plaited grey hair pinned up in a crown on the back of her head. She was very wrinkled, but her skin was clear, her cheeks pink and her eyes bright and shrewd behind a pair of rimless spectacles.

'Who's the old lady?' she whispered to a farmer standing close to her.

He grinned. 'Her? Oh, that's Elsie Tucker from Marsh Farm. Rules her family with a rod of iron, she does. She don't often get involved with the village these days, and more's the pity, 'cos we get fools like old Tenby rulin' the roost.'

The young man in front of Isabelle turned round with a grin on his face. 'She's a right one, she is. Word was, she told her grandsons if they didn't get married within the year, she'd sell the farm from under them.'

'And then, to show 'em how it's done, she went and got married herself,' chimed in another, and everyone within earshot chuckled.

'Now they've all gone and got theyselves partners,' added another. 'All 'cept Charlie, that is. He turned and ran.'

'Straight into the arms of the landlady at the Bunch of Grapes!' chipped in another and they all laughed again.

Elsie Tucker finished her consultation and called them to order. 'Major Tenby says the parish council can't take responsibility for an action group, but if the village wants to form one they'll support it. So, given the number who want to keep the shop going, are you prepared to put that support into action and form a group?'

The majority who'd won the vote didn't hesitate and roared their support.

'Good,' the old lady responded with satisfaction. 'While you're drinking your wine, Stephen and Rita'll be coming round to take your details and it would help if you can also say what you think you can do to help. Yes, Mrs Green?'

A sheep-skinned arm had been raised and a middle-class voice drawled, 'I think I speak for a number of us here, in that we'd like to support the shop, but only if we can see certain changes implemented.'

Rita clearly hadn't been expecting this. Startled, she was immediately on the defensive. 'Yes, well, of course – within reason. Those who pay the piper, as they say... I like to think I give the village what it wants.'

'That's something the action committee can look at, Mrs Green,' said Elsie Tucker crisply. 'Perhaps you'd like to put your name down for it?'

Isabelle had planned to slip away as soon as the meeting finished, but before she could squeeze to the door her neighbour pushed a glass of wine into her hand, commenting, 'Here, take this before the thirsty bunch move in. Nice to see you here, missus. Your first parish council meeting, I'll be bound. How're you settlin' in?'

To Isabelle's surprise, not only did he and his wife show every interest in staying to chat to her but a number of others came over, introduced themselves and joined the conversation. In fact, she noticed that, far from emptying, the hall was buzzing; no one seemed inclined to leave and a party atmosphere prevailed. When Isabelle's glass was empty and she started to extricate herself, someone exchanged her glass for another full one.

'Right, you lot.' Rita elbowed her way into the group, a clipboard in her hand. 'I think I know you all. Does anyone here not want me to put their name on my list?'

'What's the list for? What are you going to do with our names?' an elderly woman demanded with suspicion.

'The list is so we know who we can call upon to support our campaign. We also want volunteers for the action group; we need to get moving.'

'Who's going to run this group?' asked another. 'Major Tenby, as usual?'

'No,' said Rita patiently. 'You heard Elsie Tucker: Major Tenby doesn't want the parish council to be involved. We'll vote on who's to lead it when we know who's prepared to be on it. Right, I've got your names down. When I read them out, if you could give me your address and telephone number and tell me if you're prepared to help...'

As she went round the group, it was clear to Isabelle that while most were content to lend their support in principle, or help in some undefined way, very few felt they had the time to be on the action committee. For some reason – maybe because she still felt such an outsider – it never occurred to her that she would be asked.

'Me? I ... I don't know. I hadn't thought... I've never... I wouldn't be much use to you.'

'She's really good at art, Rita.' Paula had arrived at Isabelle's side. 'She does lovely drawings. She could do you a poster.'

A poster! Isabelle groaned. Her situation was becoming increasingly absurd. What was she doing here, in this hall? She had nothing in common with these people, nothing, no matter how nice they were. They were alien – *she* was alien, she was from another planet. She didn't belong to the village; she couldn't join an action committee and design posters; she couldn't. What would Joe say? He'd give up on her. No, she had to find her way back to where she, Isabelle Langton, had been lost and *this* was not going to be the way.

'Excellent,' said Rita, briskly. 'We'll certainly need someone; I don't think anyone in the art group would be up to it. Come and meet Elsie, Mrs Garnett. I'm hoping she'll agree to be our chairman, because once Elsie Tucker gets her teeth into something she won't let go.'

Before Isabelle could protest, Rita had turned and plunged through the crowd, beckoning her to follow.

Elsie Tucker was in conversation with another elderly lady who was tall, very much taller than Elsie, who barely reached her elbow, straight and thin, with cropped grey hair and kindly hazel eyes, and dressed very neatly, all in brown.

'Elsie – sorry to interrupt you, Nanny, but I want to introduce Mrs Garnett, here, to Elsie. She's good at designing posters and things, just what we'll need on the committee. If you'll excuse me, I'd better get on with my list before people leave without giving their details.'

And Rita whisked away, leaving Isabelle feeling her hold on reality rapidly slipping. She became aware of a sharp pair of green eyes looking up at her, seeming to read her thoughts. She blushed.

Elsie held out her hand and took Isabelle's limp

one in a firm grip. 'Mrs Garnett, pleased to meet you. I don't know whether you've met your neighbour, yet. Nanny lives at Summerstoke Manor.'

Isabelle knew all about the set-up at the manor from Paula and murmuring, 'Pleased to meet you,' turned to shake the papery, dry hand of the old lady.

Before she could explain to Elsie that it was all a mistake and not only had she never designed a poster in her life but it was the last thing she wanted to do, Elsie continued, 'I'm pleased you were here tonight, my dear, as I was going to call on you, anyway. I understand your husband's editor of the *Wessex Daily* and I wanted to ask you if he might help us in our campaign?'

She should have seen it coming. It had happened often enough when they lived in Bath, particularly when Rebecca started school. 'Do you think your husband could do a feature on our fund-raising – on our nativity play – on our parking problems – on the church roof appeal – on the use of our road as a rat run?'

At first, she'd gone to him willingly, thinking to enlist his support in what seemed really worthwhile causes; but each request was greeted with an impatient sigh, a groan or a frown, and she learned, very quickly, that a personal appeal through her would get nowhere.

He'd sneered at her for wanting to attend the meeting, so she could imagine his reaction if she asked him to help with the Post Office and if he discovered she was going to design a poster... She was certainly not going to tell him about *that*.

Her heart sinking, she began, wanly, 'Er, it

might be better to go directly to the news editor, or to features, and get them to do something on village shops and how they're under threat...' Her voice trailed away.

'What a good idea,' said Elsie. 'Think beyond the limits of our own horizons. You'll be very useful to us, Mrs Garnett.'

'Please, call me Isabelle.'

'It's time I was getting back, Elsie, so I'll say goodnight.' Nanny turned to Isabelle. 'Are you staying here any longer, Isabelle, or shall we walk back together?'

'No, I really must go, too. I've been longer than I planned. I'd be pleased to come with you.'

Saying goodnight to more people than she'd spoken to in nearly a month in Summerstoke, Isabelle left the village hall with Nanny, feeling dazed.

Nanny was a comfortable companion, and by the time they had walked up the small road that led to the High Street Isabelle felt able to blurt out her fear that Mrs Tucker and Rita Godwin might have been misled and, far from being a useful member of the action committee, she would let them down.

'Early days to worry about that, pet. Elsie Tucker's no fool and she's a good judge of character. It'll be a good way for you to meet other people in the village, won't it? You must feel very cut off from everything you know, and being by yourself for most of the day...'

'I suppose so,' Isabelle replied in a small voice. There was something about Nanny that comforted but made her want to cry and tears pricked her eyelids. Fortunately, the sound of a loud, angry wasp, coming rapidly up the High Street behind them, distracted her.

A moped, its rider crouched low over the handlebars, shot past them and turned into the drive to the Manor, the sound of the engine buzzing away into the distance through the trees.

Nanny glanced at her watch. 'Five to ten. Good boy! Goodnight, my dear. Do call on me at the manor, won't you. The Misses Merfield would like to meet you – they don't get out so much these days. And do bring your little girls.'

'Thank you. You're very kind. Er ... who was that who turned into your drive, on the moped?'

'That was Mrs Merfield's great-grandson. His father, Oliver Merfield, is our MP, you know. As he's up in London Monday to Friday, and his mother is away, making a film in America, Jamie stays with us during the week. I don't mind telling you, Isabelle, I had my doubts at first. But underneath all that teenage attitude, he's a sweet boy. He takes after his father. You've met Oliver, haven't you?'

'Yes, yes I have,' replied Isabelle.

Richard had subjected her to a stream of senseless accusations after he'd seen Oliver walking her home from the playground. It had taken nearly a week before hostilities were dropped and he finally apologised.

It was a side of him she'd never really seen before, and she didn't like it.

NOVEMBER

9

The action group settled on the following Monday evening for their first meeting, and a hapless Isabelle was informed it was to be held at her house because the village hall would have charged them, the Foresters Arms was not welcoming, Rita's flat was too small, Marsh Farm was too far out of the village, the vicarage was too small, Mrs Green had decorators in, and it would save Isabelle having to find a babysitter.

Isabelle knew Richard was going to some event that evening, in Bath, so would be unlikely to walk in on them. She hadn't told him she was on the committee and she cringed at the thought of exposing herself, or the other members, to his withering censure.

The dining room, with its wall lined for painting and floorboards nailed ready to receive the fitted carpet, was turned into a meeting room complete with wine, coffee and fizzy water for refreshment.

There were six members in all, including Isabelle and the ruddy-faced man who'd counted the votes at the public meeting and who was introduced to Isabelle by Elsie as 'my grandson, Stephen Tucker'.

'He seems a lot nicer than his brother,' thought Isabelle, as she shook his slightly damp, rather warm hand.

Elsie Tucker called them to order and was duly elected as the chair after an initial disagreement from Mrs Green, who felt Lavender Grey, as the vicar's wife, could better represent the village.

Lavender Grey was the antithesis of her husband. She was short, round and animated. Her grey-brown hair shot out of its perm in every direction; her cheeks were pink and shiny, as were her nose and chin, in spite of an attempt to dull the gleam with a smear of powder, and her eyes, small and bright, constantly darted from person to person.

She dismissed the proposal immediately. 'Goodness me, Sally, I've got quite enough to do as it is. And there are times, you know, when being the vicar's wife has its disadvantages. We're not always taken seriously. No, we need someone with Elsie's tenacity. She'll represent us admirably.'

Once the question of leadership had been settled the discussion was lively. A campaign of sorts was agreed, jobs were allocated, and after much deliberation they settled on SOPO (Save Our Post Office) as the name of the group.

'Now,' said Elsie, sitting upright in her chair and fixing a bright eye on Mrs Green, 'Over to you, Sally. At the village meeting you said if you were to support the fight for the shop's survival, you wanted a voice in the way it's run.'

Put on the spot, Sally Green went red. In her mid-forties, she was heavy and plain, carefully made up with bright-red lipstick, and with hair – once auburn, now blonde – held in place by a velvet band. Her light brown eyes were small and close together, and although she clearly needed spectacles for reading she put them on with great reluctance, snatching them off her nose whenever she could.

Isabelle had met her at Veronica's cocktail party and had not warmed towards her.

'It's just that some of us have become concerned... We know how hard Mrs Godwin works, but maybe things slip,' she spluttered.

'What things?' Rita bristled. 'Are you complaining about my stock? I'm quite happy to get things in, if people ask for them; the customer is king, as they say. But I can't carry too wide a range, I can't afford it.'

'No. Not the stock – although we think there are certain things you could make more of an effort over. No, we're more worried about how hygienic the shop is.'

'What?' Rita almost exploded and it was only with much effort that Elsie calmed her down and defused the situation sufficiently for Rita to offer to show the committee around her premises. She also agreed to conduct a survey of what produce her customers would like to see available.

When the meeting wound up and Isabelle was carrying the refreshments back to the kitchen, she wasn't altogether surprised by Sally Green, under the guise of helping, seizing the opportunity when they were alone in the kitchen to whisper dramatically, 'Didn't Veronica warn you about the rats, Isabelle?'

Isabelle frowned. 'Yes, she did, but I honestly don't know where she got the idea from. I've checked it out. She's wrong.'

'But why on earth should she bother to warn us

unless it's true?'

Isabelle shrugged, but it was puzzling her. As far as she knew the village shop was the last place Veronica would patronise, so why should she bother with it? It didn't make any sense.

'I don't fucking believe this.' Richard glared round the table.

His editors avoided his eye, their expressions ranging from bland to sullen to scared according to the level of their experience.

'This list is crap. Are you taking the mickey? No wonder our sales are dropping. We might just as well print last year's paper – no one would spot the difference. There's not a single original story here – same old pictures, same old take.' He glanced at his watch. 'I'll give you an hour to re-think. And you'd better come up with something better than this load of shit.'

He stood up and swept from the room into his office, banging the door behind him. Apart from the conference room where the daily meetings were held, his was the only enclosed space in the building.

He flung himself into his chair – the latest model of high-tech design, positioned so he could look out through a half-glass wall at the open-plan office where his cohorts toiled – put his feet up on the large, mahogany desk and brooded. A tap at the door heralded the arrival of his secretary carrying a mug of freshly brewed coffee and a sheaf of letters, which she placed in front of him.

She coughed discreetly. She was used to Richard's bad moods and, since they were seldom directed at her, wasn't intimidated. 'I've just had the secretary of the Lions' Club on the phone, Richard, confirming the arrangements for tomorrow evening. The fireworks are due to go off at seven thirty so they'd like all guests to be assembled in the marquee by seven, at the latest, for champagne and canapés.'

He growled 'Fucking fireworks' in response, so she left him to work out his bad temper on the pile of paperwork.

Richard justified the acceptance of most invitations on the grounds that out in the field he could nose out what was happening in his patch. Anyone who wanted the ear of the local editor, for whatever reason, sent him an invitation. His diary was full of lunches, dinners, openings and special events like Fireworks Night. He didn't always attend – anything a bit humble or lacking in kudos was passed on to the features editor.

Playing the scene as he did meant, on some days, he hardly saw his staff, but he had a good team of editors who only needed the occasional bollocking to keep them up to scratch. He knew the reporters and subs were afraid of him and that, he thought, was the way it should be. The newspaper world was not a cosy one: it was dog eat dog and so long as they realised he, Richard, was top dog, that was fine by him.

The telephone rang.

'It's Mrs Lester for you, Richard. Do you want to take the call?'

'Sure. Put her through.'

'Richard, hi. I'm sure you're very busy so I won't keep you. What are you doing tomorrow evening?'

'I've been invited to the fireworks bash in Bath. Why?'

'That's what I thought. Are Issy and the girls going, too?'

'No, Issy wants to go to the village one – God knows why. Why do you want to know, Vee?'

'It's just that I'm going to the Lions' do as well, with the Baineses; Hugh's in London so I'm staying over with them. We're going to dinner afterwards, at the Olive Tree, and I thought if you're going to be in town, solo, you could make up the party. How about it, Richard? It'll be such fun.'

The Baineses were a rare commodity in Bath: an old family with lots of money and lots of influence. Richard had met them a number of times, but always at large gatherings. The idea of dining with them was too good to pass up.

He settled with Vee when and where they should meet, then put the phone down to consider how he could enjoy the evening to its full and get home without hassle or expense.

There'll be a cordon of police cars round Bath, he grumbled to himself. Friday *and* fireworks; I bet I wouldn't get out of the city without being stopped, even if I didn't drink anything. I *should* be all right with a glass of champagne and a couple of glasses of wine, but it pisses me off I can't relax and have a good time. What I need is some way of whisking myself out of the danger zone. Once I'm clear of Bath, I'll be safe.

By the time the hour was up and his staff had reconvened, with some trepidation, in the conference room, he had a solution. To their amazement, he bounced into the room and looked at them benignly. 'Okay, chaps, what have we got on offer?'

Jamie loved working on *Antigone* and threw himself into the rehearsals and production work with enthusiasm. The drama teacher, who'd been off-hand when he first joined the class, was pleased with him and said so.

The performance was set for the end of November, the examiner coming to the second performance.

If only... If only Juliet would come back in time, Jamie thought over and over again. He'd asked his dad if there was any likelihood of that happening, but Oliver shook his head. 'Afraid not, old son. She hasn't mentioned anything. You'll just have to make do with me – I've written the Friday performance in my diary and told Susannah I'm not available, under any circumstances. Do you want to ask anyone else?'

Jamie frowned.

Yes, he thought, Alison.

He'd dreamed countless times of the moment he'd ask her: they'd meet at the bonfire; they'd chat; she'd suggest they meet and he'd shrug his shoulders and say, 'Love to, but I'm a bit busy the next few weeks – I'm playing Creon, in *Antigone*. I expect you've seen the posters. Hey, would you like to come to see me? We'll have a cast party afterwards, on the Friday, we could meet at that afterwards, if you fancy it?'

To his father, he simply said, 'Not really. Nanny'd probably like to come, but I think she's too old and wouldn't understand it.'

'The aunts, Grandmère?'

Jamie hesitated.

Self-consciously at first, and a little defiantly, he had found his way to Charlotte's smoking room. When, after a cautious knock, he'd gone in, he found her sitting in a deep leather armchair, smoking a cigarette in a short ivory holder, a book on her lap. The room was lined with old leather books and bound manuscripts; a small fire burned in the grate, and there was some soft, strange music playing.

'Ah, the juvenile delinquent's come to join the ancient delinquent,' she'd drawled. 'What are you smoking, or would you like one of these?' She pushed a heavy silver cigarette box towards him. 'If you're going to ruin your lungs, you might as well do it on decent tobacco.'

'Thanks, Aunt Charlotte.'

'However, I've promised your great-grandmother I won't allow you to chain-smoke, so two's your limit. We can either engage in conversation or read in silence. This evening you may choose which it is to be; the next time, I shall choose. So, which is it to be?'

Jamie thought for a moment. It would be easier to read, but he hadn't thought to bring anything and he didn't fancy the look of any of the mouldy old books in the room, so remembering the hints Nanny had dropped about Charlotte, and wondering if he could get her to describe her war experiences to him, he said, almost shyly. 'Talk, please.'

She arched her thin brows at that and large blue eyes under heavy lids scrutinised him. 'Well, you do surprise me. What shall we talk about?'

Jamie, unprepared, made a clumsy attempt to talk about the war in general, intending to bring it round to the Second World War, but she fended off his questions and forced him to do most of the talking, which hadn't been extensive, but he'd told her about Creon and she seemed interested.

He'd gone back a second time when she'd insisted they read, and a third time, when she again diverted the conversation to hear about his progress in rehearsals.

She intrigued Jamie and he wanted to impress her.

'Maybe you could ask Aunt Charlotte if she wants to come,' he said to Oliver, adding hastily, 'but not Louisa – she'd just make sarky comments – and not Grandmère – I think I'd dry if she was in the audience.'

Oliver laughed and ruffled his hair, something he hadn't done since Jamie was a little boy. 'Leave it with me. I'll sound them out.'

'Thanks. We've got our first run-through tomorrow, without scripts. It'll be really nerve-racking.'

'Would you like me to test you?'

'Wouldn't mind. I'm pretty confident I know it, but I've got a bet on with Tish.'

It being a Thursday Oliver had driven straight down from Westminster at the close of business, picking Jamie up when he got to Summerstoke. Jamie lit the sitting-room fire – a skill he'd learned from Nanny – while Oliver heated a couple of pizzas, and the two of them were relaxing in the depths of a huge squashy sofa in front of the blazing logs, munching, chatting, and half watching a late-night comedy.

Oliver, with Polly's help, had made the old doctor's house very comfortable with the furniture they'd brought down from London and some pieces picked up from a local antiques and junk shop. The sitting room, once the fire was lit and the thick, dark-red velvet curtains drawn shut, was their favourite room and they both gravitated to it.

In the weeks the house had become theirs they had established a routine. They both missed Juliet acutely, but without her dominating and distracting presence they grew closer than they had ever been.

'Are you going to the village fireworks party tomorrow night, Dad?'

'Yep. In fact, the parish council have asked me if I'll light the bonfire.'

'Cool. Have you seen the size of it? It's huge.'

The telephone rang.

Oliver glanced at his watch and pulled a face. He went to the phone sitting on a small table just inside the door, and lifted the receiver.

'Hello.' His eyes widened and he half turned to look at Jamie. 'Juliet!'

In order to meet Juliet at Heathrow, Oliver had to shift his morning appointments. Susannah had pursed her lips at the short notice and the cancellations and the rearrangements it entailed. But Oliver, driven by the tears he'd heard in Juliet's voice the last time she'd phoned from Hollywood, and the growing emptiness he felt in her absence, hadn't hesitated when she phoned.

To his very great surprise, Jamie declined the

offer to go to the airport. 'No, thanks, Dad, you meet her. I can't miss the rehearsal. I'll see her tonight.'

Juliet was equally surprised not to see Jamie, but it meant for that precious moment when she came through the Arrivals gate Oliver had her undivided attention; and nor, for once, did she look over his shoulder for anyone else who might recognise her.

'We finished the pilot yesterday,' she explained, holding his arm as they walked back to the car park, 'and of course, there were loads of parties planned for this weekend, but I just had to come back, if only for a short while. I felt so cut off from you both, Ollie, not being able to visualise where you were, what the house looks like...'

All the way back to the West Country, she was bright and talkative, describing the progress of the filming; the actors she was working with, one or two of whom had become good chums; the wardrobe mistress, who was impossible; the director, who was unpredictable; the grandness of the hotel where she was staying; and the comfort of her suite of rooms, filled with fresh flowers every day. Oliver wasn't deceived, but decided to bide his time.

Juliet approved of the doctor's house but she shook her head over the shabbiness of the kitchen and the bathroom.

'Although, if as you say the old boy is prepared to cough up to have them modernised, we could make them look really good. I'll start looking at designs.'

'You think you could live here, then?'

She cast him a look which he couldn't quite interpret, a mixture of bravado and longing, a gay adventurer casting one last wistful glance back at the harbour.

'Oh,' she replied, lightly, 'I might not get the chance. The studio's very keen on what we've done. My manager says it's okay to stay for a couple of weeks, but then I've to be back before my face gets forgotten, and they'll want me about to do whatever is needed to promote the pilot. Once the series gets the go-ahead, it's probably going to be easier for you and Jamie to come and see me.'

Feelings he was not quite able to control must have shown on his face, for she took him in her arms and held him tightly, nor did she resist when he led her to the bedroom.

They lay there together for a good half-hour after their lovemaking; not talking much, but holding each other, intermittently stroking, caressing and kissing; the depth of their need for each other sounded for this brief, magical moment.

Feeling Juliet curled up against him, relaxed and half-asleep, Oliver decided to probe a little. Gently stroking her hair, he began, 'So tell me, darling, is it all sweetness and light in Tinsel Town?'

She hesitated for a moment before replying, 'No, it's not. But then I didn't think it would be. I'm not naive.'

'I never thought you were. So tell me the best bits and the worst bits – put me in the picture.'

'The best bits are easier. The script was pretty crappy, but the chief scriptwriter was so sweet and took me out to dinner a number of times.

Actually, Ollie, everyone was really hospitable. If I didn't want to be alone in the evening, I didn't have to be – I had so many invitations to dinner, to parties, to premieres... And my hotel was lovely, very grand. I won't be able to stay there when I get back, unfortunately, but my manager's looking out for an apartment I can rent. I want him to get me somewhere on the beach – the city's pretty airless and it's impossible to do anything as simple as go out for a walk. I never thought I'd miss that.'

'A far cry from this place, then.' Oliver felt a constriction in his throat.

Juliet chuckled. 'Couldn't be more different. I'll have to take some pictures back with me. In fact, I ought to take some this evening – they don't celebrate Guy Fawkes in LA.'

'Are you sure about coming? Wouldn't you rather sleep off your jet-lag?'

'I don't get jet-lag, Ollie. I want to come and meet the local yokels. It'll be fun.'

Oliver sighed. 'Fine. You can always change your mind. I have to be there to light the bonfire at seven. Jamie says he'll be back by then.'

'I can't wait to see him.' The brittle note that had crept into Juliet's voice was replaced by one soft with longing. 'I can't believe he turned down a trip to the airport to meet his old mother because he had school work to do. Has he been brainwashed by the witches?'

'Something's affected him, but I don't think it's the old ladies. Nanny's been great with him, though; you might remember that when you see her tonight.'

239

'Oh, God, are they going to be there? That'd make a brilliant photo, a witches' coven round the bonfire – or are they standing in for the guy?'

'Juliet, they're part of the village. Please, be nice to them, for Jamie's sake, if nothing else.'

Juliet rolled over and propped her head on hand, her face alight with mischief. 'Oh, Ollie, you're so easy to tease. I can't tell you how much I've missed you and your ... your Englishness.'

He put out a hand and stroked her face. 'How much?'

She smiled down at him. 'Enough to promise to be good tonight and enough to say that I–' A shadow passed over her face and she broke off and she rolled back, sighing, and stared up at the ceiling.

'You asked me about the good and the bad of being in LA. The worst bit was feeling like a member of a different species, feeling I really didn't belong, that I spoke an alien language. Oh, they were all very nice and polite; they smiled a lot and always remembered my name – "Hi, Juliet; nice to see you, Juliet; Juliet, you look lovely; have a nice day, Juliet; I'll call you, Juliet" – but I couldn't rid myself of the suspicion it was all skin deep; that actually, in the end, no one, not even my manager, gave a damn, and if this pilot doesn't work out they'll drop me without a thought. Feeling like that makes for a very lonely existence.'

Oliver kissed her gently. 'You're very brave. You've got such guts, Juliet. But if it makes you unhappy, don't stay there. You don't have to.'

She sat up abruptly and pushed back the bed-covers. 'But I do. I've signed a contract. And anyway,' she continued forcefully, 'it's what I want. I want to be a star, Oliver, and if I have to suffer a bit on the way, so what?'

'We miss you, Jamie and I,' said Oliver, simply. 'We'd like you to come back.'

She stared at him for a moment, then shrugged. 'You've got what *you* want: Oliver Merfield, MP, resident of Summerstoke. You didn't consult *me*, there's nothing there for me. It may be awful at times, but I'm going to make it, Ollie, I am going to make it.' She gave a little, sad smile and said, more softly, 'And I miss you too, both of you, unbearably at times. But when I'm rich and famous, I'll get a first-class season ticket and come back whenever I feel like it. Now, is there a shower in that funny old bathroom, or will you run me a bath?'

Suppressing the desire to clasp Juliet in his arms and do his level best to persuade her not to go back to the States, Oliver climbed out of bed, saying lightly, 'No shower but a huge old tub, so we can share a bath if you like?'

'I'd love to. Then you can tell me what Jamie's up to.'

The children of Summerstoke had been watching the bonfire grow for nearly a month. Most of the households used it as an opportunity to dispose of their garden rubbish, and some for their unwanted household junk, too.

Guy Fawkes night was always held in the field just beyond the bridge. Owned by the Tuckers and used for occasional grazing, it was considered by the village to be part of their recreational area.

A thicket of brambles, stripped of blackberries every year, occupied the lower reaches of the field and a well-used public footpath ran along the river's edge, skirting a large muddy pond or mere, which regularly froze over in the winter, much to the delight of the children.

Charlie and Stephen Tucker had coaxed the motley collection of debris into a reasonably shaped bonfire. Charlie had emptied a number of the farm's outbuildings, prior to conversion, so the two men were able to add sufficient rubbish and dead wood to give it a chance of going up in a good blaze.

It rained hard during the morning, but by mid-afternoon the clouds had lifted and although the bonfire was dripping it was not saturated.

'Nothing a couple of cans of petrol won't cure,' Lenny Spinks said cheerfully, when he and the Tucker brothers checked it. They were going to be responsible for the bonfire, and the parish council had arranged for a firm to set up and light the fireworks. Traditionally, a group of men from the village did that, but Health and Safety, or the insurance company (nobody was sure which, but, with gloomy disgust, blamed both and the parish council for being weak and giving in), dictated the end of that tradition and was threatening, so the rumour went, the survival of the bonfire.

The ground was soggy and slippery as a result of the rain but as evening drew on the skies cleared. One by one, stars appeared and a pale, transparent half-moon hung over Summerstoke Ridge.

The gigantic pile loomed, dark and sinister, in the middle of the field, surrounded by a barrier made from orange baling twine and fencing rods. The gate was opened wide to admit cars, of which there was a growing number since the Summerstoke bonfire was well-known locally and people came from the surrounding hamlets, as well as from Summerstoke itself, for 'There'll always be those lazy tykes who'd die rather than walk,' Charlie remarked when he and his brother discussed bringing a tractor over in case any vehicles got stuck.

A table was set up by the gate to collect entrance money. This was to go towards the fireworks, but there were still those who grumbled and thought the parish council should have paid, like they always used to.

'No, they never did,' said Rita Godwin, who was collecting the entrance money. 'The manor used to pay for them.'

'Pity they don't still, then,' came the sour reply.

'You wouldn't say that if you knew the price of this little lot,' retorted Rita. 'Now, are you going to pay your pound and let the people behind you in?'

The field filled rapidly. Stalls illuminated by crooked lines of fairy lights, which periodically failed as a result of the whimsical behaviour of a loud and temperamental generator, were set up to sell mulled wine, beer and canned drinks, hot-dogs and garlic bread, roasted chestnuts, and an array of fluorescent necklaces and wands that the children snapped up with a flourish. The air was filled with their shrieks and laughter and with the buzz of animated chatter from the adults; the village was out to enjoy itself.

The last few stragglers were just making it over the bridge when Oliver arrived, chauffeuring his elderly relatives. He'd left Juliet to walk down with Jamie, chivvying them, as he left, not to be late so they could be with him when he lit the fire.

'Oh, hello there, Mr Merfield, ladies.' Charlie, leaning into the car window, nodded at the occupants. 'I've kept you a place here by the gate. The fireworks are going off over there, on the other side of the field, so if the ladies want to stay in the car, they'll get a good view.'

Mrs Merfield wound her window down. 'Is your grandmother here, this evening, Charles?'

'Wouldn't miss it for the world, Mrs Merfield. You'll find her on the mulled wine stall. She's roped in her new husband to give a hand, poor fellah.'

'I look forward to meeting him.'

'Well, if you do get out, take care. It's very slippery. I'll go and tell the Major you're here, Mr Merfield.'

Oliver smiled up at him. 'Call me Oliver, please. "Mr Merfield" makes me feel uncomfortable.'

Charlie grinned back. 'Fine. I'm Charlie Tucker, by the way.'

'Pleased to meet you.' The two men shook hands. Oliver suddenly laughed. 'Do you know, Charlie, I seem to remember us having mud-slinging battles with you one summer when we were kids – you and your brother and half the village on your side of the river, and me, my sister, and a mate on ours?'

Charlie laughed, too. 'So we did, and if I remember correctly we always won.'

244

'With those sort of odds on your side, it was hardly surprising. Nice to meet you again, Charlie. We must get together some time.'

With the assistance of Major Tenby and a few of his cohorts, Oliver and the Merfield ladies were escorted round the stalls; introductions were made; hands were shaken, and the ladies were then wrapped in rugs and ensconced on chairs placed in a prime viewing position.

Jamie spotted Alison fairly soon after he arrived in the field with his mother. She was on the hot-dog stall, cooking the sausages.

'Do you fancy a hot-dog, Juliet?'

'Not now, darling. Let's find your father.' Juliet moved into a small pool of light and looked around her, then up at the sky. 'In Los Angeles,' she said in a clear voice, to no one in particular, 'all those stars would be the lights of aeroplanes waiting to land.'

Instantly she became the object of excited curiosity and Jamie was aware of people nudging each other and whispering, 'Is that her? Is that Juliet Peters? Is that Oliver's missus?'

It didn't take long for the word to spread and for Major Tenby, on his way to meet the Vicar and his wife at the gate, to forget his mission and to push his way through the throng to her, introduce himself and offer to escort her over to Oliver.

Jamie found himself crowded out, but he was used to that and, shrugging his shoulders, turned back to the hot-dog stall. There were three people working on it: Alison, the plump woman, who had long wispy hair tied up in a bun and who seemed

245

to know all the customers – which was probably why she was burning the onions, she was chatting so much – and the mouse with big specs whom he'd met in the Manor kitchen that day.

At the end of the stall sat a tall, dark-haired youth, very pale, older than Jamie and Alison, his leg in plaster, talking to the overweight, spotty specimen he'd met at that cocktail party his dad dragged him to when they'd first arrived.

Jamie stood back and, using the crowd around the stall as a shield, watched Alison at work.

Her face was flushed with the heat of cooking; her hair was scraped up into a ponytail, which bobbed and swung as she moved; her eyes were bright, and her face was lively and friendly as she acknowledged her customers. He stared at her with admiration. She was everything he wanted in a girl – so what was he waiting for?

He would join the queue, move up to the stand and ask her for a hot-dog. She wouldn't be looking at him when he asked, she'd be concentrating on the sausages and when she heard his voice she'd look up. Their eyes would meet and hers would widen with recognition. She'd smile. 'Jamie,' she'd say, 'why haven't you been to see me? I heard you were asking after me. Why haven't you been round?' He'd make some diffident reply and she'd laugh and say, 'Don't be daft, I'd love to see you. We're having a bit of a party after the fireworks. Why don't you come along?'

The crowd around the stall grew thicker, but Jamie was enjoying his daydream so much that he was in no hurry to make a move, and stood there, jostled by the crowds, content to look on.

Oliver looked around for his wife and son. The field was now so full it was hard to make individuals out. Then he caught sight of Paula teetering through the crowd in a pair of high-heeled thigh-length boots, and carrying six hot-dogs precariously piled one on top of another.

'Paula,' he called. 'Paula!'

She tottered over to him. 'Oh, hello, Oliver. You gonna light the bonfire, then?'

'At seven. Paula, have you seen Jamie anywhere?'

'No, can't say as I 'ave. I've been queuing for ages at the hot-dog stall for the kiddies' supper. Ryan, he wants an ice lolly – can you believe it? Anyway, I didn't see Jamie around the stalls. P'raps he's waiting for you over at the bonfire.'

'Well, if you see him, tell him I'm going over there now. He should be with his mother.'

'Juliet?' Paula shrieked with disbelief, and wobbled on her heels. 'Juliet's back from Hollywood?'

'She came back this morning.'

'Oh, my God, Juliet Peters is here.' With that, she skidded on the treacherous ground, and lurched uncontrollably towards Oliver. As he grabbed her, to prevent her from losing her balance altogether, her stack of hot-dogs flew into the air and landed in quick succession on his chest, slithering down his shirt front and onto the ground.

They both stared at the sticky red trail of ketchup staining the white shirt.

'Oh, my gawd,' whispered Paula, horror-struck.

Oliver, aghast, looked down at the spreading, stinking stain, and fought to keep his cool. 'Don't worry, Paula, it was an accident.' He tried to laugh. 'Looks like I've been shot, doesn't it?'

Before he could say anything more, Major Tenby, Juliet on his arm, pushed through the crowd. 'Here you are, Oliver, I've found your lovely wife. What an honour, what an– Oh, my goodness, are you all right?'

'Oliver, what on earth have you been doing?' Juliet's voice was crisp and amused. She looked from Oliver to Paula, who had turned to stone at the sound of her idol's voice.

'An accident. Poor old Paula here skidded on the grass and her children's supper landed on my shirt.' He turned to Paula and said softly, 'Don't worry, Paula. You'd better go back and get some more; we can't have your children watching fireworks on an empty stomach. Here, you might need this.' He folded her limp fingers round a note. Turning back to the Major, he said apologetically, 'I need to change. Can the bonfire wait ten minutes?'

The Major puffed with embarrassment. 'It's nearly seven. Everyone's expecting us to start at seven.'

'I can't possibly get to the house and change and be back in less than ten minutes. Surely you can wait?' Oliver tried to keep his annoyance under control.

'If you can hang on a couple of ticks,' said Paula, suddenly coming to life, 'I live just over the bridge, I can get you a shirt.' And throwing back her head, she bellowed, 'Lenny, *Lenny!* I need you, here, quick.'

A small wiry man in his mid-thirties, his blond

hair in a long, straggling ponytail, his two front teeth missing and his arms, thick and muscular, covered in tattoos, appeared from the darkness of the field.

'What is it, my lovely?'

Paula quickly told him about the accident and, ignoring Oliver's protestations that he'd rather go back and change into one of his own shirts, sent Lenny off, running.

'It's seven o'clock now,' said the Major, scrutinising his watch by the flickering light of the nearest stall. 'And here's the vicar to say the blessing. I really don't know if we can delay...'

The tall, mournful figure of the vicar joined the circle. 'Oh dear,' he said, when told of the potential delay, 'how very unfortunate. Everyone's waiting.'

'Lenny won't be long,' Paula chipped in.

'Can you imagine, darling, what sort of shirt he's going to bring back?' murmured Juliet. 'Did you see him? It might be grotesque. You'd be a laughing stock. Why don't I light this wretched bonfire for them?'

Before Oliver could stop her, she turned to the Major with a sweet smile. 'If you're worried about the time, Major, perhaps I could light the bonfire. I know it's not the same, having your MP's wife do it rather than your MP, but...'

Major Tenby didn't hesitate. A huge beam spread across his face. 'My dear lady, I can't tell you what an honour that would be. The perfect solution.'

Jamie was jolted out of his daydream by the

sudden crackle of the loudspeaker. A hush fell and as a voice, distorted to the point of inaudibility, started to pray, one or two of the older citizens bowed their heads. He sneaked a look back at the stall. The youth was still sitting there, but the fat brat had gone; Alison and the other two women were listening to the voice and silently serving at the same time, and the queue, while not letting up in the push to buy their hot-dogs, mimed their orders.

The voice finally droned 'Amen', which was echoed, faintly and self-consciously, by the congregation. Moments later, an excited roar accompanied a *whoosh!* and an explosion of light as a sheet of flame and a million sparking, crackling outriders shot into the sky.

As the bonfire roared up, Lenny arrived back, panting.

'Bastard, they might 'ave waited,' he grumbled, handing the folded shirt to Paula who was standing, chastened, by Oliver's side. 'I was only a couple of minutes.'

'Never mind. Thanks anyway.' Oliver took the proffered shirt with relief. His own felt horrible, the sticky mess seeping through to his chest, cold and clammy, and he was relieved to see the shirt on loan was white and plain, similar to his own.

'Glad to be of service. Now, if you'll excuse me, I'd better get back to the bonfire. I dunno why they couldn't 'ave waited.' And Lenny disappeared into the crowd.

Paula took the stained shirt. 'I'll get this washed for you, Oliver. I'm so sorry, I really am.'

250

Oliver patted her arm, 'Don't worry, Paula, it was an accident.' He looked down at the shirt, puzzled. It was made from good-quality cotton and was large on him. From what he had seen of short, wiry Lenny, this couldn't be his shirt.

At that moment, Isabelle Garnett appeared out of the throng, her arm around her daughter, a pretty little girl with long blonde hair and a solemn face.

'Paula, there you are. I've just seen your mother. She's looking for you and says the children are moaning for their hot-dogs. Oh, hello, Oliver, I thought you were going to light the bonfire?'

Before Oliver could say anything, Paula turned to Isabelle with a wail, 'Oh, Isabelle, you wouldn't believe it. It were all my fault. She's here, and I've blown it – she'll never want me to clean her house – and poor Oliver, I've ruined his evening, and his shirt, and he's been so nice about it an' all and he's even given me the money for some more hot-dogs when he should be suin' me.'

'What are you talking about?' Half amused and half concerned, Isabelle put her arm round Paula.

'We had an accident.' Oliver quickly filled Isabelle in on what had happened. He could see she was trying hard not to laugh and her suppressed amusement started to work on him. 'Now, Paula, go and get those hot-dogs before the fireworks start. I'll bring this shirt back to you tomorrow.'

'Are you going to want me to come on Monday, as usual?' Paula asked, with trepidation.

'Why on earth not? I don't think Juliet would thank me for landing her with a whole load of housework on her return, do you? Don't be daft.'

251

'Thanks, Oliver. You're right, I'd better go – me mum'll be moanin' like anything.' She waved the note clutched in her hand. 'And thanks for this, Oliver. I'll pay you back.'

She turned to Isabelle as she left, 'Oh, Isabelle, I hope you don't mind. I've lent Oliver one of your hubbie's shirts.' And with that she was gone.

Oliver raised his eyebrows quizzically at Isabelle. 'I hope you don't mind.'

Isabelle smiled back. 'Of course not. I'm only glad they were there. I can't imagine what you'd have looked like in one of Lenny's.'

He laughed and shook his head.

'But I'm sorry you've been ousted from the bonfire ceremony. Was that your wife who stood in for you? Has she come back from the States?'

'Yes she came back this morning. I thought she'd collapse with jet-lag, but far from it. You must meet her.'

'I'd like that. Will she be around for a while?'

'A couple of weeks at most, I think. Where's Richard? With your other little girl?' He smiled down at the child who stood with her arm firmly round her mother's waist. 'Hello. It's Becky, isn't it?'

'Yes.' Isabelle stroked her daughter's hair. 'She's finding this all a bit strange. Clemmie's found some friends and is roaring around with them. No, Richard's not here. He's gone to a big firework event in Bath.'

The crowd round the hot-dog stall multiplied as if time, or food, was in short supply. Jamie held back and waited for the numbers to ease. He saw

Paula Spinks, the numb-brain his father employed to clean and iron for them, join the queue and press to the front.

What's she look like? thought Jamie, with disgust. Those stupid boots, and why doesn't she put her boobs away, out of sight? It's gross; Alison would never dress like that.

Suddenly the stall appeared to shut up shop. The last hot-dog was handed over, the money taken, further requests were refused, the covers went swiftly over the food, and just as Jamie thought, Right, okay, let's go, what are you waiting for? a streak of silver light soared up to the stars, then burst, sending an arc of sparkling, fizzing, crackling golden rain to spread out across the heavens. Instantly, the generator was turned off, the stalls were plunged into darkness and, illuminated only by the dancing light of the bonfire, the spectators turned their faces skywards.

Jamie edged closer to where he had seen Alison last, but when he took advantage of a particularly bright illumination to look for her, she'd gone.

'Jamie, I thought you might be here. Hi.' It was a girl's voice behind him. He turned and groaned.

Cordelia Lester, a short mohair roll-neck sweater emphasising the chubbiness of her face and her midriff, stood grinning at him.

Richard reached the VIP entrance to the marquee shortly after seven. The first part of his plan had worked like a dream – no reason for it not to; it was terribly simple. He'd left the office a little earlier than needed to get to the fireworks event and had driven to a small lane on the outskirts of

Bath, beyond the university, where he parked. Going away from the campus, the lane went down a hill and joined the main road some four miles out of Bath. During the day it was used by students, who left their cars and legged it to the university, or by dog walkers on nearby Claverton Down.

Calling a taxi on his mobile, Richard parked his car and walked back towards the university. His plan at the end of the evening was to call a cab, ostensibly to go back to Summerstoke, but he would get the cab to drop him off at the university. Perfect! He wouldn't drink much, of course he wouldn't. But at least it meant he could relax and enjoy himself, and with the day he'd had, by God, he needed to do that.

'Thanks.' He took the glass of champagne offered and looked around for Vee. It was going to be a good evening.

The Summerstoke fireworks display was spectacular but short, to the relief of some and the loud disappointment of others. But the bar resumed its sale of mulled wine and with the bonfire casting its heat and light across the field, many were inclined to linger, drinking and talking, while gangs of kids played tag in the darkness, rushing about shrieking and laughing and getting increasingly muddy.

The Merfields left shortly after the display, Oliver having arranged with Juliet for her and Jamie, who was in an unaccountably filthy mood, to meet him in the bar of the Foresters Arms, the pub in the centre of the village, where they could expect to get a decent meal.

Standing alone with Becky on the edge of the crowd, Isabelle also decided it was time to leave and went in search of Clemmie, who wailed with protest at being taken away from her game, and would have run off if Isabelle hadn't taken tight hold of her wrist. The ground, by now, was extremely muddy and treacherous, and the wriggling, protesting child made progress back to the car slow and exhausting.

Exasperated, she flung the tearful Clemmie into the child's seat, strapped Becky into hers, climbed in, slammed the car into gear and stabbed her foot on the accelerator. The engine whined, the car lurched sideways, the wheels spun. In the headlights she could see mud flying up on either side. She slammed into reverse – much the same effect. Bloody hell! she silently screamed. What now? What now? I thought these fucking four-wheel-drives could cope with anything.

She repeated the process, trying to take it more gently, willing the car to move either forwards or backwards onto firmer ground. All she succeeded in doing was to throw up more mud. She sank her head into her hands. Clemmie's wailing subsided into a whimper and Becky whispered anxiously, 'What's wrong, Mummy? Why can't we move?'

A sharp rapping on the driver's window cut short her moment of despair. She pressed the button and the window descended to reveal the angry, mud-spattered face of Charlie Tucker.

'What the hell do you think you're doing? You've covered me with– Oh no, it's you.'

Up to this point, Charlie had had a good evening.

The bonfire went up like a dream; he'd drunk plenty of his gran's mulled wine; the fireworks caused him no hassle, and he had fixed to meet a pretty brunette at the spontaneous party Lenny was having at his place, as soon as they cleared the field.

In spite of his and Stephen's concerns about cars getting stuck, they all seemed to be moving off pretty freely. Then he heard the angry whine of the Discovery, which had been parked rather closer than he would have advised to the mere, a large, marshy pool at this time of year. He went to check the stuck vehicle, wary of getting accidentally sprayed. From where he stood, it looked bogged down and it seemed the driver had given up trying, so he'd gone in to offer his help when the engine started up again and he caught the full force of the mud spray.

He was furious. And then he found himself looking into the soft blue eyes and tear-stained face of Isabelle whatsername.

'I'm sorry. I'm really sorry. It won't move forwards or backwards. I'm stuck.'

Charlie became aware of the children whimpering in the dark depths of the car as well as the look of despair on her face. He opened the door.

'Move over,' he said curtly. 'Four-wheel-drives aren't fashion accessories, you know, they're not like state-of-the-art saloon cars, and if you took the trouble to learn how to drive one you wouldn't end up in this sort of fix.'

Isabelle who, with gratitude and relief, was about to vacate the driver's seat, froze, then turned on him, stung and angry.

'Get lost. I don't need your help, Charlie Tucker, thank you very much. I'll do it myself. If we have to stay here till the morning, I'll do it without your help. You snooty, smug, arrogant bastard. All right, I'm sorry I covered you with mud, but why don't you piss off, go and have a bath or something, and send me the bill for the soap.'

The image of sending her a bill for his bar of soap tickled Charlie and he softened.

'I'm sorry, Isabelle. You're right. I shouldn't have been so rude. It was the shock of the mud shower. You can stay here all night if you want to, but I think your little girls want to get home, so why don't you move over and let me have a go?'

For a moment, it looked as if Isabelle wasn't going to move.

For such a frail-looking creature, Charlie thought, she's got a will of iron. I wonder what her old man's like. And where is he, I wonder?

Isabelle's intransigence was broken by a sobbed cry from her older daughter. 'Mummy, I want to go home.'

Not looking at him and saying nothing, Isabelle shuffled across to the passenger seat. Without further ado, Charlie swung himself into the driver's seat and, turning on the engine, set about extricating them from the quagmire.

10

Richard let himself out of the house and stood for a minute, shivering, in the porch. Perhaps this wasn't such a good idea. He was a bit hung over and suspected jogging would make it worse. Then the image of his body, naked in front of the bathroom mirror, came to mind. He'd always been proud of his physique and that, although he was now in his late forties, very late forties, he retained a muscular trimness. But he couldn't deny the body reflected in the mirror was starting to lose it; he was developing a paunch. A paunch!

He glanced across at the garage where he'd parked his Jaguar the night before. In his haste to put a distance between himself and his actions, he'd not shut the garage door. At the sight of the car, a mixture of excitement and shame momentarily reddened his face. He hadn't drunk *that* much last night but enough to put him over the limit, and the whole way home he drove with nervous carefulness. But there was very little traffic on the road and certainly no police cars. He'd got away with it.

He zipped up the jacket of his newly acquired, very classy, blue and white tracksuit and was about to set off when his eyes fell on Isabelle's car.

'Bloody hell, what's Issy been up to?'

The Discovery was parked on the far side of the courtyard, the door panels, front wheels, radiator and bonnet so caked with dried mud that the colour of the car was barely discernible.

Richard stared at it with horror. He fussed over and dusted his own car so much that it always gleamed to attention.

'Well, I hope she doesn't expect me to clean it,' he snorted and, with a shrug, turned his attention to the physical exertion ahead.

It was a cool grey morning, a touch of moisture in the air. The ground was damp underfoot and the leaves still clinging to the trees hung limp in their autumnal colours. Soft pink blooms dripped from a straggly rose bush by the gate, the grass on the lawn was bright green and glistening, a vivid red spray of hips straggled across the wall and a platoon of russet chrysanthemums paraded down the drive. Otherwise, in shades of green, gold, yellow and brown, everything was gently decaying.

He set off, the gravel drive crunching under the soles of his pristine, high-tech trainers. He'd worked out his route: at the entrance to the road he planned to turn left, jog a short way down the High Street, then cross the road and go up the small lane that led to the school. Beyond the school, where the lane ended, a footpath went over a number of fields to the river, crossed by a footbridge. Following the river on the other side, he could jog back to Summerstoke Bridge at the end of the High Street. About four miles, he reckoned, which would be a good start.

The High Street was almost deserted.

I suppose with all the shops gone, bar one, he mused, the population bugger off to Bath, or Summerbridge, or Wells on a Saturday morning.

Can't say I blame them. What this place needs is a decent supermarket.

Dodging a large cowpat in the middle of the road, he made for the little lane. Can't be many places left in Britain where the cows walk up the High Street twice a day, he thought. Now, that might make a feature: Cow v. Car. Civil war breaks out in West Country village... He sighed, heavily. That wasn't going to sell many papers. He needed something the nationals would pick up, a really strong story, preferably a good scandal that would run and run and get Head Office off his back.

It wasn't his fault circulation was falling. There just wasn't much hard news in this patch. If his readers wanted to know what was happening in the world, they went to the nationals. His readers were not the young and trendy, and it was no good his bosses insisting, 'Attract them and we win the numbers game.' No, his customers were thirty-upwards who bought the paper to read about themselves and, with any luck, find the dirt being dished on someone they knew, something to feed the gossip over a pint, or bottle of wine – hence the success of his 'name and shame' campaigns.

But, like every newspaper, he was losing readers and with falling circulation the serious advertisers were starting to drop off. The calls from head office were becoming more frequent and more threatening.

He jogged past his daughters' school, a sprawling, single-storey building of unremarkable design but surrounded, on three sides, by a generous-sized playground and playing field.

Another thorn, he thought grumpily. Little

Clemmie was fine, but Becky hadn't settled and Issy was dropping hints about sending her back to her old school in Bath. That's just crazy, he thought. It's a perfectly good school here – she'll settle in time. Anyway, I can't afford it.

He climbed a wooden stile. As he swung his leg over, his hand pressed down on a nettle growing inside the top of the post. The unexpected sting made him swear and his irritability grew, aggravated by the fact that the field, a mixture of stubble and weeds, was slippery, which made it difficult both to maintain his speed and to keep his balance.

Jogging in the city or at the Country Club was an altogether more pleasurable experience, he decided. With jogging machines in the gym, a swim afterwards, then finishing up in the bar ... certainly a lot more convivial than this.

Perhaps the move to Summerstoke had been a mistake. He was fed up with living the way they were at the moment. An electrician was playing havoc with their comfort. The floorboards were up, skirting off, and holes and channels had been carved into the walls, creating no end of dust and mess. He knew it was worse for Issy; he at least could escape to the office and spend every evening out, if he chose to. And the cost. He could see the bills mounting up, and the whole purpose of this exercise had been to realise some capital.

He reached the end of the first field and met another stile. No nettles – good – his hand was still stinging. He swung his legs over. The footpath lay, clearly delineated, across a ploughed field in which little green shoots of a new crop were visible.

Abigail hadn't been able to cope with the confusion of their new circumstances for long. She found fault with every aspect of the house; grumbled about the lack of facilities in the village; upset Issy, which seemed easy to do these days, and then dragged him out to discuss her university plans, which seemed to involve him in advancing her a considerable sum.

He had experienced a strong feeling of relief charged with an uncomfortable dose of guilt when he'd seen her off the following day, and an even greater feeling of release and even more guilt when, a few days later, she phoned to say she'd been accepted on a course at York. And then he felt bad because she *was* his daughter and he shouldn't feel like this about her.

Maybe he should invite her and Danny for Christmas. If only Issy would make more of an effort...

It was an effort crossing the field.

The reddish-brown mud was soft and before he got far the soles of his trainers doubled in size, weighed down by a thick layer the consistency of warm fudge. His attempts to continue at a brisk pace were abandoned as his shoes became heavier and heavier, squishing and squelching as he ran. In the middle of the field, he stopped and looked around for something with which to scrape the mud off. There was nothing. The soil had been well tilled; the green shoots rippled in every direction and the trees and the hedgerow bordering the field were frustratingly far off.

Snarling with frustration, all he could do was

hobble, slipping and sliding, to a stile, just visible in a gap in the high hedge on the far side. By the time he reached it the red mud had oozed right over the tops of his trainers. They were pristine no more.

He sat on the crossbar of the stile and pulled his shoes off, one at a time, poking at the impacted layers of soil on the soles and trying to wipe the uppers clean with handfuls of grass.

'Oh sod it,' he said aloud, and gave up. 'Sod it.'

The stile was damp and he could feel the cold seeping through his tracksuit. His head was starting to throb badly and as he stared around him, at the wide curving sweep of the crop field, at the vast cyclorama of the pearly-grey sky, with white puffy clouds edged with a darker grey and a few patches of powder blue, and at two birds of prey, their wings stiffly outstretched, tips curved, floating high above him, he was overcome by loathing for the countryside and everything in it.

He had, he felt, moved here with the best of intentions, but he was being asked to pay too high a price. The country was not for him. Issy, he was sure, would go back to Bath like a shot, so would Becky. But he couldn't afford it. He simply couldn't afford it! And he knew he couldn't expect much of a salary increase this winter, let alone a bonus.

He stood up with a groan. There was no way he could admit to Issy, to anyone, he'd made a mistake. He'd have to find ways of living with it, of making life more tolerable. He turned and climbed the stile into the next field, which stretched green and inviting in front of him, sloping away off in the distance down a hill. He managed to wipe considerably more mud off on the damp grass, and his spirits rose as he set off at a decent pace.

As he jogged, his head cleared. He couldn't move the family back to Bath but he could, in the pursuit of his work, quite justifiably set up an independent life-style during the week and come home at weekends. He and Issy didn't have much of a life together during the week, anyway. He left so much earlier and got back so much later, too tired to talk, or do anything but eat, drink, and go to sleep. They hardly shagged these days, either. In fact, he couldn't remember the last time he'd really fancied it.

When had they last made love? Gloomily, Richard started to count back the days. It must have been just before Vee's drinks party, when Issy made an idiot of herself over that Merfield creep.

That shook him. She used to look at him that way; he'd not seen her so alive for years. Issy never flirted and never, until he saw her with bloody Oliver Merfield, had he once doubted her. Perhaps he'd become complacent – it had certainly jolted him that night and then, the night after, when he caught them together in his headlights. He didn't really believe anything was going on, but...

They had a humdinger of a row, but even when he'd finally apologised they still hadn't had sex. That was three weeks ago! Bloody hell, when they'd first got together, it was two, three times a day! What had happened? Why hadn't he noticed before? Was his libido fading? For Christ's sake, he wasn't really middle-aged, yet – these days, late forties wasn't middle-aged...

Yes, if he came home just for weekends, it would be quality time; they might start enjoying each other again. If he didn't do something, Issy really might start looking elsewhere.

The slope in the field became more accentuated and Richard's stride increased.

When was the last time he'd had an affair? Flaming Norah, it was four, five years ago, when Issy was pregnant with Clemmie. Was he losing it?

A treacherous curve in the slope caught him unawares. His heel hit a ridge, his legs slid from under him and he crashed down full length on the grass, his weight sending up a muddy spray. He lay there, winded and hurting. Slowly, he sat up; his tracksuit was muddy and saturated; he felt bruised and shaken.

He'd had enough – there was no pleasure in this. He got stiffly to his feet and considered his options. Below, he could see the thin grey thread of the river. It was quicker to go on than climb back up the hill and retrace his steps, but he abandoned the idea of jogging the rest of the way and cautiously limped down the slope towards the footbridge.

The lower reaches of the meadow were smothered with a riot of bramble bushes, the leaves withered on the boughs, the berries black and shrivelled; molehills, some freshly dug, some long since grassed over, covered the ground, causing him to slow his pace even further – it would be just his luck to trip over one of the blasted things and sprain his ankle. Following the muddy footpath, which was running with water, he pushed his way through two large bushes, ducking under the long dangling sprays that attempted to grab his clothing, his hair, his flesh.

The footbridge had been designed to accommodate stock as well as humans and, judging from the state of the ground on his side of the river, a herd of cattle had made a good show of trampling any evidence of grass. From the edge of the bushes to the bridge, a matter of some four metres, the riverbank was a complete quagmire.

Richard stared, aghast, then at the top of his voice gave vent to every expletive in his vocabulary. It made him feel a bit better, but didn't improve his situation. He whimpered, then, sighing deeply, he took as long a stride as he could.

His feet sank deep into the gloop and it was with great difficulty that he extricated himself without falling over or losing his shoes. He took a smaller step and again sank into a morass of mud, water and ordure. Gritting his teeth, he took another step and another, feeling the mire oozing through his toes. When he reached the firmer surface of the bridge, he stopped and looked down. Below his knees, his tracksuit and trainers were invisible under a lumpy brown coating of slime.

Richard rarely cried, but for a moment tears of self-pity started to his eyes. It was so unfair, it shouldn't have been like this. Why him? Why him? And then he started to rage: sodding cows, sodding farmers, sodding countryside – if he had his way, he'd concrete the bloody lot!

He crossed the bridge, every squelching footstep adding further insult to his injured pride, and took the narrow, muddy footpath alongside the river back towards Summerstoke.

Juliet walked briskly down the High Street, savouring the air, the smells, the sounds and the look of Summerstoke itself. It couldn't be more different from Los Angeles.

At first she'd been overwhelmed by the city. It was a cliché, but everything was so big – the buildings, the cars, the hotels, the restaurants, the portions of food, the sandwiches, the people, their personalities, their voices, their smiles ... everything. She'd felt like a little girl in more ways than one. If she'd only been there for the one week of the audition, she would've come away with the impression that Hollywood was the most magical place on earth. But as time went by, she started to grow tired of the unrelenting excitement, of the pace of life it set, which seemed to insist all who flocked there must dance to its tune, no matter how facile or tawdry. Tinsel Town, La La Land – it was well named. Juliet had come to realise everyone she encountered was involved in the same conspiracy: that what they were doing, and where they were doing it was the envy of the rest of the world.

Just how homesick she became she couldn't share with anyone, not even Ollie, because to admit to it would be to admit the dream had let her down. Far from partying all the time, she declined most of her invitations because in the company of her co-conspirators she found herself feeling lonelier than she did back in her hotel watching British imports on television. She made no close friends, contrary to what she told

Oliver, and her leading man was a nightmare who terrified her with his superficial charm and his cold, obdurate rages when things didn't go to plan, his plan.

So she'd been glad to seize this chance of a break. To bask, for a brief while, in the comfort of Ollie and Jamie's love; to get her fix of England. She had to admit she'd never have thought she'd look at Summerstoke this way – as a place where it was nice to be.

As she walked down the High Street towards the river, she found herself, for the first time, admiring its long, narrow main street, bordered on either side by cottages and houses all built of the same honey-coloured stone, nothing above three storeys, all with slate roofs. Everything visible was more than a hundred years old and anything built more recently was tucked, with becoming modesty, out of sight.

She felt great surges of nostalgia as she passed St Stephen's, the Foresters Arms, the village shop. Nothing like this existed in California, except as a crude reconstruction of Olde England on a studio set.

She smiled wryly. She used to hate coming here. It had too many associations with Oliver's family, and the village had regarded her as an intruder – not good enough for the son of Sir Nicholas Merfield. She knew they all thought she'd got herself pregnant so she could entrap him. Her? How absurd!

She'd shown them. She'd refused to marry Oliver until she was ready, and everyone was forced to accept they'd got it wrong – it was Ollie who wanted *her* and she was something worth having... Being a television star, with the adulation it brought, was fun, but if LA worked out she really would be someone; she'd eclipse them all.

There weren't many people about, but she had the satisfaction of knowing those who were turned to look and admire. Her red-gold curls, brushed back into a ponytail, leaving a soft fringe framing her face; and the angora roll-necked sweater, the chunky cream cord jacket, close-fitting jeans and cream leather ankle boots made her look as if she'd stepped out of the fashion pages of *Country House and Gardens*.

Oliver had left early that morning, in spite of it being a Saturday, to catch up on missed appointments and would be gone most of the day. He'd urged her to stay in bed for as long as possible, but after he'd gone she couldn't sleep.

Finally, she got up, wandered round the house, giving it a really close inspection, and then went to wake Jamie. He responded with a grunt, rolled over, and seconds later was fast asleep again. She wondered whether to be more forceful. She wanted to spend some time with him – he hadn't been very communicative last night and there was a discernible change in him in the six weeks or so she'd been away. But Jamie, in the morning, was never much fun, so she decided to go for a brisk walk; get some much-needed fresh air and reintroduce herself to Summerstoke.

Having reached the bottom of the village, she crossed the bridge, planning to walk for a way along the river. Climbing the stile into the field, she could see a small lake of pale grey powder, the residue of the huge bonfire, being raked over by two men. A group of children rushed about, hunting for the charred remains of the fireworks, shouting with triumph every time another was found. She wandered over to have a look at the remains of the fire. Its centre still glowed red-hot but all that remained of that mountain of wood and rubbish was twisted bits of metal and an expanse of silky ash.

One of the men looked up as she approached, and she recognised him as the one with the ponytail who'd offered to lend Ollie a shirt the night before. He grinned broadly at her, displaying a wide gap where his front teeth should have been, nudged his friend and nodded. 'How do, missus.'

She smiled faintly back. His friend looked up and stopped raking. He was much taller and younger than Ponytail and by anybody's standards, thought Juliet, he was rather yummy. His face was lean and tanned, with a strong thin nose and chin; his eyes danced when he smiled at her, and even though he was shrouded in overalls she could tell he had the sort of body many aspiring actors in Hollywood would die for.

'Good morning. Enjoy the fireworks, last night?' His voice was pleasant and strong, with a slight West Country burr.

'Yes, thanks.' She smiled back at him. 'The fireworks were very impressive, but I liked the bonfire more. It was huge.'

'It was – the biggest yet. Me and Lenny, here, spent weeks building it. And you can see, eighteen hours later, there's still fire in the centre. Years past, the locals would've brought out potatoes or apples to bake in the ashes.'

'Why don't they any more?'

He shrugged and grinned, unconcerned. 'Times change. Folks are as likely to be eating frozen pizza for lunch. It's quicker than bringing potatoes out here to bake. Isn't that right, Lenny?'

'Too right, it is. Give me a pepperoni over a baked potato any day, that's what I say.'

'Still, it's a shame when old customs die out.'

'Some, maybe, but not all. At least we don't duck women for gossiping any more, and we got rid of the stocks – although you might think that's a sad loss, given the way some of the kids behave when they've had a skinful.'

'Not just the kids, Charlie,' sniggered Ponytail.

'True enough,' he laughed. 'I might've spent more time in them than out over the last ten years.' He looked at Juliet. 'If you're planning on walking along the river, it's passable but pretty muddy. Don't go over the footbridge, though. My brother's had his cows up there and the meadow's a quagmire.'

'Thanks.' She wrinkled her brow and dimpled at him. 'I didn't quite catch your name. Charlie...?'

'Charlie Tucker. And this is Lenny Spinks.'

'Pleased to meet yer, Juliet. My missus does for your old man.'

'Oh ... er, good.' There didn't seem anything else to say and, although Lenny seemed content to stand grinning at her, Charlie clearly considered the conversation at an end and turned his attention back to the bonfire.

She made as if to go, then stopped to enquire, 'Is the Foresters Arms the only pub in the village?'

271

Charlie nodded. 'Yeah.'

'Then maybe I shall see you in there?' Juliet tried to keep her remark as casual as she could, sneering at herself for asking the question at all – she'd no idea why she should want to flirt with a country bumpkin.

'Unlikely,' Charlie replied affably. 'They prefer me to take my custom elsewhere. We drink at the Bunch of Grapes, on the crossroads about a couple of miles down the road. It's a nice pub; you should try it.'

'Oh,' said Juliet, storing the information. 'Well, thanks for last night.' She turned and strode purposefully off in the direction of the footpath, her pulse rate faster than it had been ten minutes earlier.

He was right about the footpath. It wasn't too bad to begin with, running along a raised bit of the bank between the river and the pond, but when the ground levelled off the path became increasingly sticky and slippery, and the soles of her nice leather boots had no grip. Disappointed, she stopped, and as she looked further along the path, to see if there was any hope of improvement, the figure of a man appeared round a dense bramble bush fringing the route.

He looked as surprised to see her as she was to see him. He was tall and well-built, dressed in a tracksuit smeared with mud all down one side from shoulder to thigh, and both legs from the knee down were thickly caked. He had an interesting face, but it was marred by a scowl, and on first seeing him Juliet thought how very fierce he seemed.

'My goodness,' she exclaimed, 'How very muddy you are. Perhaps a walk along the river isn't such a good idea.'

His face cleared and he gave a short laugh. 'Not if you don't want to end up like me. I should have come jogging in my swimsuit or, better still, stuck to the gym.' He paused and looked at her more closely. 'You're Juliet Peters, aren't you?'

Flattered, but slightly taken aback by the directness of his tone, she chuckled deprecatingly. 'Well, yes. But you don't look like the sort of person to watch *Hunter's Way* and the other rubbish I've done.' And he didn't. His eyes were intelligent and shrewd and there was a restless vigour about him that belied the silver shot in his crop of black hair.

'No, you're right, I don't. But I've seen your photo. I edit a newspaper. You're a lot prettier than your picture.'

'Thank you.' She liked the way he said it, so matter-of-factly.

'I didn't realise you were back in the village. My spies have let me down – I thought you were stuck in Hollywood.'

'Your spies?'

He smiled at her, relaxing a little. 'Local newspapers depend on their grass-roots informants. We don't want the nationals to snatch up anything on our patch before us. Are you walking back, or are you going on?'

Juliet eyed the filthy state of his clothing. 'I think I've had enough fresh air for one day.'

'Then I'll walk back with you, if I may. My name's Richard, by the way, Richard Garnett, and before you say anything, yes, I was the brute who stole your house from under your noses, for which I most humbly apologise.'

She dimpled. 'As it happens, I'm quite glad we didn't buy anywhere. There's plenty of room for us in the doctor's house and with my plans so fluid at the moment– Oops!'

She skidded on the mud and would have gone over if Richard hadn't grabbed her.

'You better hold onto my arm or you'll end up the same way as I did, flat on your back. Here, take my non-muddy side.'

Gratefully, she took his arm and the two of them cautiously skated their way back along the path to the stile. Juliet threw a glance at the bonfire, but there was no sign of Charlie Tucker, only Ponytail throwing clods of earth onto the embers and shouting at the children.

'Were you at the bonfire last night? I didn't see you?'

'No. I had to go to one in Bath – formal invitation, and not easy to back out of. Was it any good?'

They climbed the stile and made their way over the bridge.

Juliet wrinkled her nose. 'It was quite sweet and atmospheric, I suppose, but the fireworks were rather puny.'

'Everything about this village must seem like that after Los Angeles.'

She laughed. 'Well, actually, before I bumped into you, I was drawing quite favourable comparisons between Summerstoke and LA. Have you ever been there?'

274

'A couple of times, once as a student and once on an assignment for my paper.'

'For a local paper?'

'I didn't always work for regional newspapers.' He sounded a little put out. 'My first job was on the *Express* and I'd worked my way up through the *Mail* when I was offered this editorship. I like being the boss, a big fish in a small pond, if you like. How about you?'

'Me?'

'Yeah. Big fish in small pond here in the village, or small fish in big pond in Hollywood?'

It was her turn to be put out. 'I've just completed a pilot for a new series for American television. If that's successful, I won't be a small fish.'

'Will you continue to live here, in Summerstoke?'

'My family's here, so I shall alternate between here and the States.'

He grinned. 'At last, an alternative to Jane Seymour.'

'What?'

'You probably don't know, but for years, the only film star we've had living in the orbit of my paper has been Jane Seymour. She owns a mansion on the other side of Bath and my readers have their tongues hanging out on the rare, very rare, occasions she's in occupation.'

'But she's ancient!'

'Beggars can't be choosers; she's all we've got. That is, until you came along.' He grinned even more. 'It would suit me very nicely, Juliet, if you could make sure your programme is a soar-away success.'

Juliet grinned. 'I'll do my best, believe me.'

They got as far as the shop when the vigorous clanging of the shop doorbell interrupted their conversation. A woman in her early fifties, thin, wearing tartan trousers, a purple sweater and large, tinted spectacles, rushed out. Juliet thought she recognised her from the previous evening.

'Ha, two birds with one stone,' she exclaimed. 'I've been looking out for you. I need your help.' She corrected herself. '*We* need your help – the village, that is. I said to Rob – that's my husband, only you don't see him in the shop too often 'cos his back's bad – not that I've seen either of you in the shop, although, of course, Miss Peters, that's hardly surprising since you only got here yesterday morning, from Hollywood, I'm told, and you, Mr Garnett, working all hours God sent, you're never here, are you? But I've met your wife, of course, and I was going to ask her to ask you, although Elsie said she already had, but seeing you both walk by, I thought I'd seize the moment, make hay while the sun shines, as they say.'

She paused for breath and before they could say anything more than, in Juliet's case: 'Me?' and in Richard's: 'How can I help you?', she continued, 'What I said to Rob is, we're luckier than most – villages, that is – we've got an MP, a TV star, and a newspaper editor. People listen to you; you've got clout; you can make them change their minds.'

'About what? Mrs er...?' While he was polite, there was no warmth in Richard's voice and Juliet guessed he was accustomed to being accosted in this way.

'Godwin, Rita Godwin. I run the shop and post

office, and it's the post office I need your help with. Your wife must have told you, Mr Garnett, they're closing it down.'

'She might have mentioned it.' Richard's tone was not encouraging. 'But I'm scarcely home at the moment. Are you sure they're closing it? I understood there was a commitment to back successful rural post offices?'

'Yes, but they want to close the sorting office at the back. It's the thin end of the wedge, Mr Garnett. If they close that, I lose a vital part of my income – I'm not sure I'd be able to keep going, and if I sell who's going to take over just the counters part? It's a lot of training and work for not very much return, believe me.'

'I see. Well, I'm not sure...' Richard sighed. The last thing he wanted was to become entangled in a boring, teacup-sized storm.

'Hasn't Oliver, my husband, been to see you?' interjected Juliet, smoothly. 'He's just the sort of person you need to get involved and I'm sure you'd find him very helpful.'

'Yes, he has, some time ago, before all this broke. We need to speak to him again, but in the meantime, seeing as you're back in the village, we was wondering whether we could use you for our campaign.'

'How?'

'Well, as a sort of figurehead – people will look at us twice if we've got someone like you with us. Beauty draws with a single hair, as they say.'

Bemused, Richard and Juliet stared at her.

Undeterred, she carried on. 'Then we could get Mr Garnett here to publish your picture – you

277

could be posting a letter outside the shop and SOPO could be standing in the background holding placards and waving our petition.'

'SOPO?' Juliet enquired faintly.

'It's the action committee we've formed: Save Our Post Office – SOPO.'

Juliet laughed. 'Well, I'm game. Richard?'

'With you in the frame, Juliet, it'll be a pleasure. I'll organise a photographer.'

'It will have to be soon, though. I'm only here for two weeks.'

'Fine. I'll give you a ring to fix a convenient time, and then, Mrs ... er ... Godwin, you can get your band of merry men together.'

Rita looked delighted. 'Thank you. I thought I'd be able to rely on you – people move to this village because they value the quality of life here, but it's not something we can take for granted.'

A tall, grey figure, heading for the shop, interrupted her flow. 'Morning, Vicar, I'll be right with you.'

'No hurry, Mrs Godwin, no hurry at all,' murmured the grey gentleman, nodding politely at Juliet and Richard.

'I'll wait to hear from you then, Mr Garnett. And Juliet, perhaps you'd tell Oliver I need his help? 'Scuse me.' And she whisked back into the shop, the door pinging loudly behind her.

'That's why villages need their village shop,' remarked Richard, wryly. 'They're the principal conduits of all information. Without them, one end of the village wouldn't know the business of the other end. She's probably pumping the vicar now for any little titbits.'

'You can't grumble,' replied Juliet lightly. 'You've just been handed a story.'

'Very true. Would you mind if I sent a reporter as well as a photographer? We could do a Juliet Peters profile – newcomer to village life, that sort of thing.'

'No, I don't mind.'

'Well,' he said, as they reached the gate to the Old Vicarage, 'this is where I leave you.'

She dimpled and held out her hand. 'It's been fun meeting you, Richard.'

'Yes,' he said, realising the foul humour he'd been in half an hour ago had completely evaporated. 'It's been fun.'

He walked slowly up his drive, reliving and relishing his encounter with Juliet. She really was something. With her around, life in Summerstoke suddenly seemed a better proposition. He hadn't felt so ... so stimulated for ages. Pity she was likely to be gobbled up by Hollywood but, unlike the shop, that would make good copy. In the meantime, he wouldn't mind seeing her again.

11

Isabelle stood back from the wall and critically surveyed her handiwork. She'd already spent far too long on the girls' mural, but until the electricians finished downstairs she couldn't make a start on redecorating the house.

It surprised her Richard hadn't made more of a

fuss when she suggested doing it herself – he was normally so meticulous; she'd expected him to hire the decorators Veronica Lester recommended and follow the colour schemes she'd proposed, using of course only the very best materials available.

At his request, Isabelle had sat down and costed out Veronica's suggestions. The figure made her gasp, and when she presented it to Richard she'd seen his eyes widen with shock. So she'd suggested getting in local help to plaster and prepare the walls and woodwork, and she should do the painting. Apart from insisting she consult him over the colours, he'd agreed.

'It's going to be a major task, darling, and if you feel you've bitten off more than you can chew, we can get someone in to help you. Maybe,' he'd said, looking at her thoughtfully, 'it will give you the feel for painting again.'

She flushed angrily as she remembered that remark. What did *he* know about her feel for painting? What a trite, insensitive comment. But she was looking forward to losing herself in the mindless process of roller-painting the walls and the hard physical labour the transformation of the house would involve. It would give her a purpose, something she desperately needed.

A local builder called, set the electrician to work and agreed to supply a plasterer, and Lenny was going to give her a hand with the papering. Isabelle was relieved Richard's long hours meant he was out of the house before the workmen started and couldn't criticise or query her choice of labour.

She picked up a brush and dipped it into a blob of cobalt blue. At the girls' request, there were now three princesses in this mural, one for each of them. Becky's, in pink, was in the highest tower of the castle, looking down, Rapunzel-like, at the handsome prince on his white horse poised on the edge of a chasm. Clemmie's silver princess sat astride a flying horse chasing the stars, and Isabelle's in blue, was sitting at the edge of a lake, one foot dipped into the water.

Every time Paula came to clean, she slipped upstairs to see how the painting had developed and went into ecstasies over Isabelle's handiwork. Isabelle hadn't the heart to tell her she was bored with the whole thing and couldn't wait to finish it.

She dabbed on the paint, cocked her head on one side and decided that she couldn't bear to do any more today. It's like eating a whole box of Maltesers when you're starving, she thought with a deep sigh, taking the brushes downstairs to wash through.

The electrician was sat at the kitchen table and his mate had his nose in the fridge.

'Oh, hello, Isabelle,' said the electrician, Reg Tandy. 'We was just gonna make a cuppa. Curt's lookin' for the milk.'

He was a big, square man, his trousers held in place below his belly by a tight leather belt. He was in his mid-forties, with a heavy, plain face, a thick, unruly shock of greying brown hair, and mild blue eyes behind tortoiseshell-framed glasses. He was very garrulous, with a strong West Country accent.

His mate, by contrast, was barely out of his

teens, tall, thin and pale, and smothered in acne; his hair was cut very short, his ears, nose, and lip pierced. He, too, had a thick local accent, but as he rarely spoke, interpreting what he said wasn't such a problem for Isabelle.

'There ain't none,' he said, straightening up and looking at her accusingly.

Isabelle wasn't surprised. They seemed to drink vast quantities of tea. When they first started she'd offered to make them a cup mid-morning, after lunch, and mid-afternoon, but that clearly wasn't enough and after a while she grew tired of being enslaved to their thirst and told them to help themselves.

She glanced at her watch. It was after midday. Somehow they had worked their way through the two pints delivered that morning.

'I'm sorry, I thought there was enough for the day. If you can hang on, I'll get some more from the shop – I need to post something, anyway.'

'That's very nice of you, my lovely. Ta. Thirsty work, this wirin'. But we've nearly finished, you'll be pleased to hear. I've given Bill a buzz this mornin' to tell him front two rooms is ready for plasterin'. You should 'ave them ready for your Christmas party.'

Isabelle understood him enough to throw him a grateful smile as she rinsed her brushes. 'Thanks, Reg. What about the kitchen? Are you nearly done here?'

'Not much longer. It were a problem with the two systems you've got, see. Over the years they was added to, nothin' taken out. Your house should be put into the museum of wirin', if there were such a place.' And he went off into a wheezy laugh before describing in minute detail, as he had done on many other occasions, why the wiring of the Old Vicarage was such a mess, and how lucky she was she had someone with his knowledge and experience to sort it all out and hadn't relied on some fly-by-night smart-arse electrician from the city.

At a pause for breath, she managed to say, 'I must go and get the milk for your tea before the shop shuts,' grab her coat and the letter to Joe, ready for posting, and flee.

After the cool dampness of the weekend, the weather had turned cold and frosty. The tops of the trees, just touched by the sun, had thawed and were glistening with damp, but the lower branches, the shrubs and the ground, were still frozen and white. She shivered, wrapping her coat more closely around her and hurried down the High Street.

Although the action committee had met only once, Isabelle no longer felt on the outside of village life looking in. In hindsight, she realised that what she thought were suspicious stares was simple curiosity. She'd come to like the idiosyncratic nature of the shop, and liked Rita, who called her Isabelle and greeted her with easy familiarity and included her in any conversation going.

She'd ventured to discuss the shop with Richard but he laughed at her for being on the committee, and when she asked if Veronica had ever mentioned anything about rats, he shook his head and said she was mad if she thought Vee would ever talk about anything so mundane.

The shop door pinged loudly, momentarily distracting the only customer inside and Isabelle caught a glimpse of a lovely, heart-shaped face, huge intensely blue eyes ('cobalt blue', thought Isabelle) and an abundance of copper-red curls dancing on her shoulders before she turned back to the shopkeeper.

It wasn't Rita but her husband, Rob. He was wearing his habitual cross frown and the atmosphere in the shop was as frosty as the ground outside. On the counter were two carrier bags of groceries and the up-turned contents of the woman's bag.

'It's no good,' she said, in a beautiful low, sweet voice that trembled for sympathy, 'I can't find it. I must have left it in my other bag, at home.'

Rob Godwin snorted unsympathetically.

'I'm terribly sorry, but...'

'So you'll not be wanting these things, then?'

'Oh, yes, I need them – I've got someone coming for lunch.'

'If you can't pay for them, they stay here.'

'But can't you let me owe you? You know where I live, you know who I am – I'm hardly likely to abscond without paying for them.'

'I'm sorry, missus.' Rob didn't sound in the least bit sorry. He pointed to a sign on the counter that read, 'Do not ask for credit as a refusal often offends'.

'If we start making exceptions, everyone will expect it.'

'Oh, for goodness' sake!' The plaintive note had gone from the voice. 'I'll leave them here and go and get my purse.'

'You'll have to hurry, then.' Isabelle could have sworn there was the hint of a smirk on Rob's face. 'We close for lunch in ten minutes.'

'What? Can't you wait for me to get back?'

Isabelle coughed politely. 'Excuse me, can I help?'

The woman swung round and Isabelle caught the full measure of her beauty. Swallowing a little nervously, she continued, 'I don't mean to be nosy, but you're Oliver Merfield's wife, aren't you? Only I've met him a number of times and if I can help out, I'd be pleased to. Why don't you let me lend you what's owing, then Mr Godwin can go and have his lunch? You can pay me back later.'

For a moment Isabelle felt she was being critically appraised, then Juliet dimpled with gratitude. 'Would you? Thank you so much. Yes, I'm Oliver's wife, Juliet Peters.'

'Pleased to meet you. I'm Isabelle Garnett.'

'Garnett? Oh, are you married to Richard, the editor?'

'Yes.' Isabelle was puzzled. Why should Juliet Peters know Richard – unless Oliver had mentioned him? But to her knowledge, the two men hadn't met since the Lesters' party. 'Do you know him?'

Juliet laughed. 'I met him on Saturday, returning from his jog, very muddy!'

Rob Godwin was growing impatient and cut across any further conversation. ''Scuse me, ladies, are you going to pay for these now, or am I going to put them back on the shelf?'

Isabelle hastily settled Juliet's bill, handed over Joe's letter and purchased some milk, and the

285

two women left the shop. No sooner had they done so than the key was turned in the lock behind them, the Closed sign went up, and the blue blind was pulled down.

Juliet gave vent to her indignation. 'What a horrid man! I can't believe I've offered to help their campaign. Would you believe they're expecting me to turn up for a press call tomorrow, outside the ruddy shop? It would serve them right if I found I had another engagement.'

'Oh, please don't. The post office is very important to the village. He's not often behind the counter, and his wife, Rita, is lovely. She says his bad back makes him bad-tempered.'

'Even so...'

'I haven't been here very long, I admit, but I've come to realise just how much Mrs Godwin does for the village, particularly for the older folk and for the young mums. She works so hard, but she always makes time to listen to people's problems and grumbles, and she's a real mine of information.'

'The village gossip-shop,' Juliet laughed, not really interested in the shop or Mrs Godwin and her good works. 'Don't worry, I'll do the honours. Richard phoned this morning to say a photographer and a reporter will be here tomorrow, so you can come and wave your supporter's flag then.'

Isabelle made no reply. She wasn't sure she altogether liked Juliet Peters, and she felt uncomfortable about the easy way Juliet bandied Richard's name. And why hadn't Richard told her he'd met her?

Juliet must have sensed Isabelle's lack of approval, for before they got very far she turned, with a winning smile. 'I'm very grateful to you for rescuing me, Isabelle, and I'm really pleased to meet you. We newcomers to the village must stand together – for all its apparent niceness, it's a very close-knit community and though they'll be polite, they don't make strangers welcome.'

A touch dramatic, thought Isabelle, and she asked, curiously, 'You're not really a stranger though, Juliet, are you? Your husband's family...'

Juliet tossed her head. 'When I was young and first came here with Oliver, I was treated like something that had crawled out of the woodwork.'

They had drawn parallel with the old doctor's house. Juliet put out a hand.

'Look, Isabelle, I don't know how busy you are, but please, come and have lunch with me and then I can pay you back what I owe and we can have a chat. I don't really know anyone else in the village, except Oliver's ghastly relatives. It would be nice to have a proper conversation with someone and not have to rely on the Wooden-Top Oliver's employed to do the cleaning, for my only human contact. Ollie's in London all week and Jamie, my son, is at school.'

Isabelle hesitated. She wasn't sure why, except Juliet's description of Paula made her wince. She suspected a little of Juliet's company would go a long way. But maybe she was being unfair and, after all, what exciting prospects did the afternoon hold for her? More incomprehensible conversations with Reg and Curt?

'I thought you had visitors for lunch? Surely

you don't want me as well?'

'Actually,' said Juliet candidly, 'you'd be doing me a favour, so please say yes. He's a friend of my husband's. He phoned this morning, expecting Oliver to be here – he sounded quite surprised that the MP for Mendip has to be in the House of Commons during the week. But he said he has business in Summerstoke this morning, so I invited him to lunch. I can't imagine what on earth he's doing here. As far as I know, he lives and works in London.' She looked at Isabelle pleadingly. 'I really don't know him very well – please come.'

Isabelle capitulated. 'Thank you. If you're sure? I'll just deliver this milk to my workmen – they can't function without tea – and I'll come straight over. Would you like me to bring anything? Have you got enough?'

Juliet laughed. 'I've just emptied the shop – I've got plenty. See you in a minute.'

The doctor's house was a lot smaller than the old Vicarage, but it was comfortable and warm, with pictures on the walls, rugs on the floors, heavy curtains at the windows, flowers in vases, big squashy sofas in the sitting room, and a dining room complete with polished table, matching chairs and deep red Persian carpet. At the back of the house, overlooking the garden, the kitchen was bright and welcoming in spite of its old-fashioned appearance. The house was comfortable and at ease with itself in every way the Old Vicarage wasn't.

Juliet pulled a shopping bag off a chair. 'Here, have a seat. I thought we'd eat in the kitchen. It's a bit formal in the dining room.'

'If you say so. I think it's all really nice.'

'Not bad for rented accommodation. This old gas cooker's long due for renewal, though, and there's no dishwasher. I've had to invest in Marigolds.' She grinned and Isabelle warmed to her. 'What's the Old Vicarage like? And before you start apologising for having whipped it from under our noses, don't. As I told Richard, you did me a favour. I didn't want to be lumbered with a house in Summerstoke. This suits us perfectly, particularly as I don't expect to be here very much.'

'It all looks so comfortable – not temporary at all.'

'That's Ollie, he's a natural home-maker. Most of the furniture he's bought from old junk shops, auctions, or street markets.'

'He's got a good eye,' said Isabelle, admiring the scrubbed oak table and assorted wooden chairs tucked around it.

'Yes, thank goodness. If it was up to me, we'd be sitting on tea-chests, eating off our laps and living out of suitcases. What about you, are you a home-maker?'

Isabelle wrinkled her brow thoughtfully. 'That's a good question. When I married Richard, I moved into his house; everything was in place. He didn't need me, or indeed want me, to do anything to it and I didn't mind, I wasn't bothered. Since we've moved here, it's like' – she picked her words carefully –'he's taking more of a back seat. He's very busy, of course, and has very little time, so I'm having to be more ... do more, whether I like it or not, which is good for me.' She shook her head reprovingly. 'The house is lovely. It's a real

289

mess at the moment, but when it's all finished it'll be great. You must come over.'

'I'd love to, if I'm here. Look, would you mind laying the table while I heat the soup? We've got bread, pâté and cheese. There are some tomatoes in this bag and I bought a lettuce that'll need washing, I suppose. You don't mind tinned soup, do you?' She held up a can and read, 'Cullen Skink, only the finest natural ingredients. Serving suggestion: heat through and add cream to taste.' She laughed. 'How inspiring! If Ollie was here, he'd be whipping up a cheese omelette or something – he's a good cook. Are you?'

Isabelle smiled. 'No. I can just about handle roast chicken, and spag bol, which is all the girls seem to eat. When we lived in Bath and people came to dinner, I'd cheat and get someone to do the cooking for us. I'm dreading the moment when he considers the house finished enough for us to invite people over.'

'You ought to do what a friend of mine did once, with all these posh people to dinner. He gave them an elaborate starter, then put on his coat, went out and bought everyone fish and chips from the local chippy.'

The doorbell sounded over their laughter and Juliet went to greet her guest. Moments later she returned, ushering in a tall, thin, slightly stooped man some twenty years older than either her or Juliet.

'Milo, this is my new friend, Isabelle Garnett. Our two families moved into the village at the same time. Isabelle, this is Milo Steel.'

Isabelle found her hand taken in a firm grip

and looked up at a pair of fierce blue eyes in a cadaverous face topped with an unruly mop of greying brown hair.

'Milo Steel?' Her voice was shaky. 'Milo Steel, the painter?'

The track down to Marsh Farm was long, narrow and very rough. Isabelle's Discovery lurched from pothole to pothole, like a small boat in a rough sea. She felt sick, but not because of the lurching of the vehicle: she was sick with excitement and nervousness. She had hardly slept since she'd met Milo Steel.

His father had been a giant in the art world until his death in the 1970s. Both he and his son, Milo, had studied at the college where, years later, she became a student. Milo had gone on to make a name painting the most extraordinary and dramatic canvases, influencing her and many students of her generation. It was Milo who had awarded her the Steel Prize for the year's most promising graduate.

He hadn't recognised her. That wasn't surprising, she supposed. What hurt was the way he looked at her closely, then turned to concentrate on Juliet, a baffled and disappointed look on his face. It came as a surprise, therefore, when he rang her three days later and invited her to give him a hand organising his temporary studio at Marsh Farm.

She was overwhelmed. She couldn't think of anything she'd rather do. It meant, of course, she'd have to brave another encounter with Charlie Tucker, but more daunting than that, considerably more daunting, was the fear Milo would question her about her work.

Isabelle breathed in deeply and shifted down a gear as she hit another hole, deeper and wider than the last, and put on the wipers to clear the soft drizzle intermittently blurring the windscreen. What sort of farmers were these Tuckers who couldn't even maintain their drive decently?

The track, which had been running parallel with the river, curved inland and rose slightly. Ahead was a gracious but shabby old house, surrounded by a clutter of farm buildings in varying states of decay and repair. She drove through a broken gate and into the yard, pulling round to the left, as Milo had instructed, and drawing up in front of a long, low stone barn which, from its new roof, windows and doors, had recently been converted. A battered old Volvo was parked alongside and as she turned off her ignition Milo appeared at the door and waved.

'Thanks for coming,' he said, leading her into the workshop. 'I need help to get this space organised as quickly as possible. As I mentioned on Monday, I've an exhibition in March and having to move out of my studio has set me back. It was a bit of luck meeting you. You'll know how to shift and store canvases, mix paint and clean brushes, and when not to talk. I can't pay much, I'm afraid, but I can stretch to five pounds an hour.'

She stared at him in amazement. He'd already turned his back on her and was starting to cut the bubble wrap on an outsize package.

'You want me to work for you?' she blurted.

He looked up in mild surprise. 'Why do you

think I called you? I need you. Don't say you can't do it. It doesn't have to be all day, every day – I couldn't afford that, and anyway you'll have your own work to do.'

'Yes,' said Isabelle faintly. 'Yes. I just need to think it through.'

'Fine. Here's a Stanley knife. If you could make a start on unwrapping everything, we'll stack new canvases here, finished ones here, and unfinished ones over there, at the end of the workshop.'

He was a restless, energetic man and as he talked his entire body moved animatedly. There was no minimum movement with him. When he gestured, his whole arm swept the air; he constantly ran his fingers through his thick mop of hair; paced, with great long strides, from one end of the room to the other, occasionally talking to her, but more often muttering to himself. Isabelle longed to see him at work. Would he find stillness then, or attack his painting with the same restless energy?

The workshop was ideal for an artist. It faced north, looking down the valley away from Summerstoke. A double door opened into the yard and the small window next to it was the only one on that wall. On the other side, facing the river, a window of reinforced glass ran the entire length and huge skylights punctuated the pitched roof. The floor was concrete; racks had been fixed along the wall facing the window; and a series of halogen lamps hung from the centre of the pitch.

'It's a nice space,' she commented. 'How did you find out about it? I mean, Summerstoke's a far cry from London.'

'Yes it is. Never heard of it before. But my brother, Marcus, knows the people here. He's something to do with television. Don't ask me what, or indeed how he got to know them, but he and Charlie Tucker are in cahoots over something, so he knew Charlie was developing these old farm buildings. I'm their first tenant.'

'Won't you miss being in London, in the centre of things?'

He cast her a withering look. 'Not in the slightest. When I'm working, I don't have time for anything else. In fact, being out in the wilds means I shall be free from distractions.'

'Where are you staying?'

'Here, with the Tucker tribe. Gran has moved out to a cottage in the grounds and I've got her rooms.'

'She's nice. I like her – oh!'

She had just pulled the last wrappings off a large canvas. The colours swam horizontally and vertically; shapes emerged and disappeared through translucent layers of shimmering paint.

Milo glanced at it over her shoulder and grunted, 'That's finished. It can go over there. I'll give you a hand.'

But Isabelle just stood and stared at the painting. This was what it was all about. This was what she had lost. Could she bear to work for Milo, watching him do what she should be doing but couldn't? Hadn't been able to do for the last eight years.

She felt crippled.

Something of her internal agonising must have shown on her face.

'Come on,' Milo said gruffly. 'Let's get this out

294

of the way, then we'll stop for coffee. I think we've earned it.'

'Ollie, I've had a brilliant idea. Let's have a party.'

Oliver was taken aback. Unable to return home until the following day, he'd fully expected a bored, complaining Juliet to answer the phone. But she was bubbling. 'A party? But, darling, you've only just arrived.'

'I've been here for nearly a week, Ollie. I've got to do something or I'll die of boredom.'

He was contrite. 'I'm sorry I'm not there, sweetheart. It must be difficult for you, but at least you've got Jamie.'

'Yes of course, but...'

Juliet was restless. The relief at being far from the helter-skelter world of Los Angeles had worn off, and the quiet, restorative charm of the small village she now perceived as claustrophobic and dull in the extreme.

It was fun being with Jamie, but she wasn't spending as much time with him as she wanted. He'd let her take him to school on Tuesday, and she'd been gratified by the stares and nudges. When she collected him that afternoon, after the local paper had done their stuff at the village shop, he'd introduced her to his friends.

The girl, Tish, she found rather ferocious with her pierced nose and wild appearance, and she and the boy, Adam, who smiled and chatted and seemed very charming, made her feel like ageing royalty; it was a struggle to get beyond the barrier of polite exchange.

Since then Jamie had insisted on taking his

bike, explaining that due to his erratic hours, he was better under his own steam.

Juliet, who'd never spent much time on her own before, hadn't realised how long the evenings could be, how dark they were, how quiet. As night fell she'd wander from room to room, putting on lights, the radio, the television – anything to fill up the silence, keep that blackness at bay.

On Wednesday night it was nearly eleven o'clock when she heard the waspish whine of his bike and she couldn't quite keep the sharp, anxious note out of her voice when he came in. 'Where've you been, Jamie?'

She had never asked before, and he was taken aback. 'Out with friends. Why?'

She struggled to regain her composure. 'It's late and you're on your bike. I was worried, that's all.' As he stared at her, perplexed, she attempted a lighter note. 'Are you normally this late in when you're staying with the witches?'

He frowned. 'No. I've agreed ten o'clock with Nanny, so she doesn't worry. But now you're here, it's okay, isn't it? You've never worried about the time before.'

'No. But I'm here for such a short while, I guess it would be nice to see a little more of you.'

He stared at her for a moment, then shrugged. 'I'll come straight back after my rehearsal tomorrow evening, if you like. Dad and I normally have pizzas on Thursday.'

'That'll be fun, and I'll have you all to myself – Dad's not going to be back until Friday.' Juliet tried to regain the ground she felt she'd lost. 'Come on, take those old leather things off and

296

I'll make you a sandwich. I want to hear all about this play you're so busy with.'

But Jamie was unusually reticent. He told her it was *Antigone*, but shrugged off her attempts to find out which part he was playing, so she was left with the impression that he was probably one of the chorus. He mentioned that Tish was cast as Antigone.

'Antigone? Yes, I can see that. Very appropriate.'

'What do you mean?'

'Oh,' Juliet said lightly, sensing she was walking across a minefield and unaccustomed to feeling like this with Jamie, 'feisty teenage rebel. That's what Antigone was, after all, and that's the appearance Trish presents.'

'Tish. She's really nice.' Jamie scowled as if Juliet had failed to appreciate his friend.

'I'm sure she is.' Juliet had a sudden thought and asked, teasingly, 'Is she your girlfriend?'

Jamie had claimed a couple of girls as girl-friends over the last year, but they were tokens of his post-pubescence and as such she hadn't bothered with them.

'No she's not.' Jamie replied shortly. 'She's a friend, that's all.'

'Any girlfriends on the horizon?'

The question was a casual one and Juliet was struck by Jamie's expression. He went quite pink, then, adopting the stony expression that had become all too familiar over the last couple of years, stood up and pushed his plate away, 'No, there's not. I'm going to bed now, Mum. I'm off first thing in the morning, so I'll see you tomorrow night.'

Oho, thought Juliet. A girlfriend. So that's the way the wind blows. I wonder if Ollie knows who it is? She smiled at Jamie. 'Night, darling. Give me a ring when you're on your way home and I'll get those pizzas on. Shall we go to the cinema on Saturday?'

He stopped at the doorway, 'I'm going to a party Saturday night. Sorry.'

She gave an involuntary sigh and he came back into the kitchen, looking awkward.

'Sorry, Juliet, it's just Adam said, before I knew you were coming back, he was going to have a party on Saturday and I...'

'It's all right, Jamie. Life must go on whether I'm here or not, I guess. It's just that I'm so bored. Nothing happens, and with Dad away and you not about, I'm getting the screaming habdabs.'

'You should try and get to know some of the people in the village. Why don't *you* have a bash? I bet there are people here dying to meet you.'

'Invite the local yokels? Jamie, I'm not that desperate!'

He shrugged his shoulders. 'There are one or two poshos. Dad and I went to a drinks party at that house with the fountain and all the horses. Rolling in it. You could invite them.' And with that he was gone.

Initially Juliet dismissed the idea, but after a morning roaming about the house and an afternoon in Bath shopping for things she didn't want (countless people told her they'd seen her picture in the paper, or asked for her autograph, or simply stared) the notion of a party had taken hold. After all, she'd met three people she'd happily see again

298

and there were those people Jamie mentioned; their hospitality had to be returned, even if she hadn't been a direct recipient.

There was also that dishy farmer she'd met last weekend. Milo had told her and Isabelle over lunch that he was renting a studio in Summerstoke while his own, in London, was being treated for dry rot. Charlie Tucker was Milo's landlord, so if she invited Milo she could legitimately extend the invitation to him and his wife, if he had one.

By the time she spoke to Oliver that night, she had the whole event planned.

'A drinks party, Ollie, for a few locals. And because it's a spontaneous one, no one will expect much. I'll get some nibbles from Bath tomorrow and we can pick up some wine on Saturday, when you're here.'

Oliver laughed. 'Who are you thinking of inviting?'

'Oh, those people who invited you when I was away – you'll have to tell me their names and where I'll find their number; Richard Garnett, the newspaper editor, and his wife, Isabelle; Milo, and his landlord, if he'll come.'

'It would be a good opportunity to invite some of my party workers. I owe them.'

'No way, Oliver. This is my party, to amuse me. I've been stuck by myself in this godforsaken village all week – I deserve a little light entertainment.'

Oliver laughed. 'Okay, darling, but Polly's planning to pay the old ladies a visit this weekend, we can invite her.'

'Polly!' Juliet pouted.

'Juliet, Pol's looked after Jamie a lot this year. It's the least we can do.' There was a warning note in Oliver's voice.

Juliet capitulated and so it was settled.

The following day, feeling more animated than she had all week, she set about organising her guests.

Veronica Lester was surprised but gracious about the short notice and pleased to accept, this Saturday being, unusually for them, quite free.

Isabelle was also pleased and, although she couldn't vouch for Richard, she thought he had no other plans.

Juliet had enjoyed her company at lunch with Milo, but she thought she seemed a bit colourless compared to the husband, whom she looked forward to meeting again.

Milo, whom she managed finally to pin down, said he'd be around at the weekend and he'd ask Charlie, but he didn't think there was a Mrs Charlie Tucker.

Juliet was delighted.

The light drizzle had given way to a steady downpour when, in a daze, Isabelle left the workshop to go and pick up the girls from school. She and Milo agreed, subject to her availability, she would join him after she'd dropped the girls off at school and work in the morning, while he felt he needed her. Excitement bubbled inside her. Never – it was a cliché, but oh so true – never in her wildest dreams had she imagined that by moving to Summerstoke she'd end up working for Milo Steel.

She laughed aloud. What would Joe say when

he heard? He'd be green!

About halfway along the track to the main road, the car suddenly lurched violently to one side, and as she tried to nurse it forwards the wheel started to shudder and jerk. 'Oh, bugger!' she shrieked and, pulling on the brake, tumbled out of the door into the rain. Her fears were confirmed: she had a flat tyre.

She glanced up and down the track through the sheet of rain. She could see nothing and nobody.

'Please, please, don't let him find me like this,' she whimpered, and she rushed round to the back of the car, wrenching open the rear door and throwing accumulated piles of family rubbish over the passenger seats, clearing the back, fervently hoping to find a toolbag and the jack. She couldn't remember the last time she'd changed a wheel. She'd certainly never changed one on the Discovery. There was no sign of a jack. She tugged at the cover on the spare wheel. Slippery with rain, she got it off with difficulty, but there was no sign of the toolbag.

For a moment, she stood, the rain trickling down her face, panic rising. The manual! That would tell her where to find it. Feverishly she flung open the door, rummaged in the glove compartment and pulled out the manual.

'I don't believe it! How fucking stupid!' she screamed aloud. According to the manual, she would find the jack in with the engine, and the toolbag behind one of the seats. What mighty brain thought up this arrangement? She spat.

Now she had to struggle to get the wretched bonnet open and time was ticking by.

She glanced at her watch. School would be out in ten minutes. There was no way she'd make it. She fought with the bonnet, finally finding a neat little jack, then used more precious minutes searching the back of the car before she unearthed the toolkit.

The retaining nuts on the spare wheel were stiff with lack of use, and the ten minutes had nearly gone before she pulled it free. Staggering under the weight, she threw it onto the grass verge, then dashed back to the driver's seat, fumbling in her bag for her mobile. Wonder of wonders, Paula answered.

'No problem, Isabelle. I'll take them back to mine. You can pick 'em up on your way back. Shall I phone Lenny and see if he can come over? He'd get it changed in no time.'

For a moment, Isabelle was tempted, but Lenny was probably working with Charlie that afternoon and the last thing she wanted was for Charlie Tucker to know she was in trouble again.

'No thanks, Paula. I can manage. I'll see you soon.'

Brave words, she thought. I wish it were true.

The next challenge was to get the jack in the right position. By lying flat on the muddy ground, she succeeded in inserting it under the back axle. Pushing the handle into position, she started to crank up the car. It was hard work and Isabelle thought her back would break with the strain; her arms were aching unbearably, her hands were icy-cold and slippery with rain, and covered with grease, and she had to stop every now and then to wipe her dripping nose with the

302

back of her hand.

After what seemed an eternity, the wheel was clear of the ground. The next challenge was to get the wheel nuts off. It was impossible. They were so tight that any attempt to turn them was thwarted by the wheel spinning.

'Oh shit!' she screamed.

She realised what she'd done wrong: she should have loosened the nuts when the wheel was still on the ground. But it had taken her so long to crank it up... The thought of having to go through all that again was too much and she stood and wailed.

In the middle of wailing, she heard the sound of a tractor coming down the track. Scrubbing her eyes, she prayed, 'Oh, don't let it be him, please, let it be his brother, or if you're feeling really sorry for me, God, let it be Lenny. Please!'

But God must have been off duty, because when the tractor ground to a halt it was Charlie Tucker who leaned out of the cab.

Paula phoned Lenny to tell him of Isabelle's plight and Lenny, who was with Charlie, immediately passed on the news. It was raining so hard that the two men had already decided to abandon slurrying and Charlie was about to set off back to the farm.

'No worries, Lenny. If she hasn't fixed it by the time I get there, I'll do it. Though,' he grinned, 'I'm probably the last person she'll want to see.'

So when he leaned out of the cab, he was about to make a quip about her car blocking his way and please would she move it, but at the sight of

Isabelle and the state she was in the jocular remark died on his lips.

Not only was she drenched, her hair plastered to her head, but she was absolutely filthy. Mud dripped down her front; her face was streaked with oil and dirt; her hands were filthy; and her eyes, red-rimmed with crying he guessed, stared at him defiantly.

He jumped down, but before he could say anything she waved a wheelbrace at him. 'I don't need your help, thank you very much. I can do this myself, without you sneering, so bugger off.' She turned her back on him and resolutely began to battle with the wheel.

'It'll be a bit difficult to reverse the tractor all the way back up the track with the muck-spreader on the back,' he said lightly. 'Besides, my brother'll be bringing the herd in for milking. The cows won't queue up politely to get past you.'

At the mention of the cows, she looked round fearfully.

'Listen, Isabelle, let me help you. I promise I'm not sneering at you. A puncture can happen to anyone – I've had loads – and those wheel nuts are often tightened with a machine, so it needs a bit of muscle to get them shifted.'

She made another ineffectual attempt on a nut, and the wheel spun.

Charlie shook his head. 'You'll have to get the car down, loosen the nuts when the wheel is on the ground

'I know, I know,' she hissed through gritted teeth. 'I made a mistake, I know. I was going to let it down when you turned up. If you'd been five minutes later, I'd have fixed it.'

The rain was starting to trickle down Charlie's neck and he could feel the damp permeating through his overalls. He gave a short, impatient laugh. 'Who are you kidding? Look, I'm getting soaked standing here and you're drenched. For Chrissake, give me the brace. Go and sit in my cab – it's warm in there – and let me get on with it.'

'Go and sit in your cab yourself!' She glared at him.

He glared back. 'Don't be so bloody stupid. Give me the brace.'

'Sod off.'

'Look, you stupid cow, face the facts – you're getting nowhere fast. Give me the brace.'

'If I'm a stupid cow, you're an arrogant shit-faced pig. I'll do it myself.'

Incensed, Charlie made a grab for the spanner. 'Give me the brace.'

'No, I won't. I won't.' She held onto it with both hands.

The two wrestled for possession of the brace, twisting it this way and that. In desperation Isabelle tried to push Charlie off, he slipped on his back, pulling Isabelle with him and the two tumbled to the ground, and rolled over and over, both equally determined not to let go of the tool.

The absurdity of the situation suddenly struck Charlie and as he struggled he started to laugh. The more he laughed, the more furious Isabelle became. But she was getting tired and weakening rapidly, and within minutes Charlie had the wrench. Then, out of the blue, lying on top of her and looking down at her, covered from head to foot with mud and grass, with clods of earth matting her hair and the rain and tears making little white rivulets down her grimy face, he felt an almost overwhelming desire to kiss her.

For a second they lay there, frozen, locked into each other.

Confused and ashamed, Charlie scrambled to his feet and offered his hand to pull her up, saying gruffly, 'Christ, the last time I scrapped like that with a girl was with my sister. I'm sorry – I hope I haven't hurt you.'

She ignored his hand and, getting stiffly to her feet, turned her back on him and the Discovery. She hugged her arms to her chest and stared out across the field to the river and Summerstoke beyond, not saying a word.

He stared at her back for a moment, then shrugged and started to let down the jack.

12

College was finished for the weekend and Jamie and his mates, strolling across the car park towards their bikes, were discussing Adam's party.

'There'll be some older kids there,' Adam told them. 'My parents have put my brother, Nick, in charge and he's got a girlfriend doing her last year of As at the college. So she's coming, and some of her mates.'

Jamie felt a momentary stab of excitement. Supposing Alison was among them? Then ... then at last, he'd be in with a chance.

'Hey, Jamie, those guys' – Tish nodded at two boys sitting on the wall by the gates, trying to attract his attention – 'are they mates of yours?'

Jamie's jaw dropped. What with his pre-occupation with Alison, the play, his bike, his newfound friends and Juliet's return, he'd forgotten about the desperate texts he'd sent to his old schoolmates, particularly as neither had troubled to reply.

'Yeah, they're mates from London. Look, I'll catch up with you later. Are you going down to the Ferry?'

The Ferry Inn was a pub on the river, with a large outdoor area and pool room. It was a popular meeting place for the local teenagers.

'Yeah, 'bout seven,' Tish replied. 'See you.'

Feeling slightly uncertain, Jamie went to greet his friends. 'Mark, Tim, how's things? What are you doing here?'

Mark, the older of the two, a tall, dark-haired boy, with a distinct five o'clock shadow and looking a lot older than his seventeen years, grinned. 'We decided we'd had enough of school for one day. Time we paid our old friend, Jamie, a visit, we said, didn't we, Tim?'

Tim, by contrast, was so fair and hairless he seemed bleached; his skin was pallid and covered with faint freckles, his eyelashes were almost white, making his eyes look red-rimmed, and he was shorter but a lot heavier than either of the other two. His voice was soft and unbroken.

'We did, Mark. And long overdue – we couldn't leave you pining for London much longer, could we?'

Jamie gulped. 'How did you get down here?'

Mark grinned. 'We were inventive. Your old man certainly stuck you out in the sticks. Luckily, we had a car.'

'A car? I didn't know you ... I didn't know you could drive.'

'Not officially, perhaps, but yes, I can drive. It's my mother's car. She's away for the weekend so we thought we'd take advantage, hit the open road. So we did. Next question: where to go? Easy, why not go and see our old mate?'

'I wish I'd known you were coming. Why didn't you text me?' Why didn't he feel more pleased to see them?

'We thought we'd give you a nice little surprise. You begged us to come, remember? And we were touched, weren't we, Tim? We had to wipe away the tears. Aren't you pleased to see us?'

'Hell, yeah, 'course I am, man,' Jamie replied lamely. 'I just wasn't expecting you.'

'So what gives, Jamie, my son?' Tim playfully punched Jamie's arm. 'Whad'ya got lined up for us? We've come because you asked us. Now we're here, what gives? Party, booze, girls, ganja? What goes on down here in the sticks?'

Jamie felt panic-stricken. He couldn't think of anything that would impress them. He just wanted them to go away. But he realised, with a horrible sinking feeling, they weren't going to, at least not until they were ready.

He tried to remember why he'd liked them in the

first place. He'd hung around them since he was eleven and desperate for friends. At first they'd dared him to nick sweets, then to smoke cigarettes, then drink alcohol. With them he learned to roll joints and where to buy ganja and ecstasy. Fortunately, when the three were caught smoking marijuana, he'd already handed over the pills they'd asked for, but he never once questioned why they should finger him; Jamie accepted his lot.

But now he felt differently about them, about London. He'd changed; his life had changed; he had a new set of friends, and the unexpected arrival of Mark and Tim he saw as a threat. It wasn't that the gang he now mixed with were innocents; they weren't. Plenty of illicit drinking and smoking went on, but it wasn't something to brag about, or force on the unwilling; and nicking your mother's car and boasting about it was something only twoc-heads, real delinquents, did, not over-privileged, fat-cat schoolkids.

He shifted uneasily. 'Where you guys staying?'

Mark looked at him incredulously. 'With you, you idiot. We've come to see you, for fuck's sake – nice!'

'But I don't live here in Summerbridge. I live in a village...'

'Isn't this a village? Don't tell us there are places smaller than this?' jeered Tim. 'Take us there, dipshit – I want to see the natives in their grass skirts.'

'Um ... the thing is, my mother's home and she'll say no. She's only back for a short time, see, and doesn't want any one else around. Also,' he said with a flash of inspiration, 'she'd want to know where the car came from – she'd give you the third degree.'

'That's out, then,' Mark said adamantly. 'What about this cranky old Manor where your granny lives? You told us it had a hundred rooms – or were you exaggerating a teensy weensy bit, you naughty Jamie?'

For a moment, Jamie faltered. It would be possible to conceal them in one of the rooms, if only they could be trusted not to wander. But supposing they did? Supposing they went for a slash or something, and bumped into one of the witches, or Nanny? He didn't want to be responsible for the fright it would give the old ladies and supposing one of them had a heart attack?

'No, the place is riddled with burglar alarms,' he lied. 'You'd be found out straight away.' Then he had a flash of inspiration. 'I know what, you could stay in the boathouse.'

It became one of the longest evenings in his life.

He decided not to go back to Summerstoke till the end of the evening. Juliet wouldn't expect anything else and he didn't want to risk any activity down in the boathouse until everyone had gone to bed. So they went to a café, then mooched around Summerbridge, ending up at the Ferry Inn where Mark, demanding to know what the local poison was, bought pints of Natural Dry for him and Tim and a lager for Jamie.

Jamie's friends turned up and joined them.

Initially the atmosphere was quite convivial, and Adam invited Mark and Tim to his party the following night if they were still around. But things changed. Jamie wasn't sure if it was the cider that affected them, or whether he was seeing them more clearly, but Mark and Tim became increasingly obnoxious. They made much of wanting to score that night and, when that was sorted, disappeared into the darkness of the grounds down by the river.

When they returned, Mark decided to chat up Emily, Adam's girlfriend, who'd arrived in the interim with a group of her friends; and Tim provoked an argument, at Jamie's table, over the superior merits of London as a place to live, compared to Summerbridge or anywhere similar. Since these were sentiments Jamie had expressed when he first arrived, he went hot under the collar at what an arrogant prat he must have seemed.

The atmosphere became increasingly sour. Emily and her friends suddenly got up and left and were followed, soon after, by Adam and a number of their group. As he left, Adam beckoned to Jamie.

'Sorry, Jamie, I don't like your mates. I don't want them coming to my party.'

'But you invited them... What shall I say?' Jamie stammered.

'Tell them they're uninvited. I don't mind you – you're a mate – but they're fuckin' wankers.'

Jamie trailed forlornly and reluctantly back to the table in time to see Mark return from the bar with two more brimming glasses. The whole of his group had gone now, leaving one or two people whom he didn't know talking to Mark and Tim. Sitting on the edge of the group, marginalised and miserable, he saw all suggestions to drink and cheer up as a bad joke.

It was pitch black when they returned to

Summerstoke. The sky was overcast, so there was no moonlight to guide them as Jamie led the way through the churchyard to a little oak door in the wall dividing the churchyard from the grounds of the Manor.

He had discovered the door some weeks ago, completely covered with ivy, at the back of the shrubbery, and had dismantled the lock, foreseeing occasions when being able to slip in and out of the Manor unobserved would be useful.

Hugging the shadows, they skirted the shrubbery along the edge of the lawn; the house appeared behind them, huge, dark and silent; in the distance a fox screamed; looming unexpectedly out of the darkness, nigrescent silhouettes of ornamental shrubs on the lawn took on a threatening identity, and at the boathouse the ink-black river slapped and sucked. The boys fell very quiet as Jamie led the way, and kept close. He could have sworn one of them whimpered when he swung over the ladder, but he ignored it, found the torch he kept in a plastic bag at the bottom, and lighted their way down.

'Bloody hell, is this it?' hissed Mark, looking around the boathouse. 'You're not serious?'

'You'll be fine here.' Jamie'd had enough. 'There are cushions over there and I'll bring you some food in the morning. It's the best I can do – you should have warned me you were coming.'

'Milo Steel! Ollie, I don't believe it! What on earth's he doing in Summerstoke?'

In the Manor kitchen, Oliver and Polly were drinking coffee and chatting about Juliet's party.

For a non-identical twin, Polly bore a strong resemblance to Oliver. She was tall and slim, her hair fashionably short, its honey colour enhanced with blonde streaks; she wore little make-up and her skin was clear, her grey eyes bright and intelligent. At thirty-five she showed no signs of wanting to marry, much to the consternation of her mother. She had plenty of boyfriends, but she was an independent spirit and saw no reason to exchange a fulfilling existence, running an art gallery and having fun, for domesticity and motherhood.

The old ladies at the Manor adored her and she them, so a visit from Polly was always a cause for celebration.

Juliet, on the other hand, was an old adversary and both Polly and Oliver knew she would receive a cool welcome from Juliet that evening.

Oliver knew the prime reason for his sister's dislike was her conviction that Juliet exploited him; and Juliet's hostility stemmed from the early days of their relationship when she was convinced Polly tried to persuade Oliver to drop her.

'His studio in London's temporarily out of action so he's set up in a converted barn. He got it through Marcus, apparently.'

Oliver mentioned the name lightly, aware that Polly and Milo's young half-brother, Marcus, had once been an item.

Polly appeared unaffected by the revelation. 'Goodness, who'd have thought Milo would turn up in Summerstoke? He's doing really well, you know, Ollie. My gallery would give anything to have one of his paintings. So where's his studio? Who's his landlord?'

313

'It's at Marsh Farm. Apparently, Charlie Tucker has been resurrecting the place. Do you remember us having a mud fight with him one summer? He'd secretly filled an old rowing boat with mud and, with half the village on his side, we didn't stand a chance.'

Polly laughed. 'I remember him. He was thin and wiry, younger than us, wasn't he?'

'Yeah. I met him at the firework party last weekend. He's a nice guy. Juliet's invited him to come along, too.'

'You can't do that! No, no, that won't do at all!'

Nanny who'd been listening to their conversation while making scones, looked up in horror.

Oliver and Polly stared at the old lady.

'What's wrong with inviting Charlie Tucker, Nanny?' asked Oliver.

'Have you got something against him?' chipped in Polly.

'No, of course not. He's a bit of a flibbertigibbet – not like Stephen, who's completely reliable and hard-working – but he's doing his bit to bring that farm of theirs around, I'll give him his due.'

'Then what?'

'You can't put Charlie Tucker and Hugh Lester in the same room. Definitely not!'

'Why not? Is it some village feud? Tell us, Nanny,' urged Polly, anticipating a juicy snippet of gossip.

'It's not a village feud, it's a family feud,' replied Nanny with a certain relish. 'For all they're both farmers and should be pulling together in these benighted times, the two families hate each other. And not surprising, either, seeing those Lesters nearly pushed the Tuckers into bankruptcy because they were after their land. Feelings still run very high, I'm told.'

Polly chuckled. 'Sounds like Juliet's little soirée's going to be more interesting than I'd anticipated.'

Oliver didn't share her amusement. 'Great, so I've got to phone up Charlie, or Hugh and Veronica, and say don't come. How on earth do you uninvite someone without upsetting them?'

It was a question echoed by Juliet when Oliver explained the situation on returning home. She was in the bedroom, putting the finishing touches to her make-up.

'For goodness' sake, Ollie, what do you expect me to do? I'm certainly not going to do that – for one thing, I don't know for sure Charlie will come; Milo said only that he'd ask him. If people go to parties in other people's houses they behave, don't they? Or are you saying it's different in the country, and we can't expect folk to control themselves and not to act like savages?'

'No, of course not, but it's not going to be particularly enjoyable having that sort of animosity driving the evening, is it? Anyway, I've decided to try and avert trouble by inviting a couple more people. With them here, there'll be less likelihood of an outburst.'

'Who've you invited to *my* party, without consulting me?' Juliet pouted at his reflection in the mirror.

Oliver was unperturbed. 'The vicar, the Reverend Grey, and his wife, Lavender. I know they're a bit older than most of the people we're having, but they'll chat to Charlotte and Louisa.'

'What?' Juliet almost shrieked her disbelief and, dropping her eyeliner, turned to face him. 'You've asked the old crones?'

'I've asked Charlotte and Louisa. Grandmère wouldn't come anyway and nor would Nanny, but Charlotte and Louisa always loved parties and I don't suppose they get invited to many these days.'

'And for a good reason,' muttered Juliet.

Oliver chose to ignore her. 'It's churlish not to invite them, and with the vicar and the two old dears here, it's a reasonable bet everyone will behave.' He sighed at the discontent on Juliet's face. 'Don't worry, I'll look after them. Just be nice to them, please. For my sake.'

Hearing his parents in conversation upstairs, Jamie crept along the hall and let himself out of the front door of the house, trying to conceal the large bulge in his denim jacket.

It's lucky Juliet's home, he thought, not for the first time since yesterday evening. It would have been extremely hard to smuggle food out of the Manor kitchen under Nanny's watchful eye, but Juliet always kept the fridge so stocked up she'd never miss anything.

His arrival at the boathouse was not greeted with any pleasure. Mark and Tim were huddled at the back, smoking, and looking very cold.

'About fuckin' time,' growled Mark. 'What kept you?'

'We're freezing,' complained Tim. 'If we have to spend another night here, I'm going to light a fire.'

Jamie was alarmed. 'You can't do that – this place is only made of wood. Besides, a fire would be spotted.'

'By whom?' asked Mark belligerently. 'We can't be seen from that old house. But don't worry, there's no way I'd spend another night in this hole, with or without the help of a joint or two. Lucky for us, we found your stash and now I'm starving; where's the grub you promised us?'

'Take this tray of canapés through to the sitting room, darling, and then we're set.'

Juliet was in a bubbly mood. She enjoyed parties, and at this one there'd be no competition and, more importantly, she wouldn't have to be on high alert the entire time. In Los Angeles there was always someone looking on, assessing and judging: make-up, hair, dress, manner, conversation – get one element wrong and it could be curtains.

She looked good, and she knew it. She'd scooped her hair up, leaving one or two red-gold ringlets kissing her neck and face. Long, slender gold earrings added to the air of simple sophistication, as did the dark green silk tunic with a mandarin collar, and black, tight-fitting silk trousers.

Jamie had looked in on her as she was standing in front of the mirror putting the finishing touches to her appearance.

'Nice one, Juliet,' he said appreciatively. 'See you later.'

She glanced at him. 'Do you think I need heels with this, Jamie? Or do you think I can get away with not wearing any shoes at all?'

He shrugged. 'Whatever.'

She took in the pallor of his skin, the dark shadows under his eyes, and felt a pang. 'You look tired, darling. Don't be too late back, will you?'

He stared at her, impatiently. 'Why are you fussing about me all of a sudden? I'm fine. I'll see you later.'

The guests were due to arrive at about seven and bang on the hour the doorbell rang.

Juliet glanced at Oliver, 'Don't people here realise it's the height of bad manners to arrive dead on time? I might still be in the bath.'

'Well, since you made it perfectly clear you want them all gone by nine,' grinned Oliver, making for the door, 'they're not going to waste time, are they? I bet you ten quid it's the vicar.'

It was ten pounds easily won. But Oliver was right; within half an hour most of the guests had assembled in the sitting room, Milo and Charlie being the only ones absent.

There was a certain amount of intermingling to begin with, but soon the Lesters and Richard had moved in on Juliet. Louisa and Charlotte sat close to the fire on adjacent sofas, with the vicar standing between them, tall, grey and lugubrious, his head bent low to catch what they were saying, nodding slowly and rhythmically.

Like a toy dog on the back ledge of a car, thought Oliver as he refilled glasses.

Isabelle was talking to Polly when, resplendent in a flowery chiffon blouse with ruffles and matching skirt, Lavender Grey bustled up to them.

'Now, Isabelle, this is a golden opportunity for us to raise some very influential support. I told

318

Andrew it would pay to come – he was all for staying at home and listening to the *Matthew Passion;* our daughter, Gemmy, gave it to him for his birthday. It's not going to go away, I said. You can listen to it another time. Whereas a party invitation, now that doesn't happen very often, and certainly not from our MP.'

'Hello, Mrs Grey, how are you?' Polly smiled at her. 'Still busy with your watercolours?'

'Oh, my goodness me, no, Polly. I've far too much to do.'

'Mrs Grey formed the Summerstoke Art group when I was a teenager,' Polly explained to Isabelle. 'I was her youngest recruit. Unfortunately I couldn't paint to save my life.'

'Now that's not true, Polly Merfield, and you know it.' Lavender turned to Isabelle. 'You ought to join, my dear. Paula's told me all about your mural. I'll mention it to Rita Godwin – she runs the group now.'

Isabelle gulped but before she could say anything Lavender had turned to Polly and was telling her about the shop.

Isabelle glanced at Veronica, standing, glass in hand, completely at ease, socially secure. If only, she sighed, if only I had the courage to confront her... Turning her attention back to Polly and Mrs Grey, she thought how much nicer life would be if Polly Merfield was a neighbour, rather than Veronica.

She had instantly warmed to Polly, who was calm and graceful, with an easy smile. She'd been telling Isabelle about her gallery when Mrs Grey interrupted, and Isabelle wanted to hear more.

But Lavender was right, of course. With Richard there, the Lesters, and Oliver and Juliet, she had to do something.

For all their money and influence, the Lesters were the most difficult to approach. Hugh looked good, she had to admit it, in a white linen shirt, dark blue velvet jacket and dark slacks. For once his height wasn't a disadvantage. Able to look down at Juliet, he was clearly captivated by her and doing his best to be captivating. A change, Isabelle reflected, from his usual unsmiling, arrogant self.

Veronica, resplendent in a gold crocheted jersey and black trousers, was standing a little apart talking to Richard, but all the time, Isabelle noticed, keeping one eye on her hostess, waiting for the moment when she could insinuate herself into the conversation.

She's so bloody rude, she thought, with a spurt of anger. Why does Richard put up with her? He's no self-respect! And she wondered, not for the first time, whether they'd ever been lovers.

With the party well under way and with no sign of Milo and Charlie, Oliver was beginning to breathe more easily: perhaps they weren't going to come. He glanced across at his sister, who was talking to Isabelle.

Oliver blinked. For the first time, since he'd met her, he was struck by how attractive Isabelle was. She wasn't beautiful, like Juliet, but with her hair standing out around her face like a shimmering halo, huge, sorrowful blue eyes and delicately boned features, she could have stepped out of a Fra Angelico fresco.

He was startled by his reaction; he'd met Juliet when he was eighteen and it was true to say after that he'd never paid much attention to anyone else – she eclipsed them all.

Richard, enjoying a sly destruction by Vee of the house and its décor, caught sight of Oliver staring with obvious admiration at his wife and felt a savage lick of anger. Well, he thought, casting a look at Juliet, two can play at that game.

Oliver joined his two aunts. Both ladies used the excuse of a party to dress even more outrageously and sat chatting animatedly with the vicar, who looked like a grey moth between two exotic butterflies.

'Oliver.' Louisa patted the sofa cushion beside her and he obediently sat down. 'We're having a discussion about life after death. Charlotte and I think it's a load of old hooey, but dear old Andrew, here, insists otherwise.'

'But he has to, doesn't he?' chipped in Charlotte. 'Otherwise he'd be out of a job. It's a question of pragmatism over intellect.'

'My dear lady,' the vicar started to protest.

Oliver was saved from being drawn into what was clearly a long-running argument by Polly turning to him.

'Ollie, Mrs Grey has been telling me about the village shop. It's simply dreadful news. Can't you do something?'

Oliver looked up, with a frown. 'Yes, I had an email from Elsie Bates, alerting me to the problem, last week. I've been intending to go and see Rita Godwin.'

'Didn't you see your wife's photograph in the local paper, supporting our campaign?' Lavender demanded.

Surprised, Oliver glanced across at Juliet, then back at the vicar's wife. 'No, I'm sorry, I didn't. Susannah keeps the local papers for me to go through on Friday, but I had to stay for a debate in the House, yesterday, so I won't have a chance until tomorrow.'

'Yes, but still, didn't your wife say anything to you? *She's* supporting us.'

'No, she didn't tell me. But then we've not had much chance–'

Oliver was prevented from saying anything more by a ring on the doorbell.

'Hi, Oliver,' Milo gripped him warmly by the hand. 'Long time no see – hope we're not too late. After a hard day's work, Charlie and I had to have our grub first.' And just behind Milo, grinning cheerfully and glowing larger than life, was Charlie Tucker.

When Charlie heard about Juliet's invitation, he'd hesitated. His idea of a drinks party was to go round to a mate's and crack a few cans. Somehow he didn't think this one would be like that. But he'd not much else on that evening, Oliver seemed a nice bloke and his mother, who watched every soap under the sun, shrieked when she heard Juliet Peters had invited him over.

Oliver welcomed him warmly.

Yeah, he's okay, for all that he's an MP and Conservative at that, thought Charlie, saying cheerfully, ''Lo, Oliver. Thanks for the invite.'

322

Oliver led them down the hall, murmuring, 'There'll be some people here you'll know, I'm sure, Charlie. It's not a large party, being a last-minute whim of Juliet's.'

Milo led the way into the sitting room, followed by Charlie and Oliver. The room was warm, bright and comfortable and hummed with conversation. This dipped when they entered.

Next to the fire, Charlie recognised two of the elderly Merfields with the vicar and his wife, a tall, slim woman he didn't know, and...

He blinked. It was Isabelle, but an Isabelle transformed. He'd only ever seen her soaked, or covered with mud, and there she stood, the blueness of her huge eyes accentuated by the silky dress she was wearing, her hair the colour of ripening barley.

He had barely registered her shock at seeing him and heard someone exclaim 'Milo!' when he caught the unmistakable voice of Veronica Lester, drawling 'Oh, my God.'

He turned. Staring at him, his face contorted by an angry flush, was Hugh Lester, the ghastly Veronica sneering at his side.

Charlie froze. Why hadn't he been warned? Was this somebody's idea of a joke? There was no way he was going to socialise with that bastard.

His face stony, he gave the Lesters a barely perceptible nod.

The party was small enough for everyone in the room to be affected by the atmosphere, and for a moment the loudest noise was the crackling of logs in the grate.

Juliet made the first move. 'Charlie, Milo, I'm

so glad you could make it.'

She floated over to them, kissed them both on the cheek, then took Charlie's arm.

'Charlie, I'm sure you know most of the people here, so may I introduce you to my friend Isabelle? She's new to the village, too.'

She drew Charlie over to the fireplace, where Isabelle had sunk, out of sight, onto the sofa.

Juliet's actions broke the tension. Returning to her group as soon as she could, to massage Hugh Lester's feelings, she didn't notice the horrified look on Isabelle's face.

Oliver, handing Charlie a glass, did and was surprised. And when, almost immediately, Isabelle made an excuse to go to the bathroom and left the room, he stared after her, puzzled. What on earth could she have against Charlie Tucker?

Charlie, watching Isabelle flee the room, thought about leaving himself and was about to make his excuses to Oliver when Charlotte Merfield came to his rescue.

'Charlie Tucker.' She beckoned him with a bony, crimson-tipped finger. 'Come and sit next to me. I want you to tell me what you're up to, and all about that family of yours. Is it true, now your grandmother has re-married, your mother's thinking of doing the same? And your brother? When's it going to be your turn, eh?'

'Right, then, what about this party? I'm up for a bit of a laugh!'

Jamie felt miserable. He still hadn't plucked up the courage to tell Mark and Tim they'd been barred. He'd agonised for ages about how to play it. He had to get them off his back; make 'em go back to London that evening, early enough for him to make a bit of the party, at least. He had a CD he knew Adam wanted, tucked in his shirt pocket, and some cans of Stella in his bike pannier. He knew he, at least, would be welcome.

He imagined walking into the room, the lighting low, music full on, loads of smooching couples. Alison would be sitting there, alone – no, she wasn't a saddo – chatting to a friend. He would go up to her, 'Fancy a dance?' he'd say casually. She'd look up and smile. He had to go, he simply had to.

He'd persuaded Mark and Tim to go to the cinema; they'd then gone for a pizza and were now sitting in the nearly deserted garden of the Ferry Inn, again downing pints of the local cider, the only thing they found to praise in their visit to the sticks.

'Ah, this is the stuff for proper lads!' Tim smacked his lips. 'Probably explains why you don't like it, eh Jamie? I fancy another. How about you, Mark?'

'Don't mind if I do. Trouble is I'm running short of the ready.'

'Me, too. This little jaunt has cost me more than I thought it would.' Tim turned to Jamie. 'So you'll have to treat your old mates, Jamie. Give us a bit of cash, would you?'

Jamie tried to protest, but it was no use.

'Come on, don't be such a skinflint. Juliet would never let her little boy go short.' Mark sneered and held out his hand.

Slowly Jamie dug into his pocket and felt for

the fiver nestling there. He pulled it out and threw it on the table, to receive a smack round the head from Mark.

'Ow! What the hell was that for?'

'For being a naughty little skinflint and making out you had no money. Now, about this party...'

'Why do you want to go? You didn't think much of the talent and thought the blokes were oiks. Why do you want to spend another evening with them?'

Mark shoved his face close to Jamie's. His breath smelt of rotting apples. 'For a laugh, old son; so I can get my leg over; so I can puke on the fucking lot of them; why d'ye think?'

A stab of anger made Jamie bold. 'Well, you can't. They don't want you, you'll be chucked out.'

Mark let out a hiss of anger. 'You're lying. Your mate invited us himself.'

'That was before you made such arseholes of yourselves.' Jamie didn't care any more. He just wanted them to go. 'Adam made it clear to me when he went, he doesn't want you anywhere near his party.'

Tim grabbed Jamie's jacket. 'I don't believe you, you lying bastard. I think you just want to get rid of us. Where is it? Why don't we just turn up and see if they turn us away?'

'Excellent idea, Tim. Come on, Jamie, lead the way.'

They both stood up, looking down at him. Jamie wavered. He felt sure they'd be turned away; but it was getting late, and supposing Adam's brother was not on the door? Supposing they pushed their way in? They were drunk enough and high enough not to care about other people's reactions. He'd be blamed for bringing them – he'd be out in the cold again, play or no play. And supposing Alison was there? He could see the look of contempt on her face.

'No. We're not going.'

With a movement that took Jamie unawares, Tim was behind him twisting his arm up his back. Jamie let out such a yelp of pain and surprise that the only other couple outside looked up in surprise and the man called over, 'You all right, mate?'

Tim whispered in Jamie's ear, 'Say you're okay, or I'll break your fucking arm.'

Jamie did as he was told and, relieved, the man returned his attention to his girlfriend. Moments later, with a backward glance in the boys' direction, they got up and went into the pub.

'I think we need to go and talk this over somewhere a little quieter,' suggested Mark. 'I could do with a toke. Come on, Tim, Jamie, let's go and admire the ducks.'

A jerk on his arm brought tears to Jamie's eyes and, having no choice in the matter, he allowed himself to be frogmarched down to the river's edge, beyond the reach of the pub's outdoor lighting.

With a violent thrust, Tim threw Jamie to the ground, where he lay for a moment, nursing his sore arm.

The two stood over him. 'So,' said Mark, softly, 'you're not going to take us to this party?'

'No.'

'Are you sure about that?' Tim kicked Jamie

hard in the ribs.

He cried out in pain and surprise.

'We've come all this way to see you, at your request. Is this a way to treat mates? Refuse to take us to a party we've been invited to?'

Jamie said nothing.

Tim kicked him again. 'Where's the fucking party?'

'I'm not telling you,' gasped Jamie, still winded from the last kick. 'Why don't you both fuck off out of it?'

'I believe we will,' Mark said, softly. 'I, for one, don't want to spend another night in that hell-hole by the river, and if you're not going to provide me with any crumpet to spend the night with, Jamie, I see no point in staying. I know when I'm not wanted.'

Any comfort Jamie might have derived from hearing this was cut short by Mark kicking him, saying as he did so, almost regretfully, 'Goodbye, Jamie.'

'Goodbye, Jamie.' Tim struck again.

And so it went on, interminably, it seemed, each kick accompanied by a 'Goodbye, Jamie', until suddenly the scenario had spiralled out of control into something sinister and Jamie, his whole body hurting, his head reeling with confusion and pain, thought with terror: They're going to kick me to death!

There was a loud crack, and just before he fainted Jamie heard Mark say to Tim, 'Sounded like a rib. That's enough. Let's go. We'll hit the happy homestead, leave our house-warming pressie, then boogey on back to London.'

13

Jamie was not unconscious for long. It started raining and the cold drops on his face revived him. Groaning, he sat up. His torso was rigid with pain, and blood, trickling from a cut above his eye, blurred his vision. He unzipped his jacket and cautiously examined his ribs. He felt the plastic case of the CD he'd brought for Adam, and pulled it out. It was badly cracked – that must have been the noise they thought was his ribs.

He laughed sourly. It was a small recompense, but Thirty-Six Crazy Fists had saved him from more severe injury, as had his padded leather bike jacket.

He felt his face. As well as the cut on his forehead, a large lump over his eye throbbed like crazy, his mouth was cut and swollen; blood dripped from his nose, and one cheek was so bruised it was too tender to touch.

For a few minutes he sat there weeping with a mixture of shock, self-pity, pain and helplessness. The bastards! The *bastards!* Call themselves fuckin' friends... When had they ever given him anything but grief? But they'd gone and now he was free to go to the party, to see Alison.

He staggered to his feet; quite apart from the pain, he felt groggy and sick. But that passed and slowly, painfully, he made his way across the grass to his bike.

It was hopeless. He couldn't go to any party. He'd be good for nothing and the way he looked would attract a lot of unwanted attention. That was the last thing he could cope with. All he wanted to do was get home and collapse in bed.

Fortunately, Mark and Tim had left his bike alone – one nasty little surprise less. But his relief was short-lived; with a gut-wrenching clarity, he remembered their last words.

Frantic, he forced his stiff, aching body into action, pulled on his helmet, climbed astride his bike, fumbled for his keys and turned on the engine. Roaring off, he prayed, over and over, 'Oh, please, no, no, don't let them have. Don't let them, please.'

By the time he arrived in Summerstoke, he was drenched through and shivering violently. He parked his bike inside the Manor drive out of sight from the road, and hobbled round to the churchyard, undoing his helmet as he went.

'Oh no!' he groaned aloud in despair. The little door was swinging open; he was right, they'd come back.

He ran as best he could across the grass towards the boathouse. On a slight rise of the lawn, before it dipped down to the river's edge, he saw, through the drizzle, the outline of the boathouse shrouded in a thin halo of smoke.

Weeping so much he could hardly see, Jamie threw himself forward and climbed onto the little wooden deck. The smoke was thin, but it was billowing steadily through the floorboards and curling round the summerhouse. He wiped his eyes and climbed down the ladder.

They'd started the fire in the far corner of the boathouse using, as far as Jamie could tell from the unburnt debris, ripped pages from his Nuts magazines over which they'd piled old cushions and the crumbled rubbish of their picnic breakfast. Not a very professional attempt at arson but effective enough, for as Jamie arrived a small lick of flame leaped into life and worked its way round the edge of one of the cushions.

On the other side of the river, Rita Godwin was taking Chocolate out for his evening walk. He was so fat he could only waddle, which meant he and his mistress made slow progress. The thin plume of smoke, which would have been missed by a faster walker, was spotted by the inquisitive eyes of Rita Godwin. At first she thought it might be the remnants of a bonfire, but, peering across the river through the dull dark of the evening, she could see that it came from the boathouse.

Not carrying a mobile, she had no option but to turn and hurry Chocolate as fast as she could back along the footpath, and as he saw no reason to alter his pace it was nearly half an hour later before she was on the phone demanding a fire engine be despatched to the Manor immediately.

By nine thirty the number of people at Juliet's party had diminished, but not by much. Isabelle had been the first to go. On returning from the bathroom, she had apologised, saying she didn't feel terribly well, and left, leaving Richard behind. Then Charlie made his excuses. At nine o'clock, Polly took Charlotte and Louisa home, intending to return to join Oliver and Juliet for a late supper.

The atmosphere relaxed considerably when Charlie had left, and the wine flowed. After the departure of the old ladies, Veronica started to make going noises, but Juliet said gaily, 'No, don't go yet, not unless your supper's spoiling in the oven. Ollie, Veronica's glass is empty, and so is Richard's. Open some more wine, darling.'

'If you're sure,' murmured Veronica, with a glance at her husband making himself comfortable on a sofa, looking as if he was settling in for the whole evening. 'And please, my friends call me Vee.'

So when Polly returned she found the party continuing with renewed energy. Only the vicar hovered near the door, resolutely refusing anything more to drink, gazing hopelessly at his spouse, willing her to return home with him but too well trained to say or do anything.

Lavender Grey had a mission and she wasn't going to leave until she had achieved it. The departure of half the guests, the less significant ones for her purposes (although she thought Isabelle's premature departure disappointing), made her task easier. They had only just settled in a cosier grouping round the fire, glasses replenished, when she started up.

'Well, you lot, what are you going to do about our village shop? If we don't do something we're going to lose it, and, as I said to Isabelle before she left, we have here tonight people with influence. Our MP, the local editor, landowners, even' – she threw an affectionate glance at her

332

husband, who returned it with one of great suffering – 'our Vicar, though I do accept the Church is not the power it once was. Nevertheless, you are all people of significance and the village need you to act on their behalf.'

If Juliet hadn't been so relieved at the easy passage they'd had with Charlie Tucker and the Lesters; if she'd not had her ego well and truly flattered by Hugh Lester, and to a lesser extent by Richard Garnett, and if she'd drunk less or more than she had, Lavender might have found her call to arms cut short. But Juliet was in a mood to be entertained and she could sense some good sport to be had at the expense of Lavender. So she encouraged her.

'Lavender, some more wine. You're so right. We all need to do our bit. I can't do much, of course, not being here, but I was more than happy to have my photograph used to promote your campaign.'

Richard, who would not normally have risen to Lavender's challenge, caught something of Juliet's game. 'I've done my bit – you saw the article on Thursday.'

'So now it's your turn, Ollie darling. What can you do?' Juliet didn't wait for his reply, but laughingly continued: 'We could *all* do something. Milo.'

Startled, Milo looked up from his conversation with Polly. 'Me? What on earth could I do?'

'You could paint a picture of the shop and Polly could exhibit it in her gallery and we could sell it for thousands of pounds for the action fund.'

'Juliet!' Milo was horrified.

'And Richard, you could do more: you could spearhead this campaign. After all, this isn't just any village shop, it's *our* village shop and we're influential and important people – Lavender says so. What's your action group called, Lavender?'

Lavender Grey's head was beginning to spin. She wasn't used to a lot of wine, and that last glass had been more than she wanted. 'SOPO – Save Our Post Office.'

'We could call ourselves Significant Action Group, or SAG,' chuckled Juliet.

There were cries of protest and counter-suggestions with equally absurd acronyms put forward: 'SPIV – Significant People In the Village'; 'SPAT – Significant People Acting Together'; and 'SORROW – Save Our Rural Retail Outlets Worldwide'. This last, from Richard, was greeted with a round of applause.

Lavender got unsteadily to her feet. 'Well, I'm glad you're all taking this seriously. I'll look forward to hearing what you plan to do. Now, if you'll excuse us, Juliet, Oliver, I must take Andrew home. He has a sermon to prepare, you know. P'raps we'll see you in church tomorrow, Oliver, Polly? Thank you for such a lovely evening, Juliet. So kind of you to invite us, so kind.' And with Andrew in her wake, she made her way to the hall, found her coat, and departed, still talking.

Shutting the front door Oliver heard an explosion of laughter from the sitting room. He glanced at his watch. It was nearly ten o'clock. He sighed; the rest showed no signs of going and he was hungry – the canapés Juliet had produced had long gone. Perhaps hunger would drive them away.

Re-entering the sitting room, he heard Juliet say, 'No, she's right. If you lot can't exert a bit of influence, who can? A powerful landowner, a newspaper editor, and an MP.'

'And a very lovely film star,' Hugh added.

Juliet tossed her head and laughed.

Richard watched her, fascinated. He'd been attracted to her when he met her in the village, but he hadn't realised till now how lovely she was. How on earth could she have married Oliver Merfield? She could have had anyone.

'I don't really see what *we* can do, or indeed, why we should.' Veronica shrugged. 'The village shop hardly serves the village, you know, Juliet. There's absolutely nothing there I'd want to buy. And it's so unhygienic.'

'So over to Oliver and Richard.' Juliet smiled at Richard and something fizzled in his brain, 'The MP and the editor – who can do more, I wonder?'

'Sounds like a challenge,' commented Veronica, amused.

Juliet clapped her hands. 'You're right, it does. So let's have one. Much more fun than a dreary old campaign.'

'Hold on, hold on.' Oliver was alarmed. 'I want to be taken seriously by my constituents. I'm not going to be a pawn in some stupid game you two are concocting.'

At that moment, the telephone rang and as Oliver went to answer it, Juliet turned teasingly to Richard. 'Richard, do you think you've got more influence than our MP? Are you prepared to put that to the test? Go on, I challenge you.'

Richard was prevented from replying by the

335

urgency in Oliver's voice.

'What? A fire? When? Half an hour! Why didn't you– I see... Thank you. I'll go over right away... No, please don't... I'm very grateful.'

He turned to his guests. 'I'm sorry, but I've got to go. That was Rita Godwin, she's spotted a fire at the Manor...'

Polly leaped to her feet, aghast. 'Ollie, how awful. We must go immediately.'

'Apparently she's called the fire brigade, but only just. She saw the smoke over half an hour ago.'

'Then why on earth didn't she phone earlier? The house will be ablaze. Oh, my God, Ollie!'

Polly, ashen faced, was out of the door with Oliver hard on her heels before the others had barely got to their feet.

They looked uncomfortably at one another.

'Perhaps,' ventured Richard, 'we should go and offer some help?'

'I'm not sure we could do anything but get in the fire service's way,' muttered Hugh with reluctance. 'But if you want to walk over there, Richard, I'll come with you.'

'I'm going home,' announced Milo. 'I've drunk far more than I should tonight and I've got an early start. Goodnight, most gracious of hostesses.' He kissed Juliet's hand. 'I don't usually do portraits, but one day, one day, I might do yours.'

'I'll go on home, Hugh.' Veronica turned to Richard. 'If you'd like to call in for a nightcap when the excitement's all over, Richard, you'd be most welcome.'

Within minutes, Juliet was alone.

336

'I don't believe it,' she said morosely, refilling her glass. 'The first fun night I've had in this godforsaken place, and *they* have to upstage me. Typical!'

Panicking, Jamie looked round for something he could use to scoop up the river water. Nothing, there was nothing – except his helmet, he was still carrying his helmet. He didn't hesitate. Ignoring the pain, he dropped to his knees to scoop up water, four, five times, till the fire was out and a stinking, sticky, smoky mess was left.

'So Jamie, perhaps you'd like to tell me what's been going on down here,' said a voice from above.

Whirling round, dashing the tears from his eyes, he stared up at the ghostly figure of Great-aunt Charlotte.

He froze.

'Well, Jamie? I'm waiting.' The tall, thin wraith looked down, cold, composed.

For a moment his mind went completely blank. What could he say? How could he get away with it?

'I, er ... I...' His mouth was so swollen he could hardly move his lips. He hurt so much his self-control abandoned him and he started to weep again.

'Is that fire well and truly out?'

Smudging the tears from his eyes, he stumbled over to the corner of the boathouse and pulled the dripping cushions away. The sour smell of damp, burned material filled his nostrils. He could see the corner of the building was black and stained, but the structure didn't seem charred and was not smoking. The rain, coupled with his prompt arrival, had ensured the flames hadn't set the building on fire.

He picked up his helmet, dipped it into the river and threw one last lot of water onto the cushions for good measure, then turned back to face his aunt, mumbling, 'It's out.'

'Then you had better come with me,' she said icily. She stood back to allow him to climb the ladder and it was only when, with great difficulty he manoeuvred his injured body over the railing, that she caught sight of his face.

'Jamie! What have you done to yourself? You look dreadful!'

He tried to speak, but it was all too much. Trying to wipe away the tears, blood and mucus, which were mingling freely on his cheeks, he tottered towards her.

She took his arm and, despite the fragility of her age, gripped him firmly. 'No, don't say anything now. Come on, you can lean on me. Let's get you back to the house. My poor boy, you're in a real state.'

Slowly they made their way through the drizzle to the French windows of the smoking room, from where she'd spotted Jamie running across the lawn to the river.

She helped him into a chair, then stood back, her face expressionless. 'My, my, they have given you a beating. It was "they", I take it.'

Jamie tried to speak, but she held up her hand to stop him. 'All in good time. First, I must do something about those cuts. I won't be long.'

And she wasn't, but in her absence, Jamie, reliving the horror of that evening, and realising how close the boathouse had come to burning down, wept bitter tears of self-recrimination.

She returned with a bowl of warm water and other bits and pieces, and gently sponged his wounds. She let him weep on, making no attempt to console him; but neither did she lecture him or cross-examine him. When she'd finished she sat down, lit a cigarette, and waited till he stopped crying. Finally his tears dried up and he sat there, his eyes closed, feeling so dead that he wished he were.

'Here.'

He opened his eyes.

Aunt Charlotte was offering him a lit cigarette. 'Take this. And when you're ready, perhaps you would tell me what you were doing in the boathouse, how it came to be on fire, and how you received such a terrible beating. I know the young have vivid imaginations, Jamie, but in this instance I should be grateful if you told me the truth. It would be so much simpler, in the long run. You can take your time. Nobody will disturb us here.'

Painfully, through his split lips, Jamie drew on the cigarette, then slowly told his aunt the entire story, right back to when he was caught with cannabis at his previous school. He faltered once, when he told of his decision to hide his friends in the boathouse, but she made no comment so he continued until he reached the end.

He felt exhausted, wrung out and very embarrassed. But still she said nothing. He stole a glance at her. She was sitting, as upright as ever, apparently watching the smoke from her cigarette coiling lazily in the air.

He shivered and that seemed a cue for her to come out of her reverie. She got up, putting out her cigarette. 'I'm glad the boathouse didn't burn down. It holds many memories for me. I'm going to get you a hot drink and put you to bed. I'll also give your parents a ring to say you're going to stay the night here.'

Jamie panicked. 'What will you tell them?'

'Nothing, for the moment.' She stopped, listening to a distant noise. It was the sound of the ancient doorbell, echoing through the house. 'Hmm, seems like we've got visitors. I think it's better if you stay put, Jamie. I'll be back.'

She gave him another cigarette and went. Numb as he felt, Jamie was left wondering what made his extraordinary old aunt tick.

Through the gates and into the courtyard, his heart thumping, Oliver raced, with Polly close behind. The Manor loomed in front of them, black and inscrutable. Anxiously he scanned the façade. 'I can't see anything this side, Pol. I'll run round this way, you check that way. When we've located where the fire is, we'd better get Grandmère and the others out. The fire brigade should be here any minute.'

'Shouldn't we get them out first, then see where the fire is?'

Oliver shook his head. 'You're right. I'm not thinking straight. Here.' He tugged hard on the bell-pull. 'That'll bring Nanny down. You stay here, Pol, explain what's happening. I'll go and rouse the others.'

He dashed into the house and was about to mount the stairs when Aunt Charlotte appeared through a door in the hall.

'What's going on, Oliver? This is rather late to be calling. Are you in trouble?'

'Not me, Aunt Charlotte. It's the Manor – someone spotted a fire. It's essential you all get out as quickly as possible. The fire brigade are on their way.'

And as he spoke, the approaching sound of a siren could be heard.

'A fire, Oliver? Where?' Nanny, firmly tied into a warm woollen dressing gown, appeared at the top of the stairs.

'I don't know, Nanny, but we must get everyone out.'

'You go and warn your Grandmother, dear. I'll get Miss Louisa.'

Charlotte, looking thoughtful, made her way outside and joined Polly as the first of three fire tenders, their lights flashing, pulled into the courtyard.

Attracted by the noise and lights, a number of people had congregated at the edge of the courtyard, including Mrs Godwin, Hugh Lester and the new neighbour, Richard Garnett.

The fire chief jumped out and joined Polly, leaving his team and the men in the other engines to disembark in a great display of business.

He looked up at the dark outline of the house.

They all looked up.

'We had a call saying the Manor was on fire.

Caller said the house is occupied by four elderly relatives of the local MP.'

'Well, I'm one of those elderly relatives,' said Charlotte, with some asperity, 'and I'm not aware of any fire.'

'My brother's gone in to rouse the others,' said Polly. 'We've not had a chance to check the other side of the house.'

'Right you are.' The fireman turned and issued instructions. A group of men fanned out and disappeared round the house.

A number of minutes lapsed before they re-urned with much less urgency than when they had set out.

After a brief conference, the fire chief returned to Polly and Charlotte. 'Looks like the house is untouched. One of my men thinks there might have been a fire in a boathouse at the bottom of the garden, but it's out. If you'll excuse me, I'm going to check it. Er...' He stopped. 'I thought, miss, you said your brother was getting the other ladies out of the house, only he's taking his time about it, isn't he?'

'Yes,' said Polly anxiously. 'Perhaps I'd better–'

'He's probably waiting for them to get dressed,' interjected Charlotte. 'My sisters would not dream of coming outside in their nightclothes, for goodness' sake.'

The burly man, in his padded jacket, thick boots, heavy gloves and helmet, stared disbelievingly at the tall, withered elegance standing in front of him, her red chiffon dress starting to cling damply to her thin frame and the black velvet shawl round her shoulders glistening with damp under the

342

tenders' lurid sweeps of yellow light.

'If the house had been on fire they might have burned to death.'

'Rather that than be seen undressed,' replied Charlotte. 'It's a question of priorities, isn't it? Ah, here they are. Fully clothed and not a scorch mark.'

The amazed fireman watched Mrs Merfield, in her customary black lace gown under a long black cape, pick her way across the flagstones on Oliver's arm, followed by Nanny, who had put on a serviceable trench coat over her dressing gown and Louisa, who was wearing a sky-blue cape over a silvery silk dress with high-heeled silver-strapped sandals.

'Blimey, four Miss Havershams,' the chief muttered to himself, and he hastily made off to conduct his own inspection of the boathouse.

'Pity,' muttered Hugh Lester under his breath when if became clear to the group of villagers that there was no fire.

Richard glanced at him with surprised amusement. 'A pity, Hugh? I admit I'm a bit disappointed: another scoop that isn't. Pictures of a burning house always sell newspapers, particularly when it belongs to our local MP's granny.'

Hugh grunted. 'Coming back for a nightcap?'

'Thanks.'

A fire had been lit in the drawing room of Summerstoke House and Veronica greeted them with a full decanter of vieux Armagnac. She, too, looked disappointed to hear that it had been a false alarm.

Richard raised his eyebrows. 'What is it with the Merfields? Don't you like the old dears?'

'They're very far from being old dears, Richard, believe me.' Hugh replied with a sour expression on his face. 'They're arrogant old bitches who've always lived off the fat of the land. Fortunately, there aren't too many of their kind left. Unfortunately for us, there are three in this village.'

'We were going to do a land deal with them – they've got the best pasture this side of the river,' Veronica explained. 'But at the last moment they pulled out, which made our plans to develop the stud impossible.'

'And now we've got their grandson living in the village,' said Richard lightly, swirling his brandy. 'What did you make of him and his lovely wife?'

Hugh contemplated his brandy. What did he think about Oliver Merfield and his wife? Juliet was lovely, and she knew it – totally egocentric, fun to flirt with, but nothing more. As for Oliver, there was nothing to dislike about him personally, but he was the scion of a family who'd thwarted Hugh more than once, and who seemed to think they could humiliate him with impunity.

'He's typical of his kind,' he replied finally. 'Charming, I've no doubt, but wet behind the ears. An MP in his thirties... What experience has he got to offer his electorate?'

'I should think his wife gives him a run for his money,' sneered Veronica. 'She's very lovely, I grant you that, but what a flirt! Are you going to take up her challenge, Richard?'

'What, prove I have more influence than he

344

has? I don't have to prove that Vee, it's a fact. And anyway' – Richard took the last sip of brandy with a smack of satisfaction – 'I don't usually muddy my own doorstep, nor am I the slightest bit interested in their campaign.'

Veronica got up. 'I'm going to knock up a light supper – those shop-bought canapés are hardly satisfying. Does either of you fancy some smoked salmon and scrambled eggs?'

As she left the room, Hugh reached for the decanter. 'A drop more?'

He liked Richard. He was amusing and clever, and he envied Hugh, and Hugh liked that because he knew that for all his charm, Richard would only ever get so far. He also liked Richard because he was useful, and clever though he was, he, Hugh, knew how to manipulate him. Juliet's challenge had started his brain ticking.

He poured a generous measure into Richard's glass.

Richard could feel his head starting to reel from the combination of wine, brandy and very little food, but it was a long time since he had been entertained by Hugh and Vee on his own, and it was the sort of intimacy he'd hoped for on moving to Summerstoke.

'Thank you.'

'Just how much influence do you think you have, Richard?' Hugh asked lightly.

There was something in Hugh's voice that put Richard on alert.

He replied good-humouredly, 'Not as much as some people think, Hugh, but enough. You, or more specifically some of your colleagues, have

345

experienced it over the years.'

'True, but do you think you're strong enough to take on our MP?'

Richard frowned. 'What are you getting at? Not this post office, surely?'

'Don't be stupid.' Hugh sniffed his brandy. 'No. To come straight to the point, I'd be interested, my dear Richard, to see Oliver Merfield discredited and deselected by the next election.'

Richard, almost shocked into sobriety, stared at the man sitting opposite him. 'What? Why?'

Hugh looked up from his glass, a slight smile playing on his face, his eyes cold.

He is, thought Richard, not for the first time, completely ruthless.

'Let's just say the Merfields have had things their own way for too long. I'd like to see them brought down a peg or two, and this way would give me a great deal of satisfaction. But perhaps I'm wrong, perhaps I misjudged you. I got the distinct impression you didn't like the fellow?'

All the dislike, jealousy and resentment festering in Richard's bosom found a voice. 'No, as it happens Hugh, you're right, I can't stand him.'

'Well, then.' Hugh leaned towards him, his voice soft. 'How about it? You could start with this wretched post office. He'll huff and he'll puff, but he won't blow the problem away. If head office want to close it, they will, and he'll be left with egg on his face. Round one to you. Then I'm sure you can discover something about his wife; or his son – he left his last school pretty abruptly. I'm sure you can dig up some delinquent behaviour. I don't have to teach you your job.'

346

'No, you don't.' Richard stared hard at Hugh. This was scheming on a grand scale and he felt out of his depth. 'Does Vee know about this ... this idea?'

'No. If she did she'd be behind it one hundred per cent, but this is just between you and me. And, Richard, let us be quite clear: if you take up the challenge, whatever you do, however you go about it, I don't want to be involved in any way. I've got some delicate manoeuvrings of my own on the go at the moment, and the last thing I want is to be identified with anything that discredits Oliver Merfield or his party.'

Richard shook his head, 'I'd have to be very careful – this isn't just a one-off favour, Hugh. I don't mind throwing the odd rotten apple, but a systematic campaign... Why should I?'

'Why should you stick your neck out, apart from giving me something I want? That's a fair question, Richard, and I should give you something in return.'

He swirled his glass, held it up to the firelight and watched the amber liquid settle, enjoying the game. 'It's not exactly a trade secret that your circulation is falling off, your advertising revenue is sinking to an all-time low and that your position with your bosses is under review.'

Richard felt sick. How had bloody Hugh found all that out?

Hugh, reading his friend's expression correctly, continued, smoothly, 'You're a friend, Richard. I like you. I'd like to be able to help out.'

'How?' Richard croaked. 'All newspapers are losing circulation, it's a fact.'

'True, but not all are losing their advertisers, and it's your paper's income your bosses are bothered about. If you help me with my little request, I will ensure your advertising revenue doubles in the next financial year. I can do that; you may rest assured I can. As we know there's going to be a general election next year, so get our man deselected and your job will be safe.'

14

During the night the rain eased off and the temperature began to drop. Slowly the valley of Summerstoke filled with mist rising from the river and everything, including the tall, naked figure of a man running along the footpath beside the water, was cast in a ghostly hue.

Oliver rose early on Sunday morning, in spite of having finally fallen into bed sometime after two o'clock. Having cleared away the empty glasses and wine bottles and vacuumed the sitting-room floor, he went to see if Juliet was awake. She was still sleeping soundly. He didn't bother to wake her, but quietly let himself out of the house.

Before the firemen had left the night before, the chief told Oliver that possibly a vagrant had caused the boathouse fire, but it seemed more likely, from the remnants of the magazines they'd found, to be adolescents. He had no further interest in the incident, and, although he was polite to Oliver, he made it clear he thought the call-out had been a waste of time and taxpayers' money.

Oliver had planned to wait up for Jamie. He couldn't rid himself of the suspicion that, although his son had been at a party in Summerbridge that evening, he was somehow involved. Then Charlotte rang to say Jamie, for reasons not clear to Oliver, was staying overnight at the Manor. Before confronting his son, Oliver decided, he would check out the boathouse for himself.

The lawn was wet, the air was chill and mist was swirling up from the river, cloaking the garden in a white dampness. As he approached the boathouse, the acrid smell of a spent fire and burned material assailed him. He climbed down the ladder and looked around. The fire had obviously been started in the corner: tell-tale scorch marks, blackening the white paint, reached up to the ceiling; scattered about were the charred remnants of the magazines, which probably belonged to his son; two or three singed cushions had been thrown to one side; and here and there were half-burned food wrappers, which Jamie might have taken from his kitchen.

Feeling increasingly depressed, he looked more closely at the floor, under the cushions, and in the boat. There were a large number of cigarette stubs – either Jamie had had a party down here, or he was a chain-smoker. And then he found what he had so hoped not to find.

Bleakly he walked back across the lawn to the house. By the back door, under a small bay tree, he found Jamie's helmet. It was soaked, the lining ruined.

Polly was in the kitchen, having coffee with Aunt

Charlotte and Nanny, who was sitting at the table peeling vegetables. From the sudden silence at his entry all three were obviously engrossed in a conversation which was interrupted by his arrival.

'Hi, Oliver, you're an early bird. Fancy walking with me over to Milo's studio this morning?'

'Not immediately, Pol. I need to talk to Jamie. Is he up yet?'

'He's not very well, this morning,' Nanny began tentatively.

'How do you mean, not very well? I hope he didn't get drunk at that party.'

'He didn't go.' Charlotte was brisk. 'On his way there he had an unfortunate encounter with two yobs who took it upon themselves to give young Jamie a nasty beating.'

This was completely unexpected. Oliver was horrified. 'What? Is he all right? How badly hurt is he? Where did this happen? I must go to him, right away.'

'He's asleep at the moment, pet. Best leave him that way.' Nanny was soothing. 'I've checked him over, and there's nothing but cuts and bruises, poor little fellow.'

'Sit down, Oliver. You'd better hear the whole story,' said Aunt Charlotte firmly.

'Was he involved in the boathouse fire? Was he responsible?' Oliver looked at her, feeling wretched.

'Let Aunt Charlotte tell you, Ollie, and don't leap to conclusions.' Polly got up. 'I'll pour you some coffee – you look as though you need it.'

Oliver sat quietly as Charlotte related Jamie's story.

'So you see, Oliver,' his aunt said, in con-clusion, 'he may have made a mistake in letting those two boys sleep in the boathouse without permission, but he paid very dearly for it and it was due to him that the fire was put out before it could do any significant damage.'

'They might have done some real harm, kicking him like that.'

'But they didn't Ollie, they didn't,' Polly put her arms round her brother. 'He's all right – a bit of a sight, I grant you, but he's more worried about how you and Juliet are going to react.'

Oliver, remembering his find, remained silent.

'The thing is, Ollie, what are we going to do about it? Aunt Charlotte thinks we should do nothing, and just say Jamie got beaten up on his way to the party by a couple of louts who he couldn't identify. I think we should get onto the police right away. They shouldn't get away with it – arson and assault.'

Oliver turned to his aunt. 'But you think we should let the matter rest, Aunt Charlotte. Why?'

Aunt Charlotte shrugged. 'You must do what-ever you think is right, Oliver, but because you're involved the press will be interested, and I'd rather not have the rest of the world knowing our business. We live quietly here, and I should like it to remain that way. Jamie himself is not keen to pursue them any further, either.'

'Well, I agree with Polly,' said Nanny firmly. 'They're nasty, vicious tykes and I don't think they should get away with it.'

'Oh, I'm sure they'll get their come-uppance before too long,' said Charlotte with confidence.

'It sounds as though they're headed for it. I think we should do as I suggest.'

Oliver was close to tears when he saw Jamie. The boy's face was swollen with bruising and a colourful combination of purple and red. His mouth had been split in two places, so his lips were swollen and he talked with difficulty. He was so stiff and painful that he was content to lie back on the pillows and remain as still as he could.

Gently Oliver questioned him about the incident. Jamie told the same story as Aunt Charlotte, and was adamant he didn't want to go to the police. When he urged him to change his mind, Jamie became so distressed he abandoned trying to persuade him. Oliver, his face grave, looked at his son lying on the pillows.

'There's one other thing we need to talk about, Jamie. Everything else has been explained, but this...' He produced from his pocket a small clear plastic bag with the faintest brownish residue in the bottom, and a couple of cigarette ends with cardboard filters.

'When we left London, I made you promise not to smoke marijuana again. I found this bag ground into the floor under some cushions. I know what it is, Jamie. Your headmaster showed me the bag they took off you. Be honest with me, please. Does this belong to you?'

There was silence but, from the anguished look on Jamie's face, Oliver knew he was right.

'Oh, Jamie, how could you?' He was so upset his voice shook. 'Not only have you broken your promise to me, but you've brought the stuff here!

What would have happened if the firemen had found it? A police search? How would Grandmère, Aunt Louisa and Aunt Charlotte react? And Nanny ... she's been so good to you. Is this the way to repay that kindness?'

Jamie closed his eyes and groaned. 'Dad ... Dad, I'm sorry. You've got to believe me. I got some when we first got here. I was so angry with you, I wanted to get my own back, do my own thing. But I didn't use it, honest. I hid it behind the cushions and when Mark said they'd found it and smoked the lot, I was glad because it had gone. I didn't smoke any of it, Dad. I wouldn't, not here, not now. Promise.'

Oliver looked at him, long and hard, then put a hand out and touched his cheek. 'Okay Jamie, okay. But never again. Is that understood?'

'Yes, Dad.' Jamie sniffed. 'I won't. I promise you I won't.'

Oliver gave him a tissue to wipe his eyes and stroked his head. 'Nanny tells me that there's nothing a good rest won't heal. We're meant to be having lunch here, so I'll bring the car round and take you home this afternoon. It's a nuisance I've got a party do this evening, but I'll make Juliet's excuses. Thank goodness she doesn't go back to Los Angeles till Thursday.'

But, to his father's surprise, Jamie had other ideas. Much as he loved his mother, nursing was not one of her strengths. There would be a lot of fussing and not much care, and he'd rather stay where he was. He couldn't really explain it, even to himself, but he felt safe with Nanny and Aunt Charlotte and they wouldn't hassle him; they

353

were on his side.

After his father and Polly left to go and break the news of his accident to Juliet, he closed his eyes, imagining how Alison would react to news of his accident.

She'd be shocked. 'Oh, no, not Jamie!' she'd cry. Her brilliant green eyes would widen and the tears slip silently down her cheeks.

'I must go to him. Now. I must tell him before it's too late.' (She'd heard that he was so badly beaten he was on his deathbed.)

'But you don't know him,' they'd say – he hadn't worked out who 'they' were, yet.

'I love him,' she'd sob.

He could picture her on the other side of that door, hesitant, nervous. Should she go in? What would she find? But overwhelmed by the need to see him one last time, to tell him she would always love him, she turns the handle and...

'Jamie! Oh, darling Jamie, what have they done to you?'

Her voice was soft and low, trembling with emotion. He opened his eyes.

'Hello, Mum.'

Sunday lunch at Summerstoke Manor was always a formal affair, even when the ladies had no visitors. Having wiped away her tears and satisfied herself Jamie was going to live and no bones were broken, Juliet joined Oliver and the elderly Merfields in a small drawing room.

Although it was after midday the mist had not lifted and the room was gloomy in spite of the glow from the fire that crackled in the grate.

Oliver was serving everyone with dry sherry in fine old crystal glasses – this, too, was part of the Sunday lunch ritual.

'How is the invalid, Juliet?' Mrs Merfield, sitting in her usual position by the fire, turned her dark stare on Juliet.

'He's so bruised, the poor darling, I was really shocked. I can't believe you're taking it so calmly, Ollie. Why haven't the police been told?'

'Believe me, Juliet, I was as shaken as you when I saw him this morning.' Oliver took her hand. 'But the damage is only superficial.'

'Superficial! How can you say that? His poor face...'

'The bruising looks bad, I know, but it'll fade quickly enough and there's no lasting damage. Jamie doesn't want us to go to the police. He says he wouldn't be able to identify the yobs, so what would be the point? He got very upset when I pressed him, darling, so for the moment I think we should let the matter drop.'

'Oliver's right, Juliet. What good would it do to bring the police in?' said Charlotte lightly. 'Unpleasant for everyone, I should have thought.'

'Absolutely right, Lottie,' agreed Louisa. 'And if it got out to the press...' She shuddered. 'We'd have more than PC Plod to contend with.' She turned to Juliet, a hint of malice in her voice. 'I know press and publicity are meat and drink to you, my dear, but we live quietly here and we should like it to stay that way.'

Juliet flushed angrily. 'I don't court publicity, and it hadn't occurred to me it would be an issue. So are you saying that, although Jamie's been beaten within an inch of his life, we're not going to do anything about it because you're worried your precious privacy will be disturbed?'

'It doesn't help to exaggerate, Juliet.' Mrs Merfield spoke coldly. 'I haven't seem Jamie myself, but whoever summoned the fire brigade last night put us in a ridiculous position. Jamie has said, both to Oliver and to Charlotte, he does not wish to pursue the matter, and I see no reason to call the police force out here unnecessarily, either.'

Juliet was furious. 'He's my son.'

'That is not in dispute, Juliet, but when is it you return to the United States?'

It was no good. Their cold superciliousness always made her feel cheap. It didn't matter one jot that she had youth, beauty and fame on her side, they despised her. Hating Grandmère, hating the lot of them, she could only fight back feebly. 'Thursday. But I can't help feeling that these ... these yobs were known to Jamie. Have you met the gang he hangs around with in Summerbridge? I wouldn't be at all surprised if it wasn't them who—'

She was interrupted by the arrival of Polly, accompanied by wafts of delicious cooking smells emanating from the dining room next door.

'Sorry I'm late, everyone. Nanny says lunch is served. Hi, Juliet. How's Jamie, the poor fellow? He's all colours of the rainbow, isn't he?'

'Then maybe,' said Juliet, pushing past her with ill-disguised temper, 'you should have him as an exhibit in your gallery.'

The sitting room in the Old Vicarage still bore traces of the previous occupant, the shabby wall-

356

paper and bare floorboards giving the room a depressed air in spite of a deep velveteen sofa and the colourful rugs Isabelle had scattered about. The only heating came from a large tiled fireplace with an elaborate iron gate in which Isabelle had lit a fire against the misty chillness of the morning.

She was curled up on the sofa, reading aloud to Rebecca and Clementine. The girls were waiting for Richard to get up and take them swimming, but he was slow making an appearance this morning.

'"So the little kitchen maid led the courtiers to the wood where the nightingale sang. As they went, they heard a cow mooing. 'What wonderful power for such a small bird', said a courtier."'

The girls giggled.

'"'That's not the nightingale, that's a cow,' said the little kitchen maid. 'We've a way to go yet.' So on they went. Then some frogs began to croak."'

Isabelle stopped. 'Come on, how about some croaking?'

'Croak, croak!' shouted Clemmie, while Becky enthusiastically made noises in the back of her throat.

Isabelle smiled and carried on reading. '"Beautiful,' said the courtier. 'What a lovely song.' 'That's not the nightingale, those are frogs,' said the little maid. 'Not much further now.' In the middle of the green forest the nightingale began to sing and the courtiers stood entranced. 'There, there she is,' said the little kitchen maid, pointing to a little grey bird–"'

Richard's voice, loud in complaint, echoed

down the stairs and interrupted their comfortable intimacy. 'Issy? Issy? This isn't my shirt – it's too small. Issy, whose shirt is it, and where's my coffee? Bloody hell, you should've woken me earlier.'

Isabelle put the book down with a slight sigh.

'Ooh,' wailed Clemmie, 'don't stop, Mummy.'

'Don't be silly. You want to go swimming with Daddy, don't you? You and Becky look at the pictures while I go and make his coffee.'

Isabelle picked the shirt up from the bed where Richard had tossed it and examined it. 'I don't recognise the label,' she said, frowning slightly, 'so it's not one that's shrunk in the wash.'

'Then whose is it?' he demanded, 'What's another man's shirt doing in my cupboard?'

Isabelle's face cleared. 'It's probably Oliver Merfield's.'

Before she could say any more, Richard, his brain swimming with a lethal mix of hangover and suspicion, erupted. 'Oliver Merfield? What's his shirt doing here? What have you two been up to?'

Isabelle's face went white. 'Don't be so ridiculous, Richard, and please keep your voice down – you'll upset the girls.'

'I want an explanation,' Richard hissed. 'What's that man's shirt doing here?'

'I should imagine,' replied Isabelle in a low angry voice, 'that Paula mixed up the two shirts after the fireworks and brought Oliver's back here instead of the one I lent him.'

'You lent him one of my shirts?' Richard was almost incandescent with rage.

'I'm not going to talk to you in this mood,' Isabelle said coldly. 'I've never known you to behave like this before; I don't know what's got into you.'

She stalked out of the room, shutting the door.

Richard banged his fist on the dressing table and glared at his face in the mirror. In his heart of hearts, did he believe his wife was having an affair with Oliver Merfield? No, but it didn't stop him suspecting that if the circumstances were right, he'd be in there like a shot! He thought of Hugh's proposal. He'd be playing a dangerous game, but by God, he'd nail the bastard and take pleasure in doing so.

15

'So that's it – nothing else? We just have to wait? Okay, thanks, Louis... No, no, I'm fine.' But Juliet was far from fine, and the calmness of her voice belied the fury welling up inside her. When Louis rang off, she hurled the phone down on the flag-stoned kitchen floor, screaming, 'The bastards! The bastards! How could they?'

The phone shattered, and bits of plastic, electronics and battery scattered in every direction. Juliet swung a kick at the largest piece and it spun across the floor, smashing against the stove.

'I don't believe it, I really don't believe it. Tell me, someone, am I dreaming this?' she yelled, and standing in the middle of the kitchen, fists clenched, she swore at the top of her voice. A row of shiny stainless-steel saucepans, sitting neatly on a shelf above the stove, caught her eye and dashing over she pulled each one down and hurled it across the kitchen, as if the innocuous pots were the heads of the studio bosses who by their indecision were trapping her in this kitchen, in this house, in this village.

Before the cacophony died away, Juliet fled into the hall. She needed to leave the house before she did any real damage. She didn't want to speak to anyone – *anyone!* It was fortunate Oliver was in London and Jamie was back in college after his accident, because she held them responsible, too. If it weren't for them, she wouldn't be trapped in this godforsaken dump. She pulled on her boots and grabbed a jacket. She needed to get out, find a deserted field and scream her head off.

As she banged the front door shut behind her, a stiff wind lifted her scarf. Making a furious grab at it, she snarled, 'Bloody November! What am I doing here, in this miserable place? I should be in LA, in the warmth.' Hunching her shoulders against the cold, she stomped off down the High Street in the direction of the river.

The village appeared deserted. It being nearly one o'clock, those who worked weren't about and those who didn't were home for lunch. She could hear faint shrieks of children in the school playground and the growl of distant traffic on the main road to Bath, but otherwise nothing, and, whereas before she'd drawn solace from the peace and quiet of the village, now she found it oppressive and claustrophobic.

Head down against the wind, she didn't see the vicar until it was too late. He came out of the shop, a bag of sweets in one hand and a newspaper tucked under his arm.

'Dear lady,' he began, on seeing her, 'My dear Mrs ... er, Mrs...' His hand went up to tilt a non-existent hat and the newspaper slipped. Hardly had it touched the ground when the wind whipped it into life and pages whirled and whisked away, wrapping themselves round the lamppost, the billboard, Juliet, and out into the road.

'Oh dear, oh dear... My goodness me, goodness gracious.' The Vicar, with his great heavy head, long arms and legs, made an incongruous figure flapping after his paper, but Juliet was not in a mood to be amused, nor did she make any attempt to help him. She was tempted to walk on and leave him to it but was forestalled by the breathless flow of conversation punctuating his rescue of the newspaper.

'We really don't know how to thank you. Such a pleasant evening. How kind of you. And what interesting company. I was so honoured to meet Milo Steel – Lavender thinks we were contemporaries at school together.'

He finally managed to gather all the recalcitrant pages and came back to tower over her, the crumpled paper crushed to his chest. 'It would be, er, a very great honour, Mrs, er...'

The shop doorbell momentarily distracted him and beyond him Juliet saw Charlie Tucker coming out of the shop, unwrapping a pasty. Before the vicar could turn his attention back to her, she caught Charlie's eye and mouthed a cry for help.

Charlie strolled over. 'Afternoon, Vicar, Juliet.'

He barely gave the vicar time to nod in reply before turning to Juliet. 'Lucky I bumped into you, Juliet. I was on my way to yours. You said you wanted to look around the farm and I thought, as I'm on my lunch break, now's as good a time as any. How about it?'

It was a rescue. Juliet, who had never expressed any such desire, felt her black mood shift.

'Great,' she said coolly. 'Thanks, Charlie. Now would be fine. Goodbye, Vicar. I'm glad you enjoyed the party. I think you're going to have to iron that paper before you can read it.'

They left the vicar looking mournfully at his bundle of papers.

Charlie, munching his pasty all the while, led the way to a battered white van and opened the door for Juliet.

'If I'd known I was going to give my lady a lift,' he said with a grin, 'I'd have brought the Porsche. Down you get, Duchess,' this to the spaniel curled up on the passenger seat. 'A maiden in distress needs your seat.'

He fed the dog the last corner of his pasty and dusted down the seat she'd obediently vacated.

'You've no idea how right you are,' said Juliet with feeling.

Charlie glanced at her curiously, but said nothing until he'd swung himself into the driver's seat. 'What's it to be, then, a trip round the farm? A trip round the village to shake off the vicar and then back home? Or a trip to the pub, which is where I was going?'

Juliet didn't hesitate. 'A trip to the pub, so long as it's not the Foresters Arms.'

Charlie laughed. 'If you'd wanted to drink there, you'd have drunk on your own. Come on, I'll introduce you to the Bunch of Grapes. Mind you, I don't know who'll be there and you might find some of 'em a little unsavoury.'

'I'll take my chance. Can't be worse than some of the people I've met in Summerstoke.'

'That reminds me, there's something I was wanting to ask you. Your little party on Saturday?'

'Yes?'

'Why did you invite me?'

Juliet looked at him. He was concentrating on the road ahead, a slight frown furrowing his brow. He looked lean and strong and oh, she thought, so earthy!

He felt her glance and looked at her, an eyebrow raised. 'Well?'

'Because I liked what I saw when I first met you; because you're Milo's landlord and he was coming; because I don't know many people in the village and I thought you'd be fun.'

'So you'd no idea no one in their right minds would put Hugh Lester and me in the same room? No one told you?'

'No.'

'Not even your friend from the Old Vicarage, Isabelle whatsername?'

'No. I don't think I discussed the party with her – I don't really know her that well. Anyway, how would she know about your feud?'

'She's a friend of theirs. I told her I couldn't stand 'em, so I assumed she would've told you.'

Juliet laughed. 'No, you're wrong. Besides, as I said, we hardly know each other. She's not my type – a bit too whimsical for my taste.'

Charlie grinned. 'I think I know what you mean.'

'But you still haven't said how you know her.'

An image of the mud-spattered Isabelle, clutching the wrench, lying on the grass underneath him, flashed through his mind. 'Oh, I gave her a lift once.'

The Bunch of Grapes was nearly empty so, abandoning his usual stool in the public bar, Charlie, his dog shadowing him, led Juliet through to the saloon and settled her in the deep window seat before going to the bar.

'So,' he said, placing a glass of white wine in front of her and pulling up an adjacent chair, 'why did you need rescuing? You could have gobbled up the poor old vicar and spat him out for breakfast on a good day.'

'Today wasn't a good day.' Juliet took a deep breath, but the edges of her anger were blunted and she felt able to continue with only the smallest tremor in her voice. 'I had a call from my agent. I don't know how much you know, but I've been in Hollywood making a pilot for a TV series everyone said would be a long-distance runner. He phoned today to say the studio needed more time to decide whether to back it or not, so I'm left drumming my heels, whistling to the empty air.'

'Tough.' He took a long sip from his pint. 'Is it any good?'

She relished his directness, and smiled, looking enchantingly wistful. 'It's probably crap. But then ninety per cent of television in America is, and

364

it's more intelligent than most. I suspect that will be its downfall. Americans like to watch people dumber than they are.' She took a sip of her wine. 'Trouble is, I've pinned my colours to that particular mast. If it doesn't sell... Oh, Charlie, I don't want to have to spend the rest of my days buried in Summerstoke.'

'Why should you? I'm sure there's plenty else going on. You don't strike me as the sort of person to give up so easily. You're not a loser.'

'No.' She dimpled at him. 'No, I'm not. And nor are you, are you, Charlie?'

He shrugged, leaning forward to ruffle his dog's fur. 'No, I don't think so. But I've realised things can't be taken for granted. Things worth having have to be worked for, and that applies to people, too.' He looked up with a cheerful grin. 'So what are you going to do? Go back to London?'

'I'd like to. Do you think that's awful of me? But Summerstoke, or more particularly village life, is really not me. The trouble is, I don't want to leave my son, Jamie.'

Charlie frowned. 'I heard he got a bit of a beating over the weekend. Any idea who done it?'

'No. He was due to go to a student party. *I* think it was that lot. I've met one or two of them.' She shuddered. 'Neanderthal, or what – pierced this, pierced that, and communicating only in grunts. Jamie said it wasn't any of them and refused point blank to let me call the police. But I don't believe him. Fortunately, nothing seems to be broken, but he was pretty battered.'

Charlie was sympathetic, but not terribly interested. 'Happens to us all at some point. I dropped

365

my sister off at a party in Summerbridge that night. I wonder if it was the same one?' He sipped his beer. 'I can see it's hard on you, being stuck here. You need a bit of fun. How busy is Oliver?'

'Frightfully. He works twenty-four/seven, and it's really hard on me and Jamie. Why there aren't more divorces amongst MPs' families, I don't know; we scarcely get to see him. When Parliament's sitting he's in London from Monday to Thursday, and often on Fridays. When he *is* here, he spends Friday doing constituency work and half the weekend as well. Some of it, I'm sure, is quite unnecessary – he's far too conscientious.'

'I never thought the day would come when I'd feel sympathy towards a politician, but it sounds like his shift is the same as us farmers'. We're always on call – unless of course, you're Hughie Lester and you employ people to do the grafting for you.'

'But you're not working at the moment.' Juliet dimpled at him.

'No.' Charlie smiled. 'I'm not. Another glass of wine?'

The Reverend Grey wrapped his old greatcoat round his cadaverous body, left the vicarage and made his way down to the river for his evening walk. It was dark and cold; the evening stars seemed a long way off and his breath hung heavy in the air.

It was not unusual for him to go for a walk after dark. He explained to his wife it was a good time for quiet thought while taking much-needed exercise, but his principal reason for choosing

366

that time was that he'd be less likely to meet any of his parishioners, whose needs and general conversation filled him with dismay.

He turned off the bridge and made his way along the footpath away from Summerstoke. The mere glinted back over to his left, and ahead the footpath wound between a riot of sprawling brambles. The ground was firm underfoot; the inky river slipped noiselessly to his right; the lights of the village twinkled behind him; an owl called and was answered; and thinking of the Latin translation he was about to undertake, he felt momentarily content.

A slight noise ahead caused him to break from his habitual contemplation of the ground and look up. It was the sound of footfalls – light and fast, as if someone was running towards him. He froze, and before he could melt into the dark obscurity of the bushes, the tall figure of a man swung into view. He was running and his breath came in light easy gasps, his skin silver in the starlight, and before the shocked vicar could avert his gaze, he saw the runner was completely naked.

'Oliver, come in, do.' Rita Godwin opened her front door to Oliver's knock after a delay long enough for him to wish he'd not left his coat in the car.

It was a cold, clear November night and the stars, brilliant in a dark sky, outshone the feeble glow of the street lighting outside the shop. The Godwins lived in a flat over the premises, and Rita led Oliver up a steep, narrow flight of stairs, scarcely pausing for breath the whole while.

'Thanks for coming, Oliver. That secretary of yours phoned to make me an appointment at your surgery. I haven't got time for that. We close at six on Fridays – who am I going to get to mind the shop? Rob has his darts club Friday night, and I can't afford to shut up early. And she said there was a waiting list. You're very much in demand, aren't you, Oliver? Same as me; I don't stop from the minute I get up... When do we ever get time for ourselves, eh? But you know what they say: if you want something done, ask a busy person. Here we are.'

Rita ushered him into a moderately sized sitting room directly over the front of the shop, a chink of lamplight gleaming through a gap in the bright floral curtains.

It was full of heavily stuffed leather furniture, and the walls, papered with a floral print matching the curtains, were covered with framed certificates celebrating Rob's prowess at darts, and innumerable portraits of dogs. Presumably not the same dog, but the painter had managed to blur all distinctive features so that, with lolling tongues and dewy eyes, the breeds were indistinguishable. In the centre of the room, an easel bore a half-painted canvas of a chocolate-brown head. The subject of this portrait was sprawled in front of the coals of a glowing gas fire, snoring asthmatically, his smell almost as overpowering, in that over-heated room, as the odour of the oil paint.

In a large easy chair with a headpiece and extended leg rest, sat Rob Godwin, his eyes fixed on the outsize television set in the opposite corner of the room. He briefly looked up when

368

Oliver entered, nodded, then returned his attention to the screen.

He was a big man in his fifties. His skin was grey, shiny with perspiration; the line of his chin disappeared into folds of unshaven flesh; his hair, although still untroubled by grey, was lank and thinning, and a thin green pullover, worn over a thick, red-checked shirt, emphasised the contours of his round belly.

'Turn the telly off, love,' said his wife encouragingly. 'Here's Oliver come to tell us what he can do for the shop.'

'But I'm watching me programme. I've been waitin' all day for this.' His voice was surprisingly light and querulous.

'Perhaps I should come back another time,' Oliver said politely, thinking there was nothing he'd like more than to exchange the oppressive heat of the sitting room for the cool, dark quiet of the outside. 'I'm later than I said I'd be.'

'No, no, sit down. Rob, you can turn the sound down – you don't need it to watch birds.' She turned apologetically to Oliver. 'He's mad on birds, you know. When his back's not bad, he'll sit in his hide for hours, watching them on the river. There's not much he doesn't know about the comings and goings of the birds in Summerstoke.' She laughed loudly. 'You'll have to excuse me – that's an old joke between us.'

Oliver smiled politely and nodded at the portrait. 'That's your dog, I take it?'

'Yes. I'm very pleased with it. I think I've really caught his expression – so hard with animals. I've made one or two attempts already.' She waved at

369

the walls.

Oliver murmured a polite compliment.

'I'm glad you like them. They're for sale, you know. I usually paint on a commission-only basis, but I've run out of dogs. You don't have one, do you?'

'Er, no, no, we've no pets, sadly.'

'Never mind. Dear me, I'm forgetting my manners. Would you like a cup of tea, Oliver, or a beer?'

'He'd like a beer, silly woman – no one drinks tea at this time on a Friday night. He'd rather be down the pub with his mates, wouldn't you, Oliver? I know I would.'

'I won't have either, thanks,' said Oliver hastily, ruling out anything that might prolong the visit. 'Juliet will have supper waiting.'

'Oh, you poor man, you've not had your tea yet! You must be starving.'

'No, no, I'm fine – honestly. Now, why don't you tell me what's going on with the post office? Like every other resident in Summerstoke, I was shocked to think it might close. I've put my researcher on to the minister whose remit this would be, and I'm trying to get hold of the relevant bod at the Post Office.'

It was nearly ten o'clock when Rita finally let him go. Hungry and thirsty, he was looking forward to spending what was left of the evening with Juliet.

There was a note left on the kitchen table:

Dear Ollie,
Given up waiting for you and have gone to down a

bottle with Isabelle. One bored and lonely housewife drowning her sorrows with another bored and lonely housewife. (Richard's not back till late.)
    Come and join us,
      Juliet

Oliver gave a slight, humourless laugh at Juliet describing herself as a housewife. That she most certainly was not, although, in fairness, he'd never had any expectation she would or could be. It would be nice, he thought wistfully, if just once in a while, when I come home late, she was waiting with a welcoming smile and dinner in the oven.

He made himself a cheese sandwich and weighed up the pros and cons of going straight to bed, or going over to the Garnetts and risking an encounter with Richard. He decided to take the risk. He'd not seen Juliet since her news from LA on Wednesday and he wanted to make a fuss of her.

Considering the nature of the news, Juliet – impatient, impetuous, and emotional – would normally have taken the delay very badly. Her actual reaction astonished him. She was cross, yes; fed up, yes; but she was amazingly calm when she told him about it; didn't insist on his immediate return, and made no great fuss when he told her he wouldn't be home till Friday night.

Isabelle had been surprised and pleased when Juliet phoned. Richard had been irrationally angry over Oliver's shirt and it took some time for his temper to cool. As a result she barely saw him all week and so was glad of some company.

She opened the bottle of wine Juliet brought, found a brie that didn't look too elderly and a packet of very smart cheese biscuits Richard had bought some while ago from his favourite shop in Bath.

'How are you finding Summerstoke?' enquired Juliet. 'As tedious and parochial as I am, no doubt?'

'It's not easy,' admitted Isabelle. 'But I've got this house to sort out and the girls to look after, and now I'm helping Milo it's not quite so bad.'

Juliet looked critically around the kitchen. 'This is nice. Oh, I know you've got the decorating to do, but it's got a nice feel about it. I wish we had an Aga. I know Ollie's worked wonders with the house, but it still feels like rented accommodation and I can never find anything.'

'A bit like here. I feel as if we're living under siege. So much is still in boxes.'

'Tell me about it! When I came back, I found Ollie hadn't unpacked any of my things. It was horrible. He meant it for the best, but I felt like I was someone just passing through.'

'Aren't you?'

It was a casual question and Juliet tried to take it in her stride. 'Oh,' she said, lightly, 'the studio said I can extend my leave. They've so much to sort out, they don't need me back immediately.'

'That'll please Oliver and your son.'

'Jamie, yes. I shall be glad to see a bit more of him, I admit. Did you hear he got beaten up by some thugs on his way to a party in Summerbridge?'

'Yes. Sounded awful. How is he now?'

'His bruises have almost vanished, thank God.' Juliet looked sad and, for a moment, Isabelle glimpsed a softer, kinder person. 'He's growing up so quickly, I hardly recognise my little boy. I thought he'd hate it here when Ollie brought him down, but he seems to have settled in really well.'

'But he must have been here many times before? The family home and all that.'

'Oliver's family,' replied Juliet coldly, 'are stuck-up and arrogant. I don't know if you've met them yet?'

Isabelle shook her head.

'Well, you will, and take it from me, they've not a drop of warmth in their veins, not one of them. I avoid them as much as possible, for which, believe me, they are grateful.'

'Why do you say that? Most people in the village seem to think they're all right – a bit eccentric but–'

Juliet pulled a face. 'That's because they've not married a Merfield. When I first came here, I was only seventeen and they treated me like I was something the cat brought in. I wasn't good enough for their grandson: they made that quite plain, particularly when I became pregnant. It was awful. But I showed them.'

She picked up the bottle. It was empty.

Isabelle jumped up, 'I'll get another bottle. I think Richard left one in the fridge.'

'He's very charming, your husband.' Juliet cocked her head quizzically. 'I know I'm being inquisitive, and you can tell me to mind my own business, but he's a good deal older than you, isn't he? I met Ollie when I was at school. Were you still at school when you met Richard?'

Isabelle gave a short laugh. 'No, no I wasn't. I'd just finished college.'

'And you're his first wife?'

'No, he was married before; he's got two children by his first marriage.'

'Oh? Have you met his first wife? What's she like?'

'Clare – yes, I've met her once or twice when she brought the children down to stay for the holidays. She's okay, very efficient and brisk. She's head of English at some big London comprehensive, so I suppose she'd have to be.'

'Has she married again?'

'No, she hasn't.'

Juliet sipped her wine. 'How old are his children?'

'Abigail's nineteen – she's been away on a gap year – and Dan's nearly twenty-two. He's in his last year at Warwick.'

'So how do they get on with you? Are you their wicked stepmother?'

Isabelle smiled awkwardly. She didn't want to share the ins and outs of her tortured relationship with her stepchildren with Juliet, so she was relieved when the sound of the doorbell intervened.

Both women were pleased to see Oliver and, feeling more relaxed than he had done all day, he sank into a chair and accepted the glass Isabelle pressed into his hand.

'You look tired,' she said sympathetically. 'From what Juliet says, it sounds as if you never stop. Would you like me to make you a sandwich?

We've been snacking on cheese.'

'Where've you been, Ollie? I thought you were going to come back at a decent time tonight?' Juliet was cool.

'I'm sorry.' Oliver was contrite. 'I left the office later than I'd intended and I promised to call in on Mrs Godwin; that took rather longer than I thought.'

'Doesn't that woman talk!' Juliet gave a light laugh. 'Do you have to gag her for your meetings, Isabelle?'

Isabelle shook her head. 'She's a good woman. I won't hear a word against her.'

'You wouldn't be able to – she wouldn't let you get a word in edgeways. And those terrible proverbs, or mottos, she keeps quoting – I bet she collects them from Christmas crackers. Has no one ever told her empty vessels make the most noise?' Laughing, Juliet turned to her husband. 'So you've started your campaign at last, have you, darling?'

Oliver frowned. 'It's not my campaign, Juliet, it's Mrs Godwin's and the village's. In doing what I can, I'm doing my job. I'd do the same for anyone else who came to me – no more, no less.'

'Yes, yes, very noble and all that, but you might as well leave it to Richard's paper. He's far more likely to get results than you. I don't know why you're wasting your time with village affairs.'

Isabelle flushed. 'I'd rather have Oliver pursue a cause than a newspaper. With something like this they'd run the story till they got bored, or sensed their readers were bored, then dump it, regardless of how important it was to the people involved. A lot of sound and noise, and a lot of stirring, but not achieving anything very much. Whereas, I think *you*, Oliver, would care. Maybe, in the end, you won't be able to do much, but at least you won't let go until every avenue has been exhausted. I wouldn't be worried about your motives.'

Oliver was taken by surprise. He'd never heard Isabelle speak at length before, on anything. He looked at her, touched by her evident concern. 'Thanks for that vote of confidence. In reality, if Richard's paper can stir up public reaction and make the Post Office take note, it's giving me a lot of help. Let's hope he does take it on.'

'Richard never does anything unless it's going to benefit him in some way.'

'Isabelle!' Juliet was half amused, half shocked.

'He's late back.' Oliver glanced at the old-fashioned station clock that hung on the wall over the Aga. 'Is he on a late shift or something? I guess newsmen must work very unsociable hours?'

'Unlike politicians, you mean?' Juliet turned to Isabelle. 'Don't let us keep you up, Isabelle. Chuck us out any time.'

'You're not keeping me up, not at all. It's nice to have some adult company. No, he's not actually working, Oliver, in answer to your question, although he maintains that all the socialising he does is part of work. He finishes at the office any time from about four onwards, then often goes on to some function or other. He'll be late tonight – a local magazine awards ceremony.'

'And you don't go with him?'

'I'm not often asked. But even if I was, I don't

376

enjoy watching people get drunk, so I get out of it if I can. It's sad but since we've moved we see much less of him and my little girls miss him.'

Richard, feet up on his desk, was scrolling through his personal organiser when the phone buzzed. It was Sally, his secretary. 'I've got Juliet Peters on the line for you, Richard.'

'Thanks.' He leaned back in his chair, smiling into the phone.

'Juliet, hi, Richard Garnett here... Fine, thanks. Look, I heard you've not gone back to the States yet... Yeah, they take their time, don't they? Really frustrating... Juliet, I just rang, on the off-chance, to see if you're free for lunch tomorrow... You are? Fantastic... One o'clock? Do you know Woods, in Alfred Street? Yeah, just below the Assembly Rooms. I'll meet you there... Great. I'll look forward to it.'

Richard put the phone down, well pleased, and buzzed through to his secretary. 'Sally, book a table for me at Woods, tomorrow, for two, one o'clock. Tell David I'd like one by the window and not in the fucking middle, right?'

'Fine. Oh, Richard, we've had a reminder for the Bath and West Christmas bash. Do you want tickets for you and your wife?'

'Just me, Sally, and remember to include it on my expenses, would you?'

'Of course. I'll put it in the diary.'

Richard pulled a face as he settled back in his chair. The Bath and West Christmas dinner attracted the top whack from the whole of Wessex; he'd not miss the opportunity to hobnob with that lot. Trouble was, it being a charity do, he'd have to fork out for the raffle, and at thirty pounds a ticket... Pity he couldn't claim those on expenses.

He wondered idly if Oliver Merfield would be there with Juliet. Probably – and he probably wouldn't have any trouble meeting the cost of the raffle.

Richard had spent a lot of time thinking about Hugh's proposal. The whole idea made him very nervous, but if he could pull it off... He had no doubt Hugh would deliver on the advertising, so it was up to him. If it had been anyone else, he might have pulled back, but his dislike of Oliver Merfield, quick to seed, had grown and grown, so the idea of seducing Juliet at the same time added an exciting spice to the whole affair. He was confident he'd succeed, but he'd have to be careful and oh so shrewd. The one thing he could not do was be seen to be involved on a personal level in any campaign.

So, to begin with, he spread his net wide.

His editorial staff assumed the story of the Summerstoke post office, which had been beefed up with a picture of the lovely Juliet Peters, was too small to keep their boss interested for more than one issue. To their surprise he told them he wanted to expand the coverage: reporters were to come up with other vulnerable post offices and the communities they served, and profile them in a series of features.

The first part of his plan in place, Richard turned his attention to the more delicate part of the operation.

Scrolling through his list of contacts, he came

across the number he was looking for and punched it into his mobile.

'Dave? Richard Garnett, here. Hi... Yeah, long time no see. How's things...? Freelance world tough, eh? Listen, Dave, I won't waste your time. There's a little job I need doing, cash on delivery... Yeah, but it's not me who wants to know, is that clear? A little digging, something you're good at... Oliver Merfield, MP for Mendip, recently moved from London. I want to know about him, his wife, who's the actress Juliet Peters, and his son, who until recently was at school in London. He left soon after the academic year started. I want to know if there was anything behind him leaving so soon after starting a new term... Fine. Ring my mobile or text me, okay? Oh, asap. Cheers, Dave.'

He put his mobile away then pressed his buzzer. 'Tell Neville to come and see me, Sally.'

There was a tap on his door and Neville Budd, his news editor, poked his head round. 'You wanted to see me, Richard?'

'Yep. Come in, take a seat. I want to run an idea past you.'

'Oh?' Neville came in and sat down opposite his boss. He was a short, fat man, in his late forties, with pale grey skin, yellowing eyes, a short fat nose and a chin that disappeared into his neck. His faded brown hair was thinning on top and scraped over the dome of his head. His shirt collar was greasy and his suit sagged. In every way he looked unprepossessing and unsuccessful, but Richard was well aware this concealed a sharp, restless brain and he was one of the best men on his staff.

'I want to explore the effectiveness of our politicians,' he began, 'from the paid politicians – the MPs in our patch – to the town councillors. Are they value for money? How efficiently do they get things done? Are they worth having? "Write to your MP" – is that just a waste of ink? The MP's surgery – do constituents ever get satisfaction? How hard do they work, and how effective are they? We vote them in and then we don't monitor them. The rest of us in the workforce are subject to appraisals, so why shouldn't we scrutinise our politicians in the same way? We could start with a readers' survey – you know, what has the man or woman you voted in done for you?'

Neville stared at him. 'You could make yourself very unpopular.'

Richard had thought of that, but he was confident he could shield anybody who really mattered. 'Maybe, but we're in the business of selling newspapers, not making friends, and this could produce some really good copy.'

'Yes,' replied Neville thoughtfully. 'Yes, it could.'

16

'So when Louis asked them when they thought they might have a decision, they went terribly vague and said we should know before Christmas. Christmas! What are they messing about for? I'm stuck in limbo. Louis can't put me up for anything because I'm under contract to them and no one will look at me in case I suddenly have to down tools and disappear over the horizon.'

She really is lovely, Richard thought, sipping his glass of Chablis.

'You poor thing,' he murmured sympathetically.

'And I'm so bored, Richard. Summerstoke is the dead end of nowhere. I'm fading away down here.'

If she was, it didn't show. Her copper-gold curls shone and bobbed as she spoke and her eyes were bright and sparkling with life.

No intellectual depth, he thought, but who needs it? I wonder what she's like in bed? At the thought, he felt a faint physical stirring.

'What you need is a project.' He smiled at her. 'And I don't mean an Issy sort of project, like painting the house.'

'I don't think the old doctor would let me do that, anyway, even if I wanted to, which I most certainly do not!' Juliet's dimples appeared and disappeared as she talked. Richard was aware, as Juliet apparently was not, that a number of heads had turned to stare at her.

'Have you a project in mind, Richard?'

'Have you ever tried your hand at writing? We sometimes have guest columnists in our paper. You,' he said smoothly, 'would be an attractive proposition – well-known actress, living in a village, how does it square up to living in London or living in Los Angeles? Plus the ups and downs of being an MP's wife.'

She cocked her head on one side, looking thoughtful – and adorable. Richard tried to imagine what it would be like to kiss that pretty little mouth.

'To tell you the truth,' she said, wiping her mouth on her napkin and pushing away an unfinished plate of salad. 'There are more downs than ups, in both respects. Look what happened to Jamie.'

'Yes, I heard. He's at Summerbridge, isn't he? I hope you're keeping an eye on him, it's notorious for under-age drinking and drug taking.'

Watching her closely, he saw a little furrow appear on her brow.

'Teenagers, what they put us through!' he said lightly, with an indulgent laugh. 'I know. I've got two coming out the other side, thank God.'

'Did they dabble in drugs?' She was cautious.

Richard shrugged. 'I'd be surprised if they didn't.'

The arrival of the main course interrupted them and Richard, deciding he'd gone far enough for the moment, returned to the suggestion that Juliet write a column.

Juliet looked at him shrewdly. 'Well, I suppose it could be fun, I'll think about it.'

'That's all I ask,' he grinned. 'And maybe we could have lunch again when you've decided.'

'Maybe we could.'

Juliet thought about her conversation with Richard all the way home. He was an attractive man, there was no doubt about that; the teasing, bantering quality of his conversation entertained her, and she enjoyed his evident admiration of her. But, she thought, he has a dangerous edge to him... Well, I don't have to commit myself, either to his paper or to him. Isabelle said self-interest governed everything he does, so either I kid myself he thinks I can really write an interesting column, or he's after something else.

Isabelle... Juliet had complete confidence that Oliver loved only her, but she noticed he liked Isabelle.

She, Juliet, flirted all the time, but Oliver never did and she was aware of an unfamiliar, uncomfortable feeling. She shook her head. She couldn't see what the attraction was. Indeed, thinking about it, Richard and Isabelle's relationship puzzled her, too.

Maybe strong men like weak women, or maybe they're strong women to begin with and are weakened in the process. She hadn't been weakened by her marriage to Ollie, and neither, she believed, had he.

Her thoughts flipped to Hugh Lester. He didn't have the charisma of Richard Garnett, in fact he made her shudder. She liked strong men, but she didn't like bullies and she was sure Hugh Lester fell into that category. But his ghastly wife was strong, too. Perhaps they were well matched, or maybe he was a bully because his wife was stronger than him. But as she had no plans to get to know them better, it was unlikely she would find out.

Life was becoming a little less dull, but did she want to get involved with any of this?

She sighed.

Even this far out of Bath the traffic was heavy. The road glistened with damp and, although it was not actually raining, passing traffic chucked up so much muck that she kept on having to use her wipers. The road was flanked by hedges which had lost most of their foliage and were skirted with grime; beyond them in either direction stretched fields of stubble, looking like vast tracts of wasteland under a heavy grey sky.

Juliet yearned for the shiny pavements, the bright lights and the bustle there would be in London at this time of year.

'Come up and stay with me, Juliet,' Ollie had urged. 'Jamie will be okay at the Manor, you know that. Come up for a couple of days.'

But she'd said no. He'd only a small room at Polly's and she didn't want to stay there, knowing how often she'd be on her own. She had a reasonable network of friends in London, and of course there was the theatre and the cinema. But most of her friends thought she was still in LA and she didn't want to disabuse them.

She wouldn't admit to anyone that her complaints of boredom were a cover for her anxiety. Louis hadn't said much when he'd phoned to tell her not to rush back to LA; just that the studio wanted more feedback and they'd be in touch. It had never occurred to her they might not commission the series after having gone to the expense of the pilot and when she asked Louis about it, she'd been shaken when he'd said, quite nonchalantly, it happened all the time.

Supposing she wasn't wanted? She shivered at the thought. Yes, perhaps she needed a diversion. She wanted to devote more time to Jamie. She could feel him drifting away and she really minded. But he was out almost all day every day, so a flirtation would take her mind off things. If Richard proved too difficult, there was always Charlie Tucker – now, that would be fun.

She'd had a lovely boozy lunchtime with Charlie. Leaving his van in the car park, they'd walked back to Summerstoke across the fields. It must have been about three miles, and by the time she arrived home she was dishevelled, muddy and exhausted. They'd laughed and chatted the whole time, and the afternoon in his company had gone a long way to drawing the sting of Louis's phone call. Her only frustration was that he'd made no attempt to kiss her, and left her at her front door.

Her blood was up – she tingled at the thought of him. She had no intention of having an affair with him – her sex life with Ollie was as passionate and fulfilling as she could wish – but a flirtation, that was something else.

Shortly after she got in, the phone rang. It was Louis.

Juliet felt breathless. 'Any news?'

'No, nothing. In the meantime, darling, we shouldn't let the grass grow under your sweet little feet. Will you come up for a meeting tomorrow, eleven o'clock?'

'But I thought I couldn't do anything else because of their contract?'

'That kicks in if they decide to go ahead. I obviously can't put you up for anything much, but there's no reason why you shouldn't do a commercial.'

Juliet was a mixture of outrage and horror. 'A

commercial? What are you thinking of, Louis?'

'I'm thinking of money and exposure, darling. It pays well, it's a classy little ad, which won't do your career any harm, and if they like you, it's costume fitting Thursday, shoot on Friday, and if we get the nod from LA you could be there on Monday.'

Juliet was miserable. Like a lot of her actor friends, she saw ads as the last resort, a demeaning way to make money, but Louis dismissed her objections and, although she might protest, she needed her agent too much to refuse him.

That evening she spoke to Oliver and told him about the impending job. 'So if I get it I'll be in London for three nights, if that's okay with Polly. If you can get away early on Friday, we could go to the theatre.'

'Darling, have you forgotten? It's Jamie's play on Friday night. I promised I'd go and I know, now you're around, he's desperate for you to go too.'

It was almost worth it, thought Jamie, all that grief. It bloody hurt at the time, an' I thought they were gonna kill me, but it's all worked out, dunno why.

He was on his bike, buzzing through the night, home to Summerstoke after the final dress rehearsal for *Antigone*.

Life had definitely shifted several gears since his beating. For one thing, Aunt Charlotte was amazing – he couldn't think of her as the Red Witch any more, not after that night. And, for another, when he returned to college after a couple of days off, his friends guessed who was responsible for his injuries and assumed the fight occurred when Jamie stopped them gate-crashing Adam's party. So, to his surprise, Jamie, who had tried all his life to make friends, became a minor hero, and he basked in the popularity.

The other thing making life look brighter was Juliet still being at home. He knew she was upset at the delay in returning to LA, but it meant his dream was finally coming true: she'd see him act. He'd run through it all almost as many times as he'd run through his dream of bumping into Alison and inviting her to the play, with the cast party afterwards.

Riding down the hill, he could see the lights of Summerstoke twinkling on the other side of the valley, and over to his right he could just make out a light from the farmhouse. The road took him past the entrance to Marsh Farm. He could turn off, roar down the track and stop under-neath her window. It would be dark and quiet in the farmyard. At the sound of his bike, she'd throw open her window.

'Who is it?' she'd call softly.

'Me, Jamie. I couldn't stay away any longer.'

'Jamie. At last. I've been waiting for you.'

'If I leave a ticket for you at the box office, will you come to see me in *Antigone*?'

'I'd love to, Jamie. I'd love to.'

So immersed was he in his daydreams, he didn't notice a tall figure standing in the dark shadow of a tree by the bridge, but an elderly villager, attracted by the noise of the motorbike and peering out of her bedroom window to

387

watch it pass, caught a glimpse of the naked man as he crossed the road and let out a scandalised scream.

The light was still on in the sitting room when he got home, and he found Juliet curled up on the sofa watching television, a glass of wine in her hand.

'Jamie, darling,' she said brightly, 'an awful bore, sweetheart, but I've got to go up to London first thing tomorrow. I've phoned Nanny and, of course, it's okay for you to stay there tomorrow and Thursday.'

Jamie stared at her. Had she forgotten? 'It's my first night, tomorrow night. When will you be back?'

She shrugged. 'Darling, I hope I'll be back in time to see you on Friday. I will do my level best, but if Friday's a filming day... There are no guarantees in this world, you know that. Dad will be here.'

'But I want you to come.' Jamie tried not to sound pathetic, but he was so disappointed, he wanted to cry.

'I told you, I'll do my best.'

The opening night of *Antigone* went well enough to calm the actors' jittery nerves and the audience responded loudly and enthusiastically. There were enough hiccups, however, to make the students nervous about their second performance, when the examiner was expected.

Jamie, like his friends, spent the day a bundle of nervous energy, relearning lines he already knew, checking his costume and props. At one point he found himself wandering across the stage and looking out into the empty auditorium. If only, he thought, if only he could be sure tomorrow night she'd be there, he'd feel better. But which she, Juliet or Alison? If he had to choose, would it be his mother, or the girl in his dreams? He felt choked. He shouldn't have to wish Juliet there, she should *be* there.

'Hi, Jamie.' It was Tish. 'I'll be glad when tonight's over. I'm really looking forward to tomorrow's performance. Then we'll be able to relax and really enjoy it, eh?'

'Yeah, I suppose so.'

Tish looked at him. 'You sound as nervous as I feel. You shouldn't, Jamie. You're good.'

He turned and stared at her. 'D'ye mean that?'

She looked embarrassed. 'Yeah, yeah, I do. I admit I was pissed off when you were given Creon. You'd only just joined and I thought you were really snotty. It didn't seem fair you'd been given the best part, when Adam or Mac or George could have done it. But Mr Theobald was right, they couldn't have done it as well as you. We all know that now.'

Jamie was almost speechless. 'I don't know what to say... Thanks, Tish. Thanks.'

She shrugged. 'S'all right. Are your parents coming tonight? Mine are, even though I told 'em not to. They're not going to understand a single word, but Dad says he wants to give me moral support, what with the examiner being here, an' all.'

Jamie was envious, and suddenly felt lonely.

Wouldn't it be fantastic if his family were there tonight, like Tish's, supporting him, cheering him on? 'Mine are coming tomorrow – at least, my Dad is. I don't know about ... about Juliet.'

'Do you always call your mum, Juliet?'

'Not always – she likes me to, though. I call her Mum when she pisses me off.'

Tish laughed. 'My mum would be pissed off if I called her Rosemary. Come on, let's go an' have a cup of tea – we've got some fresh supplies in.' As they left the stage, she asked casually, 'You bringing anyone to the cast party tomorrow night?'

A vision of Alison flitted across Jamie's mind. 'No, probably not. Are you?'

'Probably not.'

The auditorium was packed full of students, family and friends, determined to impress upon the examiner that *they* thought the performances were brilliant. The actors, responding to their enthusiasm, rose to the challenge.

When it was over they sat in the dressing room, exhausted and elated, high on adrenalin and the excitement of feeling the performance had been the best yet. Under the rules of the examination they were not allowed to leave the dressing room until they'd had clearance, so by the time Mr Theobald came in to give them the thumbs up, the audience had dispersed.

As he left, Mr Theobald patted Jamie on the shoulder. 'Well done. Your parents will be very proud of you. I know I was.'

Glowing, Jamie rode home. He couldn't remember anyone, ever, saying that to him before he came to Summerstoke. It was the one thing he'd dreamed of, making Juliet proud of him, and if she came tomorrow night...

It was well after ten o'clock when he let himself into the Manor, but since he had cleared his late return with Nanny, he was surprised to find her sitting at the kitchen table.

She beamed at him and before he could say anything, she said, 'Well, pet, if that examiner doesn't give you full marks, there's no justice in the world.'

Jamie stared at her. 'What do you mean? I don't understand.'

'I mean what I say – you were very good. I didn't always understand what you were saying, I must admit, but I could tell you were doing it well, and everyone around me thought so, too. I was so proud of you, Jamie.'

Jamie was completely confused. 'You were there, in the audience, tonight? But I didn't think you were ... that you...'

Nanny smiled proudly. 'I wouldn't have missed it, pet. I know you were nervous, so I thought it best not to tell you. Mrs Merfield said how good you were, and she was right. You'd absolutely nothing to be frightened of. All those words, though, dear. How did you learn all those words?'

Jamie struggled to make sense of what she had just said. 'Mrs Merfield ... you mean Grandmère was there as well?'

'She went last night, with Miss Louisa. Little Angela – you've met her, she's Stephen Tucker's fiancée – well, she works at the library, so she got us the tickets. We didn't want to frighten you by all turning up on the same night, so I went tonight, with Angela and Stephen's sister, Alison.'

Jamie thought he'd never get to sleep. His thoughts were a jumble of excited memories of the performance, the words of his teacher, the realisation that, far from being on his own, he'd had his very elderly relatives there, rooting for him, and, above all, Alison had watched him, seen him doing something of which he could be proud.

He finally drifted off to sleep, a new scenario running through his brain: *she* would seek *him* out: 'Oh, hi, Jamie. I don't know if you remember me. My name's Alison. We met in the summer, on the river. I just wanted to tell you I saw you playing Creon, and I thought you were wonderful.'

The following day he felt light-headed. He phoned home and then Juliet's mobile a number of times, but all he got was her message; the high of the previous day was gone, displaced by worry and disappointment. He'd held onto this dream for so long and now everything was in place to make it happen at last – everything but Juliet herself.

There was an excited buzz in the dressing room. With less than half an hour to curtain up, a student poked his head round the door and yelled at Jamie, 'Your dad said to tell you he's here, Jamie.'

'And my mum?'

'Not unless she's as ancient as the hills. Is that old wrinkly your grandmother?'

'No.' Jamie turned back to the mirror to conceal his disappointment. 'That's my great-aunt. She's cool, so be nice about her, if you don't mind.'

During the long opening address from the Chorus, Jamie shot a glance at where he knew his father would be sitting. Yes, there he was, leaning forward, his chin on his hands, concentrating; and there was Aunt Charlotte next to him. On his other side, the seat was empty.

A poisonous wave of disappointment, misery and bitterness engulfed him and for a moment he stood there, numb. All he wanted to do was leave. What was the point? She didn't care, so why should he?

He was aware of his cue, aware of the audience's eyes on him, aware of the silence, the tension on stage.

Fellow citizens, the state in all its majesty, is safe

The high and mighty speeches of the proud are met with mighty blows from on high, and from those blows, oh citizens, we learn wisdom

The roar of applause was deafening. Holding Tish's hand on one side and Adam's on the other, he took a bow, and another, and then another. Suddenly he realised he'd forgotten Juliet wasn't there. It didn't hurt any more. With a big grin, he lifted his hand and saluted his dad. When the curtain finally went down and they all streamed back to the dressing room, he realised he was still holding Tish's hand.

He heard her before he saw her. The bar area in

393

the foyer was packed, and as the students made their appearance the noise surged to a deafening level. Even so, he heard her.

'Yes, very good, I'm not denying it, but I don't know why they chose to do such a difficult play. Why couldn't they have chosen something modern? Much more within their grasp – and the audience's of course.'

'My mum *is* here,' he whispered to Tish. 'Shall we say hello to her and my dad? And I want you to meet Aunt Charlotte – she really is something else.'

Tish smiled up at him. 'Lead on, I can't wait.'

Firmly taking her by the hand, Jamie pushed his way through the crowd, who patted them on the back as they passed.

Around Juliet, a small circle had gathered, lapping up everything she said. Oliver and Charlotte were standing to one side talking to the principal. Jamie led Tish to them.

When Oliver saw him, he broke off and gave Jamie a big hug. 'Well done, Jamie. I'm so proud of you. It was a brilliant performance.'

'Dad, hi. You've met Tish, haven't you?'

Oliver leaned forward to shake Tish's hand. 'Yes, I remember Tish. Congratulations. You brought tears to my eyes – you were fabulous.'

Jamie turned to Aunt Charlotte who, smiling approvingly, murmured, 'Jamie, you did very well. I look forward to discussing the production with you.'

Jamie grinned. 'Thanks, Aunt Charlotte. This is my friend, Tish – she played Antigone. I wanted her to meet you.' He nodded shyly at the

394

principal. "Lo, Mr Marshall.'

'Jamie, hello. I was just saying to your father how pleased we are to have you as a student. Absolutely splendid performance, splendid. And you too, Tish. I thought you were terrific – a star in the making. I've no doubt Miss Peters will agree with me.'

Juliet, hearing her name mentioned, looked up and saw them, and as the principal reluctantly made his excuses and turned to talk to a parent who was hovering at his elbow, she left her fan club to join them.

She kissed him. 'Jamie, darling, congratulations. What a surprise.' She was animated and bright, and undeniably beautiful.

Jamie greeted her without enthusiasm. 'Hi, Mum. When did you get here? Did you see *any* of it?'

Tish, who'd been chatting to Aunt Charlotte, looked across at him.

'Of course I did, sweetheart. I got here a wee bit late, but a nice man let me in and found me a seat at the back. I hardly missed anything at all.'

'So what did you think? Did you enjoy it?'

Juliet hesitated a fraction of a second – it was just a fraction, but Jamie noticed it and in an instant, his euphoria punctured, his mood changed. Angry, hurt, he turned pale, and drawing himself up, he spat,

'You didn't like it. Fine.'

'I *did* like it. It was very interesting; you all did very well, especially you.'

'"Interesting" ... we "all did very well" did we? Thanks for that, Mum. High praise indeed. I hope my mates aren't as underwhelmed as I am.' He turned to Oliver. 'Thanks for coming, Dad. I'm off to the cast party, so I'll see you tomorrow morning. Come on, Tish, let's go.'

17

'Hey, Isabelle, have you heard about the streaker?'

Isabelle had just left the schoolyard after waving goodbye to the girls when she met Paula, her arms full of children's puffa jackets, teetering towards her. Kylie and Ryan were trailing some yards behind her and Paula turned to them with an exasperated cry: 'Come on you two, the bell's gone – yer gonna be late again!'

Isabelle waited as Paula chivvied her two offspring through the school gate, called them back to take their jackets from her, then shouted at them to run as they dawdled towards the school entrance.

She joined Isabelle with a sigh. 'Kids! I dunno what's got into them this mornin'. Mind you, I always hated Monday mornings, when I was at school. Still do, if it comes to that.'

They strolled back down the school lane.

'What were you saying about a streaker?'

'Yeah, would you believe it, here in Summerstoke!'

'You're joking.'

'No, I'm not, honest. He's been spotted a number of times, for definite, and Lenny swore he saw a naked man running along Weasel Lane after nightfall on Friday.'

Isabelle blinked. 'I can't believe it. Everybody knows everybody else in this village. Who is it?'

'Dunno. Mrs Beard, her what lives opposite us down by the bridge, says she was looking out of her bedroom window, one evenin', and she sees this fellah running away, starkers, along the footpath by the river – Sunday, that was and Mrs Godwin told us the vicar bumped into a naked man when he was out walking late a week ago last Friday. Now, if the vicar saw him, that's proof, innit?'

'And he didn't recognise him?'

'No, it was dark down by the river and as soon as the vicar saw he was naked, he looked away.'

Isabelle chuckled. 'Sensible man. I wonder who it is?'

'Well whoever it is, he better not come near me or I'll kick his goolies. Makes you think about goin' out by yourself after dark though, dunnit? Lenny thinks we ought to get a patrol up.'

Isabelle raised her eyebrows. 'That's a bit extreme, isn't it? I mean he's not approached anyone, and it sounds like he's avoiding the actual village, and after dark…'

'Well, it's not nice and he should go and do it somewhere else. Anyway, I'm just going to nip into the shop for some fags. I'll see you later, Isabelle.'

'Bye, Paula.'

It was a lovely morning. It was the very end of November, but it seemed as if autumn was reluctant to give way to the chillier note of winter. The sun shone in a peerless sky and a warm breeze sent the last remaining leaves spinning like gold coins in the air and carpeting the surface of the river and the road.

She looked forward to her mornings with Milo. Since her last encounter with Charlie, he'd given her a wide berth, so she felt quite secure walking to and from the workshop.

Milo didn't talk much; indeed, he barely acknowledged her existence and worked with an intensity Isabelle found impressive. By reputation he was eccentric and so he was – she'd found that out soon after she'd started working for him, when he'd–

Perhaps *he* was the streaker?

Isabelle's eyes widened and she started giggling. Milo might be nearly sixty, but he was tall and lean. Would he throw off his clothes and run naked in the dark? The answer had to be yes, yes, he would.

She'd arrived at his workshop shortly after nine one morning, and when she let herself in he was already hard at work, his head just visible over a stack of canvases.

She'd greeted him and he gave no sign he'd heard her, but she knew he was deaf to everything when deeply absorbed, so she'd set about cleaning brushes and preparing a grey wash. Then, without looking up, he'd barked a request for a particular colour, which she'd found and walked round the canvases dividing them, to give it to him.

She stopped dead, taken aback. Milo impatiently held out his hand. 'What are you waiting for, girl? Here, give it me.'

Wordlessly, she put the tube in his hand, then slowly backed away till she was out of sight on the other side of the canvas wall, where she started to shake with silent laughter.

Milo was painting stark naked.

Richard's campaign at the *Wessex Daily* was humming along nicely. The newspaper's postbag had never been so full. The coverage given to the issue of post offices and village shops was good while it lasted, but the majority of his readers were town-based and their interest was lukewarm. But when he implemented the second part of his plan, turning the paper's spotlight onto his readers' elected representatives, the call to arms proved irresistible.

His strategy was simple. After the opening shots setting out the paper's moral high ground along the lines of 'We workers are appraised, so why shouldn't we subject our elected representatives to the same scrutiny?' the paper encouraged readers to write in. The letters were published along with a profile of the unfortunate councillor and the results of the paper's investigation into his or her performance.

The activities of his newspaper and the consequent surge in sales excited the attention of head office, and for the first time in ages Richard was again their golden boy.

His *coup de foudre*, the three MPs on his patch, he was saving till last. He planned to be selective: one MP he guaranteed to protect, the second, particularly tiresome and unsympathetic, would have a hard time. The killing, however, was reserved for Oliver Merfield, the despised relic of an outdated social system, who'd used his connections to swan into office; who ponced about, expecting everyone to pull their forelocks ... inexperienced and ineffectual Oliver, who would not, Richard knew for a fact, be able to do anything to help the Summerstoke post office.

Dave, the freelance reporter in London, had sent him a text soon after Richard had set him digging. It had read simply: **'xpelled, possession, supply.'** He hadn't produced anything on Juliet or Oliver that the tabloids hadn't covered already, but Richard was content.

Under the guise of persuading her to write a column, he was seeing more of Juliet than he was of Isabelle. He couldn't remember having wanted a woman so much before. It had nothing to do with his marriage, except if anything did happen Isabelle would be as much to blame. She'd become increasingly withdrawn, and sex between them just was not happening. He'd no intention of jeopardising his marriage, but after that first lunch with Juliet he couldn't put her out of his mind; subsequent lunches further inflamed him, to the point where sleeping with Juliet Peters was becoming almost an obsession.

He'd committed himself to ruining her husband and was considering using her son as a weapon, but it didn't deter him. If the paper showed Oliver up as the weak vessel he was, that was hardly Richard's responsibility. And Juliet gave him the distinct impression she hoped Oliver's career in politics would be short-lived. Well, then, she would have her wish.

Richard had never failed with a woman before, and Juliet appeared to find him as attractive as other women had.

It was time to make the next move.

A new play on the first leg of a tour of the provinces was opening at the theatre in the first week of December, and Richard learned the director, better known for his films, would be there. The play had been fully booked for weeks, but the PR lady at the theatre owed him and, when pressed, came up trumps, with an invitation to join the cast for a drink after the performance.

Juliet was delighted. 'If you're sure, Richard, Isabelle wouldn't rather go with you, I'd love to. I've auditioned for Mike in the past and it would be great to meet him again.'

Without being certain how things would turn out, but determined not to leave anything to chance, Richard booked himself a room in a discreet hotel and explained to Isabelle he'd stay in Bath as he was finishing late.

'The carpet's arriving at the end of the week. It's a sort of aubergine colour.'

Isabelle and Paula were standing, mugs of tea in hand, in the middle of the empty room destined to be the 'posh' sitting room. The walls and paintwork gleamed white and bright.

'Blimey, you've done a good job.' Paula was cautious in her praise.

'You don't like it?'

'It's all a bit ... white for my taste. I like a bit of colour, I do.'

'Yes, I know what you mean. I do, too. But Richard wanted it white. He argues the colour will be provided by everything in the room – you know, pictures, books, carpet, furniture. If he had his way, I'd paint the whole house white, from top to bottom.'

Paula looked alarmed. 'You're not gonna do that are you? I mean, I know it looks nice and clean and all that, but...'

Isabelle laughed. 'No. No, I'm not. Just the rooms Richard thinks matter. You like the kitchen, don't you?'

'Yeah. It reminds me of my favourite pudding when I was a kid.'

'What was that?'

'Tinned apricots and vanilla ice cream. Yum! I love apricots – but only the tinned ones, mind. Lenny got me some fresh ones when I was expecting Ryan. Yuk!' She took a thoughtful look around the room. 'Tell you what, Isabelle, you know what you should do in here?'

'What?'

'Paint one of your castles on that wall.' She gestured to the long, blank wall facing the fireplace. 'Look lovely, it would...' Her voice trailed away in a sigh.

'I'd like to see Richard's face if I did,' Isabelle said, with a wry smile at the thought. She looked at Paula with concern. Ever since she'd arrived, Paula had seemed subdued, like Babycham without the bubbles.

'Is there something wrong Paula? You seem a bit, well, depressed. Are you all right?'

'Yeah,' replied Paula, but heavily, with another sigh. 'D'ye mind if we 'ave another cuppa, Isabelle. I need it.'

They went back to the kitchen, and Paula

slumped in a chair while Isabelle put the kettle on the hob and rinsed out the cups.

'What is it? I don't mean to pry, but can you tell me?'

Paula looked puzzled and hurt. 'I don't understand it. Rita Godwin's been like my auntie – I've been goin' to her shop since I could toddle.'

'Yes?' Isabelle's heart sank.

'Well, I went in there today on my way home at dinner time, to get some fags, and she told me she didn't want to serve me. Told me I wasn't welcome in her shop and when I asked her why, she said I knew why.'

Paula's head drooped and Isabelle watched, aghast, as a great sooty tear rolled down her cheek.

'Paula don't cry.' Isabelle couldn't bear to see her so miserable. 'Did she say anything else? Did she give you any explanation?'

Paula sniffed. 'Only when I said no, I didn't know why, she said "Rats" and turned her back on me. It was 'orrible – so humiliatin'.'

Isabelle cursed inwardly – bloody Veronica Lester! – then knelt by Paula's side. 'Listen,' she said, 'I think I know what's behind all this. Do you remember me mentioning that Veronica Lester said you told her there were rats in the shop's storeroom?'

'But I never said that. Why should I?'

'No, I believe you. But the thing is, for some reason Veronica's spreading that story. I don't know why. And I'm not the only person she told, so maybe Rita's been told that, and you can see if she thought you were responsible for spreading such a rumour she'd be furious.'

Paula's eyes widened. 'The bitch. The bitch! I bet that's her getting her own back on me – just because I walked out on her and her rotten job. I'm gonna see her right away–'

'I think it would be better if we went to see Rita, first. You need to clear that up.'

Paula looked stricken. 'She might not believe me.'

'I don't see why not. After all, as you said, she's known you since you were a baby. Come on, I'll come with you. We'll get it sorted between us, and if we go now we can do it before we pick the kids up from school.'

Paula pulled on a silvery quilted bomber jacket and wrapped a fluffy pink scarf round her neck, the only concession in her attire to the beginning of December and temperatures hovering in the low centigrade. She looked so miserable, Isabelle tried to cheer her up.

'Now the room's finished, I suppose I ought to start organising this party he keeps banging on about.'

Paula did brighten a fraction at the thought of a party.

'If you want me to lend a hand – you know, serving the drinks and things – you only have to ask. I won't charge nothing, it'd be fun.'

'Paula, I've told you, I want you to come, you and Lenny. You've both been so brilliant, you're top of my list.'

Paula looked pleased, but shook her head doubtfully. 'I dunno.'

Isabelle went to fetch the old duffle coat she had worn in her student days and had rescued in the move, eschewing the waxed jackets de rigueur among the middle classes in the country.

'Who else you gonna invite, then?'

'I'm not sure,' she said thoughtfully, pulling the coat on. 'Richard will have the main say. But I expect it will include Juliet and Oliver Merfield, if they're around, and the Lesters, I'm afraid.'

'I'd give anything to see the queen bitch's face when she sees me and Lenny have been invited to the same party,' Paula chuckled sourly.

Outside a slight wind was blowing and Paula looked longingly across at the Discovery. 'You gonna take the car?'

'No, I don't think so. It's not going to rain and I could do with the exercise.'

'If I had a car like yours, I'd drive it everywhere, whatever the weather.'

Isabelle, however, had grown to hate the Discovery, feeling it labelled her in a way she didn't want. She had taken to walking every-where, even to Milo's studio, which meant she was getting to know Summerstoke and its resi-dents in a way unimaginable a month earlier.

''Ere,' Paula's high-heeled boots sank in the gravel of the Old Vicarage drive, making her pro-gress more tottery than usual. 'Talking of Oliver and Juliet, have you heard the news what's goin' round the village?'

'No, what?'

'There's probably nothin' to it, but there's no smoke without fire, my mum says, and she was talking to Mrs Grey, the vicar's wife, who's really

405

worried about what would happen if it all came out – him being an MP an' all... And they were talkin' about it in the school playground, an' all, so it's fair got around.'

'What? Oliver's not the streaker is he?' Isabelle asked mischievously.

'No, don't be daft. No one knows who *he* is. No. It's Juliet. Word is, she's having a bit of a fling.'

Isabelle felt a twinge of fear. Irrational, she knew, because if it were Richard Paula would not be talking to her like this. But she'd seen Richard looking at Juliet and recognised the hunter in that look.

'Do you think that's likely?' she ventured. 'After all, she *is* an actress – I think they behave differently from the rest of us, they are so much more, um, emotional. I don't think she'd risk her reputation, and Oliver's, by having an affair. A flirtation, maybe, but the real thing?'

'If you knew as much as I do about the way the showbiz folks carry on... They do it all the time, you only have to pick up the papers – they're full of it.'

'That's Hollywood, not Summerstoke.'

'Yeah, but she is Hollywood, isn't she, come to Summerstoke? She's not one of us, is she? She's so beautiful, she could have any fellah she wants at the drop of a hat.'

They arrived at the shop and Paula stopped, looking uncertain and woebegone. Isabelle gave her hand an encouraging squeeze.

'Come on.'

Fortunately Rita was alone in the shop, pinning tinsel on the edge of her shelves. She looked

406

round and seeing Isabelle smiled, then froze as she saw who else had entered.

'I thought I told you, you're not welcome in my shop, Paula Spinks.'

Paula gave a little moan.

Isabelle rose to her friend's defence. 'Rita, I think there's been a misunderstanding.'

'Not by me, there hasn't.'

'Some while back, Veronica Lester told me I shouldn't use the village shop because you have rats in your basement. She told me she knew that because Paula told her.'

'That's just what I was told, so there's no misunderstanding, is there? Except I thought Paula was a friend. I've known her since she was a baby – a fine friend she's turned out to be.'

Paula whimpered.

Isabelle ploughed on. 'How well do you know Veronica Lester?'

Rita sniffed. 'I'd hardly call her a regular customer – in fact, we don't see her in here from one end of the year to the other.'

'But I bet it's no secret in the village she and Paula parted on bad terms, is it?'

For the first time, Rita looked uncertain. 'No, but...'

'When Veronica told me about the rats in the basement–'

'We haven't got a basement.'

'No, that's what Paula told me when I asked her about it. So why should Veronica Lester say Paula told her you had rats in the basement, unless she made it up?'

'Why should someone like Mrs Lester do a

thing like that?'

'But she would.' Paula could contain herself no longer. 'She's really nasty, Rita. I wouldn't put it past her to try and dish some dirt on me.'

Isabelle sighed, suddenly feeling very weary. 'She's a good friend of my husband's, Rita. I've known her for quite a while. Believe me, she's not the nicest person in the world. It's because she's telling everyone there are rats in the *basement* that I think she made it up. As you say, she rarely comes here – she assumed you had a basement. A lot of houses in the High Street have, haven't they?'

'Only the ones above St Stephen's. We're too close to the river.'

'There you go, then. The thing is, though, I think there's more to it than dropping Paula in the shit, and I've no idea what it could be.'

'It's not just Paula, it's me!' Rita retorted. 'I've been losing customers without knowing why, at a time when I can ill afford to lose 'em. I'd have appreciated it, Isabelle, if you'd told me about this in the beginning.'

Isabelle blushed. 'You're right. I'm really sorry. It's hard to ask a person you've only recently got to know whether they've got rats in their store-room. You'd have thrown me out.'

Rita stared at her for a minute, then turned to Paula, contrite.

'I'm sorry, Paula. I shouldn't have been so quick to believe Mrs Green. I didn't think. Sometimes running this shop really gets to me. Perhaps I'm getting too old for it. Maybe I should sell up.'

Something clicked in Isabelle's memory. 'Rita, you said something about selling up at the village meeting.'

'Yes, this woman called in. She runs an interior design business and said she was looking for premises.'

'Do you remember her name?'

'No, but she gave me her card. Why?'

'Do you still have it?'

'If I put it anywhere, it'll be in the back of the till.' Opening it, she rummaged through a selection of cards. 'Here we are.' She glanced at it as she handed it over. '"Marion Croucher, Interior design for the superior home." Mean anything to you?'

Isabelle bit her lip. 'Yes, it does. She's Veronica Lester's best friend.'

On the way to the school playground, Isabelle and Paula could talk of little else, but had to shelve their discussion when they were joined by a small group of mums, friends of Paula who now accepted Isabelle, if not as one of them, as someone who was not as snobbish as they'd initially thought. Their principal conversation, which normally revolved around television soaps and reality shows, was given over, with much laughter, to an enthusiastic discussion of the streaker and his identity.

Isabelle knew she could have enlightened them and put an end to it, but she felt few villagers would understand Milo, let alone tolerate his strange habits.

'Clothes are so inhibiting, Isabelle,' he'd

409

explained that first time she'd realised he was painting in the nude. 'I feel suffocated by them. Feeling the air on my body, my limbs, everything unconstricted, liberates my mind. It's a release; it enables me to focus my whole being on my painting. Have you ever swum naked?'

She had to admit she hadn't.

'You should try it. It's the most wonderful experience, especially at night. The touch of water, of air, on my skin – it's almost transcendental. Don't ask me to explain why, but I couldn't paint if I had to wear clothes all the time. Do you understand?'

No, there was no way Paula and these mums, nice as they were, would ever think he was anything but a freak, a weirdo.

The doors flung open and the children, loud in their release, streamed out.

Becky was almost always out first. Pale and wan, she would cling to Isabelle's hand till they dragged Clemmie away from her friends.

Isabelle was seriously concerned about her daughter's unhappiness and, in the face of opposition from Richard, was quietly trying to work out how she could send her back to her old school.

This afternoon was different. Becky came running across the school playground, but it was a Becky transformed. Her face was glowing with excitement and she could hardly stand still as she grabbed Isabelle's hand.

'Mummy, Mummy, I'm going to be the Virgin Mary, in our nativity, Mrs Jones says so, and I'm going to hold the Baby Jesus and Mrs Jones says would you go in and see her, please, and Annie

Russell says she wants to play with me tomorrow, at hers. Please can I go, please?'

Marvelling at the change, a bemused Isabelle allowed herself to be dragged by a chattering, excited Becky into the classroom to see the teacher.

Mrs Jones, a sensible, kindly woman in her early forties, had shared Isabelle's concern over Becky's inability to settle, but with nearly forty five- and six-year-olds in her charge, her ability to do much was limited.

'Mrs Garnett, thank you for coming to see me. Becky has told you her news, I take it?' She smiled down at the little girl, who beamed back.

'Yes. I can't... Thank you very much. I can't quite believe... She's a changed person...'

'Sometimes it just takes one little thing to make all the difference. She was wonderful when we tried it out this afternoon. Now, there's something you can do for us, if you wouldn't mind.'

'What's that?'

'Mrs Spinks tells me you paint these beautiful pictures. We're going to be doing the nativity play at St Stephen's and we thought it would be nice if we could have a background painting. You know the sort of thing – starry night, the star of Bethlehem, a hillside with sheep, and perhaps Bethlehem itself. Becky tells me you're at home most days, so I thought if you could come in and help our art group in the afternoon...?'

Becky danced all the way home, chattering and laughing with Clemmie, and Isabelle, watching her, was full of mixed emotions: heartfelt pleasure and relief at the change in her daughter; but also sensing that if she passively accepted these roles assigned her, the creative spark she hoped still flickered somewhere deep within her would be finally extinguished. Helping with the Art group, she thought, cleaning Milo's brushes, designing posters, decorating the house... Where is all this taking me? At some point, I've got to stop messing about.

It was only later, when she'd given the girls supper and plonked them in front of the television, that she thought over the afternoon and realised that behind the gigantic question of Veronica was the smaller, but no less poignant, part of her conversation with Paula about Juliet, and that she didn't know who Juliet was meant to be having a fling with.

My God, she thought, disgusted, here am I dismissing one rumour, only to be all too ready to believe in another. Is this what living in a village does to you?

Richard met Juliet in the theatre restaurant for a light supper before the performance. It was really busy, but he was given a table in a candle-lit alcove.

'A *whole* bottle of champagne?' Juliet's eyes widened as the bottle was brought to the table. 'Richard, how very decadent.'

Richard shrugged. 'You like champagne, I like champagne. Why not? We can always finish it in the interval.'

She laughed. 'Oh, Richard, I can't tell you how much I've been looking forward to this evening. I think I'll go stark staring mad if I have to stay in Summerstoke for much longer.'

'I can't have that. Have you tried writing a column yet?'

'No. It's all very well for you, but I'm not cut out for journalism. I need a ghost writer, Richard.'

He took this as an appeal. 'I'm game. December's the run-up to Christmas – lots of feel-good stories – so if you're still about, we'll have a go. It'll be fun and just what we need to liven up the paper.' He smiled at her.

'Did you ever do anything more on the Summerstoke post office campaign?'

'Do you ever read the *Wessex Daily?*'

She laughed again. 'I'm afraid I don't read the papers much, unless there's a review I'm interested in. And actually, to be quite candid, I'm not very interested in Summerstoke post office.'

'Fair enough.'

She leaned forward, her eyes twinkling. 'And nor, I think, are you.'

He smiled back. 'Well, you might be right there. That's the lot of a regional editor – we deal principally in the parochial, the trivial and the mundane.'

He refilled their glasses, watching her closely.

Momentarily she was distracted by the noisy activity of a large table nearby, where a group of twenty-somethings were taking it in turns to squash heads together, recording the occasion on their mobile phones.

He took a reflective sip. Before he made his next move, he needed to have a better understanding of how she viewed her husband.

'So how's Saint Oliver getting on? He takes his

413

job very seriously, doesn't he? Has he succeeded in riding to their rescue?'

Her laughter pealed out, causing one or two interested glances and nudges from the large table.

'Oliver Merfield, patron saint of Summerstoke! You've got it in one. He's hardly home at the moment, but if Rita Godwin or that old lady who's running their campaign, Elsie whatsername, want a word, he's theirs for the asking. The whole thing is so tedious, I shall be glad when it's over. But I suspect it's going to be a long, slow death. Oliver's addressing a meeting in the village hall this Friday. I'd have thought you'd have one of your spies there – local MP faces wrath of his constituents.' She giggled and drained her glass. 'My God, we've managed to drink most of the bottle!' She wagged a finger at him. 'You're very naughty, Richard. I want to keep a clear head this evening. It's orange juice for me from now on, do you hear?'

Her loveliness caught his breath and he had to restrain himself from leaning over the table to press his lips against hers. As it was, he picked up her hand and kissed the palm.

'Whatever you want, princess.'

'Richard, darling – what are you doing here? I didn't think you were a theatregoer. Have you brought Issy?'

Richard, pushing his way through the throng to collect their half-time drinks, froze. At any other time he would have been pleased to see Vee. Before he could say something sensible, Juliet appeared at his side.

Vee arched her brows. 'Juliet! What a surprise.

But of course,' she continued smoothly, 'Issy doesn't like the theatre, does she? And I expect you know the great man, Juliet?'

'Yes,' Juliet replied coolly, 'a little. I'm looking forward to meeting him again, afterwards. Hello, Hugh.' She smiled at Hugh, who appeared at Veronica's side carrying two large glasses of wine.

He looked startled. 'Juliet, Richard, what are you doing here?'

'Same as you, I expect,' said Richard, smoothly recovering the situation. 'What do you think of the play so far?'

'I think it's crap.' Hugh didn't bother to lower his voice and a couple nearby, deep in a discussion about the merits of the play and its performers, looked round in pained surprise.

Richard buried his face in his glass to hide his grin.

'Hugh, how can you be so dismissive?' Juliet immediately leaped to the play's defence.

While the two swapped opinions and prejudices, Vee turned to Richard. 'So you're going to the first night party as well. How nice. So are we.'

Richard concealed his dismay. 'Great. How come?'

'Hugh's on the board. We don't often come – he doesn't actually like the theatre that much–'

The bell sounded for the second act. As they moved to reclaim their seats, Juliet said apologetically to Veronica, 'Thanks for your invitation to dinner on the twenty-first, Vee. I haven't had a chance to check with Ollie's diary, but I think Parliament's in its Christmas recess by then, so it should be fine. I'll let you know for sure.'

From that point on, the evening started to unravel for Richard. For one thing, Isabelle hadn't mentioned an invitation to the Lesters' Christmas dinner party and Richard couldn't remember a time when they'd not invited him. He was alarmed.

Then, when the play was over and they gathered to meet the cast and director, Juliet became a driven creature. Eyes glittering, dimples dimpling, hair tossing, mouth smiling sweetly, voice tinkling and warm, she flattered and flirted with the director, who sat there, his eyes sunk into his head, looking grey, weary and battered.

Dismissed, Richard found a bottle of wine and sought out Veronica, whom he found standing in the middle of a small group of actors. They looked older, plainer and washed-out in their civilian clothes, politely trying not to yawn and to maintain a degree of interest as she held forth on the play's subtext.

He filled her glass at a break in the conversation and, taking advantage of his arrival, the actors melted away to regroup elsewhere.

'God, they're hard work,' she snorted, drinking deeply. 'Thanks for rescuing me, Richard.'

'My pleasure,' he murmured. Then he took the plunge. 'Vee, this dinner of yours on the twenty-first, have you sent us an invite? Isabelle hasn't mentioned it, but you know how vague she can be.'

Veronica looked at him, coolly. 'She hasn't mentioned it because I haven't invited you.'

Richard was so taken aback by the brutality of her reply that for a moment he could only gape

416

at her. He managed a shaky laugh. 'Fair enough.'

Veronica relented a little. 'I'd love you to come, Richard, but you know the rules of the game. You and Issy have been over to our place many times, but I'm still waiting to be invited back. I know you've been refurbishing the house, but still, it's nearly Christmas and you've been there since October. Hugh and I would be quite happy to sit at your kitchen table. Lord knows, we don't mind slumming it... If you must know, I feel rather hurt. I was looking forward to you living so close, but I think I've seen less of you since you moved into the village than when you lived in Bath. And what about our lunches – what's happened to those? Or is it,' she said, with a meaningful glance in Juliet's direction, 'that you've found someone else's company more to your taste?'

Richard groaned inwardly. It had never occurred to him Veronica might feel jealous, but it was true, he'd neglected their friendship, he had taken his eye off the ball... Blast Issy.

He managed a rueful smile. 'You're right, Vee. I'm sorry. I've been so busy with this current campaign, I'm hardly home. I only brought Juliet tonight because I was given these tickets and Issy didn't want to come. Between you and me, lovely though Juliet is, she's a bit of a lightweight. But you're right, I've been neglectful; lunch is long overdue.'

'I've been following your activities in the paper. A spectacular demonstration, Richard; I'm impressed. It's getting quite nasty, isn't it? How soon are you going for Oliver Merfield's jugular?'

Not knowing if Hugh had told her about their

pact, Richard gave her a conspiratorial grin. 'We turn the spotlight on our MPs next week.'

'Don't you think that gives me even more of a reason not to invite you to the dinner? I can't have two of my guests falling out – it would ruin it for everyone else.'

'Or be a source of rare entertainment.' Richard shrugged and affected indifference. 'It's your party. I didn't realise the Merfields were such chums of yours. I shall be sorry to be excluded from the table of my favourite hostess.'

Veronica made no reply, and, displeased, Richard drifted across the room to join Juliet.

He had further cause to fume when the weary actors finally released from their social obligations, and made going-home noises. Veronica and Hugh had booked a taxi and offered to share it with Juliet and Richard.

'Thank you, that's very kind.' Juliet dimpled and turned to Richard. 'I don't know if Richard has other plans?'

18

Having dropped the girls off at school, Isabelle pulled the hood of her duffle coat over her head against the cold east wind, and set off for Milo's workshop, stuffing her hands in her pockets for extra warmth. Her fingers curled round the letter from Joe that had arrived that morning. It contained a number of photographs, but she hadn't time to do more than glance at them or to read the letter before she had to bundle the children out of the house. For the first time since she started at school, Becky was the first out of the house and raced ahead down the drive.

It's a pity Richard wasn't here to see her, thought Isabelle. He could've rung me last night, the bastard. Becky was dying to tell him about her part.

She grinned, thinking about the nativity play – no politically correct sensitivity in this village. A good, old-fashioned nativity play, performed in the church. But then, there were absolutely no children in the school, as far as she could make out, who came from a different religious background, let alone other ethnic origins. A far cry from the schools she'd attended in Chatham. It seemed extraordinary, the more she thought about it, that in Summerstoke there were probably folk who'd never encountered anyone from a different racial background. She wondered if Paula, for example, had ever met a West Indian or spoken to a Sikh. She'd felt very conspicuous as a newcomer to the village. How much more difficult if she'd been a different race as well.

She paused on the bridge and gazed down into the river, letting her mind drift over the next move in the Veronica Lester affair, for with some difficulty she'd persuaded Rita to leave it to her and not to march off to Summerstoke House for a showdown. Isabelle knew Veronica could out-manoeuvre Rita with consummate ease and they would get nowhere.

The water, glossily dark, was quite high but its

movement was barely discernible, measured only by the passage of a floating leaf or feather. From an overhanging branch near the water's edge, a sudden movement caught her eye and a flash of vivid blue streaked along the surface of the water, disappearing into a bush growing out of the bank.

She gasped, straining her eyes to see where it had gone, her heart thumping with excitement. She'd never seen anything like it before, never seen such a living colour before. It must have been a kingfisher. She'd seen pictures of them, but hadn't thought they looked any more interesting than any other bird, and she wasn't very interested in birds. Why should she be? In Chatham, where she grew up, they had seagulls, pigeons and starlings, and ducks in the park and not much else, and the exotics in London Zoo, where she'd been taken once, hadn't stirred in her any emotion other than compassion.

She was so excited, she laughed at herself. The kingfisher, if that was what it was, had disappeared and was not going to show again. Reluctantly, she turned away and walked on over the bridge. She couldn't get the flash of colour out of her mind. It wasn't blue, it was something else – turquoise – a shimmering greeny blue – an iridescent combination that had clearly eluded the illustrator of her bird book. And the way it flew – so straight, so fast, just above the water.

Her mind was so full of what she'd seen that she arrived at the workshop without noticing the journey and was astounded to find it was raining and she was wet through.

Milo had agreed to wear a loincloth whenever

Isabelle was in the workshop and she had managed to persuade him, although it was against his naturist ideals, to wear one when he was out running. She knew he wasn't bothered about the village's gossip but, as she pointed out, the last thing he wanted was unpleasant publicity arising from a complaint.

He fussed around her with a small hand towel, hung her duffle coat to steam over the radiator, then, irritated by the time he'd spent away from his creation, returned to the painting he was currently absorbed in finishing.

Isabelle couldn't get the brilliance of the bird out of her mind, and as she mixed for Milo she tried to work out how one could reproduce something so elusive.

When Milo lifted his head and looked round, a signal she recognised as him needing a break, she asked if he'd ever seen a kingfisher.

'No, I don't think I have – don't get many in London. Why?'

'I think I saw one down by the bridge. It was moving so fast I just saw this flash of colour. I don't think I've ever seen anything quite like it.'

He turned and looked at her, closely. 'Hmm. Why don't you try mixing it?'

Before she could reply, he turned back to his painting, saying, 'I'm going to need some more pouzzouli – mix me up a fair amount, would you?'

Some time later, having made coffee, Isabelle remembered Joe's letter. The photographs were of an art installation he had just finished for a municipal library in Melbourne: a series of oval shapes, with a suggestion of human features carved into their smooth stone surfaces, all different colours and set at angles to each other. In front of the largest, towering way above him, Joe stood proudly grinning at the camera. 'Wow!' Isabelle was impressed.

Milo looked up, curious. 'What's that?'

Isabelle passed him the photos. 'It's my friend Joe Watts. We were students together. He went to live in Australia. This is his second big commission.'

Milo took the photographs and studied them. 'Joe Watts … can't say I know the name.' He studied them closely. 'Looks interesting.'

He handed the pictures back. Isabelle took them, saying lightly, 'Yes, he's good. Perhaps you gave the Steel award to the wrong person when you gave it to me.'

'I don't think so.' It was said dismissively, without any warmth, and he turned his back on her and resumed painting.

Isabelle flushed with shame. How could she have made such a pathetic comment? She buried herself in Joe's letter, her cheeks burning.

Joe sounded happy and full of exuberance. He'd picked up another commission immediately on the back of the library one, and his relationship with an Aussie by the name of Andy, was blooming. He joked about her working for Milo and finished with a plea that, somehow, she would find the time to pay him a visit. He really wanted her to meet Andy and to see his work for herself.

Mixing the paint to the shade of earthy red that Milo called pouzzouli, Isabelle let her imagination drift to Australia and Joe.

In a previous letter he'd described the outback to her – the desert soil was probably something like the colour she was mixing. If only she could drop everything and go to see him. Stand under that endless blue sky stretching over the infinite wilderness of rock and scrub. Oh, to have that freedom. Summerstoke – indeed, her whole life – seemed grey, lifeless, hemmed in...

A bang on the door interrupted her reverie and a man's head appeared. 'Hey, Milo.'

She'd no idea who the newcomer was. Tall, with a closely shaven head, he was in his late thirties, she guessed, well built and casually but expensively dressed. He flashed a pair of piercing blue eyes at her before advancing on Milo, who abandoned his brush and got up with a cry of pleasure. 'Marcus, my dear little bro, what are you doing here?'

'Dropped by to sort out one or two things with Charlie. We're meeting at the pub for lunch, so put some clothes on and join us.'

'Delighted to. Isabelle, may I introduce you to my little brother, Marcus Steel. Isabelle,' he explained, as his not-so-little brother firmly gripped her hand, 'is helping me get my stuff together for the exhibition.'

'Hence the loincloth.' Isabelle found herself being closely scrutinised. His gaze was intense and rather formidable. He had a bony, clever face, with a long, thin nose, and high, polished brow. He oozed energy, and, apart from his eyes, he was, in every way, unlike his brother.

'This is a first. Milo doesn't normally tolerate

assistants. Says they get in the way, cantankerous old sod.'

'It's true, they do. Isabelle's different – she knows how to mix paint and prepare canvases. Most importantly, she knows colour.'

Milo had never said this before and Isabelle was so overwhelmed she couldn't think of a response, other than to blush.

'Well, well, what a find.' Marcus held his gaze, looking intently at her for a moment, and then a smile softened and transformed his face. 'Will you join us, Isabelle?'

A thousand reasons not to flashed across her brain and every one was Charlie Tucker. She hesitated.

'Come on, Isabelle,' Milo joined in. 'I haven't bought you a drink since we started working together. It's long overdue.'

'A drink, you old skinflint?' Marcus laughed. 'You can buy her lunch.' He roamed about the studio as the two of them cleared up and got ready. 'This is a great little studio, Milo. Charlie's made a good job of it. I can see you not wanting to move back to London.'

'Well, you'd be wrong. This is all too ... open, clean, soft. The foul and filth, the noise and stench of London are meat and drink to me. The great thing about this place is there's no distraction, but if I lived here I'd have nothing to fight, nothing in me to paint.'

Isabelle's duffle coat was still steaming damp, so she left it where it was and followed Milo and Marcus across the yard to Marcus's convertible.

'Isabelle, if you wouldn't mind squeezing in the

back, the old man can have the passenger seat.'

'Less of the cheek, if you don't mind.' Milo cast a glance over his shoulder at Isabelle. 'Marcus is my half-brother, in case you're wondering about the difference in our ages. He's always been a cheeky sod. Spoilt, that's his trouble.'

The two brothers engaged in non-stop good-humoured banter and Isabelle loved listening to them. The only blot on the horizon was Charlie, but she consoled herself with the thought he'd want to have as little to do with her as she with him, and if she managed to sit nowhere near him it would be okay. And anyway, she thought, if it didn't work out, she could always make her excuses and go home.

At the end of the track, however, instead of turning towards Summerstoke, Marcus turned left and headed away from the village.

'Er, aren't you going the wrong way? Aren't we going to the Foresters Arms?' she asked, nervously.

'No. We're meeting Charlie at his local, the Bunch of Grapes, at the crossroads to Summerbridge. It's not far, two or three miles. Do you know it?'

'No,' said Isabelle faintly.

'Poor old Charlie was sweet on the landlady there. But she was raw from a broken marriage and not ready for another relationship, so she moved on.'

'He's remarkably cheerful, for a man with a broken heart,' observed Milo.

'He's resilient. He's a good man.'

Serve him right! thought Isabelle savagely. I bet

she realised what a thick-skinned, philandering bastard he is.

The Bunch of Grapes sat on a crossroads, as Marcus said. It was not large, clearly very old, built of golden sandstone with mullioned windows and a lichen-covered slate roof. A pair of chimneys breathed smoke into the grey sky, and the walls were covered with the black, bare tendrils of a creeper, its leaves shed long since.

A porch opened into a small vestibule with three doors, one on either side, and one straight ahead. Marcus opened the door to the left, and led the way into a small and cosy public bar.

A fire crackled in an inglenook fireplace, the flagstone floor was softened by rugs of indeterminate design and colour, and scattered around the room were an assortment of tables and chairs. A brown and white spaniel lay stretched in front of the fire, but as soon as Marcus walked into the room she scrambled to her feet, barking joyously.

He bent down and ruffled her ears. 'Hey, there, Duchess, old girl. Charlie looking after you, is he?'

'Twists me round her little finger,' laughed Charlie, who was sitting at the bar with Lenny. 'Hey, Marcus.' He got up from his stool and crossed the room to meet them. The two men, clasping each other by the hand and clapping each other on the back, were clearly pleased to see each other.

'Good to see you, man.' Charlie nodded at Milo. 'Hi, Milo. Welcome to my watering hole.' Then, seeing Isabelle lurking behind Milo, his eyes widened and the smile faded from his face. 'Isabelle.'

426

'Hello, Charlie,' she said, trying hard to keep her voice steady. 'Milo and Marcus persuaded me to come along, but if you're going to have a business discussion, perhaps I'd better...'

Milo and Marcus were looking at her curiously. She felt herself going red, hating Charlie all the more for ruining the occasion.

'Isabelle!'

It was Lenny. Lenny to the rescue, dear, kind Lenny, who'd spent hours helping her hang lining paper, sanding down rails and skirting boards, filling in the holes the plasterer had missed. Isabelle couldn't help but be aware she viewed Lenny and Paula in a different light from most of the village, but she didn't care. They were always so kind to her and although, admittedly, she paid for their favours, she didn't begrudge it – the amount of money they managed on filled her with shame.

The five settled round a table near the fire. Charlie went to the bar for the first round of drinks, enabling Isabelle to sit between Lenny and Milo, so it was easy for her to ignore Charlie's odious presence.

Marcus was planning some location filming at Marsh Farm, and he and Charlie were soon deep in discussion about which farm buildings he wanted to use.

Isabelle wasn't interested and chatted to Lenny, whom she hadn't seen since the incident with Paula in the shop.

'Lucky you was there, Isabelle, 'cos if it'd got back to me, I'd 'ave been round there in a flash. Who does Rita Godwin think she is, treating my missus like that?'

427

'She was upset, Lenny. Her customers were staying away in droves – or rather, the wealthier ones whom Veronica Lester had nobbled. Why do you think Veronica's doing it? Do you think she's just punishing Paula, or is it something more?'

Lenny took a pull of his cider and smacked his lips reflectively.

'Knowing 'ow she's operated in the past, I'd say it was summat more. Look at it this way: if she wanted to do for Paula, all she'd 'ave to do is spread the rumour that she'd dismissed Paula for dishonesty, and Paula wouldn't have bin able to get cleanin' work anywhere.'

Isabelle was shocked. 'That's awful. She wouldn't do that, surely?'

'You know yer friend... I wouldn't put it past her. But the thing is, Isabelle, she didn't. What I reckon – me and Charlie, that is...'

Isabelle was startled. She knew Paula would discuss it with Lenny. It had never occurred to her he'd then discuss it with Charlie.

'What we think is, she's targeting the shop. She's played this sort of trick before. When the Lesters wanted to buy Marsh Farm last summer, she put it about the dairy was havin' problems – made an anonymous phone call to the Health and Safety mob.'

'Lenny, that's awful!'

'Yep. Well nigh did for us. This woman what put in an offer, you said she's a friend of the Lester woman?'

'Yes.'

'Well, mebbe she's doin' the same thing: getting the shop to close, so her friend can nip in and buy it at a rock-bottom price. S'what she tried to do to Charlie, but he saw her off.'

'No wonder he hates the Lesters so much.' She glanced across at Charlie and surprised him staring at her.

She dropped her eyes and turned back to Lenny. 'I can't see Veronica putting herself out like that, not even for her best friend. There's got to be something more.'

Their speculation getting nowhere, the conversation turned to more inconsequential things. But then, on a peal of laughter at something Lenny said, she again caught Charlie staring at her, a puzzled look on his face.

The sandwiches they ordered arrived simultaneously with Juliet.

Juliet woke that morning long after Jamie had left for college. She stretched out in bed, not keen to get up. The sky, visible through a gap in her curtains, was dark and a silver spatter of raindrops clung to the windowpane.

She exhaled deeply and pulled a face. Not a lot to get up for, but she didn't feel like staying in bed. Her mind wandered over the previous evening's events at the theatre. She couldn't tell if Mike actually remembered her, or if he would really invite her to his next audition, but it would be worth putting in a call to Louis and alerting him. Not that Louis was very keen on her doing stage work these days. Once she'd become associated with the screen, he was not interested in the pittance the theatre paid.

Richard Garnett ... was he getting too keen?

429

What was he expecting of her? Was he serious about her writing a column? Somehow she didn't think so. Then why...? Not that he'd said anything, but the way he'd kissed her hand, and the look he'd thrown her when she accepted the Lesters' offer of a lift... She had to admit to feeling a little unnerved.

'I don't fancy him,' she said aloud. 'Anyway, he's married. And so am I,' she added, as an afterthought.

If she did fancy him, would she encourage him further? She lay back on her pillows and thought of Oliver. She'd had flirtations, plenty of them, but no affairs after she'd married him.

Before that, there had been several, but only one – at drama school with a visiting lecturer who taught experimental drama – where she'd lost it. He was married, and she'd wept buckets when he told her their affair was going nowhere. But since she'd married Ollie...

It wasn't a conscious decision – I am married, therefore I do not have affairs – and she loved people being attracted to her, loved flirtations, but she never wanted it to go any further.

Perhaps, deep down, I'm a fundamentally moral person. Or maybe I love Ollie more than I realise? Whatever the reason, Juliet didn't want to become embroiled with Richard. She would have to cool it.

So what to do?

Oliver was in London till Friday. Jamie was still playing at stand-offs, spending as much time with the Witches as with her, when he wasn't off with his friends. She knew she'd been wrong not

430

to give him what he wanted that night. He'd taken her by surprise. *She* was the actor in the family and seeing him… It was a challenge she was unprepared for. And now he was cross with her. It hurt, but there was not a lot she could say until he came off his high horse.

She thought of Isabelle, but working with Milo during the day she was hardly available. That left Charlie.

'The local yokel,' she giggled, and closed her eyes, remembering the firmness of his hand on her arm as she climbed over stiles and pushed her under barbed wire, and once, laughing, scooped her in his arms to lift her over a particularly wide patch of mud.

But when he arrived back at her house, he'd refused her invitation to go in, made no attempt to kiss her, and hadn't been in touch since, not even to return the scarf she'd left behind in his van. This she found particularly vexing – it was a trick Louis had taught her and it had never failed to work before. The scarf was returned the very next day, but someone pushed it through her letterbox without ringing the bell.

I've never chased a country bumpkin before – I've never chased anyone before, she thought. I wonder how long it'll take me to get my first kiss? Pushing back the covers, she swung out of bed. I think it's time I paid Milo a visit.

In high spirits, the thrill of the chase upon her, Juliet showered and dressed, simply but artfully, in clothes designed in London for a country weekend, then spent considerable time making herself up as naturally as she could. It was nearly one o'clock when she drove her little sports car – Ollie had bought it for her thirtieth birthday – over to Marsh Farm.

She found nobody there. Uncertain which of the buildings was Milo's studio, she picked her way round the yard, her elegant leather boots squelching in the thin layer of slurry covering everything. A sweet, sickly smell pervaded the damp air and she had to hold a tissue to her nose to stop herself gagging. Attracted by soft noises from one of the barns, she found a herd of cows blowing and snorting, lazily shifting their feet on a bed of straw, but there was nobody about.

She squelched her way over to what appeared to be the front door of the farmhouse and rang the bell. After an age, the bolts were pulled back and a plump, middle-aged woman, with faded blonde hair, soft blue eyes and a kindly face, peered round the door.

'Sorry to keep you waiting, my dear, only we don't use this door in the winter. How may I help you?'

'Sorry to bother you, but I was looking for a friend of mine, Milo Steel. I understand he has a studio in one of your workshops.'

'That's right. But I'm afraid you've just missed him. He's gone off for lunch with his brother. They're meeting my son, Charlie, at the Bunch of Grapes. You could catch him there.'

It couldn't be better. Juliet could have hugged the woman. She smiled sweetly. 'Thank you so much. Sorry to have bothered you.'

'Do you know where the Grapes is?'

'Yes, yes, I do, thanks. Bye.' She slithered back

to her car, leaving the woman staring after her, a look of concern on her amiable face.

Why she hadn't expected to see Isabelle with them, she didn't know. And why she was irritated at the sight of her, looking so comfortable and relaxed, she didn't know, either, and for a moment she stood there, all eyes on her, feeling awkward, an outsider – not a sensation she was used to.

'Hi,' she said, dimpling, retrieving the situation. 'Mind if I join you? I called at your workshop, Milo, and a very nice lady told me you were here.'

Charlie, Milo and Marcus stood up and, as Charlie went to pull in an extra chair, Milo introduced his brother. 'I'm not sure if you know Marcus, Juliet? I'm sure you must have met him before. Juliet Peters, Marcus Steel.'

She smiled at Marcus as she shook his hand. She knew who he was: Polly's old flame, who from a person of no consequence, when she'd met him previously, had become a producer in an independent production company, very much flavour of the month with commissioning editors and therefore of considerable interest to her now. 'I think we have met, haven't we? Ages ago – at one of Milo's exhibitions, probably.'

'Probably.' Marcus smiled. 'May I get you a drink? It's my round.'

As Marcus went to the bar, Milo leaned across to Juliet. 'Any particular reason you wanted to see me?'

Juliet was conscious of Charlie next to her. She could almost feel his physicality, his strength, his vigour; almost smell the fresh air that seemed to permeate his skin. Such a contrast to Milo, with his shock of grey hair and grey, lined face. She smiled demurely.

'No particular reason. I just thought it was about time I paid a visit to your workshop. Isabelle has told me so much about your work.'

Isabelle looked startled. As well she may, thought Juliet, with a secret giggle, since she's never said anything about Milo's painting.

With Marcus on one side and Charlie on the other, the lunch hour passed all too quickly for Juliet. Isabelle showed no interest in muscling in on their conversation, chatting to Lenny and Milo and leaving the other two to her.

She couldn't believe her luck. Marcus asked her about her career and what her prospects were. She told him about the pilot she'd made in LA and about *Hunter's Way*. He told her a little about the programmes he was making and his plan to use Marsh Farm as the location for a comedy drama.

A couple of times she caught Charlie's attention drifting across the table to the conversation Isabelle and Lenny were having with Milo, but nothing else punctured her enjoyment of the occasion, till Isabelle, glancing at her watch, abruptly stood up.

'I've got to go. I didn't realise it was so late. Er...' She looked around them, uncertain, then appealed to Juliet. 'I'm sorry to interrupt, but do you think you could possibly give me a lift back to Summerstoke?'

Juliet had no intention of leaving until the last

possible moment, so she smiled sweetly, but regretfully, at Isabelle.

'Sorry, Isabelle, but I've got to go on to Summerbridge and my tank's nearly empty. I reckon I've got just enough to make it to the petrol station on the main road.'

Isabelle's face did not betray her. Oh sod it, she thought crossly. Why don't I believe her?

She turned to Lenny. 'Lenny can you give me a lift? It's two fifteen and I'm meant to be at the school at two thirty.'

'School finishes at three fifteen, darlin' – you've got plenty of time. And we can always give Paula a bell, tell her to collect 'em.'

'No, I've got to go. I've promised to help with the art class. We're painting a backdrop for the nativity.'

Before Lenny had time to say anything else, Marcus stood up. 'I'll give you a lift if you like, if Charlie or Lenny can take Milo back?'

But Charlie had other ideas. 'No, I'll go. Lenny hasn't got his van here, anyway. He came with me and my van has only one passenger seat.'

She looked at him in dismay. He was the last person in the world she wanted a favour from.

'But,' she began faintly, 'You've got things to discuss with Marcus. Couldn't you just lend Lenny your car key?'

'No,' he said briskly, pulling on his jacket. 'Lenny's downed three pints of cider already. And Marcus and I have discussed as much as we can without viewing the site, so let's go.'

Without waiting for her assent, he turned to Marcus. 'I'll be about twenty minutes. If you wouldn't mind giving our Lenny a lift, I'll meet you in Milo's studio. Cheers.'

And with a farewell nod at Juliet, who, Isabelle thought, looked put out, Charlie led the way out of the pub without looking back to see if Isabelle was following.

She had no choice, and she knew it. Miserably she trailed in his wake, not losing hope some alternative might present itself. But it didn't; even the weather conspired against her – the rain sheeting across the car park – so she had to dash after him and by the time she scrambled into his van, her hair was dripping and her shirt spattered with dark wet stains.

He glanced across at her as he turned on the ignition. 'Not got a coat?'

'No,' she said coldly. 'I left it behind in Milo's workshop. I got soaked this morning – it was drying out.'

She stared out of the window, hoping to discourage further conversation and trying hard not to shiver.

Without comment, Charlie cranked up the heater and put on the blower. 'I didn't know you knew Lenny so well,' he said casually. 'You seemed pretty good mates.'

'I like him. Do you have a problem with that?'

Far from taking offence at her spiky tone, Charlie laughed. "Course not. He's a good bloke. He's my best mate, I reckon. It's just I wouldn't have thought he was your type, that's all.'

'How would you know what my type is? You know nothing about me at all.' Her feelings of ill-usage at the hands of this – this philanderer, whom she'd vowed from the very beginning to steer well clear of, came bubbling to the surface. 'From the moment you met me you've dismissed me as a useless, middle-class townie who drives a Discovery, or rather, in your opinion, *can't* drive a Discovery, and who lives in the pockets of the likes of the Lesters. Well, as it happens, you smug bastard, I have more in common with people like Lenny than you probably do!' She stopped abruptly, furious with herself. She'd meant to thank him for the lift, say nothing else, and she'd blown it.

'Oh,' – his voice was neutral – 'I think that would surprise Lenny. How do you work that one out?'

'Because, unlike you,' she spat, 'I didn't grow up surrounded by my family's acres. I grew up in a small semi – much the same size as Lenny's, but without the garden – in Chatham. I went to a sink comprehensive and when I got a place at art school, I had to work evenings and weekends to survive, because my parents didn't understand or approve and gave me no support. So what if I live in a big house now, and have enough to eat and drink, and employ Paula to clean for me? I'm still happier in the company of people like Paula and Lenny than you, or the Lesters, or all the other fat-cat farmers who strut around as if they own this part of the world.'

'Blimey!' He whistled with amazement. 'I never thought I'd hear myself condemned in the same breath as the Lesters.'

He turned off the High Street into the lane leading to the school and stopped outside the gates. He turned and said gently, 'Isabelle, I think we've–'

But she gave him no chance to say what he thought. As soon as the van came to a halt, she opened the door, coldly interrupting him. 'Thank you for my lift. I'll try to make sure you never have to put yourself out for me again.'

Then she turned and ran through the rain, into the school.

As soon as she had slammed the door of the van, Duchess reclaimed her seat. Charlie put out his hand and absentmindedly stroked the dog, watching Isabelle until she disappeared through a door without looking back.

He sighed. 'Well, Duchess, can't say I didn't try.' Feeling unaccountably depressed, he put the van into reverse, turned and drove off.

He was puzzled – puzzled by Isabelle and by his feelings, which he couldn't begin to work out. Why couldn't he shrug her off? She wasn't important to him, and she'd made it quite clear how much she despised him. Maybe that was what was bugging him?

Charlie's irrepressible sense of the ridiculous came to his rescue and his mouth twitched at being lumped in with the Lesters.

I wonder how on earth she got mixed up with them? he thought. She's not like them at all. And that husband of hers, where's he?

He remembered a tall, dark, older bloke chatting to Veronica Lester. They hadn't been introduced but then, he thought, grinning, there wasn't much introducing going on that evening. But if that was Isabelle's husband... Charlie was not impressed by that brief glimpse.

'Why am I wasting time thinking about her, Duchess?' The dog lifted her head enquiringly. 'She's a married woman, for Chrissake and not half so pretty as Juliet Merfield – now there's a cracker for you.'

He swung the van into the farm track, thinking of Juliet and then of Oliver. He liked Oliver; he wasn't sure whether he liked Juliet, but she was good fun and, he had to admit, he felt dead pleased that she seemed to find him worth bothering about.

She's dangerous goods though, Charlie, my boy. You watch your step there.

There's no danger, he answered himself. She's a married woman and I like her husband.

So why, his alter ego persisted, is it different with Isabelle?

It's not.

But his denial didn't convince him.

'Well, that proves it, don't it?' said Paula. She was curled up on their battered sofa with a pair of scissors, cutting the legs off a worn pair of jeans Ryan had outgrown – she intended to make some cut-offs for Kylie since they were all the rage now. From time to time she sipped from a can of Guinness balanced on the arm of the sofa. She'd read somewhere that Joan Collins drank Black Velvet and although Paula couldn't afford champagne, she could Guinness.

'What does?' Lenny had just recounted the lunchtime encounter at the Bunch of Grapes and was halfway through a pepperoni pizza Paula

439

produced as a late-night snack.

'Juliet turning up like that. Proves what they're saying – she's having an affair with Charlie. Poor Oliver.'

'Don't prove anything of the sort, you daft cow,' said Lenny affectionately. 'He ain't said nothing to me.'

'Well, he wouldn't, would he? Men don't talk about these things. And she's a married woman, when all's said and done.'

'Yeah, but I know Charlie. When she turned up, he didn't blink an eyelid. Oh, they all flirted with her, but you'd expect that. But that was it. No, you've got it all wrong, my flower.' A broad grin spread across his face, 'It's not Juliet Charlie fancies.' He finished his can of cider with a flourish and reached for another.

Paula stared at him. 'Lenny Spinks, what are you talkin' about?'

'What I say. It's not Juliet Charlie fancies, it's someone else.'

'Who?'

'Guess.' Lenny grinned again and took a long swig from his can.

Paula playfully waved her scissors. 'If you don't tell me right now, I'll cut your ponytail off.'

'Isabelle.'

Paula stared at him.

He chuckled, 'It's Isabelle. Charlie Tucker's got the hots for Isabelle Garnett. I saw the way he looked at her in the pub. Believe me, I'm right.'

'You're nuts, Lenny!' Paula shrieked with disbelief. 'Whad'yer know? You've got it completely wrong. The whole village is talkin' about Juliet and Charlie. Where does Isabelle come into it?'

Lenny shrugged. 'The whole village's got it wrong. It's Isabelle – I'd bet anything on that.'

'Okay, big boy, if you're so sure, let's have a bet.'

'Okay. I bet I'm right and if I'm not...' He struggled for a moment, then his eyes fell on her scissors. 'I'll let you cut my ponytail off.'

'Lenny! You never would.' Paula's eyes popped, and her beehive wobbled crazily.

'Yep. And if you're wrong and I'm right, I'll cut your beehive off.'

'Lenny, you sod! You wouldn't!' Paula shrieked with laughter and horror.

'Is it a deal? My ponytail or your beehive?'

'It's a deal. Oh, Lenny, I hope we're both wrong.'

'I'll drink to that!' Lenny waved his cider at her Guinness and chuckled.

Patting her hair thoughtfully, Paula frowned at him. 'So why are you so sure it's Isabelle and not Juliet?'

He gave her a broad grin. 'I thought yer'd never ask, my little rosebud. It's the difference between a duffle coat and a scarf.'

'How much 'ave you had to drink, Lenny Spinks?'

'Never enough. But it's what I say: the duffle coat and the scarf,' he smirked, complacently. 'The story is, my flower, Juliet leaves 'er scarf in Charlie's van–'

'That proves it – she's havin' an affair with 'im. Why else should the likes of her be in Charlie Tucker's old van? And he was seen, carryin' her

441

in his arms, kissin'...'

Lenny shrugged. 'I bet whoever saw 'em weren't that close. He gave her a lift, I dunno. Anyway, he has this scarf and what does he do? He gives it to me and asks me to drop it off at hers. Now, if he was sweet on her, he'd take it himself, wouldn't he? He wouldn't give it to someone else and lose the chance of seein' her again, would he?'

'No,' Paula agreed with reluctance, 'I suppose not. But what's a duffle coat got to do with anything?'

Lenny hugged himself with glee. 'Isabelle left her duffle coat in the old man's studio – it was wet, or something. When Charlie gets back from droppin' her off, he sees it, and what does he do? Does he ask me to take it round to Isabelle's later? No, he doesn't. He takes it, right there, himself, and goes off to give it to her, personal. There! Am I right, or am I right?'

'That don't prove nothing,' said Paula stoutly, but she nervously patted her hair.

19

'Marion? Hi, Isabelle Garnett here... Yes, I'm fine, thanks... Look, sorry to bother you, but I need a bit of advice and I wondered if... Yes, that's right, most of the rooms are ready for painting, but... Yes, I could do with some help on curtains and things. Tomorrow? That'd be brilliant ... about four thirty then? Great.'

Isabelle was not good at intrigue and plotting, but she was furious with Veronica for using Paula as a scapegoat in her machinations to ruin Rita. She was sure that was Veronica's intention – Lenny's story of her attempts to ruin the Tuckers was confirmation of how devious and unscrupulous Veronica could be.

Putting the phone down on Marion, she discovered she was trembling. Silly, she chided herself. She can't eat me.

She glanced at the clock on the kitchen wall. Nearly seven. Richard had phoned earlier to say he'd be home for supper and she'd urged him to get back in time to tuck the girls up. She really wanted Becky herself to tell him the news about the nativity, but so far there had been no chance – they'd not seen him since he'd left for work on Monday morning.

He'd come in late last night; Isabelle woke when he tripped up the still-uncarpeted stairs – the noise and his expletives echoed around the house. The girls didn't call out and he made no attempt to come into her room, so she assumed he was going to sleep in what he called his dressing room.

It took her some time to get back to sleep. Her mind went over and over the bundle of questions to which she could find no obvious answer. Why had Charlie brought her duffle coat into school like that? She'd been showing the children how to draw and cut out stars from silver paper when he'd walked in, dropped it on a chair saying, 'You might be needing this,' then turned on his heel and left, not waiting for her to thank him.

443

She didn't know how to react. Why was he so nice to her, when she'd made it clear what she thought of him? He was such a bastard. He was, but everyone seemed to like him, except the Lesters, and when had she ever agreed with them over anything?

And Veronica, what did she want with the shop? Ask Richard? Might he know?

And Richard, what was going on with him? Was he having an affair? With Veronica? Or Juliet? Was Richard having an affair with Juliet? She had to ask Paula. They'd shared a bed only twice in the last week, and she couldn't remember the last time they'd made love.

That was another odd thing: she wasn't sure she cared very much. Their early love life had been passionate and fulfilling. What had happened to it? Had she lost her sex drive? Why was she relieved when Richard slept next door? Why was he coming home so late, so often?

What should she say to Charlie when she saw him next? What had Charlie to do with anything?

Eventually she fell into a restless sleep, waking long after Richard had left for work.

'Mummy, is Dad back yet?' Becky appeared at the kitchen door, her eyes bright and excited.

'No, darling, not yet. I'll come up and run you a bath. Then you and Clemmie can be nice and clean and in your nightclothes when he does come in. Perhaps he'll read you a story.'

As she ran the bath and tidied the girls' clothes away, her mind drifted back over the morning, in the workshop with Milo. She smiled. He was such an odd character; so absorbed in his painting that nothing else mattered. She'd tried to warn him his nightly runs were causing consternation in the village, but he'd shrugged and said, 'I don't run through Summerstoke, and I'm wearing a loincloth, so why should anyone be bothered?'

Mixing for him had brought back to her how much she enjoyed paint, the smell of it, the texture of it, and how exciting even the process of mixing was, whether creating a grey to cover the canvases in preparation for him to work on, or blending a specific colour he wanted.

She asked him if she could use a discarded canvas to work out the composition of a colour. He hadn't even turned round but waved at a stash of canvases he'd abandoned. It seemed sacrilegious to paint over any of his work, but as she stood there, hesitating, he'd swung round and with great irritation told her to stop farting about. So she'd chosen the one least worked on, painted it over and, in between meeting Milo's demands, started to select the various colours she might need to reproduce the colour of the kingfisher.

The front door slammed. She went to the bathroom door. 'We're up here, Richard. I'm just putting the girls to bed.'

He made no reply but, hearing him climb the stairs, she went out onto the landing to meet him. From the expression on his face she could tell he wasn't in a good mood and her heart sank. Pretending not to notice, she said as cheerfully as she could, 'Hello, darling. I'm glad you're back before the girls are asleep. Becky has something to tell you.'

'Well, I hope it's something nice,' he growled, pushing past her and making no attempt to kiss her. 'It's not enough I'm exhausted, but that fucking honey merchant is still at it – I've got it all over the sleeve of my leather jacket. The car was parked in Pulteney Street – you'd think somebody must have seen him. Just wait till I catch him. Find me a glass of wine, would you?'

Making her way, somewhat indignantly, down to the kitchen, she heard the girls' shrieks of delight as he entered their room.

Is he taking me for granted? I haven't seen him for three days and all he can say is 'Find me a glass of wine'. I'm not his bloody skivvy!

However, she found a bottle of Merlot and left it, with a glass, on the kitchen table. Feeling depressed at the prospect of an evening with Richard in a mood, she began peeling potatoes to go with a beef stew she'd got out of the freezer.

'Did Becky tell you about the nativity?' she ventured, when he came into the kitchen. 'She's so excited, her whole attitude to school has changed.'

'Well, thank Christ for that.' His mood clearly had not much improved and he went straight for the wine bottle and poured a glass.

'I hope you're going to be able to find the time to come, Richard?'

He gave an exasperated sigh. 'Depends when it is. Until I've got this current campaign over with...'

'Richard, we're talking about your daughter, here. Becky – remember her? We scarcely see

446

you... This whole political campaign has become an obsession, I've never known you work so hard. Why?'

'Because, you idiot, I need head office to see we're a paper to be reckoned with. They're impressed with what I've done so far, but I need sales to increase sufficiently to get them off my back.' He took a large mouthful of wine and looked up at his wife, who was staring resentfully at him. He was irritated. 'What?'

'I'm not an idiot. How can I know anything about anything if you're not here to tell me? I didn't know you're having problems with head office.'

'Well, I am. And another thing, Issy, do you know Vee hasn't invited us to her Christmas party?'

'Good,' Isabelle muttered under her breath.

'And the reason for us not being invited is because we haven't had them round here.'

'No, we haven't.'

'Why haven't we? For Chrissake, they're friends of mine, Issy. They got us this house – the least we can do is invite them over to dinner.'

'But we agreed, until the decorating was finished, it would be a good idea not to have anyone over. The Christmas party was going to be the first time for everyone.'

'But the Lesters aren't everyone. No wonder Vee's put out. What have we got planned for this Saturday?'

'Nothing.'

'Then let's invite them over.' He cast an eye around the kitchen. 'This is more or less done

447

and I thought you said you'd finished the front sitting room?'

'I have. Go and have a look at it.'

'I will, in a minute. In the meantime, get on the phone and invite Vee and Hugh over for an informal supper on Saturday night. Say you've just finished decorating and they're the first to see the new-look house. Invite the Merfields, too, if you want. We owe them for that party.'

'No.'

Richard stared at her. 'What did you say?' He was not used to opposition from Isabelle.

'I said no. I don't want to.'

'Why on earth not?'

'I don't like your friend Veronica, that's why not – and I dislike Hugh, too. I don't want them in my house.'

'You stupid little girl!' shouted Richard, puce with anger. 'This is *my* house and you'll do as you're told. How fucking childish can you get?'

Before Isabelle had a chance to reply, the telephone rang and at the same time Becky's voice could be heard, calling anxiously for Isabelle.

Ignoring the phone, Isabelle started out of the room, hissing at Richard as she went, 'She was so looking forward to you coming home. You're an unbelievable, egocentric bastard. Why on earth do I let you walk all over me?'

By the time she'd settled Becky and returned downstairs, Richard was off the phone and standing in the recently decorated room. Angry though she was with him, she attempted to be placatory.

'What do you think?'

448

'It'll do for now. Maybe it was a mistake to paint it all white. We'll get Vee to advise us on some wallpaper on Saturday.' He ignored her gasp of angry disbelief and pressed on. 'That was Clare on the phone. She wants to visit friends in New Zealand over Christmas, so Abigail and possibly Danny, too, will come here. I said you'd have no objections.'

Juliet sat staring at Oliver's computer. It was no good, she couldn't think of anything to write.

'Village life compared to Los Angeles,' Richard had said. Well, Summerstoke was like living in a bloody goldfish bowl and Los Angeles was like living in a fish tank full of piranhas. What a choice. She was starting to hate the continual staring, particularly as, lately, she sensed not all of it was friendly. Even that Godwin woman, who'd been all over her when she'd first arrived back, had been almost rude to her in the shop today.

With a sigh she deleted her faint-hearted opening: 'Summerstoke is different from Los Angeles in many ways...' and, hearing Jamie clumping down the stairs, went to the door of the study to find him pulling on his leather jacket.

'You're not going out, are you, darling?'

He looked at her coolly. 'Don't worry, Mum, I won't be late.'

He had, Juliet noticed, started calling her Mum rather than Juliet and she didn't like it, but now didn't seem the best time to fight that particular battle.

'But it's Thursday night. I thought we were going to have pizzas and watch a movie. Dad's

449

not back until tomorrow.'

'I know – he's got this public meeting in the village hall. Are you going?'

'No, I don't think so,' she murmured. 'I think I'll let him get on with it.'

Jamie shrugged. 'I'm going. I think he needs all the support he can get. He was there for me when I needed him.' He picked up his crash helmet and before she could think of a suitable reply, he opened the front door. 'I'm gonna be late if I don't shoot now. I'm going bowling with Adam and Tish and that lot. Bye, Mum.' The door slammed and he was gone.

Juliet, faced with the prospect of another evening alone in front of the television, sighed and headed to the kitchen to assemble a salad for her supper.

The phone rang.

It was Richard. 'I'm in the Foresters Arms, having a lonely dinner. Fancy joining me?'

Juliet was sufficiently bored with her day to ignore the little warning bells sounding in her head. 'Isn't Isabelle with you?'

There was a slight hesitation, then a dry laugh. 'Issy and I've had what might be termed a domestic. By common consent, she's eating her stew at home and I'm running my eyes down this tasty-looking menu here, thinking how much I could do with some decent company. I've had a pig of a day.'

'So have I. Give me five minutes and I'll join you. We can cheer each other up.'

It was nearer twenty when she slipped into the empty chair at his table and dimpled at him.

450

'So,' he said pouring her a glass of wine, 'what made your day so piggish?'

'Oh,' she said, shaking her head with annoyance, 'I'm still in Jamie's bad books and it's getting very boring, particularly as he's virtually the only human being I see from one end of the day to the other. And I'm finding this prolonged silence from Los Angeles agonising. I think it's a way of breaking me down so, when they make the offer, I'll be so grateful I'll agree to anything.'

Richard looked at her thoughtfully. A bored, frustrated Juliet would more likely be up for a fling; the alacrity with which she'd accepted his invitation to dinner was a good sign. More importantly, he needed to have her where he wanted before Oliver's pillorying began in the press.

'Shall we order? I'm starving.'

'Yes, let's. Then you can tell me why you're eating here and not sitting down to a bowl of stew with your nearest and dearest.'

Richard signalled to a waiter.

'Roasted sea bass – much more exciting than the salad I was planning.' Juliet beamed at him, her ill humour quite gone. 'So tell me, Richard, what's driven you out of the house? I suspect it's all your fault. I can't imagine Isabelle throwing a paddy without good cause.'

He gave her a rueful grin. 'You'd probably be right ninety-eight per cent of the time, but on this occasion it's the other two per cent. I won't bore you with the details, but for one thing she's upset because my daughter Abigail's coming to stay with us for Christmas.'

'Why should that upset her? How old is Abigail?'

451

'She's nineteen. Not the easiest person in the world, I'm the first to admit it, but heavens above, she's my daughter and we see little enough of her. It'll be okay. No, the thing that really seemed to get her goat was a perfectly reasonable request, on my part, that we should have a small supper party on Saturday evening.' He shook his head, still amazed by Issy's reaction.

Juliet was intrigued. 'Why should that upset her? Who are you going to invite?'

'Vee and Hugh Lester. The thing is, I've known them for a long time and they've always been very sociable. I've lost count of the number of times they've invited us to dinner. We owe them, and it's beginning to bug me we've not invited them over since we moved here.'

'Sounds reasonable. What did Isabelle say?'

Richard drained his glass and poured himself another. 'She refused point blank. Said she didn't like either of them and she didn't want them in her house. *Her* house? Who pays the bloody bills?'

Juliet gave a peal of laughter. 'I can't imagine Isabelle saying that. I admit I hardly know her, but still... Are you sure she's not just premenstrual?'

Richard shrugged. 'Well, whether she is or not, I'm bloody well going to invite them. It's as much my house and she'd better remember that.'

They were interrupted by the arrival of their food, and for a while they chatted about the theatre and about television and which medium Juliet preferred working in and what her ultimate ambitions were.

'What about children?' Richard asked at one point. 'I know you've got Jamie, but you must've

452

been very young when you had him. Do you want any more?'

Juliet was thoughtful. 'I suspect Oliver would, but until I'm well established and the studio will fit themselves around me, I couldn't afford the time. It's easy for you men – you can just carry on working. Did Isabelle work before she had your little girls? She hasn't told me that much about herself.'

Richard pulled a face. 'She doesn't like talking about it. She was an artist – painted these bloody great pictures everyone drooled over.'

'What of?'

'Nothing, as far as I could see. What I mean is, they were abstract masses of colour. She stopped when she had the kids – she sort of dried up and hasn't done anything since. I've done everything I can to encourage her.'

'So what are you going to do about your supper party?'

'Go ahead and invite them, of course.' He cocked his head on one side and looked appealingly at her. 'Would you consider coming along, too, you and Oliver? I know Issy likes you both – it would be a definite sweetener if you were there.'

'And Oliver likes Isabelle. But,' said Juliet thoughtfully, 'he doesn't like either of the Lesters, and he doesn't much like you, Richard, so I don't know if I could persuade him.'

The sweet smile accompanying these words sugared the pill and Richard laughed. 'I'm sure you can make him do anything, if you've a mind to it. Do say yes.'

Another bottle of wine later, Richard paid the bill and, taking Juliet's arm, walked with her the short distance to her door. The close proximity of her body, her scent in his nostrils, the alcohol in his blood and the fire in his loins were all spurs to his libido. Stopping outside the old doctor's house he looked down at her.

'The night's young yet. How about inviting me in for a nightcap?'

She looked demurely up at him, a slight smile dancing on her lips. The impulse to crush his mouth against hers was overwhelming.

'I don't think that's a good idea, Richard, do you?'

'Why on earth not?' He lifted her hand to his lips, murmuring as he kissed her fingers, 'I think it's a very good idea.'

She removed her hand. 'For one thing, I should imagine behind the curtains opposite there's at least one inhabitant of this poxy little village watching our every move; and for another, I'm not sure a nightcap is what you really want.'

He attempted a contrite smile. 'No, you're right there. I'm very attracted to you, you know that, and I think you may feel the same way about me. We could have some fun, Juliet – it would make life so much more exciting, and no one need know.'

Juliet stared at him, no longer smiling. 'You *are* an attractive man, Richard, and you're good fun, but there is *no way* I'd have an affair with you. I'm sorry if you thought otherwise, but I do *not* fancy you, not one little bit. Older men don't turn me on, and, hard though it may be to believe, I love Ollie. There's no way I'd cheat on him like that, and certainly not with you. Sorry. Goodnight.'

Before he could react, she'd whisked through her front door and shut it behind her.

Humiliation then fury swept through Richard. He turned on his heel and walked rapidly down to the river. He was too fired up, too angry, to think of going home yet. At the bridge, he leaned against the parapet and gazed, unseeing, at the shining dark water.

The little slut, the prick-teaser, how dare she? How *dare* she! He'd show her, he'd make her sorry. Over and over again, his fevered brain tossed around the indignity of his rejection. 'Love Ollie' – pah! He'd show Oliver no mercy. This meeting of his, Friday, he'd planned to cover it, of course, but now, now he'd do more than just cover it: he'd see Oliver Merfield well and truly humiliated. As for the rest, well, little Miss Hoity-Toity would learn the consequences of messing with him. He'd screw the whole snotty lot of them.

Walking back to the Old Vicarage, his thoughts turned to Isabelle. Another thorn in his flesh, but he decided, although she was in the wrong, he'd make it up to her. His libido, battered by Juliet's rejection, needed to find solace.

Maybe, he argued as he turned into their drive, that was the problem with Isabelle: she was feeling neglected by him and was frustrated. After all, she was a young woman who was turned on by him and he hadn't made love to her in ages.

The house was in darkness when he let himself in. He stumbled up the stairs and went into their

455

bedroom. Deciding not to awaken her abruptly by putting on the light, he pulled off his clothes in the dark, slid into bed and slithered across, intending to nuzzle up to her.

He was thwarted yet again: the sheets were cold; the bed was empty.

Juliet leaned against the front door, trembling. How could she have been so stupid? She knew he was dangerous, she just hadn't seen that move coming so quickly. Why had she ever thought a flirtation with him would be fun? She thought of all the times she'd been out with him, and blushed. Yes, she'd had fun, but what on earth had she imagined the endgame would be? What she'd said to Richard was true: she did love Ollie; she didn't want, didn't need, another lover.

She suddenly thought of Charlie Tucker and blushed more deeply. Thank goodness she'd made no moves there. What was she playing at? It was being stuck in this wretched house, this awful village. Ollie hadn't thought of her when he moved them all down here, lock, stock and barrel.

Angry with herself, angry with Oliver, she walked into the kitchen.

Jamie had left her a note on the kitchen table.

Dear Mum
Where are you? Tried your mobile but you've switched it off. Looloo wants you to call him tonight.
Love Jamie

Juliet suddenly felt breathless and her head spun. She poured herself a glass of cold water and looked at her watch. A little after 11 pm – not too late for Louis. With a slight tremble, she dialled his number.

'Louis' – she tried to make her voice sound as normal as possible – 'it's Juliet. I hope it's not too late, but I had a message you wanted to speak to me tonight?'

'Juliet, darling. How are you, my sweet?'

'Oh, fine,' she replied lightly. 'My teeth have been ground to stumps with the frustration of being stuck here, but otherwise...'

'Well, grind no longer.'

'You've heard something?' Juliet could hardly speak.

'Got an email this evening from Ed. I wanted to talk to him asap, but I needed to get your reactions first. You had your mobile switched off, naughty girl.'

'There's only a patchy signal in this village – it wasn't switched off.' Juliet suddenly felt nervous. 'What's it about? My reactions to what, Louis?'

'How's your American accent these days, darling?'

'It would get by. Why?'

'It would seem' – Louis's voice gave nothing away – 'our brothers and sisters over the ocean reacted negatively to what they perceived as a foreign accent. To put it bluntly, my sweet, according to Ed your dulcet tones had an adverse effect on the approval ratings.'

Juliet felt sick.

'The studio say it's because it's the lead – a minor part wouldn't have attracted the same level of discontent.'

457

'But the whole point about the story is that she's English. You can't play an English person with an American accent!' she croaked.

'Yes, well, I've got to speak to him, as I said. But in the meantime, we need to go along with their request.'

'What's that? Cut me out? Rewrite so I'm playing a minor role?'

'No, no, Juliet – calm down. It's not that bad, yet. They like everything else about you; Ed was really warm. No, they want you to fly out there and be ready in the dubbing studio on Monday.'

'For what?'

'To dub your voice with an American accent.'

She was speechless and so taken aback it took her some time to process the implications of the request.

'Juliet? Are you still with me? Look on the bright side: they're not saying no and it's going to be another ten days' work in LA. We can set up other meetings for you, so if this does go to the wall, we can put you up for other things – you'll be on the spot.'

She took a deep breath. 'Let me get this right, Louis. It's now Thursday night and they want me to be ready to start dubbing my voice on Monday. Are they going to give me any coaching? What sort of American accent are they after? I haven't done one for ages – I'm going to be really rusty.'

Louis's voice was cool. 'You've got three, four days before you have to do it. If you want this job, you'll have to do a bit of intensive revision. I'll meet you at Heathrow on Saturday morning with your tickets. I'll give you another ring after

458

I've spoken to Ed. For Chrissake, we've got so far, don't fall at this hurdle, darling. And look on the bright side. You'll be back for Christmas.'

A heavy, damp grey mist, blanketing everything, discouraged parents from lingering to chat in the playground at the start of the school day. But Isabelle, anxious to talk to Paula, dawdled in the school entrance, wrapping her duffle coat round her against the chill.

It was the first foggy day of the season, and in spite of her gloomy frame of mind, Isabelle allowed her thoughts to be distracted by the effects of the mist.

For one thing, there was no birdsong, apart from the startled scolding of a blackbird in a nearby laurel bush, and even human sound was muffled. Grey shapes would emerge out of the mist, hurrying towards the school and only when they were a few feet away was she able to identify anyone – the parents wrapped against the seeping dampness, the children squeaking with the novelty, their breath hanging on the air.

The water vapour transmuted into tiny droplets on everything it touched – the intricate filigree of the cobwebs hung with diamante, and while the upper branches of the trees were invisible, the lower boughs glistened black.

The weather suited Isabelle's mood.

Last night's fight had been bad and when Richard left for the Foresters Arms, she'd been really angry with him; but by degrees remorse had set in. It was his first night home for days; she should have been more understanding about the Lesters;

she'd no right to kick up a fuss about Abigail coming to stay, and she shouldn't have taken any notice of his objections to the sitting room.

She'd chucked the beef stew away – neglected on the stove, it had dried up – poured herself a glass of wine, and sat at the kitchen table, brooding on the course of their quarrel. It was nearly ten o'clock when she decided she'd have to be the one to make a conciliatory move, so, checking the girls were safely asleep, she'd grabbed her coat and slipped out of the house, thinking to meet Richard on his return from the pub.

It was less than five minutes to the Foresters Arms. The front door opened into a glass-panelled lobby and there she hovered, trying to spot him. The lighting in the room was discreet, but each table had its own lamp and the pub wasn't busy, which gave her a clear view of Richard sitting at a table, deep in conversation with Juliet.

For a moment she had stood there, frozen. Juliet? What was Richard doing there with Juliet? Was it planned? Isabelle couldn't imagine Juliet eating out alone. What were they up to? Then she remembered Paula said Juliet was having an affair with someone.

She'd left the pub and run all the way home. Standing alone in the kitchen, trembling all over, she fought to clear her thoughts and work out her next move. It was no good; she couldn't face another battle with him that night. So, rather than risk Richard joining her, she slipped into the girls' room and bedded down there, although she slept little, her mind a ferment.

Richard had gone to work before they'd woken

460

in the morning, but Isabelle found a curt note telling her he was going to invite the Lesters to dinner on Saturday night.

Isabelle knew on Friday Paula went straight to clean at the Manor after dropping her kids off, but she couldn't wait till the end of the afternoon to ask her about Juliet, and it wasn't something she felt she could ask on a mobile.

The morning bell had just rung when through the mist ran two small, boisterous figures, followed by the unmistakable figure of Paula, resplendent in her silver bomber jacket and thigh-length silver boots.

'Bye, Ryan, bye, Kylie. You be a good boy, now, Ryan. I don't want that Mrs Jones on my case again. D'ye hear?'

But if Ryan heard, he didn't reply and the school door slammed shut in his fond parent's face.

'Oh, hello, Isabelle.' Paula beamed. 'I was hopin' to catch you this afternoon. You waitin' for someone?'

'Just you, as it happens. I'll walk down the lane with you. I know you're going off to the Merfields', but I wanted a quick word.' Isabelle tried to sound cheerful, but Paula picked up the wobble in her voice.

'You sound a bit mizzy. You all right?'

'Yeah. Just a bit tired, you know.'

'Yeah, tell me about it! Lenny's decided he's gonna cheer me up – it's me birthday tomorrer, so we're gonna have a few mates over for a drink and some pizzas.' Paula paused for a moment before continuing, slightly self-consciously, 'I

461

know your hubby'll probably have other ideas, but I'd love it if you could come, Isabelle.'

Isabelle thought of Richard's note and the awful evening in store. To be invited to Paula's was to rub salt in the wound. She'd give anything to be able to walk out of the house and go to the Spinkses', but... 'I'd love to come, Paula, but I know Richard's arranged something else. If I can get out of it, I will. What time?'

'Oh, six thirty, seven. Bring your two, if you like. Mine won't be in bed and they can watch telly together.'

'Thanks, Paula, I really *would* like to come.'

They were reaching the end of the lane, and as Isabelle dithered, Paula got in first.

'D'ye mind if I ask you somethin'?'

'No, what?'

'What d'ye think of Charlie Tucker? I mean, really think? D'ye fancy him?'

This question so took Isabelle by surprise that she stopped, gave a short laugh then snorted, 'Charlie Tucker? I hardly know him. I know he's your Lenny's great mate and everything, but from what I've seen, I think he's a complacent, self-satisfied bastard and I wouldn't touch him with a bargepole. Why?'

Paula turned and stared curiously at her. 'My goodness, so you don't like him, then?'

'No. Why?'

'Oh, no reason, really. Did you know it's going round the village that he's havin' it off with Juliet Peters?'

'What? You're kidding?' Isabelle was stunned.

'No, I'm not, honest. My mum got it off the

462

Vicar's wife, who got it off Rita, who heard it from someone who actually saw them in the fields, her in his arms, kissin' passionately.'

Isabelle was lost for words. Why was it so completely unexpected? Why did she feel so choked?

'Oh my God, look at the time. I must shoot. What was it you wanted to ask me?'

'What?'

'You was waitin' for me – you said you had somethin' to ask.'

'Oh, yes, sorry, Paula. It's not important; actually, you've answered my question anyway. Look, I'll catch up with you later. Are you going to the meeting tonight?'

'I wouldn't miss Oliver for the world. Poor Oliver – who'd have a film star for a wife with all her goings on? It's not right.'

During the course of Friday, Richard made a phone call.

'Vee, hi, it's Richard here... Fine, and you...? Great... Listen Vee, there are a couple of things I wanted to ask you... No, no, I understood perfectly... Absolutely. The thing is, I know it's bloody short notice, but Issy seems unable to get her act together. Any chance of you coming over to supper tomorrow – just a casual affair, feet under the kitchen table? She's just finished the first stage of decorating and I'd welcome a second opinion. I think she's stuck... I know, I know, Saturday's always difficult and I know how much in demand you are... You will? Great! I look forward to being able to catch up with you ... perhaps we could play squash next week...? Yeah? Fine, well– Oh, yes, there is something else. It's in the nature of a small favour. Tonight, at the village hall, Oliver Merfield's speaking to the masses. Can you lend me a couple of bodies, just for an hour. Let's say I need a small recruiting party – I'll make it worth their while... Let me explain...'

The mist hung around for most of the day, symptomatic of the way Isabelle felt: cold and depressed, unable to see what she ought to do, or be clear about what she really thought about Richard.

The village seemed sure Juliet was having a fling with Charlie; Isabelle was convinced it was Richard. Was she having affairs with both? Neither? She'd have to confront Richard, but she didn't know if she could trust him to tell her the truth; and if the truth was that he'd been cheating on her, what then?

The morning dragged, interminably.

Charlie poked his head round the door of Milo's workshop at lunchtime to invite them over to the farmhouse for a bowl of soup. Milo had gone, but Isabelle turned her back on him with an icy 'No, thank you', and trudged back to the Old Vicarage to find the plumber in the throes of installing a new central-heating system and the water turned off.

Marion was due at four thirty, but the plumber assured Isabelle he'd nearly finished and everything would be up and running for the weekend. So she took an apple for her lunch and went for a walk along the river, leaving Summerstoke and Marsh Farm behind her.

The mist was thicker along the riverbank;

hedges, brambles, bushes, trees, everything dripped and the sodden ground squelched underfoot. She could make out the grey water of the river slipping along, the mist swirling a foot above it. The reddish earth of the riverbank opposite reminded her of the colour she'd been mixing for Milo when Charlie invited them for lunch. The bank was pockmarked with small holes and studded with clumps of reed, wilting and sinking back into the water. The odd briar with rosehips, now dark and wizened, splayed out over the surface and it was on one of these that Isabelle saw the kingfisher.

She stopped, hardly daring to breath in case it heard her and was frightened off. She stared at it; stared, trying to impress on her mind, absorb with her whole being, the colour of it – that blue, that iridescent blue, with the bird's breast the colour of the red earth. With a flash that caught her by surprise, the bird dropped onto the surface of the water and then, silver in its long, thin beak, streaked away up the river, out of sight.

For a while she stood there, seeing nothing but the colour now implanted in her memory. With a sigh, she turned and walked slowly back to face the rest of the day and Marion Croucher.

'Issy, darling, how are you? You look quite pale and thin, my dear, if you don't mind me saying so. Is Richard overworking you with all this house-decorating? I must say, when Vee told me you were going to take it on, I was aghast. A house this size – my dear, you really could do with some professional help.' Isabelle groaned inwardly.

465

Marion was a full-on sort of person, whose poisonous barbs were contained within sweeps of effusiveness. Her heavy face, immaculately made up, was wreathed in smiles, but her small eyes, cold, greedy and bright, darted everywhere.

Isabelle gave her tea, then showed her round the house, trying all the while to work out how best to broach the subject of the shop.

'What you need in here is excitement in your drapes to counteract the startling whiteness of the room. I've got a sample of a fabric which would be perfect – it's at home, but I could easily drop it round. It's a lovely floral weave on silk; or I have a more flamboyant taffeta and you could have cushions and a sofa in co-ordinating velvets...'

'Sounds lovely, Marion. Er, do you keep much stock at home? I suppose it must take up a lot of room. Have you ever thought of opening a shop?' All she had to do was keep her nerve, sound innocent, interested. Oh, God, she thought, don't let me blow this.

Fortunately, Marion picked up the bait. 'Believe me, Issy, I'd love to. The thing is to find the right premises at the right price. Not so easy, you know.'

'Where would you want to be based? In Bath, I suppose?'

'Far too expensive – and there are plenty of interior-design shops there, anyway. No, I've decided to look for a shop in a village.'

'Like Summerstoke?'

'Like Summerstoke. In fact' – Marion's eyes gleamed – 'as you're a friend I don't mind telling

466

you, but it really mustn't go any further, I've made an offer for the shop in the village.'

'The village shop?' Isabelle's eyes were wide with innocence. 'That would be ideal, Marion. But I didn't know they're going to sell?'

'Perhaps not at the moment, but we can wait. I don't think they can keep going much longer. Village stores just aren't viable now, you know.'

'We?'

'Pardon?'

'You said "we". Have you got a partner? I thought you worked alone.'

Marion hesitated, 'Well, yes, I do. But I'm going to need some sort of partner if I'm to buy a shop.'

'Of course. Have you got one? 'Cos if you haven't, I'd love to help.' Isabelle squirmed.

Patronisingly, Marion smiled at her. 'Well, maybe when it's up and running you could give me a hand, Issy – you're quite artistic. But the sort of partner I need is someone with capital to invest and I don't think you have that, have you?'

'No,' replied Isabelle, sounding as humble as she could manage. 'So have you found someone? Or can't you say?'

Marion's smile broadened. 'I have, and I shouldn't say. Seeing as it's you, Issy dear, I'll tell you – but you mustn't tell anyone else yet. We want to get the deal through first.'

Isabelle held her breath. She didn't want to seem too eager, but...

Marion leant forward, conspiratorially. 'It's Vee. She's going to buy the shop and I'm going to stock and run it. I can't wait.'

20

In the children's playground next to the village hall, Jamie sat on a swing, moodily smoking a cigarette, the collar of his biker's jacket pulled up against the pervasive chill of the evening air. He was feeling pissed off. Why was life so bloody complicated? Maybe he'd played his cards badly. He'd been on such a high after *Antigone*, he wasn't thinking straight, so when, at the cast party, Tish asked him if he really fancied anyone he told her about Alison. He shouldn't have, he really shouldn't, he realised that now. To be fair, she then told him about this guy she wanted to go out with, but after that, and subsequently, she seemed subdued and he missed the easiness between them, the good laughs they'd had together.

It wasn't as if he and Alison were going anywhere. True, she'd seen him triumph, but the scene where she came up to him, told him she'd watched him, thought him magnificent, then shyly confessed her secret passion for him – that just hadn't happened and those scenes were becoming harder to conjure up; he didn't seem to have either the imagination or the appetite for them any more.

If only he could crack it with Tish... But how could he do it without sounding like a complete prat? 'Oh, Tish, that girl I told you about? It was unreal, I was fantasising, it was a daydream.'

How wet can you get?

'Nothing's happened and nothing will, because' – and he knew this was true, at least – 'I like you, Tish, and not just as a friend.'

He sighed heavily and tossed his cigarette butt into the air, watching its glowing end arc through the gloom and land with a slight fizzle on the ground.

'Naughty boy,' said a soft voice behind him. 'That's no way to treat a kiddies' playground. Who's gonna pick it up, then?'

Jamie started and turned round.

He hadn't noticed the two men standing a short distance away. They were both quite slight and wore quilted jackets, their hands shoved into their pockets and woollen hats pulled low over their brows against the damp evening air. The orange light of the solitary lamp illuminating the playground cast deep shadows, making it difficult for Jamie to make out their faces or their ages. Nervously he stood up, letting the seat of the swing bang against the backs of his legs. There was nobody else around; the village hall was still in darkness, the meeting not due to start for at least another hour.

Before he could say or do anything, one of the men moved towards him.

'Here,' he said in a more friendly tone, ''ave one of mine. Probably better than the rubbish you're smokin'.' His accent was not local. 'Here, take the packet. Go on, I'm not gonna bite yer.'

Jamie decided the best way out of this was the line of least resistance. 'Cheers, mate,' he said as nonchalantly as he could and took a cigarette from the proffered packet.

'Nah, keep 'em.' The man waved a hand as Jamie tried to hand the packet back. 'I've got plenty more, duty-free. How're yer doin', then? My name's Pete, by the way, and this is my mate Stefan. He's Polish so he don't speak much English.'

'Hi,' replied Jamie, his voice croaking slightly with nerves. 'I'm Jamie.'

'Nice to meet you, Jamie. What are you up to this evening, then?'

'Not a lot.' Jamie couldn't work out where this was going.

'That's what we thought when we saw you – someone with not a lot on tonight. Well, how would you like to help Stefan and me earn a couple of bob? Strictly legit, of course.'

'Doing what?'

'Can you keep yer mouth shut?'

Jamie nodded.

'A geezer's speakin' at the village hall tonight and Stefan and me, we've been asked to liven things up for him. But there's just the two of us, so if you was to come and bring a mate, say, there'd be a tenner apiece for your trouble.'

Jamie went cold. 'Liven things up?'

'Yeah, you know, heckle, shout him down. He's a politician so he'll be used to it. You can copy me and Stefan. It won't be for long – we'll get ejected pretty smartish, then you'll be on your way, ten quid the richer. Can't be bad, eh?'

Jamie thought quickly. If he refused, the chances were this bloke would go looking for someone else. 'Yeah, all right. I've got a mate –

470

I'll text him to come over. He don't live in the village, though.'

'Then he won't be recognised. What about you? Everyone know yer face, do they?'

'No. I'm new here, and I don't hang around the village much. What about you?'

'We're local, in a manner of speakin'.'

'So why, if you don't mind me asking,' said Jamie, his mouth dry, but trying to sound as casual as possible, 'why do you want to wreck this meeting?'

'Fair question.' The man shrugged. 'Our boss wants to do a friend a favour and she's paying us handsome for our efforts.' His manner became brisk. 'Right, we'll meet you and your mate back here at seven. The meeting's due to start at seven thirty, so we'll give you a bit of coaching. Then we'll split up and go in separately – don't want to raise suspicions too soon, do we? Come on, Stefan, I'm ready for that pint you owe me.'

Shaken, Jamie watched the men disappear into the gloom. What should he do? They were going to wreck his dad's meeting; he had to do something. He couldn't contact his father, who was doing his surgery until seven. Juliet would be no use. She'd been in London all day with some voice coach and had only just got home, so she was in a tizz, packing.

There was only one person he could think of who'd help: Aunt Charlotte.

It was just before seven when, standing on Summerstoke Bridge, Jamie heard the sound he'd been waiting for, the thin, mosquito whine of a

471

moped coming down Summerstoke Ridge – except there were two of them. Seconds later the first stopped by Jamie, and Adam pushed his visor up. 'Hi, Jamie. We got here as quickly as we could.'

By this time the second bike had pulled over. It was Tish. 'Hi, Jamie,' she said shyly. 'I hope you don't mind me coming along, but I was having a drink with Adam when he got your message. I thought maybe I could help, too.'

Jamie was touched. 'Thanks, Tish.' Then he had a brain-wave. 'Actually, there is something you can do...'

They parked the bikes at the bottom of the High Street and took a short cut to the village hall down a dark alleyway leading to a small housing estate behind the High Street, where Jamie filled them in on what had happened.

'So, Adam, you and me go and meet these guys now. When we get into the hall, Aunt Charlotte says we must make sure we're not sitting anywhere near them; we don't want them nobbling us if we don't play along. And if they're stuck by themselves, they'll be isolated and, she reckons, unable to do too much.'

'So what do you want me to do?' Tish asked.

Jamie turned to her. 'Tish, you don't have to do this, honestly. I'll understand...'

'What?'

'Don't come with us. Be outside the hall when the meeting starts. These guys are sure they're gonna be ejected. When they are, I want you to follow them, I want to know where they came from. If we know where they go afterwards, it'll be a start.'

'Supposing they just go to the pub? Isn't that the most likely?'

'Then you can text us and I'll come and take your place till they leave. They've gotta go sometime.'

'Wicked!' she breathed excitedly. 'I'm up for that.'

But immediately Jamie had second thoughts. 'No, you mustn't. I'm so stupid, I must be fuckin' mad.'

'What d'ye mean? I told you, it's cool.'

Adam shook his head. 'No, Jamie's right, Tish. Supposing those men cottoned on to you following them? Supposing they walked out of the village, or had a car?' He turned to Jamie. 'I've a suggestion. Tish and me'll swop. She can go to the meeting with you. I don't suppose they'll object too much if the friend turns out to be a girl.'

Adam was right. Apart from the initial raised eyebrows when they saw Tish, whom Jamie, with a slight lump in his throat, introduced as his girlfriend, they raised no objections, provided she shouted as loud as the rest of them.

After a discussion about the things they could yell, and agreeing to take their cue from Pete, they settled on meeting at the back of the car park of the Foresters Arms when they'd been ejected from the hall, and Pete would give them the promised tenners.

The lights were streaming from the hall by this time, and people were starting to gather at the doorway.

'Go and join the queue, then, mate.' Pete nudged Jamie and Jamie, with a glance at Tish, who gave him a small smile, did as he was told. Seconds later he saw Tish join the throngs behind him, then Pete and lastly Stefan.

There was a slight hold-up going into the hall, which made those caught out in the damp night air grumble vigorously.

Rita Godwin had set up a table inside the door and was insisting that all comers write down their names and addresses.

Jamie grinned. He'd heard Aunt Charlotte on the phone to Mrs Godwin, warning her about the potential trouble and telling her to get everyone to sign in. 'It may well be they will give false names and addresses, Rita... Yes, of course you're the postmistress, and that's why I'm proposing you do this. You'll know if the address is false, so straight away we'll have identified the trouble-makers... Excellent. Now, can you organise a couple of the men to mark them – you know, go and sit by them so when... Yes, that's the idea. We get rid of them as soon as they start anything.'

'Why you makin' us sign in, like this, Rita Godwin?' moaned a thin, elderly man in front of Jamie. 'You knows who I am – why should I sign to get into my own village hall? It's bloomin cold outside. Don't you know that?'

'Sorry, Mr Shaughnessy, it's the police. They say it's for security, because we've got an MP coming tonight,' Rita replied glibly.

Jamie signed in, then made his way to the empty seats at the front of the hall. Tish was also at the front, sitting on the other side of the aisle. The hall was filling rapidly; the meeting was going to be well attended. Jamie glanced over his shoulder and spotted Aunt Charlotte sitting next to Nanny and talking to the fair-haired woman they'd met when they first came to Summerstoke. Behind them he recognised the Tuckers from Marsh Farm. Alison, sitting at the far end of the row, was listening to Nanny and Alison's mother and brother. Then she laughed and Jamie felt his heart lurch.

He turned away and, leaning forward, looked across at Tish. She was so unlike Alison: her hair was dark, short and spiky, whereas Alison's was long and blonde and silky; her eyes were round, dark and merry, Alison's were larger, more oval and flashed green; the two were more or less the same height. Tish was chunkier, but she was as pretty, in a different sort of way and even her pierced nose, he thought, was attractive. She was looking very serious, but when she caught Jamie looking across at her she gave a broad grin in response to his.

I'm glad she's here, thought Jamie.

Just before seven thirty, a man carrying a professional-looking camera and bag made his way to the front. 'Looks like we've got the press in,' muttered the man next to Jamie.

Rita Godwin was worried. It was true she knew all the addresses in her postal area, but these days she didn't know all the occupants by sight and it had proved harder to identify the potential troublemakers than she or Charlotte Merfield had anticipated. Not only that, but close to seven thirty the queue waiting to get in had become increasingly impatient and a number had pushed on through, waving aside her objections, saying they would sign on the way out.

There were only a few stragglers left and, seeing Charlie Tucker next in the line, she jumped up. 'Charlie, do us a favour. Take my place, would you? I must go and have a word with your gran. Don't let people in unless they sign, right?'

She pushed her way out of the hall, hurried round to the back entrance and into the kitchen, where Elsie was having a cup of tea with Oliver. They looked up as Rita poked her head round the door.

'Elsie, Oliver, a quick word, if you don't mind.'

She quickly filled them in.

Amazed as he was to hear of the plot and Jamie's involvement, Oliver wasted no time in fruitless speculation. 'Who've you got standing by to deal with the troublemakers?' he asked.

'I've got Tom Batts and Findlay Spence,' replied Rita. 'I thought I'd sit them next to the men so they can pounce as soon as they start up, but now I'm not sure who these people are, and not only that but the press are here.'

'The press?' Elsie frowned. 'Of course, Sally Green would have told them. I just hope we can keep any trouble to a minimum. Most unfortunate.'

'I suggest we get Tom and Findlay to stand at the back. Is there anyone else we can rope in?' Oliver was calm, but inwardly he cursed, particularly at the presence of the press. This was the last thing he wanted to happen on his own doorstep. He was well aware of the *Wessex Daily's* current campaign to bring MPs to account. Richard Garnett, he seethed, will rub his hands with glee.

'Stephen's in the hall,' said Elsie, 'so, Rita, tell him to sit at the end of a row, and tell Charlie, if he turns up, to do the same.'

'He's there now – he's minding the register for me.'

'Good.' Oliver smiled. 'Thank you very much, ladies. Let's hope it's not going to be too much of a bumpy ride.'

Apart from a teenager lurking in the gloom beyond the lights of the hall's entrance, there was no one waiting when Rita rejoined Charlie and gave him his gran's instructions.

As he pushed his way into the crowded hall, Charlie's mind was only half on the evening ahead. Sitting at the table, supervising the signatures, an elderly lady whom he recognised as Miss Whitfield, a retired teacher from the village school, wagged her finger at him. 'I'm surprised at you, Charlie Tucker. Fancy having the nerve to show your face here. Carrying on like that, and she a married woman with her husband away from home, as he is. No good will come of it, mark my words. You're a loose cannon, that's your trouble. Time you settled down.'

With a loud sniff, she moved on before Charlie could collect his wits enough to find out what she meant.

He knew the village loved nothing so much as a good gossip, but he couldn't think what he'd done to set this one off. Perhaps someone saw him rolling on the ground with Isabelle and misunderstood the situation ... but he'd have spotted anyone on the track to Marsh Farm. Perhaps someone had seen him take the duffle coat into school and leaped to some daft conclusion. He felt very uncomfortable. He was used to village gossip, but Isabelle, poor girl, how would she cope with it?

Ironic, he thought, grimly, that she can't stand my guts.

Isabelle was sitting in the middle of the hall. If she hadn't been on the action committee, she wouldn't have come to the meeting, much as she wanted to support Oliver.

Shutting the door on Marion, sorting out the girls' tea, and organising the babysitter had all been accomplished on automatic pilot while her thoughts were a jumbled mess.

Veronica had started the campaign of rumours because she wanted to buy the shop. What should Isabelle do with that information? Confront Veronica? She'd just laugh, even if she didn't deny it. And the Lesters were coming to supper tomorrow night. Did she have the nerve to leave them to it and go to Paula's?

She'd tried to take a stand with Richard but he'd brushed her objections aside. He didn't respect her wishes, he didn't respect her – that was pretty obvious. But if she wasn't there for his supper party, she was making a bigger statement than just not liking his friends. Was she ready to do that?

And if Juliet and Oliver were also going to be there – she assumed Richard would invite them... She really liked Oliver, and he would be the only reason she'd put up with it, but having seen Richard and Juliet together, could she act naturally with Juliet? And why had she been so shocked at the thought of Charlie's involvement with Juliet? Why hadn't she been relieved? She'd just begun to think she might have been wrong about him, but if he was the sort who played around with other people's wives, she could dismiss him as the untrustworthy, arrogant shit she'd always thought him to be.

If only there was someone to advise her; if only Joe wasn't so far away. Sitting in the village hall, in the middle of a crush of cheerful, chatting people, all of whom seemed to know each other, she felt as lonely as she'd ever felt.

Her reverie was interrupted by Nanny and Charlotte Merfield sitting down next to her.

On Isabelle's other side the chair was taken by a youngish man who looked familiar and who, when Elsie Tucker introduced Oliver Merfield to everyone, drew out a notebook.

Neville Budd, features editor of the *Wessex Daily*, had drawn Chris Gorman to one side just before he left the office. Chris Gorman was not in the best of moods. He knew he was considered the paper's best news reporter, so why Richard had suddenly decided he, Chris, was to cover such a non-event as a minor MP talking to some group in a miserable little village, way out of Bath, on a Friday night, he did not know.

'Jake Woods is on pics. He'll meet you there.'
'I know, I know.'
'Richard briefed him himself.'

'What?' This was unusual. An assistant editor or a reporter would normally do that. The great white bastard, as Richard was known, rarely spoke to the photographers, let alone indicated he knew who they were.

'Why?'

Neville shrugged. 'I have a pricking in my thumbs... And he's picked you to go although I've got any number of juniors kicking their heels. Any special briefing?'

Chris wrinkled his brow. 'As you might expect: pay particular attention to any complaints the village have about their MP – Richard wants us to nail him, if we can. I won't shed any tears over that – he's a fuckin' Conservative with silver spoons dripping out of every orifice.'

Neville nodded. 'Fine, but make sure you stay to the bitter end, okay? I want to find out what's driving our glorious leader's obsession and I've got a hunch about tonight.'

Oliver had been an MP for the better part of six months and was used to addressing meetings. It felt, he admitted to himself, a little odd to be addressing people who had watched him grow up and among whom he now lived, and he wished he had better news for them, but he was confident he could put the more positive side of his message across, deal with any hecklers, and ensure the meeting ended on a positive note.

'I don't suppose we know why they want to stir things up?' he asked Elsie, when Rita had left.

'I don't, but perhaps, your son will be able to shed some light later.' She glanced at her watch.

'It's seven thirty. Do you want a little more time to gather your thoughts?'

'No. No, I don't want to give anyone grounds for criticism. Come on, Mrs Bates, lead the way.'

Elsie smiled. 'Very few people call me by my correct name. I'm still Elsie Tucker to most of the village. Thank you for the courtesy, Oliver. Ron's in the audience, so I hope you get an opportunity to meet him later.'

The applause was enthusiastic when Elsie introduced Oliver, and he relaxed a fraction. Whatever drove the troublemakers, the majority of the villagers bore him no ill-will.

Briefly he sketched out the problem the action committee had presented him with and the various enquiries he'd made.

'So basically, I've some good news and some bad news for you.'

'Typical bloody politician,' somebody growled.

Although he'd been warned, the heckle, coming as it did from this warm and interested group of listeners, took him by surprise and for a moment he faltered, before regaining his momentum.

He smiled. 'Fair comment. I'll try not to sound too much like a politician, so I'll start with the bad news first, although it affects Mrs Godwin more immediately than the community as a whole. The sorting office is to close. There's absolutely nothing anyone can do to save it. It's Post Office policy to consolidate their sorting offices, and rural sorting offices, like the one we have here, are all going.'

'Useless, that's what you are. Wet behind the ears!'

That voice again. Oliver tried to identify the speaker, then from another part of the room came a cry of 'Resign! Go back to London. No bloody good!'

The disruption had a ripple effect around the room. Heads were turned, necks craned, one or two people started to mutter, both for and against Oliver.

'I knew it. He's far too young – who's gonna listen to him?' An elderly gentleman sitting near the front grumbled aloud to his neighbour.

'Typical politician – all hot air,' growled a young farmer leaning against the wall at the back.

'You'd think he'd have made more of an effort, wouldn't you?' replied the young woman to whom this was addressed. 'How we gonna manage without our post office?'

'We're not going to lose it. You should listen to what he's saying, Lisa Judd, instead of sounding off as usual!' hissed a woman nearby.

'You shut your face, Annie Smith. I'll say what I like.'

Oliver raised his voice. 'The post office is not going to close. Rest assured. It is simply the sorting office that–'

But the hecklers, sensing the restlessness in the hall would work to their advantage, didn't let him finish.

'Lies – it's all lies!' the first voice jeered. 'Don't believe a word he says.'

'How dare you say that, young man?' Nanny, incensed, stood up and shook her fist at the heckler. 'How dare you?'

Unfortunately her standing up was the cue for

others to jump up as well.

'It's a free country. He can say what he bloody well likes,' shouted the first young woman.

'Well, I want to hear what our MP has to say, so why don't you just sit down and shut up!' snarled the second woman, getting to her feet.

'Come and make me!'

'Please, we're not getting–' Oliver began again, trying to restore peace.

'No bloody good. Go back to London. Go back to where you come from, bloody foreigner!'

The second voice sounded foreign to Oliver. Ironic, he thought.

'I've come to tell you there's good news,' he continued.

'Come down here, making promises you can't keep. Wet, that's what you are!' Pete was on his feet looking around the room as he shouted, looking for his two young recruits.

Jamie, upset at the way the meeting had got so quickly out of hand, shrank down in his seat.

'Boo!' shouted Stefan.

'Resign!' shouted Lisa Judd, provocatively making a two-fingered gesture to Annie Smith.

Infuriated, Annie Smith attempted to launch herself through the chairs. Several went crashing and there were loud protests from her neighbours, but Annie's partner, holding onto the elastic of her tracksuit trousers, prevented her from getting anywhere near Lisa Judd.

'This is disgraceful!' thundered Aunt Charlotte, pulling herself up to her full height.

Lavender Grey tugged urgently at her husband's sleeve. 'Do something. There's going to be a fight if we don't do something.'

The vicar, looking terribly unhappy, stood up. 'Er, ladies, ladies, please...'

'No blooty goot!' Stefan was on his feet now, as well.

'You've let us down, Oliver!' the young farmer shouted, grinning all over his face. He'd thought it was going to be a dull old meeting – this was more like!

'No he ain't!' shrieked Rita Godwin, 'He's worked bloomin' hard.'

'What's he done, then? Nothing!' shouted someone else.

'You're all hot air, Lisa Judd.'

'Please,' said the vicar, helplessly regarding his flock. 'Please... Let us–'

'Pray?' muttered Charlie, pushing his way down the aisle to help Tom Batts with one of the hecklers. 'Not now, Vicar, not now. God wouldn't be able to hear you.'

The hall was in turmoil, with people shouting for Oliver to speak, many standing the better to make their views known.

And all the time Oliver was aware of the photographer's flashes.

It looked as if the meeting was descending into chaos. Oliver could not make himself heard over the mêlée, so, for want of a better solution, he scrambled onto the table and, cupping his hands, bellowed, loud and deep, 'Sto-o-op!'

It did the trick. In the sudden, surprised silence that followed, Pete and Stefan were pounced upon. They quickly capitulated and were frog-marched out of the hall.

Looking slightly self-conscious, Lisa Judd and her partner fell silent and resumed their slouched positions against the wall, arms folded, chins jutting defiantly.

Looking down on the ruffled, vexed and excited faces, Oliver held up his hand and, gradually, the talking and buzzing subsided sufficiently for him to make himself heard.

'Well,' he said ruefully, 'I wasn't expecting such a baptism of fire. I'm really sorry for the disturbance.' He shook his head. 'It seems odd to have hecklers at what should have been a straightforward meeting about the village shop, but we'd been warned to expect trouble – though why anyone should want you not to have a proper discussion with me, I don't know.'

There was a lot of tut-tutting, murmuring and muttering at this. Then Charlie shouted, 'Come on, then, Oliver, what have you got to tell us? Spit it out, good or bad. I'm listening.'

Others took up his appeal until finally calm was restored and Oliver, climbing down from the table, was able to continue.

The photographer, he noticed, was nowhere to be seen.

'Thank you.' He smiled warmly at the sea of faces. 'After that bit of excitement I'm sure we all could do with a cup of tea.'

'Or something stronger!' Lenny shouted from the back of the hall.

There was laughter and some cheering.

'The most important thing I want to say is you are really lucky in Summerstoke. Okay, you're going to lose the sorting office – as I said, there's nothing anyone can do about that – but you've got your post office, you've got your shop. There are many villages in this constituency who've lost theirs, and once they're gone they're very difficult to get back. I know you've heard it all before, and why should you trust a politician? But as it stands, both the office of the deputy prime minister and the Post Office themselves state they are committed to keeping rural post offices like ours open.'

A buzz went round the hall.

Someone shouted, 'And you believe them?'

Oliver sighed. 'I sympathise, I really do. But we've an election next year and a government is much more assiduous about keeping promises in an election year. But, and let us be absolutely clear about this, the shop will close if we don't use it. "If we don't use it, we'll lose it," as Mrs Grey is constantly telling us, and she's absolutely right.'

The applause was vigorous as he sat down. He looked across at Jamie and gave him an affectionate smile. Jamie grinned back.

Elsie took over the meeting and fielded a number of questions.

Then Rita stood up. 'Before everyone goes, please may I say something?' She looked around. 'I'm very grateful for the trouble Oliver has gone to for us, but I know, from the way my business has dropped off the last six months, some of you are thinking: Why should I buy stuff from Rita Godwin when she's got rats in her basement?'

She paused as a low murmur rippled round the room, then continued, 'So what I want to say is

486

this: I've no rats, like I've no basement. If you want to come and check out my stockroom, you're welcome. The person who's been spreadin' this rumour has her reasons. She isn't here tonight, otherwise I'd call her a liar to her face, but you all know me, I deal straight with people. There's only one rat around here, and she ain't to be found in my shop.'

As the meeting broke up, Isabelle turned to her neighbour, who was still scribbling in his note-book. 'Which paper do you write for?'

'*Wessex Daily.*' He looked at her, interested. 'What did you make of tonight's showing?'

She frowned. 'I thought Oliver Merfield came across very well. He's right. The shop's survival is up to us. As to that lunatic fringe early on, if you were a decent, investigative paper, you'd want to find out who those men were. Who sent them? Why did they want to wreck the evening?'

'Good question. Why do you think they did?'

'I've no idea. But I noticed your photographer disappeared almost as soon as the hecklers did. He wasn't interested in pictures of a comfortable, constructive discussion with our MP, was he?'

Chris Gorman shrugged. 'He's out to get a good picture.'

'Even if it doesn't reflect the true nature of the evening? We had a pleasant, positive discussion tonight, but what will his picture say? "Riot as MP addresses his constituents"?'

'Why should our paper be interested in reporting something that isn't true?'

Isabelle turned to look at him. 'Because your

487

paper has an agenda. It's not interested in the truth, it's interested in humiliating Oliver Merfield.'

Chris was fascinated. 'Why on earth should you think that?'

'Because,' said Isabelle, 'your paper's whole campaign isn't really about assessing politicians, is it? It's about upping your circulation, and we all know good news stories don't sell newspapers. I suspect this meeting was deliberately sabotaged to give your paper a thumping good story. You can prove me wrong – tell the story how it was... Somehow I don't think your editor will be interested.' And looking at his face, Isabelle knew she was right.

'Wait.' He put out his hand. 'What's your name? I'm sure I've met you before, somewhere.'

Sick and dispirited, she replied, 'My name is Isabelle Garnett. We probably met at the *Wessex Daily*'s Christmas party last year.'

The meeting broke up shortly after eight thirty. As soon as it was over Jamie checked his mobile, pushed his way across to Tish and hissed, 'Let's go. I've had a message from Adam.'

His dad was surrounded by people wanting to chat, so, pushing his way towards the door, he whispered to Aunt Charlotte 'See you and Dad back at the Manor.'

Charlotte nodded and resumed her conversation with the Tucker family, including, Jamie noted with a slight pang, Alison. But he didn't hesitate and, grabbing Tish's hand, negotiated his way through the throng streaming out.

They'd received directions from Adam, so once on the High Street they turned right, went past the Foresters Arms, Jamie's house and a row of other houses, then past Summerstoke House on the edge of the village and up the hill, into the darkness beyond the street lights.

On one side of the road was a high stone wall, on the other a thick hedge. There was no sign of habitation, or of people, apart from the occasional car which swept down the hill momentarily blinding them with its headlights, tyres swishing on the damp surface. They said very little, but the dark, and a sensation of not knowing where they were headed affected them both, and when Jamie stopped and tucked Tish's arm into his she didn't draw back.

Ahead, on a bend in the road, a car's lights momentarily picked up the white paint of a gatepost and as they drew parallel with it a shadow stepped out of the hedge.

'You took your time,' Adam said cheerfully. 'I thought I was gonna freeze to death.'

'Sorry, mate. We couldn't get out until the meeting finished and God, didn't they go on! What happened?'

Adam grinned at them through the darkness. 'They came out of the hall bellowin' their heads off, then they started laughin' and walked off – took no notice of me. I kept my distance, but they didn't turn round. Then they started ranting about you two – it was easy to hear them 'cos there was no one else about and they didn't bother to keep their voices down. When they got to the pub, I thought they were gonna walk

489

straight past, but they changed their minds and turned back – gave me a fuckin' scare, I must say, 'cos I thought they were bound to see me, but they didn't seem to, so I walked on to that church gate and waited for them to come out. They didn't stay in the pub long. Either they weren't served or they downed their drink in one. They walked up the road and I followed. I tell yer, it was fair spooky when we left the village, but they was jabberin' on, so I didn't need to keep too close, which was just as well, 'cos every time a car came past, it lit me up like a fuckin' star turn. Anyway, they got as far as here, then disappeared down that drive. I've been watching ever since, but they haven't come out again.'

'Nice one, man.' Jamie slapped him on the shoulder.

'Where are we?' Tish asked, wandering across the road to look down the drive.

'Haven't a clue,' said Jamie, crossing to join her.

With the aid of the light from their mobile phones they found a smartly decorated sign on a five-barred gate which said simply, 'Home Farm'.

Back at the hall, Oliver, puzzled, had gone to join his aunt. 'Where's Jamie?'

'Unfinished business,' said Charlotte cryptically. 'He said he'd join us back at the Manor, so if you've finished I suggest that's where we go. I could do with a gin, I must say.' In a softer voice, she said, 'Try and persuade that nice little neighbour of ours to come back with us. I don't know, but I think she could do with a bit of

490

company right now.'

Oliver followed his aunt's gaze. Isabelle was standing next to Nanny, listening to her conversation with Elsie and Ronald Bates, Elsie's new husband, a jolly, bald-headed elderly man. She looked stricken: her eyes were large and tragic, her face pale and drawn. Oliver had wanted to finish at the hall and get back to Juliet, but the sight of Isabelle looking so unhappy affected him.

He moved over to her. 'Hi, Isabelle. We're going back to the Manor. Do you fancy coming with us? My aunt would be so pleased if you'd join us for a drink.'

He was startled by her look of anguish.

'Thanks, Oliver, that's really kind, but I must get back to the girls. I promised the babysitter I wouldn't be longer than an hour, so I'm late already. But I'll see you tomorrow night, won't I?'

He blinked. 'Tomorrow night? I don't think so.'

She stared at him blankly. 'But I thought Richard was going to invite you, you and Juliet?'

'Not to my knowledge. Anyway, Juliet won't be here. I'm putting her on the plane for Los Angeles tomorrow morning, and then Jamie and I are going to stay with Polly; we're having a weekend in London.'

To his consternation, Isabelle turned even paler and her eyes filled with tears. He touched her arm. 'Isabelle, are you all right? Do come back with us.'

She broke away, 'No, no. It's all right, I'm just tired, that's all. Tell Juliet ... tell Juliet I hope she gets what she wants; with all my heart I hope

491

that. I'll see you soon, Oliver. Well done tonight. I thought you came up trumps. Bye.' And with another farewell which encompassed the rest of the group, she almost ran out of the hall.

Both Aunt Charlotte and Nanny watched her departure, then turned, glanced at each other, and at Oliver, who was staring after Isabelle, a perplexed frown on his face.

Isabelle ran as if pursued by demons, tears pouring down her face. She couldn't sort out what was worse: the fear her husband had unscrupulously set out to destroy Oliver Merfield's credibility, or the thought she'd have to spend the following evening alone with him, Veronica and Hugh.

Charlie, stacking chairs at the back of the hall, straightened up in time to see Isabelle rush past, tears spilling down her cheeks. His first inclination was to run after her, but he stopped himself.

Whoa, there, Charlie boy. You're not her favourite person, remember?

But he was troubled and wondered if some gossipy old nosy parker like Miss Whitfield had said something. If there was a rumour doing the rounds, he had to find out what it was.

Lenny and Paula were drifting out, chatting to a couple of friends.

Paula called out gleefully, 'Did you hear what Rita Godwin said about Veronica Lester, Charlie, in front of everybody? "There's only one rat around here, and she ain't to be found in my shop." I wish Veronica'd heard that, I really wish she had.' She chuckled at the thought.

Lenny put his arm round her waist and gave

her a squeeze, grinning at Charlie, 'Hey, boss, wanna come over and sink a few cans?'

'Don't mind if I do, Lenny,' he replied. 'I'll be along shortly. I want a few words with Rita first.'

Rita, inevitably, was thick in conversation with anybody and everybody, even after the Merfield party left, and Charlie cleared away all the chairs, swept the floor, turned out the lights in the lavatories and tidied the kitchen, and still she was talking to his gran. He loitered by the door, willing Ron to come and collect his indefatigable grandmother.

Elsie looked up and saw him. 'You don't have to wait for me, Charlie. Ron's sitting in the car outside. I must say, you've done a thoroughly good job clearing up – I didn't think you knew how to use a broom!'

'Very funny, Gran. As it happens, I wanted to have a word with Rita, but if you two are gonna to be witterin' on all night...'

'No, I'm done, my boy: I've tried poor Ronald's patience long enough. Good night, Rita. I think it's been a good evening – this shop advisory group is definitely the way forward. Goodnight, Charlie.'

Finally Charlie had Rita's attention, and for a second he was tongue-tied. It was one thing to know the village shop, in the form of Rita Godwin, was the epicentre of almost all the gossip in the village, but he didn't know how to tap that knowledge without making things worse.

'Yes, Charlie? What is it?'

He decided to come straight to the point. 'Er ... thing is, Rita, Miss Whitfield said a funny thing to me this evening and I'd like to know what she meant by it.'

'How should I know?' Rita's tone was not sympathetic.

Charlie flushed. 'Well, of course you might not, but as was said this evening, the old people in the village rely on you, and they confide in you, so if anything's been said about me I thought you might know.'

'I keep my own counsel about what's said to me, Charlie Tucker. I hear all, see all, and say nowt.' Rita's mouth folded into a thin, tight line, as if to demonstrate the truth of that.

Charlie played his trump card. 'Well, perhaps I'll ask Mum. Maybe she knows.'

Charlie's mother, Jenny, was Rita's best friend, a soft-hearted, sweet woman whom everybody, with the possible exception of Elsie, adored. It did the trick.

'No, don't ask your mum – she'll just worry and get upset. I admit I've heard something, and if it's true I'm very disappointed in you, Charlie Tucker. I know you haven't had it easy, but carrying on with a married woman – and she isn't the first, is she? – isn't the way to behave, particularly as we owe him so much. Your chickens will come home to roost, mark my words. How you could look him in the face this evening, I do not know.'

Charlie was completely confused. 'Who? Look who in the face?'

'Why, Oliver, of course. Oliver Merfield. It's shameful, you carrying on with his wife. I know she's a film star, but she's no better than she should be. She's not changed, not from the first moment she came to the village – seventeen she was then, tossing her red hair like she was telling us all where to get off, the young madam!'

Charlie gave a loud crack of laughter, stopping Rita in mid-flow.

'Juliet? I'm meant to be having a fling with Juliet Peters? Rita, you *are* joking?'

Rita was disconcerted. 'How can you deny it? You was seen holding her in your arms, kissing her. You're not denying that?'

'Oh, but I am. I am! At a guess, this comes from the time I walked her back from the Grapes. I lifted her over a puddle, but kiss her? No, definitely not. No.' Charlie shook his head, grinning with relief from ear to ear. 'I'm not having an affair with her. Get real, Rita. I'm a simple farmhand. If Juliet Peters was going to have an affair with someone, it wouldn't be with the likes of me.'

'And you're sure he said his boss was paying him?' Oliver asked, his face grave.

'Yeah. He said the boss was doing it as a favour for a friend,' Jamie replied.

He, Tish and Adam had joined Oliver in the kitchen of the Manor. To the silent awe of Jamie's friends, Mrs Merfield, clad in black lace and looking as if she'd stepped out of *Dance of the Vampires* had deigned to join them. She was sitting at the head of the table with her sisters, who were dressed in drifting layers of pale blue in Louisa's case, and emerald green in Charlotte's, on either side of her.

Nanny brought in some bottles of beer for the

three teenagers, and sat down.

Mrs Merfield turned her hooded eyes on Adam. 'You don't think they met anyone at the Foresters Arms?' In spite of her imperious manner, her voice was friendly.

Adam, who didn't think, even in his dreams, he'd ever met anyone quite like Jamie's grandmother, was certain. 'No, Mrs Merfield. They were in there for such a short time, and when they came out, they didn't mention it. I could hear more or less what they was saying, and if they'd met someone I'm sure they'd have said something.'

'Home Farm.' Oliver shook his head. 'Doesn't mean anything to me. Maybe Rita can tell us who lives there.'

'There isn't a Home Farm in the village, any more,' observed Charlotte.

'It was pulled down yonks ago,' chipped in Louisa.

'By Père Lester, wasn't it?' Charlotte looked at Mrs Merfield for confirmation.

'No, Lottie, by the superbrat when his father died.' Louisa tittered. 'True to form, he chucked the farm manager out, pulled the old house down and built his stables.'

'Yes, that's right.' Mrs Merfield nodded. 'But I think the complex is still called Home Farm. There are a number of cottages used, I believe, by Mr Lester's employees.'

'So, Oliver, it looks as if the finger is pointing rather firmly at Hugh Lester.' Charlotte took a sip from a large gin and tonic. 'Can you understand why he should behave in such a way? I know he's not popular in the village, but why risk his reputation like this? What has he got against you?'

'And wouldn't he run the risk of criminal prosecution?' Louisa drummed her long, painted fingernails on the table in her excitement. 'Isn't there such a thing as incitement to violence?'

For a moment the only sound in the kitchen was the gentle gurgling of the Aga and the quiet ticking of the clock.

'Well,' said Oliver wearily, 'I can't do a lot about this before Monday.'

'But I can find out from Mrs Godwin whether anyone called Pete, or Stefan – was it, Jamie? – lives at Home Farm,' said Nanny. 'Now you'd better get home to Juliet, dear. She must be wondering what on earth has happened to you.'

'Thanks, Nanny.' Oliver swallowed the last of his drink and stood up. 'Charlotte, I can't thank you enough for your part in all of this.'

She shrugged her thin, elegant shoulders. 'Me? I didn't do anything. It was Jamie.'

'Yes, I know.' Oliver turned to his son. 'Jamie, if it hadn't have been for your quick thinking and the help of your two friends here, things would have been much, much worse for me this evening. I'm so proud of you. Adam, Tish, I don't know how to thank you. Jamie's lucky to have such friends.'

A short while later only Nanny and the Merfield ladies remained.

'Well!' Nanny poured a measure of whisky into her warm milk. 'What an evening!'

'I'm sorry I missed it.' Louisa rose to her feet to

fix herself another gin and tonic. 'These village meetings are usually such a ghastly non-event. Top up, anyone?'

'So Juliet's off to the States, tomorrow,' said Charlotte, deceptively lightly, looking at Nanny. 'You know, Nanny, we really must have Isabelle Garnett to tea. What neglectful neighbours we've been.'

Nanny shook her head reprovingly. 'We must. She seemed upset about something this evening, didn't she, poor little thing.'

'There's something going on here,' interjected Louisa. 'What are you two hinting at?'

'Oh, nothing, dear.' Charlotte smiled at her sister. 'Only when, at the end of the meeting, Oliver told Isabelle he couldn't go to dinner with her tomorrow night, she looked as though she was going to burst into tears.'

'And Oliver himself looked very upset,' added Nanny, sadly shaking her head. 'Dear, oh dear, I wonder what on earth is going on?'

21

There were still two hours to go before sunrise when Oliver, Juliet and Jamie set out for Heathrow. It was pitch black and the air was damp and cold.

Juliet shivered. 'I'm looking forward to enjoying the sun, I can tell you.'

'I thought you didn't get to see the sun in Los

Angeles, on account of the pollution,' growled Jamie, stretching out on the back seat and plugging his headphones into his ears.

The roads were empty and the drive uneventful. Juliet, like Jamie, dozed for most of the way and Oliver was left to his thoughts.

He knew Juliet was meant to be going for just ten days, but she hinted there might be pressure for her to stay on and make herself known to other studios and casting directors. He had no doubt that, if she did, it might be a long time before she came back – Summerstoke held no attraction for her.

If she did return, maybe he should bite the financial bullet and find a small flat in London so she could stay up there as much as she liked. Initially his prime concern had been not to abandon Jamie, but Jamie seemed to have fallen on his feet, particularly with the occupants of the Manor. Indeed, thought Oliver, Juliet complains he seems to prefer their company to hers.

Yes, he would do that. He'd take advantage of the slight respite the Christmas recess gave him to find somewhere.

His thoughts turned to the events of the previous evening. Why should Hugh Lester want to disrupt the meeting about the village shop? Unless it was to discredit him, and why should he wish to do that? Oliver would have to ring the branch chairman. It was no good the party courting the Lesters for donations if they were undermining their MP. He'd give Nanny a ring when he got to Polly's. If she could confirm the hecklers were Lester's employees, Andrew Hill ought to know.

And what about Isabelle? Her face, and those large blue eyes staring at him so tragically, had haunted his dreams the whole night. What was that all about?

Juliet stirred. 'Are we nearly there yet? What time is it?'

'It's nearly seven thirty. Look, you can see the sky lightening. Be dawn soon. We'll be there in less than half an hour.'

'Good. I shall be glad to be on the plane. This is always the worst part of any journey, getting to the airport.'

'And saying goodbye,' Oliver added lightly.

She put her hand on his knee. 'Oh, Ollie, I don't need to say that. I wish you could come with me. Promise, if I have to stay out there you'll come over?'

'I'll do my best, I promise. We're going to miss you. We've grown used to having you in Summerstoke.'

'I'll miss you, Ollie darling, but I don't think I'm going to miss Summerstoke. There's simply nothing to do there, nothing ever happens, the people are so dull.'

'I thought you got on with Isabelle Garnett?'

'She's sweet enough, but I didn't see much of her. Truthfully, I found her a bit of a wet blanket.'

'She seemed upset last night. Are things okay with her?'

Juliet shrugged, uninterested, 'I've no idea, but I wouldn't trust Richard further than I could throw him.' And, as they were arriving at the airport, the subject was dropped.

'I really liked your friends, Jamie. It must have taken some nerve for Adam to follow those men the way he did.'

As Juliet headed for Los Angeles, Oliver and Jamie headed for Shepherd's Bush.

It was the first opportunity they'd had to go over the events of the night before and they'd discussed every detail, speculating till they reached a standstill. But there was something else Oliver was curious about.

'Yeah, they're cool.'

Oliver glanced at Jamie, 'You can tell me to mind your own business, and I won't be offended. You and Tish, are you an item? Only after *Antigone*, I thought...'

Jamie sighed heavily. 'No, we're not. I'd like to, Dad, but I blew it, and I don't know what to do about it. I think she likes me, but, well, I don't know.'

'From the little I saw last night, I think she does. But how did you blow it? Can you tell me?'

Jamie groaned and screwed up his face. 'I feel such a prat. I told her about this other girl I really fancied, that's all.'

'Not such a clever move, old son.'

'Tell me about it.'

'Is there another girl?'

'Yes – no, not really. I met someone ages ago, and I had a crush on her, that's all. But then, when I gave Tish that crap, she told me there was someone *she* really fancies, so she and I... We got nowhere. We're just friends.'

'And does she really have someone else on the scene?'

'Not that I know of. Adam says he's never heard of anyone, and he and Tish are great mates.'

'It doesn't sound so bad. But you have to make the first move. Write her a letter, tell her how much you like her, and that she's more important to you than this other girl. I'm sure you can think of what to say.'

'A letter? No way!' Jamie looked aghast. 'Maybe I could try and send her a text.'

'Maybe.' Oliver laughed. 'Have you ever written a letter in your life, Jamie?'

'I've written thank-you letters, remember? You always sat over me till I'd done them.'

'And what agony it was, for both of us.' He manoeuvred the car down a side street. 'So what are you going to do with your day? Are you going to try and catch up with friends from your old school?'

Jamie shrugged. 'Maybe. I'll probably go down Portobello, see what gives.'

'Just so long as you don't make any arrangements for this evening. Polly's cooking us dinner.'

'That's cool... Dad?'

'Yes?'

Jamie was suddenly diffident. 'I know I've given Mum – Juliet – a hard time recently, but I really don't want her to go to Los Angeles – you know, for a long time. It's horrible of me, I know, but I really don't want her to get this stupid part.'

Oliver squeezed his son's hand. 'Nor do I, Jamie; nor do I.'

'Bye, Paula. See you later.'

The holly wreath Rita had hung in the middle

of the shop door wobbled precariously as Isabelle closed the door behind her. She had just started back up the High Street when a familiar voice stopped her.

'Issy, darling, I do hope that's not tonight's supper you've just bought?'

Isabelle wheeled round. Perfectly seated astride a tall, glossy bay, Veronica Lester smiled down at Isabelle.

'What?' hissed Isabelle.

At the venom in her voice, the horse side-stepped and gave a distressed whinny.

'Whoa, there, boy, whoa there.' Veronica reined him in, patting his neck. She looked reproachfully at Isabelle. 'He's highly strung – you made him jump.' She waited a second for Isabelle to apologise but, as no apology was forthcoming, continued coldly, 'I'm glad I bumped into you, Issy – I was going to give you a ring. I've a raspberry mousse in my freezer, surplus to requirements. I wondered if you'd like me to drop it round for supper tonight. I know cooking isn't your favourite activity.'

There was a faint ting behind them; unnoticed by either, Paula came out of the shop.

Isabelle found her voice. 'No, it's not. So it's lucky for me that I'm *not* cooking tonight.'

'Pardon?' Veronica was as much puzzled by the tone of Isabelle's voice as by what she was saying.

'There is no way' – Isabelle almost choked with emotion – 'I would sit down to eat with you, or my rotten husband, let alone cook for you.'

Paula tiptoed back to the shop door; seconds later she returned with Rita, Jenny Tucker and a

503

couple of other shoppers. The small group stood and watched in silence.

Veronica tried to keep her temper and calm Isabelle, but succeeded only in sounding patronising. 'Why are you so upset? If you're worried about Richard, don't be. It's not serious – he told me himself he found her lightweight. She's a typical actress – makes a pass at any good-looking man. Believe me, it's just a fling.'

'I don't need you to tell me what to think about my fucking husband. He's beneath contempt. He'd destroy a person's reputation and livelihood as easily as you would. He has as little regard for decent hard-working people as you have. No wonder you like each other – you're both immoral, bloodsucking predators, rotten to the core!'

Emerging from the gate of the vicarage, the Reverend Grey, headed for the shop to collect his *Telegraph* and daily allowance of pear drops. He stopped at a discreet distance when he saw two ladies apparently in the throes of a heated exchange. Raised voices, arguments, fights of any sort, unnerved him, so he stood there, hesitating, wondering whether to cross the road and give them a wide berth, or whether, as a man of the cloth and therefore of peace, he should intervene.

Before he'd decided on his best course of action, Nanny appeared at his side. She was also on her way to the shop, intending to ask Rita about Home Farm.

'What's going on, Vicar?' she said quietly, concerned at Isabelle's distress.

'Ah ... um ... I really am not quite sure, Mrs, er...' he dithered.

504

The numbers of the onlookers was swelled by Lenny, who, strolling to the shop to buy cigarettes, was drawn by the sound of the altercation and by the sight of his wife in the small crowd, and by Lavender Grey, returning home from her duties at the doctor's surgery. She, too, stopped, startled by the sight of a woman on a horse shouting at someone on the pavement. She couldn't see who else was involved in the quarrel, because the horse obstructed her view, so she edged along the street, then noticed her husband standing next to Nanny, a trapped look on his face.

She turned her attention back to the fracas and, to her great surprise, saw that the two protagonists yelling at each other like fishwives were none other than Isabelle Garnett and Veronica Lester.

'What the hell are you talking about, Issy? Whoa, boy, whoa.' The horse did not at all like his mistress shouting, and side-stepped again, snorted, and tossed his head. 'What have I ever done to you but put up with you, been nice to you, had you as a guest in my house more times than I can count?'

'And the thought of all that chokes me. But it's not what you've done to me, Veronica. It's what you were prepared to do to Rita Godwin, what you did to Paula Spinks—'

'Oh, for Chrissake, you're getting hysterical. What interest have I in people like that? Honestly—'

'I'll tell you what interest you have.' Isabelle was so angry that she was shaking, but her voice was loud and strong. 'You spread a rumour that Rita Godwin had rats in her basement – you

505

advised people not to shop there – and you said it was Paula who'd told you.'

'So?' Veronica's voice was silky, dangerous. 'Paula said lots of things. I believed her.'

'You made it up. She never said any such thing.'

Veronica gave a brittle laugh. 'Honestly, Issy, if you're going to believe that little slut rather than me... Why on earth should I make it up? I've got better things to do with my time. I'm not in the slightest bit interested in Mrs Godwin or her grubby little shop.'

Paula and Rita reacted angrily, but Veronica and Isabelle were too immersed in their quarrel to notice anybody else and both offended parties fell silent on Isabelle's next words.

'But that's not true, is it, Veronica? You *are* interested in the shop – so interested, you're planning to buy it if Mrs Godwin's forced to sell.'

'You don't know what you're talking about.' But for the first time Veronica's voice lacked conviction.

'Yes, I do. I've had it from the horse's mouth, to use an appropriate cliché. Marion Croucher told me about your partnership. You're to buy the premises, she's to buy the stock and run it as an interior design shop. She's so stupid she thinks it will work; but you're not stupid, are you, Veronica? An interior design shop, here, in Summerstoke? I wouldn't give it more than a couple of months, and then there you are, sitting pretty, with a nice little investment on your hands.'

Veronica's face was an ugly red. 'I'm not staying here to listen to any more of this rubbish,' she spat. 'You can tell your husband we won't be coming to supper tonight.'

'And you can stuff your raspberry mousse up your backside!'

With a furious snarl Veronica dug her heels into her horse's ribs and, with a shrill whinny of protest, he shot up the road accompanied by the cheers of the assembled crowd, apart from the vicar, who looked thoroughly confused.

Isabelle turned and registered her audience for the first time. Her mouth fell open, she burst into tears, dropping her shopping and ran, without thinking where she was going, down the road, over the bridge, over the stile, into the field, to the edge of the river where she stood, sobbing and shaking.

'Isabelle ... Isabelle, what is it?' His voice was gentle and kind. He touched her shoulder. She turned, understanding instinctively that the comfort and support she so desperately needed would be found in his arms.

On the Portobello Road, Jamie had stopped by a stall selling CDs and was rummaging through a stack. Tish liked Nirvana, and if he could find a copy of *Hoarmoanin* she'd be over the moon. He thought about the suggestion he should write her a letter. Dad meant well, but there was no way Jamie'd do that. He'd text her – yeah, when he got back to Aunt Polly's, he'd text her.

'Hey, it's Jamie Merfield!'

Jamie looked up and recognised a couple of boys from his old school.

'Hi, how y'are doin', man?'

'Fine, fine. How's things with you lot?'

'Not so bad. What's life like in the sticks?'

Jamie thought for a bit, then nodded. 'It's cool. I like it.'

'Did you hear what happened to your mates, Mark Sedbury and Tim Fishwick?'

'No. We don't keep in touch.'

'They've both been expelled. Happened a few weeks back – the fuzz caught Mark driving well over the limit. He'd nicked his mum's car. Seems him and Tim were also had for being in possession. Stupid bastards.'

'Yeah,' said Jamie, thinking of Aunt Charlotte's prophecy. 'Stupid bastards.'

Folded in Charlie's comforting embrace Isabelle sobbed till she had no more tears left and then she became aware of two conflicting emotions: she was in the arms of the man she most wanted to avoid in the world, but, amazingly, she liked it there and, treacherously, she had no wish to change the situation.

But she couldn't stay there for ever and her nose was running.

'I'm sorry,' she said in a small voice. 'I need a tissue.'

Charlie released one arm and rummaged in the pocket of his overalls. 'If I were a gent,' he said ruefully, 'I'd produce an immaculate silk hand-kerchief for the lady. As it is, I've only got this.'

'This' was an oily rag.

Isabelle smiled weakly. 'No, thanks. I must have something I can use.' Delving into the depths of her duffle coat, she found a crumpled tissue.

Having blown her nose she looked up at him, suddenly feeling very shy, and very aware of his arm draped round her shoulders, of his body close to hers, and of the frisson of pleasure it gave her. In vain did she attempt to assert all her previous condemnation of him – that he was a notorious flirt, an arrogant, self-centred bastard who'd written her off as a woolly-headed Lester acolyte.

Now here she was, in his arms, and liking it!

She looked down, flushing slightly. 'I'm sorry. You must think I spend my whole time getting into one mess or another.'

'No, I don't, and don't be sorry. I'm just glad I saw you. Can you tell me what's wrong?'

His voice was so unusually gentle that Isabelle was tempted to unburden herself completely. It was a struggle not to. She had longed to find someone she could confide in, but she had never, in a million years, thought it would be Charlie Tucker.

'Why're you being so nice to me?' she demanded, with a bit of her old spark. 'I don't deserve it – I've been perfectly horrid to you.'

'Probably with some justification,' he replied with a grin. 'What did you call me, "an arrogant shit"? I didn't mean to be, but I can see how it came across and I'm sorry.'

'No, I'm sorry,' said Isabelle wretchedly. 'I'm so pig-headed.'

'Yes,' said Charlie, remembering the fight over the wheel brace, 'you are. But you've got spirit; you stand up for yourself – that's nothing to be sorry for. So what's upset you?'

Isabelle couldn't bring herself to talk about Richard, but she told him about her confron-

509

tation with Veronica Lester.

'And then,' she concluded, 'I turned round and it seemed as if the whole village had gathered to listen. I was shaking so much, all I could do was drop my shopping and run—You're laughing!'

Charlie was trying to suppress it, but he couldn't, and throwing back his head he laughed out loud. 'Fantastic, bloody fantastic! Isabelle, you've done something I bet the whole village has longed to do for the last twenty years – told Veronica Lester to stuff her raspberry mousse up her backside.' And he laughed till the tears rolled down his cheeks.

Isabelle, still shaken by the incident, didn't know how to react at first, but Charlie's mirth was infectious and by degrees she relaxed and was able to smile, then laugh, herself.

He gave her a hug. 'That's better. Come on, I'll give you a lift back. My van's on the side of the road there. I saw you running over the bridge as I came out of our drive.'

Isabelle's altercation with Veronica had provided enough juicy material to satisfy the village's thirst for gossip for the foreseeable future, so when Charlie let her off to retrieve her shopping, she received a heroine's welcome from everyone in the shop, to her great embarrassment.

Dealing with Veronica, however, was only half the battle. There was still Richard, and she knew that particular encounter was going to be very nasty. He was due home late in the afternoon and she wanted to get the girls out of the way. When, therefore, everyone was finally driven out of the shop by Rob, who came in wanting to know why Rita hadn't closed for lunch, she diffidently approached Paula. 'I know it's your birthday today, and you've probably got plans, but I wondered if you could have the girls for the afternoon – or at least round about tea-time. There's something I've got to do, and it would be easier if they weren't around.'

Apart from a curious glance, Paula didn't hesitate. ''Course not, no probs. Bring them over after they've had their dinner. Lenny's puttin' the finishing touches to our outdoor Christmas decorations so we can 'ave them lit for the party tonight, then we're all goin' up to the farm. Stephen's got a delivery of some Highland cattle, and there's a couple of calves, he says, so we're gonna take the kiddies to look at them. Your girls would love that. And then we're staying to tea – Jenny's baked me a birthday cake.'

'Oh, I didn't want to interfere with anything you've got planned.'

'Don't be daft, girl,' chipped in Lenny. 'The more the merrier. They can stay with us till after the party at ours. You are comin', aren't yer?'

'Yes,' Isabelle said with a brightness she was far from feeling. 'Definitely.'

Richard climbed into his Jaguar, humming slightly. It was all coming together nicely. Jake had come up trumps with his photographs: some good close-ups of angry villagers; Oliver looking bewildered; and an excellent wide shot of the hall in turmoil, faces turned, shouting at Oliver.

Barring a local murder or fatal train crash,

which would drive everything else off the front page, his lead story for Monday was settled: Oliver Merfield faces the wrath of his own village.

For some obscure reason, it took some persuasion to get Chris Gorman to write the story to go with the pictures. If he had ambitions to go and work for a national, he'd better start shedding a few scruples, Richard told him, sending him back to do a third rewrite. But with a judicious bit of editing, and some non-attributable quotes, Richard managed to get the story he wanted.

On an adjoining page he'd slipped in a small story of his own, one that made Neville Budd raise his cautious eyebrows.

He glanced at his watch. Just after four – he was late. That was Gorman's fault. I'd better give Issy a ring, he thought, see if there's anything she wants picked up for tonight.

He'd been taken aback by her show of defiance. He knew full well she didn't particularly like the Lesters, but she'd always got on with it. What had caused that little outburst, the night before last, he'd no idea, and she was asleep by the time he got back last night so he'd had no chance to tackle her further. But he was confident she'd be over it by now and wouldn't embarrass him this evening.

The answer-phone was on and her mobile didn't respond. He frowned. If there was anything needed, he could always shoot out to that supermarket beyond Summerbridge, but it would be a bloody nuisance, especially when all the shops of Bath were at his fingertips.

He was looking forward to the evening. His

vanity had been badly jolted by Juliet's rejection, but the knowledge that his revenge would be sweet and unexpected, and that, at the same time, he'd give Hugh what he wanted, was a considerable consolation.

The only downside about this evening was having chosen some excellent wine; he'd have to hang back on the booze, because Abigail had inveigled him into picking her up from York tomorrow. He'd have to make an early start, something he didn't want to do sozzled.

It would be a long drive, but Abigail's skills in emotional blackmail were second to none. She was going to stay with her mother for a few days before coming down to his place for Christmas, so the plan was to drop her off in London, and stay the night there. Monday, when the office should be humming with the Oliver Merfield story, was his day off, and he planned to return in a leisurely fashion from the big city.

Sunday evening with Clare, his ex, also promised to be fun. She and he had somehow survived divorce to remain on friendly terms and he was looking forward to a good gossip. Maybe he'd put aside a bottle of wine he'd got for this evening and take it with him.

He parked his car in the garage, picked up the case of bottles from the boot and let himself into the house.

The hall was in darkness. In fact, there were no lights on anywhere, and the house was silent. But he'd noticed the Discovery parked in the drive so Issy couldn't have gone anywhere, and as it was now dark outside, it seemed unlikely that she'd taken the girls out for a walk or to the playground.

'Becky! Clemmie!'

Normally his call would have invoked an enthusiastic response from his little girls, but on this occasion ... nothing.

Frowning, he made his way down the hall to the kitchen and, balancing the case of wine under one arm, he managed to open the door.

Isabelle was sitting at the kitchen table, her back to him, concentrating on a small sheet of paper. The sole light in the kitchen came from a desk lamp she'd set up on the kitchen table. In front of her were two jars of water, one clear, one murky brown, a mug containing brushes, and lots of pots of different coloured paints.

'Issy,' he complained. 'You might have opened the door for me.'

She didn't turn round and it was then he noticed that there was nothing in the kitchen to indicate she was getting ready for the dinner party: no saucepans bubbling on the Aga, no half-chopped vegetables, no sign of meat in preparation, no cheese on the sideboard, nothing.

He dropped the box on the table and turned to her. 'What's happening? Where are the girls? Why aren't you getting ready for dinner?' And then, exasperated, 'What *are* you doing?'

She looked at her painting, gave a little grunt, placed the brush she was using in the jar of clean water and started to put the lids back on the pots of paint.

'I'm painting a birthday card,' she said, calmly. 'The girls are having tea with a friend, and there is going to be no dinner party.'

'What d'ye mean, no dinner party? I hope you're not playing some stupid game, Issy, because I'm not in the mood for it.'

She looked up at him for the first time. 'I'm not the one who plays stupid games, Richard. There will be no dinner party because Juliet and Oliver, Veronica and Hugh have said they're not coming.'

'What? What d'ye mean? I wasn't expecting the Merfields, but Hugh and Vee ... what did you say to them? I can't believe this! What are you up to?'

Ignoring his explosive reaction, she stood up, placed her painting on the side of the dresser and, taking the paintbrushes over to the sink, proceeded to rinse them.

'Oliver told me Juliet has gone to the States and he's staying in London,' she replied finally, cold and controlled. 'I think that's just as well, don't you? Considering the way you're behaving. Destroying people's lives is just one big game to you, isn't it, Richard?'

She turned the tap off and faced him. 'It's taken me a long time to realise it, but you're totally without principle. The fact that you were prepared to have Oliver here to supper, fully intending to fuck his wife – if you haven't done so already – and knowing that he's about to be crucified in your paper – something you've orchestrated because it amuses you or, more probably because newspaper sales and dancing to head office's tune is more important to you than people's careers' or reputations – makes me feel so sick I can hardly bear to be in the same room as you, let alone speak to you.'

'What the fuck are you talking about? Where

515

have you got these ridiculous ideas from?' Richard tried to bluster.

How did she know about Juliet? How much did she know about his campaign against Oliver? While she was still quite wide of the mark, her accusations were too close for comfort. She had to be guessing, and if he shouted loud enough he could crack her certainty and get things back under his control.

'It's no use blustering, or denying anything. I was at the village meeting last night; I saw your thugs in action, and I watched your photographer get just the pictures you wanted and then leave.'

'You're talking rubbish. What thugs? Nothing to do with me.'

'No?'

Her cold, unwavering stare unnerved him and he bellowed, *'No!* No, it's not. I don't know *what* you're on about.'

'Well, I guess I'll suspend judgement till next week, when the papers come out. Then I'll know. I just hope, Richard, hope so much, I'm wrong. Until then, I don't want you to come anywhere near me.'

Before he could say anything more, she stalked past him, out of the kitchen, picking up her painting as she went; seconds later he heard the front door slam.

After her departure, Richard sat in a state of shock, trying to untangle what had passed between them.

She didn't say anything about Vee or Hugh, he thought. What the fuck has she said to them?

516

What the bloody hell is she up to? She can't make ultimatums like this – who does she think she is?

He decided the best course of action would be to phone Vee. If she knew nothing of his deal with Hugh, Vee loaning him a pair of thugs might not go down too well; more importantly, he needed to know if Vee had told Issy about his involvement in breaking up the meeting. He needed to keep Vee sweet because, while he didn't think Issy would broadcast his actions, an angry Vee could be vicious, particularly if she was still labouring under the impression he was having it off with Juliet Peters. Knowing what she did, she could pull the proverbial rug from under his feet.

'Vee, hi, it's Richard here. I've just walked into a major domestic. Can *you* tell me what's going on? Issy says you're not coming over tonight. Why's that?'

Her voice sounded cold, unfriendly. 'Hello Richard. No, we're not coming. I'm afraid Issy was so rude to me today that I see little point in pretending a friendship that clearly is not there.'

'Issy rude to you? What did she say, Vee? No,' his voice changed, becoming quite bitter, 'you don't have to tell me. She knows how important you ... your friendship is to me. It's not you she's getting at Vee, it's me. She's out to destroy me and everything I care about.'

'I'm sorry to hear that, Richard,' Veronica's tone softened. 'She certainly was absolutely ghastly to me – I couldn't possibly repeat what she said. But you? Why on earth do you think she's out to destroy you?'

517

For a moment, Richard hesitated; he wasn't sure how much he could trust Vee. Then, affecting a broken, low voice, he continued. 'It's too complicated to explain over the phone. But she's gone off somewhere with the girls. I need someone to talk to, Vee. Obviously this evening has been ruined for us all, but would you and Hugh consider being my guests at the Casillero del Diablo? I gave them a rave review so they owe me.'

The Casillero del Diablo was *the* restaurant of the moment and a table, particularly on a Saturday night, would be gold dust.

There was silence on the other end of the phone and then Vee said, with all the sympathy Richard could wish for, 'Poor Richard, you must be feeling completely wretched. I'd love to come. Hugh's not here, though. He went out on business. I'll leave him a note so if he comes back early, he'll know where to find us. What time?'

Isabelle walked out of her house, her legs so wobbly they hardly supported her. She could have told Richard to go then and there, but supposing she'd made a huge mistake? She didn't think so but, so far, all her evidence was circumstantial. For the sake of her little girls, if nothing else, she had to give him the chance to prove her wrong.

The front of the Spinkses' cottage was transformed into an electric wonderland of fairy lights, nodding reindeer, an illuminated Father Christmas climbing up the front wall of the cottage, winking stars, dripping icicles and a flashing 'Happy Christmas' emblazoned across the front of the cottage. Caught unawares, Isabelle threw back her head and laughed.

Paula answered the door, a crown of tinsel in her hair, a can of Guinness in her hand. She shrieked when she saw Isabelle. 'Isabelle, you've come! Brilliant!'

Isabelle smiled. 'Happy birthday, Paula. Here, I've a card for you.'

She was ushered into the Spinkses' tiny sitting room. It was full of laughter and noise; every available space was occupied; someone made room for Isabelle to sit on a patch of threadbare carpet; someone else thrust a can of beer in her hand and someone else gave her a slice of pizza. The stereo was booming; overhead she could hear children, including her two, shrieking and laughing. Every now and then a loud thump on the ceiling made the paper chains looped across the room shake crazily.

She started to breathe more easily.

Glancing up, she saw Charlie, squashed on a sofa, looking at her.

His eyes twinkled and he smiled.

She blushed and smiled shyly back.

Fortunately for Richard he was able to call in his favour, so a couple of hours later he and Veronica were ushered to a table in the expensively discreet, candle-lit dining room of the Casillero del Diablo.

Veronica looked around with satisfaction. 'This is nice. I must say, Richard, you're one of the few people I know who can transform a disaster-laden evening into a real treat. Now, tell me' – she leaned forward, her long nose twitching slightly – 'what's

519

happened? Why has Issy gone off the deep end like this? Is she, you know, unwell?'

'I think you might have hit on it, Vee. She's been behaving increasingly oddly since we moved to Summerstoke – look how she insisted on painting the entire house herself, for a start.'

During their conversation, it became clear to Richard that Hugh hadn't told her about their agreement, nor had Vee told anyone about the 'favour' she'd done him and nor was she likely to.

'For goodness' sake, Richard, darling, why should I do that? What sort of position would that put me in?'

He breathed out.

He told her about Isabelle's ultimatum. 'Thing is, Vee, she's made it quite clear if I publish a photograph discrediting Oliver Merfield in any way, it'll be the end of our marriage as far as she's concerned.'

Veronica's eyes almost popped out of her head. 'What an extraordinary thing to do. Are you sure she's not just being difficult because of ... you know, because of you and Juliet?'

Richard stared at her as blankly as he could manage. 'Me and Juliet?'

'Don't be naive, Richard – I saw the two of you together last Tuesday, for goodness' sake.'

'And I've taken her out to lunch a couple of times, but that doesn't mean I'm having an affair with her, Vee, or that I want to. I told you, she's very decorative and I enjoy her company – up to a point – but that's it. She's very cloying. Give me an intelligent woman's company every time.'

Veronica gave him a searching look and he held

her gaze.

'Believe me, Vee, I have no interest in Juliet.'

Veronica appeared satisfied and smiled. 'Good, because I have no interest in becoming an accomplice in your amours, Richard. But if that is the case, and I take it Issy knows it is, the question remains to be asked, why's she protecting Oliver Merfield?'

'Damned if I know.'

'She's prepared to sacrifice her marriage to *you*, defending *him*. What does that say to you? Because I certainly know what it says to me, Richard. You need to wake up!'

22

There was no sign of Richard when Isabelle got up early on Sunday morning. He had disappeared, presumably to York, without a word. She had spent a sleepless night, worrying about what he was going to do, about the implications for them both if he went ahead and published anti-Oliver photographs. And if he didn't ... what then?

Mechanically she went through the routine of washing and dressing, then rousing the girls. Oliver's prospective humiliation weighed heavily on her. She didn't know what to do – whether to try and warn him so he was, at the very least, prepared. But then, she thought, if Richard did retract, she'd have exposed him unnecessarily, and wasn't there such a thing as wifely loyalty? If he did publish, how could she continue to live in the village? The Merfields were an old Summer-stoke family; Oliver was popular; Richard's actions wouldn't be easily forgiven; she'd be held responsible for not having stopped him.

At this point, her gloomy reflections turned to fury. Typical fucking selfish bastard – he doesn't think beyond the end of his nose; doesn't stop to think about the effect of his actions on anyone else, not even his own sodding family!

She liked living in the village; she hadn't wanted to come here, but now the thought of leaving was awful. And Becky and Clemmie were happy here; Clemmie had made loads of friends and Becky was just coming into her own. Was Richard going to destroy that? Not if she could help it. No way!

She stared out of the kitchen window, feeling bleak and desolate.

Perverse Nature had decided she wasn't ready for winter yet and the sun shone, warm and bright, the sky a clear, speedwell blue.

'Come on,' she said to the girls after breakfast, 'Let's go for a walk. Where would you like to go? Along the river? We might, if we're very quiet, see the kingfisher I told you about.'

Clemmie was all for that, but Becky had other ideas.

'Mum, please, *please* can we go to the farm? Alison said I can have a ride on Bumble next time I go. It was too dark yesterday teatime. He's lovely, Mum, round and fat, and he ate a carrot from my hand. Please say yes, Mum, then you can see those cows they've just got – they're huge!'

'They've got horns *this* big,' said Clemmie, stretching her arms wide.

'But not the babies – they're so sweet.'

'I want one of them. They've got faces like teddy bears.'

Isabelle tried to raise objections – her emotions were in such turmoil, she was trying to put all thoughts of Charlie Tucker on hold. At Paula's party she'd barely exchanged more than two words with him, stubbornly ignoring the ache she felt, the desperate need to creep back into the comforting circle of his arms. The thought of going to the farm, running the real risk of bumping into him and not being able to contain herself...

'No, they're not expecting us... We should wait to be invited... It's too far for Clemmie to walk... They'll be busy – it's a working farm.'

But the girls' eagerness for another visit capped all her objections, and when Isabelle put in a cautious call Jenny Tucker was so welcoming that she could object no longer.

Walking through the village, Isabelle was aware of how much life had changed since they'd moved to Summerstoke. She no longer felt like a stranger, and this morning even people whom she knew only by sight nodded and smiled at her. It brought a lump to her throat. When the newspaper came out it would be a different story.

They paused by the gate into the Spinkses' front garden. The glorious light-show of the night before was now a tawdry skeleton of plastic and glass.

Lenny was up a stepladder, a pile of lights hanging from the top, banging them into position.

'Hi, Isabelle,' he called cheerfully. 'Good party last night, weren't it? Paula's mum found some more fairy lights at the car-boot sale this morning. The more the merrier, I say.'

Isabelle laughed. 'Or "In for a penny, in for a pound," as Mrs Godwin would say.'

'D'ye want me to get some for you? I'll come and put 'em up for you – no probs. Some of them reindeer would look smart in your garden.'

Ignoring her daughters' pleas to have a herd of electric reindeer on her lawn, she satisfied Lenny by accepting his offer to help her rig some fairy lights in a tree by the gate, then steered her two girls over the bridge and down the farm track.

Christmas – oh, God!

Christmas in their new house. It should have been so exciting; she could feel the bubble of anticipation growing daily in the girls. Already the school was filling with strings of tinfoil stars, toilet rolls transformed into Father Christmases with the aid of crêpe paper and cotton wool, and painted snow scenes, nativity scenes and Christmas trees.

She and Richard hadn't even discussed where they'd put the Christmas tree.

Her mind went back to the miserable artificial tree her mother had pulled out every year and decorated with no joy; putting it away again, with great relief, on Boxing Day. Her first Christmas with Richard, she remembered, he'd bought her the largest tree he could find and had teased her to find enough decorations to cover it. They'd been so happy.

At the farmyard gate, they were met by a slender young girl carrying a saddle. She had long blonde hair swept back in a ponytail, wide green eyes and a delicate face with the sort of bone structure, Isabelle reflected, that would one day make her quite beautiful.

She smiled at them. 'Hi. I heard you were coming over, so I thought I'd get Bumble ready. I'm Alison, by the way. I know you work with Milo, but we've never met, have we?'

'No, we haven't. It's very kind of you to do this for the girls. I don't think Becky's talked of anything else since she met Bumble.'

Alison laughed. 'I started about the same age. I warn you, horse mania's a terrible thing.'

The girls spent an ecstatic hour with Alison, taking it in turns to sit on the back of the fattest pony Isabelle had ever seen.

When the saddle was removed and the good-natured Bumble taken back to his stable, Alison invited Isabelle and the girls into the house.

Isabelle hung back. 'No we couldn't, it's too much – you've been so kind already.'

'Oh, please,' Alison insisted, 'you must. Nothing's too much for the person who told Veronica Lester to stuff a raspberry mousse up her backside.' She chuckled. 'Brilliant! I promised Mum I'd bring you inside.'

'How do you know about that?' She stopped. Had Charlie told them how he'd found her in tears, by the river?

'Mum was there, she heard it all. And it's all over the village – a story like that will run and run for yonks.'

A small red car turned into the yard at speed and screeched on its brakes, its wheels spitting mud.

Alison smiled. 'It's Gran. She and Ron have been to church. You know my gran, don't you?'

'Yes, I met her at the shop action meetings – she's an amazing person.'

'You can say that again. I hope I've got mental faculties like hers if I ever get to that age.'

Watching the diminutive form of Elsie get out of the car, it occurred to Isabelle that *here* was someone in whom she could confide, someone she could trust.

She turned to Alison. 'Er, Alison, I'd like a quick word with your gran. D'you think you could give the girls some squash or water or something? I won't be long.'

'No probs. See you in a min. Come on, you two, let's go and raid my mum's fridge.'

Hesitantly, Isabelle approached Elsie, who climbed stiffly out of the car, talking to her husband.

It was Ron who saw her first. 'Hello, my dear. What a very pleasant surprise. Been visiting the Highland cattle, eh? I think they're going to be quite an attraction, don't you?'

'Alison's been giving my girls rides on her pony. We might have to leave the cattle to another day – we've been here rather a long time already,' smiled Isabelle. Then, to Elsie, 'Alison's taken them to get a drink, so I wondered, Mrs Bates, whether I could have a word? Um ... I won't take up much of your time, but...'

Elsie looked at her shrewdly, then turned to

Ron. 'Go and tell Jenny to put the kettle on, there's a dear. Won't be long.'

Ron headed off, and Elsie turned back to Isabelle. 'It's a lovely day and I'm stiff from sitting on church pews. Let's walk down to the river and you can tell me what's on your mind, my dear. I suspect it's something more than telling Mrs Lester what to do with her frozen desserts.'

Slowly, painfully, Isabelle described her suspicions about Richard's involvement in the attack on Oliver. Elsie was a good listener, betraying few emotions and asking few questions.

When Isabelle fell silent, Elsie looked searchingly at her and then said gently, 'This is a huge accusation you're making, my dear. Are you sure you're right?'

'I'm nearly a hundred per cent sure. But I have to wait for the paper to come out to be absolutely sure, and then it'll be too late. What do I do?'

'These men, you think your husband hired them?'

Isabelle shook her head, weary with thinking. 'I don't know. Are they local? Did you recognise them? If they are, well, he's hardly been in the village since we moved here – he doesn't know anyone, except for the Lesters, of course, and the Merfields.'

'We can find out if they're local – Rita kept a register, remember – and if they are, we might be able to find out who set them on. But in the meantime, what to do about Oliver? I think, my dear, it would be a good idea if he were to be forewarned. Forewarned is forearmed. It's also a question of what *we* do. Of course, the *Wessex Daily* isn't the

527

only newspaper in our neck of the woods.'

'But it's the only local daily, and by the time the weekly ones come out the damage to Oliver's reputation will have been done,' Isabelle said wretchedly.

'It all depends how much you're prepared to fight, Isabelle,' said Elsie, rather grimly. 'Any campaigning we do in support of Oliver is going to be seen as a little local affair, but if we go on to prove your husband exploited his position *and* incited people to violence, then, you can see, as he's an editor of a newspaper, it becomes a much bigger story.'

'Yes,' said Isabelle in a small voice. 'Yes, I see. But he's still my husband, Mrs Bates, and he's my children's father. It wouldn't be an embarrassment he'd get over in time, like Oliver. It would destroy him.'

'Can you get hold of him? Could you not point this out to him? Persuade him that it's bound to come out. He's not thinking straight, is he? If you're right and we can identify those men, it's not going to be difficult to trace them back to him. And you can be sure of the village being robust in their defence of Oliver – their description of the meeting will be very different. It's the sort of thing the Press Council would take up, I'm sure. Can you not ensure he changes his mind?'

'Yes, yes you're right. Thank you. I should have thought of all that myself, but I've been in such a state of confusion. Thank you.'

'In the meantime, I'll go and have a chat with Rita, see what we can find out about those two men; we need to muster our defences in case your husband proves intransigent. With Oliver's help, we built up a lot of goodwill towards the shop on Friday. He's a good MP and I won't have anyone say different.'

Richard drove all the way to York in the icy fury that had descended during dinner with Vee the night before. Of course Vee was right. How could he have been so blind? He'd been so busy trying to get his leg over Juliet, he hadn't noticed his wife playing a similar game with that prick. If only he could see Oliver's face when the paper came out tomorrow. And Juliet's, for that matter. He'd hesitated about playing that little joker; but now ... now they deserved everything he could throw at them.

He laughed grimly. How appropriate that Oliver Merfield, losing his job, guaranteed Richard his. He thought briefly of Hugh Lester. By his actions, he'd become Hugh's creature. Not the best position to be in...

And he and Issy?

For the first time since he decided to marry her, he thought long and hard about Issy and their relationship. Every now and then little bubbles of anger broke through at the realisation she was prepared to put their relationship on the line to protect Oliver Merfield; that she thought she could coerce him into changing his mind about the front page.

He reached York shortly after midday to find Abigail hadn't even begun to pack. It was a couple of hours later when an exasperated Richard finally set off with his daughter for London.

'You'd better give your mother a ring, Abi, tell her we're not going to get to hers till about seven.'

'My battery's flat. I need to use yours, Dad.'

Richard reached into his pocket and produced his phone. 'Here.'

'Thanks. Hey, Dad, this is new, isn't it?'

'Yeah. Like it? It's an MP3 player as well as being able to download videos and all the usual stuff.'

'Awesome!'

The afternoon shift was coming to an end at the *Wessex Daily*. It had been a dull old day and, with the cover story set by Richard the day before and nothing occurring to displace it, Neville Budd was about to round off the day with the final conference. He was gathering up his papers when an excited gasp from one of the junior subs attracted his attention.

It fell to the lot of the junior subs working the Sunday shift to trawl the national papers looking for stories with a sufficient local slant to be worth following up.

The sub looked up, her face glowing with excitement. 'Neville? Neville, look at this.'

Without much expectation, Neville wandered over.

'What is it, Laura?' She was halfway through one of the minor Sundays, one which paid more attention to gossip and scantily clad celebrities than it did to news. She pointed to a small photograph in a gossip column.

The caption read: 'Who's the new man in Juliet

Peters' life?'

He peered at the photograph and then shouted, 'Bloody hell, I don't believe it!'

Picking up the paper he made his way through to Richard's office, the only place where he could use the phone without being overheard.

The reporter took his time to answer.

'Chris, it's me, Neville. About that conversation with Mrs G, I want you in here. We've found the fucking missing link... I don't give a toss that it's a Sunday and you're still in your pyjamas. We need to be on top of this, Chris. I tell you, I don't think it's a storm that's about to break over our heads, it's going to be a fucking tsunami.'

Isabelle tried all afternoon to reach Richard on his mobile but without success. He'd turned it off – unusual for him. In desperation, she phoned Clare and left a message for him to phone as soon as he could. She also tried calling Oliver, but again without success.

The afternoon ticked so slowly by she felt each minute tightening every nerve in her body. Frustrated, unable to do anything, afraid to go far from the phone in case Richard or Oliver should return her call, she sat next to it and wrote a long, desperate letter to Joe, finding some solace in detailing everything that had happened.

Elsie, who had gone to the Manor after having seen Rita, called round at the end of the afternoon to find out if Isabelle had spoken to Richard, and to tell her the two men had come from the farm cottages used by the Lesters for their grooms.

'The Lesters?' Isabelle stared at her. 'Is that a coincidence?'

'No,' said Elsie grimly. 'From what I understand, they told young Jamie Merfield their boss was doing a friend a favour. You said your husband's a friend of the Lesters.'

'Yes.' Isabelle nodded, feeling sick to the bottom of her soul. This was the confirmation she needed, but so did not want. 'Yes, they've been friends longer than I've known Richard. But why should those men tell Jamie Merfield? I don't understand – what's he got to do with this?'

Elsie shook her head. 'I don't know the ins and outs of it, but it seems they were trying to recruit a couple of others to swell their numbers. He must have looked a likely candidate – you know, sullen teenager, probably loitering where he shouldn't. It was unlucky for them they picked him.' She gave a humourless laugh, then her voice softened. 'This is very hard for you, Isabelle. It's not just your husband and Oliver with a lot at stake, is it?'

'No,' replied Isabelle miserably. 'It's not.'

Elsie patted her hand. 'You've made a place for yourself in this village's heart, dear, remember that. Oh, one other thing: have you thought of asking at the Manor how Oliver can be contacted?'

Isabelle kicked herself. It was so bloody obvious – why hadn't she thought of it?

The traffic into London was heavy and it was well after seven when Richard drew up outside Clare's house in Camden.

She was much the same age as Richard, tall, thin and intelligent, with a dominant nose and shrewd light-brown eyes.

She smiled at him cheerfully as he followed Abigail in, and gave him a peck on the cheek.

'My, you look as if you could do with a drink. Gin and tonic, or straight to the wine? I've got a casserole in the oven, so we can eat in about an hour. Abigail, I've been fielding the telephone for you all afternoon – there's loads of messages for you on the pad in the hall. Why didn't you have your mobile on?'

'Battery's flat. Ta, Mum.' Abigail disappeared.

'I'll have a G and T, thanks. Shall I fix it?'

'Help yourself. Oh, by the way, there's a message for you, too.'

'Oh?'

'Isabelle. She sounded distinctly wobbly, I must say. She said she's been trying to get you on your mobile all afternoon, but you're switched off. Honestly, you and Abi, what a pair!'

Richard frowned with impatience. 'That's ridiculous. I keep my phone on all the time, in case the paper wants me for anything. What's she on about?'

'Well, whatever... I think you should ring her, asap, though.'

Richard put his hand in his pocket for his phone.

'Bugger, where is it? Abi? Abi?'

Abigail's voice floated back. 'I'm on the phone, Dad. What is it?'

'What have you done with my mobile? You had it in the car.'

533

'I haven't done anything with it. It's probably still there.'

Richard found it in the glove compartment, where Abigail had put it when she grew bored playing with it. It was switched off.

Clare looked at him curiously as he stomped back into the kitchen. 'My, you look out of sorts. Did you phone Isabelle?'

'Not yet. I need that drink first.'

'I don't want to interfere, Richard, but is everything okay between you two? I've never heard her quite so wound up.'

'She's becoming impossible,' Richard growled, 'and now she's trying to interfere with the way I run my newspaper.'

'What?'

'She's always moaned when I run campaigns – honest, the way she goes on, you'd think I was crucifying saints when I nail drunk drivers. This particular little episode, for some reason, has really got her goat and she more or less told me that, unless I change my cover story tomorrow, she and I are through!'

Clare stared at him. 'Isabelle threatened that? Are you sure? What's the campaign all about?'

'Oh, we've been looking at how effective local politicians are in meeting their electorate's needs. Pretty boring stuff, really, but the sort of thing we should be doing – holding our elected representatives to account.'

'So why on earth is Isabelle so upset she's threatening you with divorce? Come on, Richard, tell me the truth.'

Richard swallowed the rest of his drink before

replying. 'The truth is she's soft on the local MP. He's a smarmy sort of chap, still wet behind the ears, Tory, not much older than her. We covered a meeting held in our village, where the villagers nearly lynched him because he'd done sweet FA to prevent their one and only shop closing. The picture in tomorrow's paper shows that.'

Clare was incredulous. 'And Isabelle wants you not to run the story? You're joking!'

Richard got up and poured himself another gin. 'It's no joke. So if I don't give in, Clare, if I don't compromise my professional integrity, I shall find myself homeless, no wife, no little girls.'

In the event, it was several drinks later before Richard, urged on by Clare suggesting Isabelle might be having second thoughts, phoned his wife.

Isabelle finally got hold of Oliver when he returned to Summerstoke, and when Richard rang she'd just shown him out, clearly shaken by what she'd told him. Sitting on the bottom step of the staircase, her head in her hands, she sprang up at the first ring and picked up the receiver with a trembling hand.

'Richard, thank goodness! It's after nine and I've been phoning you since two. Where've you been? Why haven't you phoned me before?'

'I've been to York and, anyway, I got the distinct impression you'd told me I was to have nothing further to do with you.' His voice was hostile.

'Listen, Richard. It's important we talk through ... talk through what will happen if you print those pictures tomorrow.' Isabelle's teeth were chattering so much she had to stop to regain her composure. It was vital that she didn't lose her cool, that she spelled out the danger he was in.

'Listen, Issy, if the only reason you've phoned me is to get me to change my mind, you're wasting your breath. I don't know what's gone on between you and Oliver Merfield–'

'What?'

'And I think it's quite extraordinary you're prepared to put our marriage on the line to protect him.'

'What?'

'But, believe it or not, I value my professional integrity above most other things and tomorrow's front page stays as it is. Got it?'

Isabelle struggled for a second, but it was no good. She exploded. 'Yes, I've got it. I've got it all right. You're stupid, Richard. I didn't realise it till now, but actually, you're stupid. You can't see beyond the end of your nose. You're so busy justifying the shit you throw at everybody else, you don't see the danger you're in. So Oliver has a nasty moment, but people have got short memories, unless you're determined to keep this campaign up, week after week. But what happens to you when the word gets out – as it surely will, unless you're prepared to stop a lot of mouths – that you've perverted the truth and that you're pursuing him for personal reasons?'

'What are you on about?'

'What happens to you when it gets out that it was *you* behind the hecklers at the village hall, courtesy of the Lesters?'

'What?'

536

'Quite apart from getting into bed with Oliver Merfield's wife—'

'You're fuckin' crazy!'

'I don't think so. If you don't change that front page Richard, I'd say you're the crazy one. Professional integrity? Don't make me laugh – it's professional suicide!' She banged the phone down and slumped to the floor. There was nothing more she could do.

Richard woke in the early hours of the morning. In spite of the cold night air, he was perspiring heavily; little rivulets coursed through the hairs on his chest; small pools of sweat collected in his armpits, his groin, his navel. He was terribly thirsty and his mouth felt sour, his tongue swollen. Bugger it, he'd drunk too much last night, even for him. And as if to prove this, when he turned his head to read the bedside clock, the darkness swam in front of his eyes. It was four thirty. He turned on his side and tried to get back to sleep. It was no good. His bladder was calling for relief and he desperately needed a drink of water, so he staggered to the bathroom, had a pee and, emptying the tooth mug, filled it with water, drank, filled it again and took it back to bed.

He might have relieved the needs of his body, but the physical activity had woken him up. He lay in the darkness, his mind relentlessly sweeping backwards and forwards over the conversation with Issy.

'Stupid' – he was the 'stupid one' – 'professional integrity', it was a phrase he liked to use, a useful cloak – 'professional suicide', was it? Was it?

Nobody knew about his deal with Hugh – and Hugh wouldn't say anything. And Vee... Vee would never tell anyone about the two men – but Issy knew. How did she know? And if she knew, how many other people knew, too? What had Vee said to her men? Could they be trusted to keep their mouths shut? He should have offered them more. If they tracked the two men down ... they: who might 'they' be? He shivered. He didn't need to answer that. He lived and worked in a piranha-infested profession; any display of weakness and he'd be dead meat.

He sat up in bed, all thought of sleep gone. He'd been so keen on scoring against Oliver, he was in danger of giving away an own goal. He picked up the clock. It was nearly six. Neville and the chief sub would have been at work for the best part of an hour, sending stuff to the printers, putting the final touches to the paper, including anything from the Sundays. He imagined the consternation it would cause if he phoned and told them to hold the front page till he got there.

'But fuck 'em.'

His head swam dangerously as he swung his legs over the edge of the bed. Six o'clock. Even if he wasn't over the limit, which he suspected he still was, and even if he drove like the devil, he'd have to contend with the London rush hour. No, there was no way he could get there – realistically, that is – until eight thirty, nine. The paper would be on the presses by then.

He groaned aloud. He had no option but to give Neville a ring, tell him to scrap the cover story and find a decent substitute. He had to throw himself

538

on Neville's mercy. But, somehow, 'Neville' and 'mercy' didn't sit reassuringly together.

Neville was sitting at Richard's desk when a junior sub poked his head round the door.

'Hey, Nev, it's the chief. He wants to speak with you, urgent.'

Neville looked up from the paper he was studying. For a moment he stared at the sub, his face impassive.

'Does he now?' he said softly. 'Hmm. Tell him I seem to have left the office for the moment. Tell him you'll give him the message when you find me. Okay?' He smiled.

'Okay,' the sub grinned back.

23

Jamie's bike stuttered to a stop in the car park of the Ferry Inn. It was only just after seven o'clock in the evening and the car park was empty except for a motorbike.

The flutterings in his stomach increased tenfold. Oh God, she's here already, he thought as he locked his bike and took off his helmet. This is no dream, this is for real. Christ, I'm not ready for this!

He'd sent her a text the day before and she'd texted back almost immediately. Further texting led to an arrangement to meet in the beer garden at seven thirty, and Jamie decided to turn up early so he would have time to calm himself down. Discovering Tish was already there had the reverse effect. Slowly he walked through the car park to the garden, wondering how he could be sweating like a pig on a winter's night.

He saw her before she saw him, sitting at a table illuminated by the outside lights. Awesome, she's wearing a skirt. I've never seen her in a skirt before – she looks fantastic!

His mouth went dry and he didn't know how his legs carried him across the grass. She turned and saw him and immediately her face burst into life with a smile.

'Hey, Jamie, over here,' she called, half rising and waving to him, although she was the only person in the garden.

He quickened his pace, then stopped short of the table and stood there, not knowing what to do, how to greet her. Should he hug her? Kiss her? Or just sit down with a noncommittal 'Hi'? The seconds seemed to stretch as he stood there, frozen with indecision.

Tish solved the problem by jumping up and throwing her arms around him.

Amazing, he thought, how warm she feels.

'Hey, Tish,' he said, suddenly completely at ease, hugging her tightly. 'It's great to see you. I've been looking forward to this.'

'Me too,' she said joyously.

When they finally broke apart, Jamie took her hand. 'Tish,' he said tentatively, at first, but the warmth of the hug lingered on, renewing his confidence, 'there *is* no other girl, it was a daydream. You, you're real. You're the one I care about, you're my mate, the person I count on, but more than that, the one I look out for, the one I love.'

'Oh, Jamie,' Tish's voice was as gentle as he'd ever heard it. 'I'm so glad. I feel the same way. I nearly died when you said there was someone else. And then when you texted and said we should meet, we should talk... I was gonna tell you what I felt, whatever you said.'

Taking her in his arms, Jamie thought he would burst with happiness. This was real. This was Tish. His girlfriend.

The *Wessex Daily* arrived in the village shop at around midday, but Isabelle, feeling so sick she could hardly swallow a cup of tea, couldn't wait till then. While the children were eating their cereal, she slipped upstairs to Richard's computer and, with trembling fingers, went on the paper's website.

It was as bad as she'd feared – worse. The whole front page was filled with a huge picture of Oliver apparently trying to placate an angry mob, with the banner headline 'Village turn on local MP'.

She didn't have time to see more. Becky shouted impatiently from downstairs, 'Come on, Mum. We've got carol practice this morning; I want to get there early.'

At more or less the same time, Oliver looked at the pictures on his computer. His face was grim.

He'd spent most of Sunday evening in long conversations with his branch chairman and with Central Office, and it had been decided the best course of action was to carry on as normal, which meant going to London and being in the House on Monday afternoon.

When they'd returned from London yesterday evening, Jamie had gone straight out to meet Tish and had returned in such a glow of happiness, Oliver decided to wait until breakfast before he told him the *Wessex Daily* were devoting their front page to Oliver Merfield, the MP, who'd let his constituents down and faced an angry mob.

'So what are we gonna do, Dad? Just sit and take the shit? Is that what your bosses want? I don't believe it!' Jamie was close to tears, disguising the fact by angrily stuffing books into an already bulging school bag.

'You've got to see it from the party's point of view, Jamie,' Oliver said gently. 'As far as Central Office is concerned, it'll be a nasty little story about the uselessness of one of their most junior MPs. It's not that important – we're about six months off a general election so I'll just have to work much harder within the constituency to convince those who don't know otherwise that there isn't a word of truth in it and I'm the best MP they've ever had.' He smiled at his son. 'It'll blow over, Jamie.'

'But you're letting them get away with it. That's so unfair.'

'We'll have to see. I suspect there'll be quite a groundswell of anger from people for being misrepresented – I think the redoubtable Elsie Bates and my grandmother are putting their heads together as we speak. And I think it's quite probable the editor will be called to account.

He's behaved very badly, stupid man, and it doesn't need me to point the finger for him to be exposed. So, although it's going to be an unpleasant few days, in the long run we'll be the survivors, Jamie, you'll see.'

Isabelle walked the girls to school that morning, feeling like a condemned criminal with a few hours left before her execution. She doubted anybody else would be bothered to look up the local paper on the internet, so she had till midday to live what was left of her normal life.

Paula breezed up to her in the playground as she was leaving for Milo's workshop.

'Isabelle, I meant to pop round to see you yesterday, only I had such a hangover...' She laughed, happily, 'I must've had more than ten Bacardi Breezers, then, after you left, Lenny insisted we polish off his bottle of Jack Daniel's. I was pie-eyed when we fell into bed.'

Isabelle tried to smile. 'It was a nice party. Thanks very much for asking me. The girls had a great time, too. Clemmie didn't want to go home, but then she never does.'

'It's lovely the way she and Kylie are such great mates. Er, Isabelle...' Paula hesitated.

'Yes?'

'That card you gave me, did you really mean it? Only, I'd understand if you haven't got the time... The card's so cool, I'm gonna frame it.'

Isabelle smiled, warmly this time. 'No, I mean it. If that's what you'd like and Lenny's okay about it. Castles, princesses, unicorns, dragons – choose your wall and I'll paint whatever you fancy.'

Paula was almost overcome at the thought. 'I've never had a real painting before. Isabelle, you're the best!'

By eleven thirty, Isabelle could bear it no longer. She'd been unable to lose herself in work, the studio felt hot and stuffy, and she was dizzy with the combined smells of paint and spirit. It was still too early for the paper delivery, but she had to get out, go for a walk, calm herself down; so she made an excuse about feeling unwell and left. To her relief, Milo made no fuss and hardly seemed to notice her going.

Unlike the day before, the sky was a leaden, uniform grey. A cold wind blew, carrying a hint of rain. Isabelle huddled inside her duffle coat and at the end of the farm track crossed the road, making for the riverbank where she'd seen the kingfisher and where she'd sobbed in Charlie's arms. That all seemed so long ago, even though it was only the day before yesterday. He couldn't come to her rescue now. There was no rescue to be had – how could there be? She was the wife of the man who'd destroyed Oliver Merfield's reputation.

It was as if the kingfisher had been waiting for her. He perched on a small branch overhanging the silvery-black water, his head tilted, his beak towards her, long and thin, rapier-like. She froze, hardly daring to breathe in case she disturbed him, willing him not to fly off.

The bird sat there, apparently unperturbed by her presence. His brilliance was extraordinary in the dank and dripping surroundings of the riverbank and she gazed and gazed, her eyes wide, her brain trying to unlock the elusive properties of that iridescent colour.

As if aware he was being scrutinised, the bird flicked round on his branch and showed her his magnificent rusty-red breast. Then without warning he took off, winging up the river, but he didn't go far and landed on another overhanging branch.

Isabelle slowly walked towards him. When she was nearly abreast of him he sped off once more, but again for only a short distance, appearing to wait for her until she nearly caught him up, when he flew off again. In this way Isabelle, spellbound, followed the kingfisher for some way along the riverbank, her misery temporarily forgotten, her senses mesmerised by the enchanting bird.

Finally he landed on a thin branch of willow on the opposite side of the river and waited until she stood at the edge of the bank, watching him, enraptured.

Cocking his head to one side, then the other, the kingfisher seemed to be appraising her. As she watched he began gently bouncing up and down on the branch; then without warning, with a shrill shriek and with Exocet-like speed, he streaked off, a flash of blue just above the surface of the water, back the way they had come.

Isabelle watched till the bird was out of sight. For a few minutes she stood there, staring down the river, feeling odd, almost disembodied; then slowly she retraced her steps, her eyes fixed on the river all the way, in case she should see the kingfisher again.

'Your husband's gone to town,' said Rita grimly, as she handed the newspaper over. 'There's more inside. Take a look.'

Trembling, Isabelle opened the paper. A double-page spread devoted to the meeting was full of pictures of angry faces, including a close-up of Nanny looking distressed, with a caption that read, 'Elderly resident joins in the protest'.

'That's rich, that is!' Rita stabbed a finger at the offending paragraph. 'What a cheek! Just wait till Nanny sees it! But what I don't understand is, you were there, you know what happened. Why didn't you tell your husband how it was? No one's going to take this lying down, Isabelle. It's immoral. Your husband, for one, isn't going to be able to show his face in the village.'

'No,' said Isabelle wretchedly. 'No, he's ruined everything; for all of us.'

'He's certainly dug out the dirt,' continued Rita, turning a page and pointed at another headline over a much smaller item. 'Where did that come from? I've never heard nothin' – no one's said nothin' to me.'

Ashen-faced, Isabelle read the offending item. Captioned 'MP's son dealt in drugs', it read:

Villagers of Summerstoke were reeling after learning the son of their MP was expelled from school for drugs. It was a double whammy for the folk of this sleepy village, who have already attacked their MP for failing them in their post office campaign. 'We're bitterly disappointed in him,' said one resident. 'I've two teenage children

– we don't want drugs brought into this village.'

Somehow she got herself out of the shop and stumbled home. Letting herself in, she slammed the door behind her and, leaning against it, sobbed great, painful, convulsive gasps of shame and pity. How could he? How could he bring Jamie into it? He'd stooped so low, lower than she could ever imagine. What damage had he done, not just to Oliver but to Oliver's son? How could he? And why? Why? Not just to sell newspapers. There was more to it than that, there had to be.

Her tears eventually dried, and dully she looked up. The house was silent, holding its breath, waiting for her next move. She had grown to love this house, to feel it was hers, and now she was going to lose it and it was all Richard's fault.

All his fault. Bastard!

She straightened up and wandered into the room she had so recently finished painting. White, all white – sterile: that was her relationship with Richard, devoid of anything, blank.

The anger stirring within her suddenly ignited, erupting like a volcano, carrying her out of the empty room to the cellar, where her paints and brushes had been stored against the day when she would, as Richard always so patronisingly put it, start her painting again.

Start?

She'd start, all right. And she'd start in there; she'd expunge him from that room and from her life if she could.

She took a large, wedge-shaped brush, dipped it into a pot of paint and, with the aid of a stepladder, painted an arc of ultramarine across the wall. She opened another pot, and, dipping her hands into the paint, started to rub on splodges of vermilion.

Chris Gorman, lounging in a chair in Richard's office, watched Neville Budd, sitting in Richard's seat, tap in a number and wait. After a few seconds Neville's whole demeanour changed: he stiffened, his eyes widened, he licked his lips and flickered a glance across at Chris, nodding slightly. Chris leaned forward, alert, poised, straining to catch the voice at the other end of the phone.

'Mr Tranter, Neville Budd here, news editor, *Wessex Daily*... Yes, you're right, we have met... Thing is, Mr Tranter, we have a bit of a problem on our hands. I think you need to be aware of a situation that's arisen here and is getting hotter by the minute. If we're not careful, we're going to have the whole rat pack down on the *Wessex Daily*... No, he's not in till four thirty and in fact, sir – and I hate to say this – this is all breaking over *his* head. Let me explain.'

In his dingy office in the bowels of Norman Shaw South, Oliver Merfield sat, his head in his hands, looking at the pages of the *Wessex Daily* Susannah had faxed to him.

Bloody Richard Garnett! he thought bitterly. Poor Jamie, why's he been dragged into the ring? Why? Why? If it had just been the pictures he could have dismissed it all as some sort of stupid vendetta, but in printing the story about Jamie the paper had gone for his jugular. What could he

548

do? The paper daren't print Jamie's name, but as he was Oliver's only child they might just as well have emblazoned it across the front page. It was a double hit. Wondering how he could protect his son from all the consequent fallout, Oliver thought of Juliet in Los Angeles. Maybe he should resign and take Jamie with him to live in the States – make a fresh start.

It was quite probable, he thought bitterly, he wouldn't have to resign. The chances were, when this news got out, the local party would want another candidate to fight the next election, one without baggage.

But Oliver wasn't a loser. He wouldn't flee the field without giving battle. His horror and disgust gave way to fury. He thumped his fist on the desk. What sort of example am I giving Jamie if I just capitulate? And for Chrissake how would Jamie cope if he thought he'd cost me my job? He leaped to his feet and angrily paced the tiny office. Dammit, Richard Garnett isn't going to get away with this! What a complete and utter bastard! May he bloody rot in hell! He kicked his desk so hard, the plywood veneer splintered.

The clock on the wall showed nearly two o'clock. Time to go.

As he emerged into the street, a man moved in front of him and there was a camera flash. Oliver frowned. The *Wessex Daily* had only been out for a couple of hours and surely a local spat would be of no interest to the national press.

''Scuse me, Mr Merfield,' the reporter said politely, 'but I wonder if I could ask you a few questions?'

'Sure. What about?' Oliver tried a pleasant smile, his heart thumping so hard it hurt.

'This picture.'

He held out a newspaper cutting.

'I don't know whether you're aware of it, but it appeared in yesterday's *Sunday's Chat.*' He showed it to Oliver. 'I wonder if you recognise either of the persons involved?'

Again Oliver was aware of the camera flash as he peered at the cutting. His mouth went dry. It was a picture of Juliet leaning forward, gazing intently at a man kissing her hand. Her expression was hard to read, but the photograph suggested an intimacy beyond friendship.

Oh, Juliet, Juliet! Oliver groaned inwardly.

To the reporter he said, as lightly as he could manage, 'Yes, I know both of them. That's my wife having dinner with a neighbour of ours, Richard Garnett. I can't imagine why *Sunday's Chat* should find it of the slightest interest.'

With something of a flourish, the reporter produced another cutting. 'This came out a couple of hours ago. I guess it's as much of a surprise as the picture of Richard Garnett and your wife. Would you care to comment?'

It was one of the pictures Susannah had emailed him earlier.

He said coldly, 'There's no truth in that story. For whatever reason, Richard Garnett is playing a dangerous game. It would take very little effort to go to Summerstoke and find out that the meeting, apart from a disruptive element who were ejected by the villagers themselves early on, was conducted in an orderly and constructive manner.'

'Are you saying Richard Garnett set you up?'
Oliver was silent.
'That he employed what you call the "disruptive element" so he could get these photographs?'
Oliver remained silent.
'And he did so because he was determined to discredit you because he was having an affair with your wife?'
Oliver tried to keep a clear head. If he said nothing, the press would take his silence as confirmation. 'Juliet, oh Juliet!' He felt sick to his soul.
'I think the latter explanation is unlikely. He is a friend of my wife's that's all.'
'Which is why he also ran the story on your son? Strange sort of friend. Is there any truth in that allegation, by the way?'
'You should know better than to ask me a question like that.' Oliver was dismissive. 'Now, if you'll excuse me, I'm about to miss the afternoon session in the House.'
It was a thin debate that afternoon and Oliver found a seat easily enough, but he couldn't concentrate on the issues being discussed.
Where had that photograph of Juliet and Richard come from? Were they having an affair? He really didn't think so – Juliet had flirtations but never anything more. She was self-serving in everything she did, and Oliver couldn't see what she'd gain from an affair with Richard, unless she was in love with him, and Oliver believed, implicitly, that if Juliet loved anyone else apart from herself she loved him. But beyond all that ... that tackiness, the question had to be asked: had

Juliet, in one of her tête-à-têtes, told Richard about Jamie? He had to speak to her. He glanced at his watch. Barely three o'clock – she wouldn't be awake yet.

He thought of Richard Garnett. What had he, Oliver, done to make Richard go out on such a limb? Poor Isabelle. What would she make of all this?

He thought of her huge, tragic eyes, her wan face, her brave attempts to make light of her appalling husband's actions when she had spelled out, yesterday evening, what she feared was going to happen. She'd had no idea Richard was going to finger Jamie, and she, he guessed, would be nearly as upset as he. How would she cope with the press pack baying for her husband's blood? Because now they'd got hold of that photo there would be no stopping them. And how would she react when they thrust the picture of Juliet and Richard into her hands?

And Jamie, how would he react to the photo? Would he think his mother had betrayed him?

For the first time Oliver felt angry with Juliet. How could she have been so thoughtless? She'd put them all in the shit.

It was no good. He couldn't stay and act as if nothing had happened.

Making his excuses, he slid along the banquettes and, taking the underground passage, made his way back to his office.

From the winking light on his answer-phone, he could tell it was full. He didn't listen to any of the messages. Instead, he phoned Summerstoke Manor.

Charlotte answered, and after a brief exchange Oliver told her he was returning to Summerstoke that night.

'Jamie's in the front line, Aunt Charlotte. I'll phone the College so they know precisely what's going on. It's possible no one in Summerbridge will have seen the story yet – the *Wessex Daily* isn't a local paper there, after all. And there's a strong chance Jamie won't have seen his mum's photograph, but you can be sure someone will show it to him. I need to preempt that and soften the blow somehow. Juliet isn't to blame, and I need to be with him to make sure he understands. Oh, and Charlotte, would you ask Nanny to go round and see if Isabelle's all right?'

Jamie froze; the chocolate biscuit in his mouth turned to a tasteless mix of grease and dust. He stared at the newspaper pushed under his nose.

'It's your mum, isn't it? She's Juliet Peters, isn't she?'

Jamie hardly knew his interrogator, a boy from the year below him. It was the mid-afternoon break. He and Tish had met in the college canteen to plan what they could do about the *Wessex Daily*'s campaign against his father, when the boy approached him with the newspaper.

'What is it, Jamie? Let's see.' Tish pulled the newspaper towards her.

'It *is* her, isn't it?' the boy persisted.

'Yes, so what?' Jamie growled. 'He's a friend of ours – it doesn't mean anything. When you're well known these pictures get taken all the time, for Chrissake. Now, if you've not got anything of

553

more interest to me, you can push off.'

The boy pulled a face. 'Okay, okay. Can I have my paper back?'

'You can have it minus this.' Jamie ripped the page out, ignoring the boy's protests. 'I don't want you going round spreading filthy insinuations. Now get lost.'

The boy scowled at him then turned and walked away, saying defiantly, 'You can keep it – everyone's seen it, anyway, an' it's obvious what they're up to.'

Tish and Jamie stared at the picture.

'Who is he?' Tish finally asked.

Jamie shrugged. 'Dunno.'

'But I thought you said–'

'If I'd said anything else, it would've made things worse, wouldn't it?' Jamie couldn't keep the anger out of his voice. 'If it's not enough some fuckin' newspaper is dishing the dirt on my dad, here's my mum doing it, too. I thought I couldn't bear it if she had to stay in the States, but I tell you, Tish, I couldn't bear it if she came back.'

The sullen grey day had given way to the gloom of early evening when Elsie emerged from her cottage, trim in a smart wool overcoat and woollen trilby.

'Off out, Gran?' Charlie took a break from his labours and smiled at the old lady as she crossed the yard to her car, drawing on her gloves, a newspaper tucked under one arm. He and Lenny were filling a skip with rubbish from an outhouse Charlie planned to convert into a holiday cottage.

'I've had a call from Mrs Godwin at the shop. Seems the place is crawling with the television and press and she needs help to deal with them.'

'What's going on?'

'Have you seen the local paper today?'

'No, I don't usually bother with it. Why?'

Elsie handed it to him. 'Have a quick look while I turn the car round.'

Charlie whistled when he saw the front page, and Lenny, peering over his shoulder, was equally astonished. 'Well I never, was they at the same meeting as us?'

Charlie turned to the inside pages. 'Here, Lenny, here's a nice one of you: "Angry villager shouts Merfield down".'

Lenny was not amused. 'Bloody 'ell, what do they think they're playin' at?'

'That,' said Elsie grimly, holding her hand out for the paper, 'is a question we should all be asking. And have a look at this little billet-doux.' She folded the paper open at another page and passed it to them, her lips pursed.

The two men read the brief article.

Lenny chuckled, but Charlie was shocked. 'God, that's playing rough.'

'Isn't it? I don't know how much the press have got hold of, but if they're here in numbers, as Rita Godwin suggests, there's going to be a right royal battle and it's not going to be very pleasant for anyone, especially poor Isabelle.'

Charlie stared at her. 'Isabelle? What's any of this got to do with her?'

'I'll tell you later. Must go. Bye.'

Unsettled, he gazed after her car as it hurtled

555

out of the farmyard in a cloud of exhaust fumes and dirt.

Lenny's mobile rang.

''Ello, darlin', what can I do for you...? No, I ain't seen her... I'll go and have a look and ring yer back, okay?'

He glanced at Charlie 'That was my missus. She's a tad worried 'cos Isabelle didn't pick her girls up from school. She's got 'em back at ours and wants me to go and see if Isabelle's with Milo and forgot the time.'

He'd barely finished speaking before Charlie was running across the yard to the workshop.

Milo looked up, irritated by the abrupt arrival. 'I say, Charlie, you might make less of a noise. You've completely broken my concentration.'

'Is Isabelle here?' Charlie's voice was sharp.

'No. She doesn't work here in the afternoons. I thought you knew that. I need a period of un-interrupted work, Charlie. Uninterrupted.' He was becoming increasingly annoyed.

'Sorry, Milo. It's just that she hasn't collected her kids from school and we wondered if she might still be here.'

'Far from it. She left early – said she wasn't feeling well.' Milo wasn't interested and was aching to get back to his work. 'She probably went to bed and fell asleep. Has anybody checked at her house?'

Lenny asked Paula the same question when he phoned her back, and reported the answer to Charlie. 'Paula's had her hands full with all the kiddies, but she tried phoning her on the mobile and the land line, and got no answer from either,

556

which is why she thought she might be up here.'

'Right, let's go.' Charlie started to head for his van.

'Where we goin', boss?'

'Over to her place, of course. It's not like her to forget her kids. And remember what Elsie said. I need to see she's all right.' His face furrowed with anxiety, he clambered into the cab.

'Oho,' Lenny said, softly, stroking his ponytail. 'If you ain't right, boy, you can shave yer whole bloomin' head.'

At the shop, Elsie pushed her way through a crowd of locals attracted by the television crew and the number of reporters milling about. Some, whom she recognised from the meeting, were being interviewed. She went from one to the other, hissing in their ears, 'I hope you're setting the record straight.'

She got inside in time to hear Rita say, 'No, I don't know nothing about drugs. What's that got to do with anything? Someone who shall be nameless put it about that we had rats in our basement. Rats! I ask you. And I haven't even got a basement. I told them that at the meeting, after Oliver finished his speech– Oh, Elsie, I'm glad you've got here. This gentleman's from the *Daily Mail* and the BBC's waiting outside to talk to us.' She turned to the reporter. 'Mrs Bates is the chair of our action group. She knows what's going on, probably better than me.'

Elsie, anticipating what she would be asked, determined to tell the reporter what she knew, and what she'd been told about the two hecklers, and about the *Wessex Daily*'s skewed and un-truthful reporting of the event. She ticked him off for suggesting anything involving Oliver Mer-field's son was anybody else's business and scorned the suggestion that people in the village felt betrayed because they hadn't been told.

She had not, however, expected to be asked about an alleged affair between Juliet Peters and Richard Garnett. For the first time in a long while, Elsie was rendered speechless.

By the time the scrum had subsided, she was really concerned about Isabelle. The poor girl hadn't mentioned anything about her husband's liaison with Oliver's wife. If this had just come out, how must she be feeling? And how was she coping with this feeding frenzy, for, vultures that they were, the press would have flocked to her house?

'Rita, have you seen Isabelle Garnett today?'

Rita sniffed. 'Yes, I have. She came in this mor-ning, just after the papers were out. I must say, I'm very disappointed in her, and I told her as much. She could've stopped all those lies being printed.'

'She did as much as she could and more, Rita. You were quite wrong to say what you did. The poor girl needs our support, not our disapproval. I must go straight over and see how she is.'

Lavender Grey stood looking down at her hus-band with something approaching exasperation.

'I can't believe you haven't been to see her, Andrew. You changed your text in church yester-day to lecture the village about loving our neighbours. Well, there wasn't much love expressed towards her in the surgery today, I can tell you. So typical of people – one minute she's a heroine for exposing Veronica Lester, and the next she's vilified for not having stopped those lies being printed in the paper. She's a sweet girl, Andrew. We need to make it quite clear to the village that whatever *he* may or may not have done, *she* has our support. People will respect that.'

The vicar looked wearily at his wife. 'I sometimes think, my dear, your vision of my standing in the community dates from another century. The people in this village will remember Isabelle Garnett for telling Veronica Lester what to do with a raspberry mousse long after they've forgotten my sermon on brotherly love.'

Lavender's mouth twitched. 'Yes, well... But do go and see her. She must be mortified by this coverage and as shocked as the rest of us by the insinuations about poor little Jamie Merfield. I don't suppose she has much influence over what her husband does at work. I know I don't.'

Heaving himself out of the armchair where he had been snoozing until his wife bustled in, the Reverend Grey chuckled, a dry, dusty chuckle which rose from deep within his chest and shook his whole frame. 'Which is why, my love, I'm going out into the cold, on a dreary evening, to see a parishioner who has never attended my church, to tell her that all's right with the world, even though I don't believe it.'

Lavender made to speak, but he held up his hand.

'But you're right. She's a nice little thing. She's

559

gentle and kind and she looks like one of the angels in the stained glass of the west window, so hold your peace, I'll go and comfort her as best I can. "Come to me, all who labour and are heavy laden, and I will give you rest", eh?'

It was shortly after four o'clock when Richard's old Jaguar pulled up in front of the brightly illuminated offices of the *Wessex Daily*. One of the directors' spaces was occupied. Richard raised his brows in surprise. Bob Tranter? What was he doing here? It was not like him to come down unannounced, and Richard's mobile had been silent all day. That, in itself, wasn't unusual. Neville Budd wouldn't bother him unless there was a crisis, but Bob Tranter, unannounced, could certainly be classified as that.

Richard's hangover hadn't cleared until midday so he'd left London after lunch. He'd toyed with the idea of ringing Issy, but decided to hold off until he'd seen his newspaper. He was puzzled Neville hadn't bothered to phone him back that morning, but at least he could tell Issy he'd tried.

Issy... What to do with Issy? He didn't want his marriage to come to an end, but clearly it had reached crisis point – at least from Issy's point of view. He'd ring her after the news meeting and suggest he go home to discuss things with her. And, he thought grimly, find out precisely what was going on between her and Oliver Merfield.

He strolled through the entrance, nodded to the receptionist in the foyer, who stared at him like a trapped rabbit, tapped in the code on the inner door that let him into the newspaper offices and pushed. Nothing happened. The door remained shut. He tapped in his code again. Again, nothing. He pushed the door, cursing irritably, then turned to the receptionist who regarded him with the same frozen expression.

'What the fuck's wrong with this door? It's not reading my code. Open it for me, would you?'

'I'm sorry, Mr Garnett,' she squeaked nervously, 'but the codes were changed this afternoon. Mr Tranter has asked you to wait for him here, in the foyer.'

'What?' Richard roared.

The reception and the office seemed to go silent as if everyone and everything were waiting for the next few minutes to be played out.

'Open that door,' he croaked, summoning all his strength to exert his authority but feeling it ebb away at the feet of this minion.

'Richard, nice to see you.' With a slight swish, the inner door closed behind Bob Tranter.

Some fifteen years younger than Richard, with plump, shiny features lightly tanned, cold eyes and a smile to match, he was an executive with a capital E from the tips of his coiffed hair to the toes of his shiny leather shoes.

With a well-oiled movement he glided forward, shook Richard's hand and steered him back to the entrance, talking the entire time. 'How are you? I thought we'd go out for tea, somewhere nice. We need to chat. No need to worry about the afternoon meeting – Neville's got that in hand. We'll take my car.'

Sitting on the leather upholstery in the back of Bob's car, staring at the greasy pores of the driver's neck, aware of the brightly lit city streets as they made their way to a smart but discreet hotel on the outskirts of Bath, listening to Bob's inconsequential social chatter, Richard felt as if he'd entered a surreal world. Nothing was as it seemed. He could have been in a tumbril, on his way to the guillotine – the only thing missing was the jeering crowds; those had been left behind at the office.

He was under no illusions: he was for the chop. No doubt he would be allowed back to collect his personal effects, and then the whole organisation would turn its back on him, the paper would come out tomorrow, the hole created by his departure would be filled, and it would be as if he'd never been. And all done so discreetly – so discreetly – with Bob maintaining this seamless, inane, small talk, sending the message that Richard had to play the game to the bitter end and not make any intemperate comment in front of the chauffeur.

There was just one surprise for him.

Having lambasted Richard for bringing the paper's integrity into question; berated him for the way he had abused his position; told him the paper would publicly disassociate itself from him in the event of any prosecution following not only the use of an unsubstantiated story involving a minor, but, more significantly, his employment of hecklers to fabricate a story – and having said all this while working his way through a plate of dainty sandwiches – Bob Tranter had just reached for a chocolate éclair when he stopped.

'I would have gone to my grave, Richard, puzzled someone with your professionalism and intellect should have run such risks. It just didn't stack up. And then I was shown this.'

He pulled out a newspaper cutting from his file and placed it on the table in front of Richard.

Richard stared at the picture of himself and Juliet.

'A lovely bit of stuff, I grant you, but, oh, Richard, you've been well and truly caught with your pants down, and I'm afraid things are going to get worse.' He spread his hands, almost apologetically. 'I'm afraid the big boys are on to this. We couldn't stop them. The story's too good – you must see that? You're a newspaperman, you know the score. It's ironic, isn't it? You've become the story that's going to make us the bucks.'

24

Isabelle ignored the bell, the hammering on the door, and the knocking on the window. She had closed all the downstairs shutters when the first of the press arrived, and returned to her work, illuminating the wall with a couple of angle poise lamps.

Immersed in her painting, she lost all track of time or place. The single arc of blue had been joined, complemented, blended, and leaped free of a mass of colour and shapes. Sometimes she used her brushes, sometimes her hands, sometimes a rag. Her face, hands and body were covered with smudges of paint. She had no thought for anything else – her anger, her pain, her loss, all were subsumed by the need to paint.

Finally, as she stepped back to look at her work, she became aware of a familiar voice calling.

'Isabelle? Isabelle, it's me, Charlie.'

Charlie.

For a moment she stood there, feeling slowly creeping back into her numbed mind.

Charlie.

She was so exhausted she wanted to lie down on the floor amid her paint pots and go to sleep, dreaming of the time he'd put his arms round her and held her.

'Isabelle, open the door. It's going to be all right, I promise you.'

Oh, Charlie... There was only one way he could make things all right and that was ... that was... It was so impossible it was painful to think about.

Slowly she walked to the front door and unlocked it.

To her shocked brain it seemed half the village had gathered on her doorstep: Elsie, Rita, Nanny, Lenny, the vicar – and Charlie.

'Isabelle?' someone asked, shaken by her paint-spattered, wild appearance.

Charlie pushed his way through and put his arm round her.

'We were worried,' he said gently. 'You forgot to pick the girls up.'

'Oh, my God!' Isabelle was horrified. 'What time is it? Where are they? Are they safe?'

Lenny piped up, 'Paula's got 'em – they're right as rain. She's given 'em their tea.'

Elsie took Isabelle's hand. 'Let's all go inside, dear. You're shivering.'

In a daze, Isabelle let herself be led into the one room that was blazing with light.

There was a brief, stunned silence as they all stared at the painting. Then:

'Bugger me!' said Lenny.

'My goodness!' said the vicar.

'My God!' said Rita.

'Well, I never!' said Nanny.

'Gracious!' said Elsie.

'Fantastic!' said Charlie. He threw back his head and laughed. 'What is it with you, Isabelle Garnett? You come up on the inside and take me by surprise every single time.'

'Langton. My name is Isabelle Langton.'

Then suddenly everyone was talking. Rita told Isabelle she wasn't to worry about the newspaper – everyone would understand she couldn't prevent it. Elsie squeezed her hand and told her she knew about Juliet and Richard. Nanny thought it would be a good idea if Isabelle went and had some supper at the Manor, where Oliver was going to join them, and that Oliver had phoned and particularly told them to look after her. Lenny said he'd drop the girls round to the Manor, if that was what she wanted. And the vicar said something about 'the comfortable words', looking very uncomfortable, then left, saying he would call the next day as she was in such good hands, casting a meaningful look at Charlie, whereupon Charlie removed his arm, which had been round Isabelle's shoulders all this time.

'I'm not sure I know what's going on, and I'll

doubt I'll find out with this lot fussing round you,' he muttered. 'Are you going to be at the workshop tomorrow?'

Isabelle nodded.

'I'll take you to the pub for lunch – if you want to go, that is?'

Again Isabelle nodded; she was beyond speech. The one thing she knew was that she didn't want Charlie to leave. But he had to – she was a married woman with other, more pressing, matters requiring her attention.

Jamie was nowhere to be seen when Oliver joined the ladies, who were as always, resplendently dressed for dinner, and sipping gin and tonic.

'Thanks, Aunt Charlotte.' Oliver accepted a drink gratefully. 'Has Jamie come home yet?'

'Yes, he has,' replied his grandmother evenly. 'He came back a good hour ago. He's in his room.'

'How is he?' Oliver asked anxiously.

'Not good, the poor lamb,' replied Nanny. 'He insisted on seeing that ... that paper as soon as he got in. He's very upset.'

'Hardly surprising,' commented Charlotte. 'He'd been prepared for the worst as far as the pictures were concerned, but the drugs story was totally unexpected.'

'And someone had shown him the picture of Juliet.' Louisa studied her long, exquisitely painted, pale pink nails. 'I rather think he blames her for letting the cat out of the bag. One can sympathise...'

'Yes,' said Oliver wretchedly. 'I'd better go and

566

talk to him, if you'll excuse me.'

'Do.' Mrs Merfield stretched out a withered arm encased in black lace and said with unusual warmth, 'He won't speak to any of us, not even Nanny. We've grown very fond of him, Oliver – I'd like both of you to know that. As far as we're concerned, everyone makes mistakes and must be allowed to put those mistakes behind them. His home is here, in this village, with us, for as long as he needs us.'

'Thank you, Grandmère.' Oliver's voice was husky.

'I've invited Isabelle and her children to join us for dinner. She's so upset, poor thing, I don't think she should be on her own this evening.'

'You're right, Nanny, she is a poor thing. At least we've got you behind us. She's got nobody.'

Oliver tapped on his son's bedroom door. 'Jamie, it's Dad. May I come in?'

After a couple of seconds a key was turned and the door slowly opened. Jamie's face was swollen and blotchy, and Oliver's heart went out to him.

He held out his arms. 'Oh, Jamie...'

The boy fell into his father's embrace and wept afresh. Oliver, holding him tight, found himself crying, too.

When the storm had passed, they sat side by side on the bed.

'I'm sorry, Dad, I'm really sorry. I've fucked it up for you, haven't I?'

'No, you haven't. You certainly haven't. I'm the one who should be saying sorry to you.'

'What?' Jamie stared at Oliver. 'How do you

567

work that out? I'm the one who got expelled, remember?'

'Yes, and you paid for your mistake. If I'd been anyone else, that would have been the end of it, but I'm a public figure and the target of a particularly malicious attack. They used you to get at me, which is desperately unfair, and I'm sorry, Jamie, I really am.'

'How did they find out about me? Was it Mum? She's such a fuckin' blabbermouth.'

'Now, Jamie, is that likely? Your mother loves you very much.'

'Does she?' replied Jamie bitterly. 'I don't see much evidence. I don't think she loves me and I don't think she loves you, Dad. Have you seen that picture of her with that man? D'you know who he is?'

'Yes, I have seen it, and yes, I do know who he is.' Oliver gave a sad smile. 'Strangely enough, Oliver, I think the photograph is going to help us win through.'

'How?'

'Because the man with your mum is the newspaper editor who's been orchestrating this campaign against me. He's been conducting a very personal vendetta and I couldn't understand why. Now I do. This photograph has exposed him. The national press are on to it already, and in the next few days it will all come out. We just have to hold up our heads and sit tight.'

'Was Mum having an affair with him, then? Is that what you're saying? So she must have told him about me? How can you be so calm about it all?' Jamie, no longer weepy, was furious.

'Jamie, I know your mother.' Oliver shook his head wearily. 'I don't think for one moment she would ever do anything to hurt either of us.'

'That photograph says different.'

'It may look incriminating, but then those photographs of the meeting at the village hall made *me* look a complete idiot.'

Jamie said nothing, but from the look on his face Oliver knew he had a long way to go to convince him of Juliet's innocence.

If Juliet *was* innocent, that is.

'No problem, Andrew, I'll be with you in about thirty minutes. Bye.'

Hugh Lester replaced the phone and, humming lightly, went into the kitchen, where Veronica was loading the dishwasher.

She looked up, eyebrows raised. Humming, for Hugh, was usually strictly post-coital.

'My God, darling, you look like the cat that's got the cream. Who was that?'

'Andrew Hill. He wants me to call over to his place.'

'At eight thirty in the evening? It must be urgent.'

'Yep. I reckon he's ready to tell me the chairmanship of the Land Association is in the bag. The closing date for nominations is Thursday and I, my darling, am the front runner, by a long way. So, yes, what with the billet-doux in today's paper' – his pleasure at Oliver Merfield's treatment by the *Wessex Daily* had surprised even Veronica – 'I *am* feeling well pleased. Justifiably so. I'll see you later. Put some champagne on ice.'

The whole way over to Andrew Hill's, Hugh's high good humour did not abate. Clever Richard. He'd done it! Merfield was well and truly humiliated – those pictures had nailed him, and he wouldn't be able to show his face in the village again. As for the story about his son's nasty little habit, a stroke of genius. Good old Richard. Having done that, what else might he not achieve for Hugh, once Hugh was running the Landowners?

He turned his Land-Rover Sport into Andrew Hill's courtyard, parked and knocked on the front door. The hall light went on and Andrew Hill answered the door.

'Evening, Andrew.' Hugh was bubbling with excitement. Andrew Hill, however, was distinctly lack-lustre in his greeting.

He followed the chairman into his study and took the seat offered. But he was not invited to have a drink, or offered one of those rather good Havana cigars pressed on him on previous occasions.

He'd barely had time to register these omissions, when Andrew Hill picked up a newspaper from his desk. 'Have you seen the *Wessex Daily* today, Hugh?'

'Yes, as a matter of fact I have.' Hugh tried adopting a sympathetic tone. 'Your man made rather a mess of things, didn't he?'

'Did he?'

'Well, according to these photographs he did. Terrible mess. You must be pretty cut up about it.'

'We are, Hugh, we are.'

Hugh was starting to feel somewhat uncomfortable. He'd expected Andrew to get stuck into the chairmanship nominations for the Landowners, not faff around talking about Oliver. But there was no point wasting this golden opportunity to put the boot in. 'It must be dreadful to discover your MP's such a lame duck,' he said smoothly. 'His behaviour can't inspire any confidence in the electorate, let alone your members. I assume you're going to have him de-selected?'

'Is that what you'd like to happen?'

'Me? My wishes hardly come into it, but I suppose if I'm considering contributing to Conservative Party funds, I need to know the representative has your confidence, one hundred per cent.'

'Well, he does.'

'Pardon?'

'He does have our confidence, one hundred per cent. However, you do not.'

'Pardon?'

Andrew Hill tapped the newspaper. 'We've good evidence these hecklers weren't genuine dissenters. They were set up so the *Wessex Daily* could get the photographs they needed to discredit Oliver Merfield.'

Hugh stared at him. 'What?'

'And it turns out, these hecklers are men in your employ, Hugh. What do you say to that?'

'Bollocks!'

After supper, Oliver walked Isabelle and the girls home. Isabelle was almost transparent with fatigue, and he hesitated to burden her with further discussion, but there was one area that needed to be broached.

'It was a bit like a war cabinet, this evening,' he began lightly. 'Us all sitting round the table with Grandmère at the head, presiding over tactics.'

'She certainly is a formidable woman.' Isabelle was impressed by the Merfield ladies, and thought wistfully how wonderful it would be to belong to such a family. 'In fact, I'd go so far as to say the women of your family are amazing. They weren't in the slightest bit fazed by the accusations against Jamie, were they?'

'No, of course not. I told them all about it when we first came here.'

'But they were so upfront about it, and told him to be, too. They'll see anyone off, you can be sure of that. I wouldn't be in your chairman's shoes for anything. What do you think he'll do? He can't hold Jamie's drugs thing against you, can he?'

'He ticked me off for not telling him about it – apparently, neither I nor my family have the right to privacy. But no, now the whole sorry saga of Richard's campaign is unfolding, it's unlikely my position will be threatened.'

'So what can he do about the Lesters' involvement? As far as I know Hugh Lester isn't a paid-up member of any party, although the Conservatives would seem to be his natural home.'

'Thanks very much!'

Isabelle laughed. 'Sorry, Oliver, but you know what I mean.'

'Yes. Thing is, we've been courting Hugh Lester for a fat donation; one I understand he's about to give. He may not be a member, but if you're one of the elite circle of donors you can expect to be very well treated, and that's probably what he and his wife are after. I suspect the chairman will tell him to stuff his donation – putting it more elegantly, of course.'

'Which means Hugh and Veronica become social pariahs, at least as far as you lot are concerned?'

'Yes, but we lot have influence beyond our party interests, remember that. This is a shire, Isabelle. Form counts for a great deal. What Hugh has done is bad form. He'll find invitations to all sorts of social functions, private or otherwise, withdrawn or not forthcoming. That's where Grand-mère comes into her own.'

'Blimey. It's like a rural mafia.'

He laughed. 'It's a powerful network of influence, but there's nothing criminal about it.'

They reached the end of the Manor drive and turned into the High Street. In the reassuring glow of the streetlights, the girls danced ahead.

'Isabelle,' Oliver began hesitantly, 'that photograph... In all probability, it doesn't mean what it seems to mean. I know Juliet.'

'And I know Richard,' replied Isabelle in a low voice. 'It didn't come as such a shock, Oliver. I don't know where or when that photo was taken, but they've seen each other on more than one occasion, I know they have.'

'Because they're both egocentric people: they're driven by what *they* want at any given time, without thinking about the impact on anyone else. Juliet would be out for a good time. As she saw it, stuck here in the country she had the right to seek entertainment where she could. It doesn't mean she'd contemplate having an affair with anyone. A flirtation, maybe, but an affair? No.'

Isabelle stopped and looked sadly up at him. 'That's the difference between them. You may be right – they may not have done anything. But Richard wanted to. Not only would he contemplate it, he'd do his level best to make it happen and it would only be a matter of time before he got his way. He always does.'

'Do you think that was behind his attempt to destroy me? Jealousy? Rather than because he got carried away trying to boost his sales?'

'Possibly. I don't know. Whatever it was, it's destroyed us.'

Oliver could think of nothing reassuring to say, and in silence they turned into the Old Vicarage's drive.

'Are you expecting him home this evening?'

'I don't know. He might have phoned, but I haven't picked up any messages.'

'Have you thought what you're going to do?'

'Endlessly.' She gave a deep sigh. 'And what about you?'

'I'm going to phone Juliet tonight.'

'Will she... I'm sorry Oliver, this is so awful, but will she tell you the truth?'

'I've never known her not to. She's never bothered to make things up, however hurtful the truth might be.'

'I guess I want you to tell me what she says,' said Isabelle awkwardly. She stopped at the front door and looked up at the dark house. 'Well, we got this house by unfair means. It's quite possible we'll have to sell it. How would you like to have first offer?'

'Veronica? Veronica? Where the devil are you?'

She had just settled down to watch the news, a glass of wine in her hand, when she heard the front door crash open and Hugh bellowing in the hall.

'I'm in the sitting room. What on earth are you shouting like that for?'

Hugh appeared in the doorway. His face was livid.

Veronica looked at him, startled. 'Why, darling, whatever's the matter?'

'What have you been up to?'

He was so incandescent with fury he could barely spit the words out.

'Me? Nothing. Why? What on earth is this?'

'Nothing? Are you sure? Did you not tell Pete and Stefan to liven things up at Oliver Merfield's little meeting on Friday?'

Veronica's mouth dropped open.

'I've been to see them. They told me you wanted to do a friend a favour. That little favour, Vee, has cost me dear. Do you know what this is?' He waggled a piece of paper in front of her.

She shook her head.

'It's a cheque, Vee, a cheque for our tickets to the Bath and West Christmas dinner. It's been returned. It would seem our presence there is no longer welcome.'

Veronica found her voice. 'But that's outrageous! How did he...? He can't do that. What's it

575

got to do with him?'

'Oh, he can, and he has. Socially, we're dead meat, Vee, Hill made that quite clear. No more invitations to things that matter, and certainly no possibility of being elected chairman of the Landowners. In fact, I'll be lucky if I'm not asked to resign from the committee.'

'He can't do that. He can't! He's coming to our dinner party.' A note of hysteria entered Vee's voice.

'Dinner party! You can forget that. Just wait and see, one by one your friends will find some excuse not to come. We're out in the cold, Vee. What the fuck did you think you were doing? They thought it was *me!* Offering a donation to the party with one hand, and wrecking their man's public meeting with the other. Hill was hopping mad. I've never been so humiliated in all my life! I *told* Richard bloody Garnett not to implicate me in any way, and then you ... you have to stick your nose in and compromise me in the most comprehensive way. It was such a stupid thing to do, I can't imagine why you, of all people, didn't think it through. Are you so infatuated with Richard Garnett you'll do anything he asks you? Tell me, Vee, are you? Are you?'

For the first time, in thirty years, Veronica burst into tears.

It was nearly midnight when Oliver got through to Juliet. She had just come out of her first session in the dubbing studio and was not in the best of moods.

'I'm sorry, Ollie, it's been a hard day and I've

576

got to study the next bit of script before this evening. What is it? Can't it wait?'

'No, Juliet, it can't. A picture of you and Richard Garnett has appeared in a Sunday rag.'

'Oh?' Juliet didn't sound in the least interested.

'The thing is, for reasons too complicated to go into now, it's going to be in all the nationals tomorrow, and not only am I under siege, but Jamie has seen it and is really upset.'

'But that's ridiculous! Why on earth should the press–?'

'The thing is, Juliet, I've always believed you tell me the truth. I need you to tell me the truth now. It's really important, darling. You must understand.'

'You sound so melodramatic, Ollie. What is it? Listen, I really don't have much time. What is it you want to know?'

Oliver took a deep breath. 'Are you having, or have you had, an affair with Richard Garnett?'

There was a silence on the other end of the phone and in that silence, Oliver went cold. He'd been so sure of her … supposing...?

'Ollie, you should know me better.' Her voice was crisp. 'You're an idiot if you think I'd have an affair with Richard Garnett – or with anyone else, for that matter. I've been out with him on the odd occasion, sure – he was good fun. But that's as far as it goes, and if he says different it just is not true. He tried it on, but I told him to get lost. It sounds like a lot of fuss about nothing. Ollie, I love you. Please give me a little credit. Now I've really got to go. I'll ring you later and we can talk then. Bye, darling. Love to Jamie.'

'Juliet, there's something else I need to know–'
But she'd gone. Oliver stared at the phone in his hand. He believed her denial, but he didn't know whether to cry from sheer relief or from exasperation that Juliet could be so blithely unaware of the damage caused by her behaviour, the destructive fall out, the level of hurt inflicted, however unintentionally, on those caught up in her wake and on Jamie in particular.

Shortly after nine, when Isabelle had finally turned out the light in the girls' room, she heard someone knocking at the door.

Puzzled, she went down the stairs. If it had been Richard he'd have let himself in, and she couldn't think who else it could be. Unless it was another bloody reporter.

'Who is it?'

The answer took her completely by surprise.

'It's Milo.'

He stood in her doorway, naked apart from his loincloth, and, nodding at her, walked straight past her without waiting to be invited in. 'Charlie tells me you've been painting. May I see it?'

Silently she took him into the room and turned the lights on.

He grunted and stood in the middle of the floor, staring at the wall in silence.

Isabelle stole a glance at him. His face was impassive. She felt so nervous she could hardly breathe. She argued she didn't give a damn if he didn't think it was any good but she knew she did, she did bloody care.

She felt weak.

Milo grunted again, then turned to her. 'I'd say that was worth waiting, how many years for? There's only one problem.'

'Oh? What?'

'I can't see how we're going to get it up to London.'

Charlie had told him about Isabelle's extraordinary painting over supper at Marsh Farm. Milo feigned nothing more than polite interest, but in truth he was really excited.

Isabelle would have been amazed to learn that Milo had been covertly watching her first tentative dabblings. He remembered her talent and couldn't, wouldn't, believe something so huge could have vanished altogether. He'd grown fond of her, but that wasn't the point. His whole life was committed to his painting and he couldn't conceive of anyone abandoning their talent as Isabelle appeared to have done.

When he'd finished his evening stint in the studio he decided to run over to the Old Vicarage and take a look for himself. Reaching the bridge, he turned into the High Street.

Paula, drawing the curtains in her children's bedroom, saw the tall, apparently naked figure as he momentarily ran under a street light.

'It's the streaker!' she squeaked and ran to the top of the stairs. 'Lenny, Lenny, quick, it's the streaker. After him!'

Lenny, about to relax in front of the telly, appeared at the bottom of the stairs in his stockinged feet. 'What's that, Paula? What yer on about?'

'It's the streaker,' shrieked Paula, clomping down the stairs as fast as her high-heeled furry mules would let her. 'He just went past, going up the High Street, as bold as anything. After him.'

'This is daft, I'll never catch him up,' grumbled Lenny, but he pulled on the wellington boots he'd discarded by the door and, urged on by Paula, hurried off after the streaker.

Milo had nearly reached the Old Vicarage when a couple came out of the Foresters Arms. They stopped in their tracks at the sight of a tall, apparently naked man turning into the Old Vicarage driveway. 'It's him!' whispered the woman in fascinated horror. 'It's the streaker and he's gone into the Garnetts'. What shall we do? Go after him?'

'We should get the police,' said her companion, who'd no intention of tackling a naked man, and probably a lunatic, for all he knew. 'Or the vicar,' he added, prompted by the sight of the church opposite.

'Yes, he'd know what to do. Come on, quick, before he does anything.'

'Like what?' said her companion. Following her across the road, he met Lenny hurrying along, accompanied by a couple of others who had been similarly disturbed by sightings of the streaker.

They had a hurried consultation. Half of them elected to go and get the vicar and phone the community policeman, and the other half, led by Lenny, concerned for Isabelle's safety, decided to go and check out the grounds of the Old Vicarage.

'Supposing,' said one of Lenny's party as they cautiously moved up the drive, 'Supposing the streaker turns out to be her old man?'

'Oh lord,' whispered another, 'you've got a point there. This streaker only appeared after they moved here, didn't he?'

When they reached the house they decided to fan out and search the grounds before alarming Isabelle. They found nothing, and had re-assembled a little distance from the house when the rest of the party arrived, accompanied by a very unhappy vicar and the community police-man, who was tut-tutting under his breath about the unorthodox nature of the gathering.

Isabelle had just made Milo a whisky toddy when the doorbell rang.

'Who on earth can it be *this* time?' she muttered, going to the door.

When she opened it and saw a crowd assembled on her doorstep for the second time that evening, she could only gape.

'You all right, Isabelle?' asked Lenny, 'Only the streaker was seen runnin' into–'

'If you will allow me.' The constable pushed his way forward. 'Sorry to disturb you, madam, but it's as this gentleman said: a naked person was seen running into your–'

His mouth dropped open. Lenny gave a strangulated cry, 'Milo!' and the group behind him gasped, gawped and giggled.

Milo had appeared in the hallway behind Isabelle, and, as she slightly obscured their view, it appeared he was indeed naked.

'I think,' said Isabelle calmly, 'You must be referring to my friend Milo Steel. He was out jogging this evening and came to view a painting. But a streaker he is not.'

Milo joined her in the doorway and the cotton

loincloth ('Like one of those sumo wrestling things,' Lenny told Paula later) was visible to all.

The constable looked very uncomfortable. "Scuse me, sir, but we've had a number of reports over the last few weeks of someone streaking through the village. Er, do you always wear that, er, thing when you jog?'

'I don't jog, constable,' said Milo coldly, 'I run. I run every day of my working life, and I wouldn't dream of running through a village, naked. I'm not a fool.'

'No sir, I'm not suggesting... But there have been people who've seen you – that is, someone, without anything on. The vicar, here, for example.' He consulted his notebook. 'You, or rather, Mrs Grey, reported an incident on the footpath by the river, didn't you, sir? Do you recognise this person as that man?'

At this the Reverend Grey looked tortured. Milo Steel was a great man – and they'd been at school together. True, he had seen him, but it was dark, he might have been mistaken...

Truthfulness vied with loyalty in his brain. Loyalty won.

'Er no, no. What I mean is, I may have been mistaken about the nudity, erm ... but I didn't look closely, you know, and besides, constable, I was at school with Milo Steel – we went to the same prep school, you know. If it had been him, I'm sure I'd have recognised him.'

That settled the matter. The constable closed his notebook. 'Sorry to have troubled you, madam, sir. It's obviously been a false alarm. I'm sure I don't have to remind you, sir, that it *is* an offence to appear on the public highway un-clothed.'

'Thank you, Constable,' Milo drawled, bored by the whole encounter. 'I must be off, Isabelle. I'll see you in the morning.'

The small crowd parted to let him through, staring in stunned silence as he ran off down the drive, his bare feet making a light, crunchy sound on the gravel, his long, thin body luminous in the moonlight.

'He's nuts!' murmured someone as they started to drift away, and Isabelle, overcome by fatigue and all the conflicting emotions of the long, long day, hastily shut the door and collapsed in a heap of hysterical laughter.

'Shall I order you a taxi, Richard?'

The owner of Richard's favourite wine bar viewed his last customer with a mixture of exas-peration and concern. Richard Garnett was a good customer, but if he took offence at being asked to leave before he was ready, sooner or later the bar would receive a stinging write-up. Still, enough was enough. It was nearly midnight and Richard had been sitting alone at the bar, drinking deeply, since mid-evening.

Not that he appeared drunk. The only thing different about him this evening was the absence of his usual entourage of sycophants and social-ites, and when everyone left the bar, he made no effort to engage the staff in conversation.

He looked up and the proprietor was taken aback by his haggard face.

'Yeah, order me a taxi, Dave. You're right: it's

time I was off. How much do I owe you?'

Monday night being quiet, the taxi was outside in no time and he walked, with only the slightest stagger, out into the night.

Dave pulled a face as he drew the shutter down. 'Obviously had a bad day,' he commented to the remaining barman. 'Perhaps he's human, after all.'

Richard told the cabbie to drop him off in a street adjacent to where he'd parked his car, and slumped back in the seat.

He hadn't decided on his next move, but as he had to speak to Issy, he thought he'd go home. It was his house, after all – she couldn't prevent him from sleeping there.

His talk with Bob Tranter had been conducted with ruthless efficiency. He was no longer the editor of the *Wessex Daily*. In spite of his conduct, the company were inclined to be generous and, in view of his long service with them, he would receive a generous lump sum as a pay-off, but only on condition that in any interviews he gave he made it clear the newspaper itself had not been involved in any impropriety.

He'd then been escorted back to his office, where a skeleton staff watched in silence as he was allowed to remove his personal effects. No one approached him, no one said they were sorry, no one said goodbye.

He'd driven to the outskirts of Bath, left the car and taken a taxi back in. The last thing he wanted to do that evening was face Issy and tell her she'd been right. So he'd gone to the wine bar and tried to drink himself into oblivion. Except his brain wouldn't let him, and wouldn't let him escape from the humiliation of what had happened but went over and over every single detail from the moment, the awful moment, when he realised the key code had been changed and he was locked out of his own office.

He paid the taxi off.

It was completely silent up here on the edge of the city. The sky was black beyond the street lights which were spaced far apart among the trees, and through flickering shadows he walked to his car. At one point he thought someone was following him, but when he turned he could see no one in the darkness beyond. When he reached his car, he looked round again: no one about. He climbed in and, breathing deeply, turned on the ignition and drove off.

He had turned onto the main road and was headed towards Summerstoke when a pair of headlights leaped up behind him. Seconds later a flashing blue light scoured his car's dark interior. His stomach turned to water, his legs jellified, his muscles went slack, and his breath came light and fast as the police car signalled him to pull over.

25

'Room Service? It's room 1403 here. I'd like a chicken Caesar and a bottle of sparkling water, please, right away. Thanks.'

Although she detested her room and her hotel

(the studio had expressed their regrets but her former accommodation was no longer available, and after all it was only for ten days, so she could manage, couldn't she?) the idea of phoning around to find some insincere jerk to spend the evening with was much less attractive.

Juliet had been in Hollywood for a week and she was far from happy. Quite apart from her sub-standard accommodation, the studio's treatment of her was less attentive. Of course they were all rushing around trying to make this programme work for some nameless moron in a viewing studio, a stupid button at his fingertips to press every time he felt a teensy bit uncomfortable. But she felt like yesterday's flavour and, increasingly, she had the impression they were just going through the motions.

The news from England did nothing to help, either. She'd been dismissive about the affair when she'd spoken to Ollie, but she'd phoned Louis and at her request he emailed the press coverage as it appeared.

She'd been really indignant when she saw the coverage of Oliver's meeting in Summerstoke in the *Wessex Daily*, but the picture of her and Richard she'd rejected as not worthy of comment.

But the following day, Louis had sent the story about Jamie. She was so shocked she phoned the studio to say she was sick, and if Louis hadn't phoned her and told her, in no uncertain terms, to pull herself together, she'd have taken the next available flight home.

When she'd finally got hold of Ollie, their conversation was terse.

586

'Well, did you tell Richard about Jamie?'

'No, Ollie, of course not. I wouldn't – he's my son. I'm not that stupid.'

'Did you ever talk about Jamie?'

She tried to remember. 'After Jamie got beaten up, we talked about him, of course we did. I remember Richard saying how unsavoury Summerbridge was, and we touched briefly on drugs and alcohol as problems besetting all teenagers. Richard talked about his two, but that was it, Oliver, that was it. How is Jamie?'

'I thought you'd never ask.'

'Oliver, that's unfair. I think about him all the time.'

'He's doing fine. The principal of the college is being great – he's seen the press off and he says Jamie's coping really well.'

'Thank goodness. I'd hoped Jamie would text me or ring. Will you tell him to? I really want to speak to him myself.'

'He doesn't want to talk to you right now, Juliet.'

And the conversation ended with Juliet in tears.

The press interest seemed to grow rather than diminish and she felt increasingly helpless. She made a number of further attempts to speak to Ollie, but he wasn't available and didn't return her calls, something he'd never done before.

'How they can make so much mileage out of so little, I don't know!' she raged to Louis. 'How many times do I have to deny it before they believe me, and get off my case?'

'You should know, my sweet, they're not interested in what really happened. They've got the bit between their teeth. Press man abusing his power, drugs, adultery – they don't want to upset a good story, and I'm afraid the decline and fall of lover boy is a good story.'

Through gritted teeth, Isabelle said for the twentieth time, 'He was *not* my lover, for Chrissake!'

'Darling, who cares? Has anyone approached you from the American press?'

'No,' replied Juliet in a small voice, guessing Louis would see the lack of press interest in Hollywood as much more of an indictment.

He sighed. 'As far as things here go, you'll just have to sit tight. You're back next week and by then the hounds of hell will have moved on to another story. At least Oliver's come out of it with flying colours.'

Juliet was toying with her Caesar salad when the phone rang. Without enthusiasm she answered it, but when she heard the voice on the other end, her manner changed. 'Ollie! Oh, Ollie, why haven't you phoned me before?'

'I've been busy.' His voice sounded distant, cool. 'And so have you. How's it going?'

For a second, Juliet hesitated. She longed to tell him how awful it all was, how mindless she found the whole process of dubbing, that she felt marginalised and homesick.

'It's going well, I think. The director seems really pleased and the pictures look good. We should have it finished by the weekend and my manager's keen to set up some meetings with other casting directors. He says even if this series is a non-starter, the pilot will be really useful as a show reel.'

'So when do you think you'll come home?'

'I want to be back for Christmas.'

'Yes?'

'Yes, of course I do. Ollie, are you all right? Only you sound very... Well, you don't sound very warm.'

'I've had a hell of a week.'

'Yes, I know, darling, and I'm sorry, really sorry. Louis sent me the press cuttings; I can see how awful it's been for you, and for Jamie. But it's all right now, isn't it? As far as I can tell, everyone's saying how wonderful you are and how badly Richard's behaved. I know they've been going on about him and me, but I told you, Ollie, there's absolutely nothing in it.'

'I don't think I'm the one you have to convince, Juliet. Jamie...'

'What about him?'

'Quite apart from the widely held belief that it was you who told Richard about his expulsion, he's affected by what he reads in the papers about his mother. He's very angry.'

'Angry with me?' Juliet drooped. She couldn't bear Ollie's rather formal tone any longer, and knowing Jamie, her little Jamie, who had always worshipped her without question, was angry with her was too much. 'Ollie, please, it's not my fault. You've got to tell him—'

'I've tried, but he thinks I can't see beyond the end of my nose. And maybe he's right. I've been thinking till my brain hurts, but maybe I have to accept the inevitable. The way I want to live my

589

life, with my wife and son, is just not compatible with the way you want to live yours. I've been selfish, trying to impose a lifestyle on you, one you don't want and can't handle, which is why this business with Richard blew up. You can't live in Summerstoke; I was wrong to think you could. You're happy where you are, and that's what I've got to accept, so maybe–'

With fierce desperation, Juliet rallied. 'Don't say another word. You're wrong, Ollie, and so is Jamie.' Her voice cracked and the tears welled up in her eyes and slipped down her cheeks. 'I'm *not* happy here. I want to come home, to you and Jamie. I want to see you *now*. I want you to put your arms round me. I want you to tell me you still love me.' Juliet sobbed, without restraint. 'I need you, Ollie. I need you.'

There was silence on the other end of the phone, then Oliver, sadly and softly, asked, 'But do you love me, Juliet? Do you love me?'

'Your name?'

The justices' clerk glanced up at the packed public gallery, and the press bench full of reporters, then turned to Richard, standing in the well of the magistrates' court.

He'd never imagined humiliation quite like this. His descent was complete; after this he could fall no further, and it was all because ... why? How on earth had he got to this position?

'Name?' The clerk asked again, a trifle impatiently.

'Richard Edward Garnett.'

Richard Edward Garnett – what the fuck was

590

he doing here? He didn't belong here, not him, not him. The press were having a field day. Chris Gorman was here, and he recognised one or two others from the nationals. He could imagine the headlines: 'Hoist by his own petard... Taste of his own medicine'. There would be no mercy; he'd handed them a gift.

'Date of birth?'

'Twelfth, fourth, nineteen fifty-eight.' He was nearly fifty and he was done for, at least in the newspaper business, and all for what? Juliet? No, it had begun before she came on the scene. It was the honey that had started it. From something so small, so insignificant, as honey smeared on his car door, he could trace his journey to this courtroom.

'And your address is The Old Vicarage, Summerstoke, Somerset, BA11 2QZ?'

'No, not any more.'

He and Issy had split. Once the paper had come out there was no going back, she had made that quite clear when she collected him from the police station.

'I've a temporary address in London. Fifteen Boxwood Road, Camden.'

Clare had let him use her spare room and since she was going to be away for Christmas, Abigail and Danny would rally round, she said. Some hope! Abigail was over the moon at the thought of not having to go to Summerstoke and immediately plunged into party plans, and in the brief conversation he had with Danny, it was clear his son's main concern was that his money supply might have run dry.

He'd lost everything, and it was all through his

591

own bloody, unbelievable stupidity. He couldn't blame anyone else, much as he'd like to. Issy had warned him and she'd been right. Life was going to change drastically for her, too. They'd have to sell the house; he'd have to negotiate with Issy to see his little girls; it had all happened so quickly that he hadn't even had a chance to see them. There'd be no happy family Christmas for any of them, particularly if he was imprisoned. His solicitor had spelled it out: he was so far over the limit the magistrates might send him to prison. Unlikely, but they might want to make an example of him.

The words of his wife, at dinner one night at the Lesters', floated through his brain: 'they're just ordinary people who've made a mistake. You're shoving them in the stocks. I hope *you* never get caught doing something wrong.'

Richard shivered.

The children's voices wandered through the tune of the last carol, their piping notes filling the candle-lit gloom of St Stephen's. Balanced against the pulpit behind the crib was the cardboard screen painted by Isabelle and her myriad small helpers, showing a dark hillside dotted with sheep and a sky full of stars and angels.

Looking positively angelic, Ryan stood by Becky's side, a faithful and mute Joseph. Becky, cradling a doll in her arms, and with a sweetly serious expression on her face, exhorted the congregation of mums and dads to 'Come and adore Him'.

Isabelle, along with many other parents, felt for

her hanky.

It had been an awful few days. Somehow she had got through – knowing a lot of people in the village wished her well had helped. She often asked herself if she'd done the right thing as far as the children were concerned. Richard should have been with her, watching them perform in the nativity play, but he wasn't, he was in court, something she was quite unable to explain when Becky asked if Daddy was going to see her as the Virgin Mary.

The two girls had seen so little of Richard since they'd moved to Summerstoke, Isabelle doubted they would miss him very much on a daily basis. It was at the important events in their lives that they looked to see him, to share things with him, and Isabelle didn't know how to tell them their lives had changed irrevocably. With Christmas so close, they'd no time at all to adjust to their new circumstances.

As she dabbed her eyes, Nanny's thin dry hand folded over hers and gave it a reassuring squeeze. 'You all right, pet?' she whispered.

Isabelle nodded and managed a watery smile.

The ladies at the Manor had taken her under their wing, and not a day went by without a call, or an invitation to tea or to supper. Isabelle was convinced it was due to their unwavering support that the village accepted she'd had nothing to do with Richard's attack on Oliver and Jamie.

Elsie Bates led a determined counter-blast against the *Wessex Daily's* report and on Wednesday there was much jubilation in the village when a feature in a national paper on the abuse of press power gave their version of the events in the village hall.

Ironically, Isabelle was further vindicated by the speculation about Juliet's relationship with Richard. Village gossip agreed she had probably been kept in the dark by her husband about a lot of things, and, as the wronged wife, she received a lot of sympathy she didn't want. She did her best, for Oliver's sake, to pour cold water on that speculation, but it was an uphill battle – the village had taken against Juliet, condemning her as a poor wife and a poor mother, whose neglect had caused her son to stray into drug-taking in the first place.

It was with great relief that Isabelle was able to slip over to Milo's studio and lose herself in painting. He made no reference to the scene outside her house, and paid her no particular attention, but when she arrived at work a couple of mornings after he'd seen her painting, she'd found a fresh canvas set up at the opposite end of the studio from where he was working.

Hardly bothering to greet her, he said, 'You'd better get started on that – you've a lot of catching up to do. I don't need anything for the moment, so you needn't fuss about me.'

By Friday, the day of Richard's court appearance and the nativity play, she'd seen nothing of Charlie, for which she was relieved. She felt too raw to trust herself with him, and the promised tête-a-tête in the pub, at lunchtime on Tuesday, had not materialised because she went to collect Richard from the police station.

That was awful. She had hoped she'd be able to

keep her husband's final humiliation away from the public gaze, but had reckoned without the tenacity of the press. He was in their sights, and wherever he went they followed. He had been spotted in Dave's bar that night; his taxi was followed; he was seen getting into his car, well over the limit... And when he emerged from the police station the following morning, the pack were waiting for him.

He packed a suitcase and Isabelle gave him a lift to the station after he called in at the school to kiss his little girls goodbye. In the afternoon, Elsie collected her and the children. She did so again on Wednesday and Thursday, and Nanny called round in the mornings and walked with her and the children to school. It felt like she was living in a permanently numbed state, and only when she was painting could she forget everything.

Fortunately, the school needed her help with their Christmas preparations, and each afternoon she became absorbed in finishing the nativity scene, decorating the school hall for the Christmas party, supervising the making of cards and calendars, and helping the smaller children wrap little presents for the bran tub. Getting to know her, the children loved her for her quiet appreciation of their efforts, her skill, her patience and her gentle prettiness, and Clemmie and Becky basked in the newfound popularity of their mum.

By Friday she was exhausted and, accompanying Nanny to St Stephen's, she could scarcely put one foot in front of the other. But watching the innocent simplicity of the nativity and receiving a great warm beam from Becky as the play finished, the fog in her brain lifted and, although the tears poured down her cheeks, she was filled with great excitement, the excitement of new beginnings.

She beamed back.

The Reverend Grey, in the middle of his last amen, caught sight of the beam and was momentarily thrown. He glanced nervously over his shoulder at the west window. The angel was still there.

'All right, I admit I was wrong about Juliet and Charlie, but then so was half the village,' said Paula over her shoulder to Lenny, as she tottered up the garden path carrying four bulging carrier bags of shopping. 'But you still 'aven't proved nothin' about Charlie and Isabelle, and that was part of the bet,' she continued, pushing open the door and taking the bags into the kitchen, where she dropped them on the floor. 'What's more, no one else has said nothin'.'

Lenny staggered into the kitchen after her, his arms round a large cardboard box, which he banged down on the table, making it wobble precariously. He grinned, a wide, knowing grin.

'That don't mean I ain't right, my little flower.'

'Have you asked Charlie?' Paula started to unpack the groceries. Lenny wandered over to a cupboard and came back with two cans, one of Guinness and one of cider. He sat down and cracked them both open, pushing one across to Paula.

'No, but—'

''Cos I asked Isabelle.' Paula took an appreciative slurp of her Guinness. She picked up the box of crackers she'd just unpacked and looked at them critically. 'Magic tricks. Ryan's gonna have fun with these.'

Lenny stared at her. 'You never?'

'I did, and she says she can't stand 'im. So there, Mr Lenny Spinks.' She carefully extracted an iced Christmas cake from its wrapping and set it on the table.

'I dunno why you get Christmas cake, Paula. None of us likes it.'

'It's traditional, ain't it? Christmas wouldn't be Christmas without Christmas cake. I've got a chocolate log as well, though. You like that, don't you?'

'S'all right. When did you ask her?'

'Last Friday mornin'. She said he was an arrogant bastard and she wouldn't touch him with a barge-pole.'

Lenny was disconcerted. 'She might have said that, but she didn't *mean* it.'

'When's Isabelle ever said anythin' she doesn't mean?' Paula squatted down and peered into the overflowing fridge. 'I dunno how we're gonna get that turkey in here, Lenny. You're just gonna have to stick it out the back and hope this cold weather carries on. Hey, wouldn't it be great if we had snow? We've never had a white Christmas, as long as I can remember. The kiddies would love it.'

'Yeah,' Lenny chuckled. 'I remember skimming down Dawson's field on me mum's tin tray when I were not much older than Ryan. A good laugh it was.' He took another swig of cider. 'I'll put the turkey out in a minute. Have you got summat for the kids? They don't like turkey.'

'It was on offer and was a darn sight cheaper than chicken, and it goes a lot further. If they don't want it, I've got some dippers in the freezer.' She took a sip from her can and looked at him, challengingly. 'If you want to cut my hair off, Lenny, go ahead. But your ponytail goes as well.'

Returning her look, Lenny finished his cider then said thoughtfully, 'You wouldn't look the same, Paula, without yer beehive. It's just you, somehow, darlin'.'

She smiled happily. 'And you wouldn't look the same Lenny without yer ponytail.'

'Shall we call it quits, then, sweetheart?'

'Yeah, let's. Shall I get us another couple of cans? We'll drink to it. Then we can get on with decorating the tree before Mum gets back with the kids. She took 'em to see Father Christmas at the late-night opening in Summerbridge.'

Paula went to the cupboard and returned with two more cans.

'I'm right, though.' Lenny cracked open his can and licked the bubbles of fizz from the top, 'It's Isabelle and Charlie, you just wait an' see.'

'Ollie! Ollie!'

Through a sea of emerging passengers negotiating their laden luggage trolleys, Oliver could see Juliet waving. Even at that early hour of the morning, her loveliness made people turn and stare. But she had eyes only for him and the love Oliver had always borne her welled up again at the sight of her.

She ran to him and he wrapped his arms round her. Holding each other tight, they stood there, too emotionally charged to say anything. Finally he released his hold and she stood back to look at him, tears trembling on the tips of her long lashes.

'Oh, Ollie,' she whispered, 'I do so love you.'

On the journey back to Summerstoke, Oliver filled her in on everything that had happened since her departure.

'The heat's off now, thank God. I don't know what possessed Richard Garnett, but it was almost Shakespearian, his headlong rush to destruction.'

Juliet stared out at the passing landscape. 'I'm sorry,' she finally said, in a small voice, 'really sorry for my part.'

Oliver reached across and squeezed her hand. 'It's not going to be easy. There will always be people quick to condemn, but if we hold our heads up and stick together, Juliet, we'll get through.'

'Have Richard and Isabelle split up for good?'

'As far as Isabelle's concerned, yes. She's the one we should all feel concern for, darling – she's the innocent victim. It's none of my business, but I don't know how she's going to manage financially, quite apart from the emotional upheaval for her and the girls. I don't suppose it'll be easy for him to find another job.'

'Will they sell the house?'

'She's given me first refusal.'

Juliet was silent for a moment, then asked in a subdued voice, 'Are you going to take her up on it?'

For a reply, Oliver took a file out of the glove

compartment. 'Here, take a look.'

The file contained the particulars of several small flats in central London. Wonderingly, Juliet sifted through them.

'I don't know whether you like the look of any of those, darling, but I've decided that, if we're to have a fighting chance, I can't leave you languishing down in Summerstoke when you're not in Hollywood. All this business between you and Richard might not have happened if I'd been more sensitive. You're a town mouse, not a country mouse.'

'Mouse!'

Oliver grinned, 'Yes, well, anyone more unlike... But I've decided, and I hope you'll agree, to sell our house in Barnes and buy a flat. Jamie will carry on at the Manor during the week and we'll continue to rent the old doctor's house – we might even buy it, if he offers. I'll spend weekends and holidays in Summerstoke, and I hope I'll be able to persuade you to be with me there, part of the time at least.'

'Oh, Ollie, I won't need much persuading, promise. Our own flat in London! Brilliant!' Her face glowed with excitement and then she said, soberly, 'This is very hard for me to say, and I've had a struggle accepting it myself. I confess, I thought I'd die if I didn't get this series; I didn't want to come back a failure. My whole life I've set my sights on Hollywood, on being a film star, you know that, but this last trip was simply horrible. I don't think I'm cut out for it, I really don't – leastways, not without you to keep me sane.'

'I can't tell you how much it means to me to hear

you say that,' replied Oliver softly. 'And Jamie, when he calms down, will be over the moon.'

The smile went out of her face. 'Jamie ... is he really so cross with me?'

'Yes, I'm afraid so. But you have to remember he loves you and, although he'll give you a hard time, at heart he wants to forgive you. May I give you a bit of advice?'

'I'm listening.'

'Jamie has a nice little girlfriend.'

'Not Tish, the one with ironmongery in her nose?'

'Yes, Tish. And I think she's sweet and very good for Jamie. I know you don't like her, but give her a chance, Juliet. Be nice to her, don't try and overwhelm her, befriend her, and you'll see, Jamie will start to thaw.'

Juliet snorted, but said nothing.

'You'll meet her tomorrow, in any event. Grandmère's having a party.'

'What?'

'A party. It must be the first one they've had at the Manor for decades and the old dears are very excited about it, so please, Juliet, be nice.'

'I will, I will. I'll be the returning prodigal, the repentant sinner; I'll go round with ashes on my head and eating 'umble pie...'

Oliver chuckled. 'That'll be the day.'

'But why the party? I can't imagine it's to celebrate my return to the fold.'

'No. They don't know you're back. I didn't have time to tell them, sweetheart; it was very short notice.'

'I know.' Juliet's voice suddenly went gruff. 'I

601

suddenly couldn't bear it any longer. I was lucky to get the flight.'

Oliver smiled. It was a long time since he'd felt so happy. 'Yes, you were, and it's great you're back in time for Grandmère's party. She decided one was long overdue and she's invited the whole Tucker clan. I don't know whether you know any of them, but they're great favourites with the old ladies. Milo's coming, possibly his brother Marcus, Isabelle, and Polly, who's at the Manor already.'

Juliet received the news of the guest list in silence. The Tuckers – that meant that Charlie would be there. For a moment her skin tingled, then she glanced at Oliver's profile, at his strong, lean face, the arch of his nose, and his hair, the colour of honey, flopping over his eyes.

He could do with a haircut, she thought, and smiled.

26

Isabelle was in bed when she thought she heard the faint diesel chug of a taxi. She hadn't been asleep. Although it was still dark outside, it was nearly eight o'clock and the birds had been busy with their early-morning conversations for some while.

Her mind was too occupied to let her sleep on, even though it was the first day of the Christmas holidays and Milo wasn't expecting her at the studio. Richard had phoned last night. He was due back in court for sentencing early in January, and by mutual agreement he was going to stay in London till then. It was a miserable prospect, explaining to the girls he wasn't going to be there for Christmas, but better than going through the charade of happy families. Still, Christmas wasn't going to be easy. There'd be just the three of them – perhaps she'd cancel the turkey on order. The girls didn't like it, anyway; they'd be happier with a roast chicken.

Her thoughts turned to the prospect of the party at the Manor that evening. They had been insistent she went, but she really was not in the party mood, partly, she had to admit, because Charlie would be there. What would she do? How would she cope? She so wanted to see him she trembled at the thought, and then grew angry with herself for being so feeble.

You've just shut the door on one bastard, she upbraided herself. Why are you so ready to let in another?

She couldn't answer and lay there taunting herself with the fact he'd not been near her since Richard left, and on the face of it she'd no evidence to think he cared about her at all. He had a reputation, after all... She was probably just another of his flirtations. How humiliating!

The brassy clamour of the doorbell startled her. She scrambled out of bed and, pulling an old woollen sweater over her pyjamas, padded down the stairs, assuming it was the postman's van she had heard, although it seemed early for a special delivery.

It wasn't the postman. Two men, both very tanned, stood there, a couple of suitcases at their side. Before she could collect her wits, one of them beamed at her and held out his arms. 'Hi, Isabelle.'

It was Joe.

'It was your last letter. I realised things were getting out of hand and I thought, if Mohammed won't come to the mountain, the mountain must go to Mohammed, or something like that.'

Joe and his boyfriend, Andy, were sitting at the kitchen table having consumed the enormous fry-up Isabelle had made them. Attracted by the noise of their arrival, the two girls joined them and quickly made firm friends with the gentle and rather shy Andy. He told them he was a carpenter.

'Like Joseph, my husband,' said Becky gravely, and she proceeded to bring him a number of broken items of furniture from her dolls house. These he was fixing with a tube of glue while listening to the flow of conversation between Joe and Isabelle.

'We've got two weeks. I want to show Andy my roots, but if it's okay with you, Isabelle, we'd like to spend most of the time here, with you.'

'Christmas?'

'If that's okay?'

Isabelle didn't know whether to laugh or cry. 'Joe, I can't imagine a nicer Christmas present.'

That afternoon, she was sitting at the kitchen table with the girls making Christmas cards, with Joe and Andy asleep upstairs, when she heard the doorbell ring.

To her very great surprise, it was Juliet.

Juliet tried to smile. 'Hello, Isabelle.'

'I thought you were still in Los Angeles?' Isabelle was cool and unwelcoming.

Juliet blushed. 'I decided I needed to be here. I got back yesterday. Er ... may I come in?'

Isabelle hesitated. She didn't want to listen to a series of excuses or exonerating explanations.

'Please, Isabelle, I've got to talk to you.'

'But I'm not sure I want to talk to you,' Isabelle replied in a cold, quiet voice.

'No, I'm not surprised. Nor does Jamie.' Juliet looked so miserable that Isabelle felt almost sorry for her.

She opened the door wider. 'Come in. I'm making cards in the kitchen with the girls. Wait for me in there,' indicating the sitting room. 'I'll settle them and get us some tea.'

'Well, Juliet,' Isabelle handed her a mug. 'What is it you want to say?'

Juliet bit her lip. 'Just that I'm really sorry, Isabelle. Believe me, I wouldn't deliberately do anything to hurt you.'

'Then you and I have completely different ideas of what you do and don't do to friends. I know we weren't close, but I wouldn't dream of embarking on a flirtation with your husband, even if I thought the two of you were miserable.'

'But it wasn't like that, believe me.' Juliet looked thoroughly uncomfortable. 'I had lunch with Richard a couple of times because he wanted to discuss my writing a guest column. And then we went to the theatre together because he said he had tickets, but you'd said you didn't want to go, and the director was someone I'd worked with before, so I *really* didn't think you'd mind.'

'He didn't mention anything about the theatre to me,' said Isabelle coldly. 'He'd probably planned the whole thing. But what about the time you had dinner together at the local pub? Was that planned, too?'

'No, it wasn't, honestly. He just phoned and said he was eating there alone and would I like to keep him company, that's all. It was no more than that. Why should it be? I'm married to Ollie, and I love him. I wouldn't dream of hurting him – or you, Isabelle.'

'But that photograph suggests something else.'

'I know it does, but there was no something else. Believe me, Isabelle, we flirted, but that's all. Please believe me.'

She looked so sincere, so repentant, Isabelle unbent a little. Undoubtedly Richard had been the driving force, but Juliet wasn't completely innocent. Looking at her beautiful face, the picture of contrition, her eyes wide and shiny with a hint of tears, Isabelle couldn't help admiring the skill with which she played the penitent.

But she had called round. It couldn't have been easy and Isabelle had to give her credit for that.

She shrugged, then sighed. 'Fine. Then there's nothing more to be said. You've such a lovely husband, Juliet, I don't know why you should jeopardise what you've got, when you've got so much.'

'No,' Juliet said humbly. 'I don't know why, either.'

In the yard of Marsh Farm, the Tucker family, in their party finery, were sorting out who was going in which vehicle.

'Al and Alison, you go with Jeff and Jenny.' Marshalling her troops, Elsie was in her element.

Al, Alison's boyfriend, was back from university, a tall, pale youth with eyes and hair so black they accentuated the pallor of his skin. A long thin red scar, running the length of his face, and an earring added to the singularity of his appearance, but his fierce expression melted when he smiled, which he did a lot when he was with the Tuckers and particularly when he was with Alison.

Jeff Babbington, Jenny Tucker's fiancé, laughed. 'Right, that's us four sorted. Elsie, are you going to let Stephen drive your car and take you, Ron and Ange?'

'Certainly. But what about Charlie?'

The question cast a pall of silence. Charlie had been in such an odd mood over the last week, one way and another they'd all been affected.

'I don't think he's in the mood for partying,' volunteered Stephen. 'Fair bit my head off when I come in from the milkin' and asked if he was done, only I needed to use the tractor to shift some bales.'

'Something's got under his skin, all right,' frowned Alison. 'I'd have thought he'd jump at the chance of some free booze, but when I asked if he was coming tonight, he grunted and said hobnobbing with the gentry wasn't his scene.'

'But he liked Oliver.' Jenny sounded anxious. 'And I know he's not always seen eye to eye with

Mrs Merfield, but that's in the past. I don't feel happy at us all going and leaving him behind. It's not right.'

'It's a pity Milo's already over there – he's quite thick with Charlie, he could've persuaded him,' said Alison. 'So what are we gonna do? It's nearly six thirty already, and that's when we're expected.'

'Where's Charlie now?' asked Elsie.

'In the outhouse, fiddling with some wiring, last time I saw him.' Stephen got to his feet. 'Come on. We can be the advance party. The rest of you can sort Charlie out – he never listens to me.'

'Stephen, that's not true,' his mother protested. 'Of course he does.'

'Stephen's right,' said Elsie crisply. 'Off you go, all of you. You can leave Charlie to me.'

'But, love,' said Ron, concerned, 'how will you get there?'

'Charlie can bring me.'

'In his old van, Gran?'

'Why not, Alison? I'm not completely past it,' her gran replied acerbically.

Elsie let the noise of the departing vehicles die away before she went in search of Charlie.

He was, as Stephen said, chipping away at the wall in the outhouse. 'Charlie.'

He jumped at the sound of her voice and wheeled round. 'Gran, what are you doing here? Why aren't you off with the others?'

'I could ask you the same question. What are you doing out here? Aren't you going to the party?'

An expression which Elsie could only describe as mulish, settled on Charlie's face. 'It's not my sort of scene, Gran. I'm not cosy with the Merfields

608

like the rest of you. I shan't be missed.'

'I beg to differ. As the others have gone, I need you to take me. If you don't go, I don't. It's far too far for me to walk.'

Charlie folded his arms and looked mutinous. 'This is blackmail, Gran.'

'Possibly. But I wanted to have a little chat with you, anyway.'

Charlie was instantly on his guard. 'What about?'

'Isabelle.'

Elsie was watching Charlie closely. His eyes, avoiding hers, inspected the floor of the outhouse.

'Why do you want to talk to me about Isabelle Garnett?'

'Isabelle Langton now. That's what she wants to be called.'

Charlie shrugged in feigned indifference. 'What's it to me what she wants to be called?'

'Because, Charlie, dear, it's an expression of her independence. She's putting everything behind her. She's starting a new life for her and her little girls.'

'So?'

'So, Charlie, I may be old-fashioned, but I'm not narrow-minded. Times have changed, and, thank goodness, we're not trapped, any more, by stifling convention. I'm not blind, my lad. You've grown up in front of my eyes. There's not a gesture, an expression, a mood on you, that I don't know what it means.'

'Gran–'

'In spite of the fact that I see you as the

609

wriggler, the wheeler-dealer, the quick-fix merchant–'

'Thanks, Gran!'

'–you're basically honest, straightforward, and caring.'

'Thanks.'

'And that's what Isabelle needs.'

'What?' Charlie's head jerked up and he fixed a fierce gaze on his grandmother. 'What are you saying?'

'I'm saying, my boy' said Elsie gently, 'I can see Isabelle is very vulnerable at the moment. You care for her and she cares for you.'

'How do you know that? She hates me, she thinks I'm an arrogant bastard–'

'Don't be silly. Of course she doesn't, and you know it. So tell me, what's made you so miserable these last few days? Why aren't you helping her? Why aren't you there for her? I know it's early days and she has tremendous problems to overcome, but it makes it all the more important she knows she can turn to you if she needs you, doesn't it?'

'Gran,' Charlie groaned, 'you mean well, but it's not that simple. Isabelle and me, we're worlds apart. Oliver's much more suited–'

'Oliver?' Elsie was startled. 'What's he got to do with anything?'

'He's got to do with Isabelle, that's what. Word is, he's right for her, the Merfield ladies have given it their seal of approval – they've taken her under their wing. And they're right; he's a nice bloke, and he's got money, he's got class. I can't compete, Gran.'

She looked at him, amazed, then slowly shook her head.

'Charlie, my dear boy, you've got it all wrong. Oliver hasn't finished with Juliet, not by a long chalk. If people are talking about him and Isabelle, they've got it very wrong. Those two have been clinging to the wreckage, that's all. Believe me.'

'Then why' – Charlie looked at her fiercely – 'has Isabelle not got in touch with me? We had a sort of date on Tuesday – she wasn't here and there was no word. If she'd wanted me, she'd have got in touch, surely?'

'On Tuesday,' said Elsie reprovingly, 'she had to go and collect her husband from the police station and deal with all of that. Of course she didn't keep her date with you. And have you made any effort to get in touch with her? Even just to ask how she is?'

Charlie sagged.

Elsie put out her hand, 'Come on, Charlie. A quick wash and brush-up. It's not too late.'

As he was about to leave for the party, a loud knocking brought Oliver to his front door. It was Rita Godwin, clutching a flat parcel wrapped in Christmas paper.

'Ingratitude is the worst of vices, as they say, and I'm really grateful to you, Oliver, for everything you did. I know you'll say you was just doing your job, but service without reward is punishment, so I'd like you to have this – I know you admired it. Happy Christmas.'

As Oliver closed the door, Juliet joined him,

pulling on her gloves.

'What have you got there, darling?'

'It's a present from Mrs Godwin. A sort of thank you, I guess.

'Well, don't just stand there staring at it. Open it.'

Oliver pulled off the wrappings and revealed a painting, in thick brown oils, of a dog's head.

Juliet goggled. 'My God, what's that?'

'That, my love, is a portrait of Chocolate, Mrs Godwin's dog. It's the first gift I've ever been given as a politician. Do you think I should declare it as a work of art?'

'If you did that,' giggled Juliet, 'there definitely would be questions in the House about your fitness to stand.'

Paula opened the door to the Tuckers and, having shown them where to stow their coats, led the way to the drawing room where the party was assembling.

The room twinkled with candlelight; huge sprays of holly, laden with red berries, filled every vase; Christmas cards jostled for room on the mantelpiece and the bookcases; a long table, covered with a white cloth, had been set near the door and laid out with glasses, bottles of wine, spirits of every description, mixers, and jugs of fruit juice; and all around the room were dishes of olives, crisps, crystallised fruit, dates, and nuts. A Yule log was spitting gently in the fireplace, bathing the people gathered round it in a warm glow.

In her chair, closest to the fire, sat Mrs Merfield, as upright as ever, in an elegant lacy black dress. By her side sat Charlotte, looking brilliant in a purple chiffon gown and with a purple streak in her silvery hair. Oliver was introducing them to Marcus, who'd just arrived ahead of Milo, and on the other side of the fire Juliet was doing her best with Jamie, Tish and Louisa.

Amid the mêlée of greetings, Oliver noticed there were absentees. 'Where are Charlie,' he asked, 'and Elsie?'

'They're coming along in a minute,' Alison informed him. 'Charlie got delayed so Gran decided to wait for him.'

'Right. Now, what can I get you all to drink? Jamie, old son, give us a hand.'

Jamie was very aware of Alison's arrival in the room and standing in front of her now, with her big green eyes fixed on him, he felt himself blush. She'd been the object of his dreams for so long, the whole situation felt unreal. He glanced across at Tish, who was still chatting to his mother, then back at Alison.

'Can I get you a drink?' he croaked.

'Hi, Jamie, we meet again.' She smiled at him. 'This is my boyfriend, Al. Al, this is Jamie Merfield. I met Jamie playing at shipwrecks on the river in the summer.' As Jamie and Al nodded at each other, Alison continued, 'I saw you and your girlfriend in *Antigone*, Jamie. I thought you were both really good.'

'Thanks.' Jamie could feel the blush receding. 'Thanks a lot. I'll get Tish to come over and say hello. Er, Al, we've got some beer if you'd prefer it to all that wine and stuff.'

'Cheers, mate. I think that's what Ali would

prefer, too.'

'Yes, please.'

Jamie went to fetch their beers, feeling quite light-headed. He was free; the spell had lifted. She was very pretty, but she wasn't for him, he could see that, and he had no regrets, no regrets at all. He had Tish and he was happy.

'Juliet.' Marcus joined her as Jamie pulled Tish away and Louisa turned to talk to Jenny and to Jeff Babington. 'This is an unexpected pleasure, I must say. I didn't expect to see you here. I thought you were still filming.'

'No.' She smiled up at him. 'It's finished and, to be honest, I don't think it's going to happen.'

'I'm sorry. You must be very disappointed.'

She looked thoughtful. 'I suppose so, but not as much as I thought I would. Hollywood isn't all it's cracked up to be and having so many wanna-bees all in the same melting pot, one loses sight of what makes a good actor. In fact, that seems to be the least important consideration in the whole ball game, and I'm not sure I want to play.'

'Does that mean you're going to be looking for work over here?'

'Yes. As soon as I get the all-clear from my agent, I'm seriously in the market place.' She smiled at him. 'Any suggestions?'

'Well, as it happens, yes. We're going to be casting our comedy drama series immediately in the New Year. I'd like you to read for it if you're interested.'

Joe was insistent that Isabelle should still go to the Merfields' party.

'We've been travelling non-stop for the better part of two days, and we need to get some shut-eye. I can wait to meet them all – there's plenty of time.'

'But I'd much rather stay here with you and Andy.'

'No, you wouldn't, and Becky and Clemmie are looking forward to dressing up. Anyway, I thought you liked them all? With one exception, of course, and he's hardly likely to give you a hard time with everyone else there, is he?'

Isabelle blushed. 'Charlie? No, no I suppose not.' She gulped. 'Actually Joe, I think I might have been a bit... I, I think he's probably nicer than I made out. He...'

Isabelle was aware of Joe staring at her and she blushed even more deeply, but before either could say anything the doorbell rang.

It was Polly, with Milo dressed, immaculately, in a dark-blue velvet suit. Startled but pleased to see them, she welcomed them in.

Milo got straight to the point. 'I've had Polly at my workshop today. She's seen the painting you're working on there and I told her about your mural. Mind if we have a look? This way, Polly.'

Not waiting for a response, he led Polly, who cast an apologetic look at Isabelle, into the room with the mural.

Joe entered the room behind them.

'Milo, Polly, meet my friend Joe Watts. He's just turned up from Australia, with his partner. They're going to be here for two weeks.'

Responding to the pleasure in Isabelle's voice, Polly greeted Joe warmly.

Milo nodded. 'The sculptor, eh?' And he turned back to his study of the painting.

Polly turned and, stepping back to get a good look, gasped. At that, Isabelle, murmuring she had to get ready and they could let themselves out when they'd done, fled to the kitchen, pulling Joe with her.

'What's up?' he asked, as she sat trembling at the table, 'Who's she? Isn't Milo Steel something else? You're a brave girl. I'd be terrified working for him!'

'That's Polly Merfield – I think I told you in one of my letters, she runs a gallery in London. Why's Milo brought her here?'

'To see your painting, you ass. Anyone with any artistic sense will see it's a beaut.'

She looked at him with a faint smile. 'You're becoming an Aussie. Oh, Joe, you and Andy seem so sorted. I'm in such a mess.'

'It may seem like that at the moment, but if you ask me, you've got quite a lot going for you and it's not at all what I expected.'

'What do you mean?'

He grinned. 'Go to your party. We'll talk after that.'

Polly and Milo lingered by the painting and Isabelle heard her daughters insisting Andy go with them to have a look, too.

She smiled. 'I've never known Becky take to someone so quickly. Your Andy's rather special.'

Joe smiled happily back. 'He is, isn't he? Now, you'd better get off. And be brave – your painting's really special, too.'

Becky and Clemmie were chatting to Polly.

'Oh yes,' Isabelle heard Becky say, 'it's very good, but I prefer the one she's painted in our bedroom. That's beautiful. It's got a castle and princesses – it's magic. She's gonna paint one for my friend Ryan's mum, too.'

'I like this bestest,' chipped in Clemmie sturdily. 'It's like mine. I like painting, lots. Would you like to see some?'

'Not now, Clemmie.' Taking a deep breath, Isabelle went to Polly's rescue. 'We've got a party to go to.'

'If you're ready, we'll walk with you.' Polly smiled at her and then turned back to the wall, looking serious. 'This really is something, Isabelle. Quite remarkable.'

'Told you so,' said Milo. 'So what are you going to do about it?'

'Milo!' Isabelle and Polly protested as one voice, Isabelle with embarrassment, Polly with laughter.

'Come on, Isabelle,' said Polly. 'Let's talk on the way to the Manor. It's nearly seven and Grandmère hates guests to be very late.' She turned to Joe and Andy. 'I know Isabelle said you want to crash out, but if you'd like to come to the party you'd be very welcome.'

'Thanks, but no. We need to build up our energy for Isabelle's bash. We'll meet you all at that, I hope.'

No one could have looked more startled than Isabelle. 'My bash?' she said faintly.

'Sure.' Joe grinned. 'You mentioned it so many times in your letters, it's just got to happen, and Andy and I are very good at throwing parties. You can't deny me. I've set my heart on having a bop with Paula.'

By the time they arrived at the Manor, Isabelle was fizzing with excitement. Polly had said that, subject to her partner's agreement, she'd like to include four pieces of Isabelle's work in her gallery's summer exhibition and she wanted to have the mural photographed.

The party was buzzing. Clemmie and Becky were immediately set to work by Nanny to carry around plates of delicious little strips of chicken, savoury puffs of pastry, prunes wrapped in bacon, and sundry other delicacies.

Isabelle cast her eyes quickly round the room. No sign of Charlie. But her eyes widened at the sight of the tall, pale young man standing next to Alison. She went and touched him on the arm.

'Anthony!' He turned. 'That last time I saw you was at your parents', in the summer. What are you doing here?'

Al looked startled. 'Isabelle! Er' – he lowered his voice – 'please don't call me Anthony. I left that name behind when I left home. Call me Al.'

'Sorry, Al. But tell me, how are you? The last I heard, you'd had an accident on your bike.'

'I did. But I'm better now, thanks. You know Alison, don't you? She's my girlfriend.'

'Yes, yes I do. Oh, I can't tell you how pleased I am that you ... you've...'

'Escaped my dreadful parents?'

'Yes.'

They both laughed.

'You're looking very sparkly.' Oliver smiled as

he handed her a glass of wine.

'Yes. Suddenly, Oliver, everything's looking brighter. My best friend, Joe, has turned up from Australia and he and his partner are going to stay over Christmas. And' – Isabelle was bursting to tell someone – 'Polly's going to exhibit my paintings in her gallery's summer exhibition.'

His eyes widened appreciatively. 'You must be good: Pol's very protective of her gallery's reputation. Well done, Isabelle. I'm really pleased for you.'

'Thanks, Oliver.' She smiled, then said lightly, 'You must be pleased to have Juliet back.'

'Yes.' Oliver looked grave. 'I'm afraid meeting Juliet wouldn't be high on your wish list, would it? I'm sorry. If it's any help, she's very remorseful.'

'Yes, she told me as much this afternoon.'

'She came to see you?' Oliver looked startled.

'Yes, didn't she tell you? She came to apologise and to explain.'

'Juliet did?' Oliver's expression softened. 'For what it's worth, I'm glad she did. She's not irredeemably self-centred.'

As if she knew they were talking about her, Juliet drifted across the room to join them, slipped her arm round Oliver's waist and smiled almost shyly at Isabelle.

'Hi, Isabelle, and congratulations.'

'Congratulations?'

'Yes, Milo and Polly are talking about your painting. It sounds amazing.'

They were interrupted by the arrival of Elsie, followed by Charlie.

Isabelle froze. This time there was no convenient sofa to sink into and hide.

'Charlie, Elsie,' Oliver greeted them. 'Come in. I think you know everyone here.'

Charlie nodded, smiling at the assembled guests. Then his eyes caught Isabelle's.

For a moment they stood, both uncertain, both looking for something. Finding it, they smiled, first tentatively, and then with a thrill of happiness and excitement.

Elsie alone noticed this exchange and was satisfied with what she saw.

'So you and Juliet have made it up?' As soon as he could, Charlie was at Isabelle's side, Juliet having left her and joined Marcus and Milo.

'Not exactly. She asked me to forgive her. I forgave her, but it doesn't mean we're about to become bosom pals.'

'Isabelle,' Charlie said quietly, touching her arm, 'you can tell me to get lost if you want, but I'd like to talk to you, somewhere quiet.'

That light touch had an electrifying effect. Tingling all over, hardly able to breathe, she looked at him. He was gazing down at her with such a serious expression, her heart flipped.

'Yes, where?'

'Let's slip outside for a moment, if you wouldn't be too cold?'

Quietly they left the room and he took her hand and led her out into the back garden. For a moment they stood there, gazing up at the sky, their fingers interlocked, their breaths intermingling in the frosty air.

'Did you know it was the winter solstice today,

the shortest day of the year? I always used to think on the longest night there should be no moon, but look, it's half full, see?'

'It's lovely.' Isabelle gazed up at the shimmering half-moon, with faint, high clouds scudding across it, and at the sky, full of stars. Then she sighed. 'The longest night? This has been the longest week of my entire life.'

He put his arm round her and she relaxed against him, feeling the warmth of him, the strength of him. 'The days get longer from this point, Isabelle, and life will get better. It will.' He turned her to him and, gently caressing her face, looked into her eyes and said softly, 'Oh, Isabelle, I can't believe this. I told myself I was mad even to think about you.'

'And I thought I was dreaming it all, that you ... that you dismissed me as utterly useless the moment we met.'

'And you told me I was an arrogant bastard, and I was no better than the Lesters,' he chuckled. 'That hurt.'

Isabelle laughed, too, then broke off. 'The thing is, Charlie, it's all so new, so raw. I need time. Everything's happening so quickly: the newspaper stories, Richard's arrest, my painting, you. I stopped loving Richard a long time ago, but I didn't allow myself to realise it until all this happened. And then, before I knew it, there was you. It was all so confusing.'

She looked up at his strong, lean face, his skin silvery in the moonlight, his eyes dark pools. 'I need to know it's not just a knee-jerk reaction not just for my sake and for yours, but for the children. I need to tread very carefully. Do you understand?'

'Yes,' he said gently, 'I understand. I'm a blasted impatient person most of the time, Isabelle, but I'll wait for as long as it takes. But there's one thing I can't wait for any longer.'

'What's that?' she said faintly.

'This,' he said. And enfolding her in his arms, he bent down and kissed her, a long and tender kiss that felt like for ever.

The moon sailed high in the heavens; an owl hooted; a dog barked; the kingfisher slept, his head tucked under his wing, on a willow branch above the dark flow of water.

Paula, escaping down the back corridor to have a quick fag, stopped short in her tracks.

'Blimey,' she said, under her breath. 'Well! Well I never did. Who'd 'ave thought it? Lenny was right all along. Blimey!'

The publishers hope that this book has given you enjoyable reading. Large Print Books are especially designed to be as easy to see and hold as possible. If you wish a complete list of our books please ask at your local library or write directly to:

Magna Large Print Books
Magna House, Long Preston,
Skipton, North Yorkshire.
BD23 4ND

This Large Print Book for the partially sighted, who cannot read normal print, is published under the auspices of

THE ULVERSCROFT FOUNDATION

THE ULVERSCROFT FOUNDATION

... we hope that you have enjoyed this Large Print Book. Please think for a moment about those people who have worse eyesight problems than you ... and are unable to even read or enjoy Large Print, without great difficulty.

You can help them by sending a donation, large or small to:

The Ulverscroft Foundation, 1, The Green, Bradgate Road, Anstey, Leicestershire, LE7 7FU, England.
or request a copy of our brochure for more details.

The Foundation will use all your help to assist those people who are handicapped by various sight problems and need special attention.

Thank you very much for your help.